EXILE

FORGE BOOKS BY JAMES SWALLOW

EXILE

JAMES SWALLOW

A TOM DOHERTY ASSOCIATES BOOK

NEW YORK

This is a work of fiction. All of the characters, organizations, and events portrayed in this novel are either products of the author's imagination or are used fictitiously.

EXILE

A Forge Book
Published by Tom Doherty Associates
175 Fifth Avenue
New York, NY 10010

www.tor-forge.com

Forge® is a registered trademark of Macmillan Publishing Group, LLC.

The Library of Congress Cataloging-in-Publication Data is available upon request.

ISBN 978-0-7653-9514-6 (hardcover)
ISBN 978-0-7653-9516-0 (ebook)

Our books may be purchased in bulk for promotional, educational, or business use. Please contact your local bookseller or the Macmillan Corporate and Premium Sales Department at 1-800-221-7945, extension 5442, or by email at MacmillanSpecialMarkets@macmillan.com.

First published in Great Britain by Zaffre Publishing, an imprint of Bonnier Zaffre, a Bonnier Publishing company

First U.S. Edition: May 2019

Printed in the United States of America

0 9 8 7 6 5 4 3 2 1

For my friends, who helped me get here.

EXILE

— ONE —

There was a peculiar stillness in the air, and it made the night seem like a solid mass laid over the low, dusty cityscape. With the balcony windows half open, little of the oppressive, blood-warm heat from the faded day had diminished inside the mansion. Each time Welldone Amadayo moved, he felt his expensive Chinese silk shirt sticking to his back. The temperature, a steady drumbeat of fear, was making him sweat, and he absently ran a long-fingered hand over the dark worry lines of his oval face.

The screen on the wall above his desk was blank except for a blue square surrounding a coiled arrow, which turned in an endless circle as the voice-over-Internet-protocol software in his computer worked to connect him. Amadayo peered at the stubby digital camera clipped to the frame of the screen, watching the slow blink of a crimson light diode. He experienced a moment of brief panic, and his hands fluttered over the shirt, readjusting it in an attempt to portray himself in a more casual fashion. After a moment he gave up and hissed through his teeth. The arrow continued the endless chasing of its own tail.

Amadayo thought about sitting down, then discarded the idea. He glanced at the closed door behind him, then away. Every second of waiting was eroding his calm. He looked through the slatted blinds leading outside to the balcony. Beyond, a soft aura of light was cast from the windows of his home and the watery shimmer of the swimming pool, but the glow petered out as it reached the high walls and acacia trees surrounding his private compound.

Past that lay the clutter of the city of Mogadishu, the scattered specks of illumination in constellations of orange light that escaped from the windows of red-roofed apartment buildings and sodium-lit streets. If he stood there, he might be able to pick out the line of darkness where the seashore began, but Amadayo stayed inside more often these days, and he had an arsenal of lies for anyone who wanted to know the reason why.

Finally, he decided to loosen the shirt, to make himself look as if he were completely relaxed. He sat and stared into the camera, schooling his expression, glimpsing his reflection in the dark portions of the screen. He was experienced at this sort of thing, he reminded himself. There was no reason to be concerned.

The turning arrow vanished and the blinking red light became a steady green. Suddenly there was a white man on the screen, outlined against a wide room made of yellow Italian stone. Shafts of daylight from a setting sun cut across the background. *"Mr. Amadayo,"* began the man. *"Greetings."*

"Doctor," Amadayo corrected him automatically. He had paid a good amount for the framed university degree hanging on his wall, and it was second nature for him to remind anyone who addressed him as that. "Mr. Brett. A pleasure, as always." He showed a practiced grin.

Brett inclined his head, his eyes flicking away to glance at something that the camera on his end didn't show, then back once more. *"Dr. Amadayo,"* he began again. *"Forgive me for disrupting your evening, but as I am sure you understand, my employers are eager to communicate their concerns to you. And you have been rather difficult to reach over recent weeks."* Brett's accent was like the BBC World Service radio broadcasts Amadayo had listened to in his youth, every word balanced, cut to length and positioned in exactly the right place. There was a strangely soulless, machine-like quality to the man, which Amadayo found slightly unsettling. His milk-pale face, his straw-like hair and watery blue eyes seemed unnatural. He reminded the Somalian of albino children he had seen in Tanzania, and Amadayo half-wondered if, like them, the Englishman's body parts would be worth money if made into charms post-mortem.

He nodded and widened his smile for the camera. "It is I who should be begging your forgiveness!" Amadayo faked a contrite tone. He shook his head. "So much work to be done here, you know? So many people with needs to be dealt with and hands held out. It takes up all of my time."

"That is why we agreed to have you work as our representative in So-malia, because of your connections," said Brett. Personally, Amadayo had always thought of himself as a partner more than an employee, but he let that go for the moment. *"But we are concerned about a lack of visible progress."*

"Oh?" Amadayo raised an eyebrow. Outwardly he maintained an air of quiet concern, but his heart was racing. The shirt stuck to his back like a second skin. "I have done everything the Combine has asked of me—"

"We prefer you not to use that name again," Brett snapped, with a wince.

Amadayo bristled at the Englishman's tone and pressed on, masking his worry with a rising anger. "How long have I been helping you in my nation? Your past transactions in Puntland and elsewhere—who ensured that those would proceed without issue?"

"And you have been paid handsomely for your brokerage," came the reply, *"That guarded compound where you sit? My employer's money made it possible for you to live in such luxury. And safety."*

There was a threat buried in the words, but Amadayo didn't waste time on it. This man was half a world away, and the things that Amadayo *did* fear were far closer than he was.

But then Brett looked out of the screen at him, and it was as if the pale man reached into his thoughts and pulled that fear out across the distance. *"You enjoy your comfortable life, doctor. You like to say you are the man who knows all the names, the one with a friend in every town and village. But how much of that is true?"* He came closer until his face nearly filled the screen. *"You promised stability. You told my employers your influence could make that happen. But it has not."*

Amadayo blinked, briefly lost for words.

When Brett spoke again, the cultured accent had become acidic and accusatory. *"You were employed because you pledged to bring us some measure of constancy in that cesspool of a country. But somehow, despite all your promises, despite all the people you claim to hold sway over, terrorism and piracy are on the increase once again. How is that possible, if you are working so hard for us?"*

"I—" Amadayo sucked in a breath and marshalled a tirade to throw back at the pale foreigner. But before he could shape it, a crackling ripple of noise reached his ears. Gunfire, close at hand.

He bolted from the chair and took two quick steps toward the balcony door, in time to catch the sound of an echoing crash from the front gate. Amadayo gingerly leaned out and saw flashlights bobbing at the far end of the sandy driveway. A handful of his security men were sprinting in the direction of the commotion.

Looking down, he found a lanky guard with an AK-47 assault rifle circling warily around the edge of the poolside two stories below. Amadayo shouted out an urgent cry in the local Benadir dialect. "You! Tell me what is going on out here!"

The guard halted and showed him a shrug. "Not sure, doctor-sir. Someone at the gate, but I don't know—" The younger man's words mingled with a low subsonic *crack* that cut him off mid-thought, as half of his face was abruptly ripped away in a fluid jet of crimson. The guard tottered and tumbled into the pool, a gush of blood staining the grubby tiles and clouding the water.

More shots rose in a chorus and Amadayo tore his gaze from the dead man in time to see the gate crumple as a cattle truck rammed it open. Yellow sparks of muzzle flare erupted all along the line of the acacias and Amadayo flinched, ducking back into the room.

"What was that noise?" Brett asked lazily.

Amadayo tore a drawer from a nearby cabinet and pulled an old World War II-vintage Tokarev pistol from among the papers inside. He kneaded the weapon and spun in place to glare at the little camera. "You have done this?" He stalked toward the screen, wishing it was a window through which he could send a bullet. "You sent them?"

"Sent who?" The Englishman didn't show the slightest flicker of alarm. He sat and watched as if he were in the audience at a theater, indifferently observing some uninvolving drama.

A random spray of automatic fire hosed across the stone balustrade outside and splintered the wooden balcony doors, causing Amadayo to cry out. Spurred into motion by the shots, he ran across the room and levered open a trapdoor in the floor. Beneath it was a safe, and inside that a bag containing a few gold bars, wads of American dollars and forged identity papers. Amadayo stared at the bag, knowing what it represented. If he removed it, it would be tantamount to admitting defeat, like a pilot taking a parachute before abandoning his aircraft to smash into a hillside.

The shooting outside tailed off to nothing, and Amadayo heard the low, indistinct rumble of a man's voice. He held his breath, straining to listen.

After the gate was breached and the initial exchange of automatic fire ended, a dangerous, loaded silence descended on the compound. The bulk of Amadayo's guards were Yemeni, ex-military who had fled the civil war in their own country and crossed the Gulf of Aden in search of better odds. The doctor thought that made them a smarter choice for his protection detail than the locals: they were trained soldiers but also lacked connections to the web of clan obligations and rivalries that were a matter of course for his fellow Somalis. They could keep him safe from the criminals who took issue with his actions, or the Al Shabaab militants who considered him an ungodly apostate. But what he had failed to take into account was that these men were also *survivors*, who knew full well when the deck was stacked against them.

The guards drew back into cover behind lines of ornamental planters and low stone walls, weighing their chances. Half their number had already been killed in the opening exchange.

The cattle truck that had rammed the gate retreated and dozens of armed men flowed in through the gap it left. They toted beaten, battle-worn versions of the same Kalashnikov rifles that the guards carried, one or two sporting grimy rocket-propelled grenade launchers or PKM machine guns with heavy box magazines. At first glance they resembled the gangs who prowled the lawless provinces, or the *burcad badeed* pirates from outside the city—but unlike those rabble they moved with something approaching self-control. The Yemeni guards had expected shouting and wildfire shooting, but not discipline.

The invaders' ranks parted to allow their commander to advance into view. Heavyset, he was a densely muscled street fighter with a broken nose and a face that shone like polished teak. A curved scar began at the right corner of his mouth and described a semicircle up his cheek to end above the brow, with the effect of permanently pulling his expression into a narrow glare. The iris of his right eye was damaged, permanently wide and black like a shark's. He marched slowly up the driveway, the heavy iron ingot of a Desert Eagle semi-automatic dangling at the end of his arm, and found a place to stand out in the open.

He took a breath and gestured with the big pistol. "Look at me," he called. A few wary heads bobbed up from behind cover, vanishing as fast as they had risen. "Who does not know my name?" He cast around, waiting for someone to reply. "Ask those with you, if you do not." The gun went back into a leather holster strapped across his chest. "Do you want to oppose me? Do you understand what that will mean?"

Thirty meters away, the brother of the youth whose body now floated in the pink water of Amadayo's swimming pool sighted down his AK-47. He knew the name of the big man.

Abur Ramaas.

He knew who he was and what was said about him but, in that moment, his grief was in control. The dead guard's brother rested the weapon atop a concrete urn and framed the man's chest in the ring of his rifle's iron sights. Teeth gritted, he broke the silence with a shot that the poorly maintained gun sent well wide of the mark. Ramaas heard the wasp-drone of the round passing by and glanced after it, making a disgusted face.

The next shot came from one of his men atop the compound's outer wall, the spindly length of a Dragunov sniper rifle in his hands. The weapon chugged and the guard joined his brother.

Ramaas sighed. "Anyone else?"

Slowly, hands rose and guns clattered to the ground.

"We execute them?" said Guhaad. He was trying not to seem eager about the prospect, but to Ramaas the other man was like a hungry dog always pulling on its chain, desperate to taste blood.

He shook his head. "Take their weapons and let them leave. It's a good lesson for the others." Ramaas didn't add that dozens of dead bodies piled on the mansion's piebald lawns would draw the wrong kind of attention. A handful of killings could be ignored under the cover of night in Mogadishu, but the open massacre of a dozen disarmed soldiers . . . that might force the men who pretended to govern the fragmented city into action. They would feel the need to be seen to do something, and Ramaas did not wish that. He wanted them to remain comfortable and complacent, until the moment he knifed them in their beds.

Guhaad grimaced, showing teeth that were stained orange from too much khat leaf. Ramaas had outgrown partaking of the narcotic, but his second-in-command liked it as much as the younger bandits did, chewing it to keep him alert and awake all hours of the night. Ramaas indulged him, though. Guhaad *was* his war dog, after all. Brutal and violent at the snap of his fingers, Guhaad was the club in Ramaas's hands for battering down his foes. He just lacked the insight to think more than a day ahead.

"No sign of the army," said another voice, as Ramaas's other weapon approached. The rifleman's name was Zayd, and he was the careful knife to Guhaad's blunt instrument. The two of them looked similar enough to be brothers, both of rangy build with long arms and legs, both from clans in the south, but the way they carried themselves made the divergent nature of their characters obvious. Zayd was sly and cold-eyed where Guhaad forever teetered on the edge of fury.

Ramaas nodded. "They won't come." He nodded toward the house, its doors yawning open and unguarded. "In there, he is calling for them right now." He shook his head. "They won't come," he repeated.

Amadayo snapped his cell phone shut and gripped it in his hands. The men in the federal government who owed him favors were suddenly *unavailable,* as if a peculiar malaise had struck them down all at once. From out of nowhere, his name had become a filthy thing, a word that no one wanted to utter.

How had this happened? He tossed away the phone and went for

the pistol again. "Ramaas. The pirate is in my home." Amadayo said
it aloud, cementing the horrible truth of it in reality. "He's come to
end me."

*"I think we can consider this the conclusion of our working relation-
ship,"* said Brett, reaching for a control off-screen.

"No!" Amadayo shouted at him, eyes wide with panic. "You think
I am a man who cannot produce results? I will show you!" He bran-
dished the pistol. "You will learn!"

Outside the room, floorboards creaked under the weight of heavy
boots, and Amadayo surrendered to action over reason. Swearing a
curse, he unloaded the Tokarev into the closed door, mashing the trigger as fast as he could, bullets crunching through the wood in a desperate attempt to kill whomever was on the other side.

Without warning, the gun's slide locked open with a hollow click
and Amadayo started, staring down at the weapon in his hand. The
magazine was empty, brass shells scattered at his feet, cordite smoke
curling around the barrel.

The bullet-punctured door burst open, sagging on its hinges, and
Ramaas filled the room. Amadayo staggered back, but in a single quick
stride the bigger man was upon him and he was disarmed with a backhand slap that knocked the Tokarev to the floor.

"You have never shown me respect," Ramaas growled, the words
low like a leopard's snarl.

Amadayo gathered spittle in his mouth as a retort, but then thought
better of the act and swallowed it as he locked gazes with the other
man's dead eye.

"You brought this on yourself," Ramaas told him. "You should have
left the country when your wife and daughter did."

"My . . . ?" Amadayo's legs turned to water and he had to grasp the
back of a chair to remain standing. "What did you do to them?"

Ramaas ignored the question. "Everyone hates you," he explained.
"Because you are a jackal that cannot be killed cleanly. Because you
have made yourself necessary." He shook his head. "Not for much
longer." He glanced at the screen and the camera, as if noticing it for
the first time, then returned his attention to his prey. "I have heard
what you said to the other weak men about *stability* and *community*.

Those are just the words you use for the chains you put about people's necks."

Amadayo blinked fear-sweat from his eyes. For months now, he had been actively suppressing information about Ramaas's activities in Somalia, paying bribes to stop them from being talked about too widely, while all along trying fruitlessly to find a way to subdue him. He had feared what would happen if his fading grip on things became apparent.

Somalia's disordered state of the nation was both opportunity and burden to Amadayo. He had used it to ingratiate himself with politicians in the government and rich outside interests, who even now were drawing future plans about how they might exploit the country's untapped reserves of oil and natural gas. Ramaas threatened all of that.

At first he had been nothing more than a blip on Amadayo's radar, one more bandit warlord among a population of smugglers and pirates. That underestimation had been his biggest miscalculation. Day after day, Amadayo got word of new alliances between Ramaas's band of brigands and the antagonistic clans in Puntland, Galmudug and elsewhere. Even worse, it was said that the ruthless Al Shabaab Islamists had found a kind of accord with the man. He was undercutting the work that Amadayo had spent painstaking years constructing. Every thug he had sent to kill Ramaas never returned. Most, he feared, had switched sides and given their fealty to the warlord instead—Somalians always respected strength. As Amadayo searched Ramaas's scarred face for some ounce of humanity, he knew that here and now, the warlord had all the power over him.

"The clan elders are sick of you," Ramaas was saying. "They mock you in Haradheere. Like a woman who lies with any man, they say, the biggest *dhillo* in Mogadishu." He prodded him in the chest with a thick finger, and nodded toward the camera. "In the pocket of the *gaal.*"

"I am no whore!" Amadayo dredged up what little of his defiance still remained, but the outburst drained him and he folded.

Ramaas saw it, a hunter knowing his prey had given up, and nodded. "Time for you to go."

Was he being given a way out? Amadayo took a wary step toward the door, but an angry-looking man in a bright red soccer shirt was barring the way.

"You've been lucky," Ramaas told him. "Getting to here." He surveyed the room. "I want to see if you are still lucky." The warlord fished in a pocket and produced three careworn playing cards, each bent into a curve. He showed Amadayo their faces; the Jack of Spades, the Jack of Clubs and the Queen of Hearts. "Find her."

Amadayo knew the game, and he knew it was a trick, but Ramaas was already laying the cards out on the desk, moving them about with a deftness at odds with his heavy boxer's hands. When he was done, he drew back a step and waited.

One chance in three, Amadayo reasoned. He had no other choice but to play along. Reaching out, he tapped the middle card, and he heard the outlaw in the soccer shirt give a derisive snort.

Ramaas gave an indulgent nod and let Amadayo flip the card over. The pale face of the Jack of Clubs pictured there reminded him of Brett's studied features.

"Come, mister-doctor. I want to show you something." A smile played around Ramaas's mouth and he pushed Amadayo in the direction of the balcony.

He reluctantly allowed himself to be directed outside. His eyes darted around, searching for anything that could be a method of escape. Below them, the warlord's men were already looting the house, walking in empty-handed and out again with anything of value they could carry. Amadayo stifled a moan of dread.

A heavy hand landed on his shoulder. "You see that?" Ramaas pointed out toward the city. "It was never yours to begin with. You were a fool to think otherwise." He paused. "Do you believe in a God? Do you think he looks well upon you?" Amadayo didn't know what to say, but he suspected Ramaas knew the answer to his questions already.

"Brother, please," Amadayo whispered, pleading. "You are going to let me go?"

"No." With a vicious shove, Ramaas's hand clamped around Amadayo's neck, his thumb choking him as it pressed into the soft flesh of his throat.

He stumbled back and collapsed against the bullet-pocked balustrade, but Ramaas kept up the pressure, forcing him over the edge until his torso was hanging out over the drop. Amadayo's hands came up, flailing and scratching, fright overwhelming him as he realized that this would be his end.

Ramaas grabbed at his belt for leverage and tipped him over the edge. Amadayo spun and landed hard against the tiled patio surrounding the murky swimming pool, bones breaking against the concrete. Agony blinded him and blood spread around his body, soaking into the silk shirt.

"Boss." Zayd glanced at the twitching body on the ground and looked up at the balcony where Ramaas was wiping sweat from his fingers. He pointed down at Amadayo. "Still alive."

"Oh." Almost as an afterthought, Ramaas removed the Desert Eagle from its holster and blind-fired four rounds into the dying man. The reports of the heavy-caliber pistol echoed like claps of thunder, and then the matter of Welldone Amadayo was dealt with. "Get up here," said the warlord.

Zayd's head bobbed on his thin neck and he shouldered his rifle on its strap, making his way in through the house. Expressionless, his gaze ran over the expensive furniture and the garish paintings on the walls. Every square meter of the place was crammed with overblown, gaudy clutter. Zayd looked away—Amadayo's home was full of hollow things that only had value to rich fools, but like the man himself they were worthless. There was nothing here that had been earned through sweat and toil, only by guile and lies.

The other outlaws were in the process of stripping the place. What could be sold on would be used to fund their group. The remainder would be left for those gathering outside the gates—the people who had been forced to live in the shadow of Amadayo's offensive wealth—to take and do with as they saw fit. Zayd pushed past a man on the stairs laden down with armfuls of colorful women's clothes, and found his way to the dead politician's office.

Inside, he came upon Guhaad emptying a bag across the floor. Small bars of gold thudded on the thick carpet and his eyes widened. Zayd ignored him and looked to Ramaas, as the warlord pulled on a fist-sized plastic ball mounted on a television screen.

He drew it toward him, and the device cracked, trailing out wires. "You liked the show?" he asked it.

On the screen, a well-dressed foreigner cocked his head like a curious dog. "*It seems as though you have dealt with a problem that we both shared. Perhaps you would be interested in accepting the position that has just been vacated?*"

Ramaas gave a grumbling chuckle and shot a look at Guhaad, who belatedly shared a rough snigger. Zayd's expression remained blank. Little amused him, and certainly not some pale-skinned *gaal* who talked at them like he thought they were all fools.

"Messenger," Ramaas said to the white man. "Go and tell your masters that I am in charge here now." Then with a jerk of his wrist he wrenched the camera the rest of the way from the wall and tossed it onto the desk. The screen flickered and went blank.

Zayd nudged the camera ball with a finger, ensuring it was dead. Next to it, he saw the warlord's cards lying in a line. He flipped over the two that were still face down and found a pair of identical Jacks. "Amadayo should not have played this game," he noted, handing the cards back to the warlord.

"So true," said Ramaas. "Greed makes a man overstate his chances. He knew chance did not favor him, and yet still he played on. You see the arrogance of that? To the end, Amadayo believed the rules of the world did not apply to him."

"What do you want me for?" said Zayd.

Ramaas studied the computer on Amadayo's desk. They had men who were knowledgeable about such things, and the machine would go to them just as the spoils from the house would go to the rank-and-file of the outlaws. Ramaas looked Zayd up and down. "You are no bigger than the late mister-doctor. His clothes are very fine. Go to his rooms, gather some up. Take what you like."

"Why?"

"You are going on a vital journey." He nodded in the direction of the screen. "There is more work to be done." He leaned in and spoke quietly. "Only you can do this for me, brother." The rest went unspoken. It would not be the first time that Zayd had carried the warlord's flag for him. There were few to whom Ramaas was willing to give such an honor.

From across the room, wood crunched and splintered as Guhaad bodily shoved a rack of shelves aside, to reveal a hidden compartment behind it. He broke open the lock on the metal door with the butt of his rifle and slid it open. "Boss. Look here!"

Ramaas reached inside and came back with plastic-wrapped bricks of American dollars in high denominations. He gave a nod. "Empty it. Amadayo will be generous in his passing." Zayd watched him lay a hand on Guhaad's shoulder. "I can rely on you to keep things in order while we are gone?"

"We?" Guhaad shot a look in Zayd's direction, confused and annoyed all at once. He didn't like the idea of being left out of something.

Ramaas was already shaking his head. "I need your strong hand here while I am away." He had a way of managing the thug's moods that the rifleman could never comprehend. "Zayd has a mission, and so do I. These things are significant, brother. I could have sent you two alone to do this thing today, but I did not. I am here. You know why?"

"It is important to do some things in person," Guhaad replied, remembering other lessons he had been taught. "A man must be seen to do the deed." A thought occurred to him. "That's why you let the Yemenis live. To say what you did."

Ramaas nodded. "All men should live by a code. A set of principles." He released his grip and walked away, turning the bale of money over in his hands. "Just a few more things need to be done. There are ropes that hold us tethered which need to be cut."

"And then?" asked Zayd. It was rare for him to even think of questioning Ramaas's orders, but the need to know pushed at him. Each day they were moving closer to some goal that only Ramaas saw clearly.

"*Waaq* will provide," said the warlord, using the Cushitic name for God. Zayd cared very little for religion, but he kept that to himself rather than offend his Muslim brothers in the war band. For his part, Ramaas held to the old Oromo folk beliefs and no one had the courage to challenge him on them. More than once, Zayd had heard him talk of *Mission* and of *Duty*. Ramaas could be compelling when he wished to be, then terrifying, turning from one to another like the rise and fall of ocean waves.

"We are change," he told them, speaking with such certainty that it seemed as though his desires were already fact. "We are the storm that will sweep over our nation. Believe that." Then he smiled, squeezing the fat bundle of dollar bills in his fist. "But to make it happen, we will need more of *this*."

like the P90 better." Jurgen Goss raised his hands up in front of him and mimed holding the Belgian-made submachine gun. He aimed across the cramped interior of the ill-lit office and drew a bead on an equally insubstantial enemy. *"Brap Brap!* Good grouping!" He lolled back in his chair and it creaked under his weight as he chuckled. "And you must love the cool plastic ammo magazine. See the bullets go, one-two-three . . ."

"Good for a close-up dance, I'll give you that." Sitting on the edge of Goss's untidy desk, Marc Dane shrugged. "But I'd prefer something with more stopping power."

"Assault rifle?"

Dane nodded. "Assault rifle. SCAR-L, 5.56mm NATO with an extended mag, ACOG sight. And a laser designator. I like the laser."

"Slower to reload," Goss noted. He shifted forward. The Austrian was doughy, and he tried to ignore how his girth tended to pool around him in the too-small chair. But he was sick of trying to have new office furniture sent in from procurement.

"You don't need to keep reloading if you actually hit your target first time, yeah?" Dane told him. "You know what your trouble is?"

"You're going to tell me," Goss sighed.

The Brit made a hosing motion with his hand. "Too much spray-and-pray."

"Put enough lead in the air and someone is going to die," he countered.

"Yeah," Dane said pointedly. "Your teammates, if we're stupid enough to be in your line of sight."

Goss rolled his eyes. "You are not going to let me forget that, ever?" Earlier that month they had ignominiously lost an online tournament to a collective of foul-mouthed Texan high-schoolers, after Jurgen's lack of weapon control had caused a match-ending blue-on-blue incident. "I'm sure I'd do much better if I had a real gun."

A shadow passed over Dane's face and the other man's mood shifted. "It's not as much fun as you'd think."

Goss didn't press the point. The Brit could be an odd sort at times. For the most part, he was good natured and hard working, even in the face of the grinding bureaucracy of the office's labors. Fast with a joke and funny, too—but then he could change, as quickly as a cloud across the sun, becoming sullen and withdrawn.

Like the technician, Dane was in his mid-thirties, but that was where the similarity ended. Goss had an unkempt shock of oily black hair that rose up from a high forehead and a face better suited to a schoolboy than a grown man, whereas Dane's dirty blond look and stubbly beard framed a wolfish expression that was too serious by half. Goss was, if he was honest with himself, letting his body run to flab with too much desk work and not enough exercise. Dane looked rail thin, but it was mostly whipcord muscle.

He knew only a little about where the other man had come from prior to joining the United Nations investigation team in Croatia, mostly rumors about him leaving the British security services under less than ideal circumstances. Goss didn't pry. In his experience, the English thought asking any kind of personal question was crass.

He decided to change the subject. "Are you coming for a beer after work?"

"Nah. The Whites are playing Dinamo Zagreb tonight," Dane said, referring to the city of Split's premier football team. "Pubs will be full of shouty fans. You know how they get."

"But Croatians don't wreck the place when their team lose, not like your hooligans," Goss countered. He took in the walls around them with a gesture. "We are in Split, not London. Don't you know? It's a cultured town."

"Fuck off, mate." Dane gave a brief smile at the mild dig. Goss had learned early on that the Brit missed his home and would use it to jokingly needle him.

"What did you say?" The question was a rough bark, dragging both men's attention around to the alcove where Goss's prized espresso machine sat.

The Austrian's heart sank. The squat, square-headed form of Senior Police Inspector Franko Horvat stood there toying with a bowl-shaped coffee cup, glaring at the two of them.

The man had an unpleasant habit of sneaking up on you. He wore a gray sports jacket and unmatched trousers that were two decades out of date, and a permanently irritated air that made him seem like he was always picking a fight. He usually was.

Horvat waved the cup at Goss. "What are you saying about Split? I was born here. You're making an insult to me?" The policeman's breath smelled of stale tobacco.

"He's joking," Dane told him. "*It is Austrian humor, yah?*" He said the last few words in a bad imitation of Goss's clipped accent, defusing the moment.

Goss blinked, thankful for the other man's intervention. He found Horvat and most of the other Croat police officers to be quite intimidating, and it was a continual source of dismay to him that their unit was forced to share a building with them. When Jurgen Goss had come to work for the UN he had hoped it would be in some gleaming glass-and-steel office space in Vienna or New York City, not a grimly functional police precinct in Split.

"How does this work again?" Horvat fiddled with the espresso machine, mashing artlessly at the controls, and Goss sprang out of his chair to stop him from breaking it.

"Let me," he insisted.

Horvat thrust the cup into his hands and smiled victoriously. "You make it. You do it well. Like a good wife."

Dane jerked a finger at the ceiling. "You've got a coffee machine up on your floor," he told the policeman. "But you still keep coming down here. Why is that?"

"Not working." Horvat didn't even try to sell the lie. Goss suspected the real reason was half that the policeman was too cheap to pay for it, and half that he liked showing his face around the UN investigator team, to continually remind them whose turf they were on. He leered at Dane. "You find any bombs today?"

"You arrest any of your mates?" Dane shot back. It was widely speculated that Horvat's extended tenure in the Policija was more down to his connections in the criminal world than those in law enforcement, but the man was so slippery that nothing stuck to him. Still, he got the Brit's inference and his toothy grin snapped off.

"*Mislite da ste pametni.*" Whatever it was Horvat said, Goss didn't doubt that it was something insulting. "You must come upstairs," Horvat added with a snort, his small eyes narrowing. "See real police work for a change." He tapped himself on the chest. "You will see an important man do his job." He pointed a nicotine-stained finger at the wall, where a map of the Adriatic Sea and the countries surrounding it was studded with pins and taped-up data sheets. "Not that."

Along the top of the map frame was the investigation team's designation: *Division of Nuclear Security (NSNS Field Operations #7)— International Atomic Energy Agency.* Beneath that, a logo depicted the orbits of electrons around a nucleus surrounded by a pair of olive branches.

Goss bristled at Horvat's offhand dismissal of their work, but he expected little more from the man. Horvat's idea of policing was pushing suspects down staircases, taking bribes and blaming crimes on immigrants, and he lacked the sophistication to handle the idea of bigger threats to the world at large.

Once, Goss had tried to explain to him what the NSNS were doing in Croatia. The country was a choke point for clandestine smuggling routes from Russia and its former Soviet satellite states, a gateway port to the rest of the world through which illegal trade flowed as freely as honest commerce. Much of those proscribed goods were weapons from the mountain of military material created by the USSR during the Cold War—and not just bullets and rifles. Enriched uranium, plutonium rods from fast breeder reactors, atomic waste, all kinds of fissile materials—a whole bestiary of radioactive horrors that might be used to create a dirty bomb, or even an actual nuclear device.

Field Ops Unit #7 was one of many NSNS groups around the world, watching for traffic in nuclear technologies and hardware, constantly gathering intelligence and coordinating with the UN member states to make sure humanity's worst weapons stayed bottled up. But all Franko Horvat saw was a bunch of foreigners in his territory, getting in the way, draining resources and showing nothing for it.

Goss poured out a generous amount of rich Arabica blend into a plastic cup—having learned the hard way that Horvat never returned the mugs he "borrowed"—and passed it to him. "Here." *Now go away.* The rest of the sentence was unspoken, but it hung there in the silence.

Horvat sipped the brew and turned to leave, but he couldn't resist a last taunt before he walked away. "You should go home," he told Dane. "Back to English-land. You're a waste of time here."

"Please tell me you spat in that," Dane snapped, when Horvat was out of earshot. "Why do you even give that ratbag the time of day?"

Goss scowled at his own inability to get rid of the policeman. The last time he had tried to do so, the Austrian's little Fiat 500 had inexplicably been broken into the very next day, and Horvat had taken great pleasure in lecturing him about the consequences of "unfriendliness."

"It is easier than getting into an argument with the man," he said.

"Way I hear it, he's based his entire bloody career on that." Dane shook his head and glared in the direction of the door. "I hate blokes like him. Always got to be taking the piss."

Horvat's departing insult angered the Brit far more than Goss realized, and he wondered why. There were other rumors about Marc Dane, and the reasons why he was working for the NSNS. *He wasn't allowed to go back home. He had been involved in a fatal incident. He had been cashiered as a MI6 field officer.* Goss couldn't help but wonder which one was true.

"Have you got those notes for me?" Dane snapped back to business, back to the reason he had actually come to Goss's desk in the first place.

He nodded, pulling a file from atop a pile of other investigation dossiers. Dane flipped it open and scowled at a sheet of paper bearing the crest of the Royal Canadian Mounted Police. The information written there was clearly not what he wanted. "It's like you said," Goss told him. "There are some suspected connections with organized crime groups in Quebec, but nothing actionable."

Dane blew out a breath. "More data. No conclusions, just more data." He forced a grateful smile. "Thanks, Jurgen. I appreciate the effort." The Englishman took a look at the Cabot diver's watch on his wrist and shot to his feet. "Ah. Gotta go. Briefing."

"Have fun," Goss said lamely. "I have to finish up here."

"I'm sure Schrader will listen. Fourth time's the charm," Dane told him, the dour tone of his words saying exactly the opposite.

The operations meeting was getting started as Marc slipped into the back of the room, but he wasn't stealthy enough to avoid getting a slow-eyed look from the man standing at the lectern. Maarten de Wit was Field Office #7's deputy chief investigator, a tall and shaven-headed Dutchman with a perpetually hangdog expression and a low monotone voice. He looked out over the half-dozen people in the room and frowned.

The Powerpoint display on the projector screen behind him had a photo of an articulated cargo truck on it, and from the glimpses of police uniforms in the corners of the frame, Marc guessed it was from a stop-and-search.

"We were fortunate, we caught this one," de Wit was saying. "By chance. The border officers were looking for undocumented migrants." He tapped a button on the lectern and the picture changed to the interior of the truck. A dozen oil drums were visible, each one wrapped in a sheet of thick plastic. "Contaminated metal slurry," he went on. "Very high levels of cadmium and caesium. Driver has been detained, but as usual the paperwork connecting him to his employers is all make-believe."

"Where was he going?" The question came from one of the local liaison team up at the front of the room.

"To meet a cargo ship. We know the driver wasn't the only one. We'll lean on him to get more information."

"All right." A severe woman in a dark pantsuit stood up from the front row and waved de Wit away, taking his place at the lectern. In her late forties and briskly mannered, Gesa Schrader was investigator-in-charge and Marc's ultimate superior in the NSNS field team.

Formerly a ranking member of the *Bundeskriminalamt*, Germany's Federal Criminal Police Office, Schrader was what Marc considered to be the literal embodiment of the phrase "no-nonsense." He'd been working with the NSNS for months now, and in all that time he couldn't recall ever seeing the woman show anything like actual emotion.

"Every attempt we make to cut off this pipeline fails. We strangle one route, another opens." Schrader's eyes scanned the faces before her. "I am tired of telling head office in Vienna that we have caught another small fish. Narrow the focus, ladies and gentlemen. We are going to stem the flow of this toxic waste, and we will do it with purpose and speed." She took a breath and her lips thinned. "We all understand why we are here. The mission is in the name. The Division of Nuclear Security." Schrader nodded to herself. "That means that every last drop of reactor effluent that crosses our path, every criminal polluter who thinks he can skirt the law, every dumper and trafficker, is our target." She pointed at the image on the screen. "This poisonous material is seeping out of Central and Northern Asia, it is being transited through the Balkans, and we are still guessing at where it ends its journey. But wherever it goes, it makes the earth turn black and die. We are going to stop it. Make sure this waste is dealt with safely, *properly*." Schrader stepped away from the lectern, signaling that she was winding up her statement. "I've spoken with Europol and our friends upstairs in the Policija, and they will lend us whatever support we need. This tip-off could be the breakthrough we've been waiting for. I want your best efforts on this. Nothing less will suffice."

De Wit got up and raised his hands. "Individual assignments and new taskings will be passed out this afternoon. Each of you will have leads to follow."

Marc felt his spirits drop, and he opened his mouth to speak, then thought better of it. But he was too slow to avoid being seen by Schrader. "You have a question, Dane?"

Her tone was telling him that he should shake his head and say *no, ma'am* like a good, obedient officer—but then he remembered all the effort he had put into the investigation he was currently working on and that went away. "What about our active caseloads?"

"As of now," said de Wit, "this illegal shipping route *is* our caseload."

"Look, I get how important it is, but I don't want to abandon what I'm working on. I've got some . . . promising tips." Marc could almost hear the eye rolls coming from certain people in the room.

"I thought your investigation had stalled," said Schrader, dismissing the other investigators with a wave of the hand. "The Kurjak brothers are staying off the radar."

Marc shook his head, standing his ground as the rest of the team filed out. "The Kurjaks are active. Which means they're a viable security threat." He chose his words deliberately.

Originally a minor-league Serbian group in the wide network of Eastern *bratva* gangs, the Kurjaks had made a name for themselves in the 1990s as smugglers and money launderers; but they had come to the notice of the International Atomic Energy Agency in the wake of the Gulf War, when representatives of the gang had offered nuclear materials on the black market, allegedly recovered from secret Iraqi weapons labs. The Kurjaks started a lucrative sideline in selling Red Mercury, a rare accelerant compound that was exceedingly hard to synthesize but, if properly utilized, could magnify the destructive power of even the smallest, crudest nuclear device into something truly devastating. Militants, terrorists and rebels clamored for the opportunity to bid for the material, believing that possession of it would be the first step toward building a bomb that could make the world tremble.

However, those murderous ambitions were dented by one simple fact. It was all a lie.

Red Mercury was fiction, samples of it faked using crimson-colored fluid and radioactive sources stolen from old X-ray machines. No such compound existed, and nothing real was capable of the incredible list of capabilities its sellers claimed for it. But the Kurjaks were superlative liars, and their nuke scam made them a lot of money, over and over again, as they shopped it to any terror group eager to cause mass destruction.

Marc had to admit that he had a tiny fraction of grudging admiration for the Serbs. After all, you needed a special kind of greed and unbelievable audacity to run a con on people like al-Qaeda or the Shining Path.

Inevitably, because of their actions, the Kurjaks gained a long line of ruthless killers who put the criminals on their shit-lists, and so they moved like ghosts through the Balkan states, never staying in the same place for more than a couple of days. But they remained a constant thorn in the side of the IAEA and the NSNS. Their fake deals and the fog of rumors they put up clogged the work of tracking down the possibility of *real* loose nukes from the former Warsaw Pact states. Thanks to them, manpower was continually being wasted on sorting false leads from actual ones.

Marc Dane had been tracking their movements for some time, trying to tighten the noose. He was getting closer, he was certain of it. Pattern analysis had always been one of his strongest skills, and little by little Marc constructed a frame for the Serbian gang's movements. They ebbed and flowed down the Adriatic coast, migrating south to warmer climes in the winter and moving north again in the spring. Right now, he believed that the Kurjaks were lying low in Croatia, maybe even in this city. The problem was, no one else in Field Office #7 shared his conviction.

De Wit hinted that Europol was willing to let the Kurjaks run out the clock on their own. Eventually, he reasoned, their past would catch up to them and one of the terrorists they had swindled would deal with them permanently. "These things have a way of working themselves out," he said.

Marc disagreed. "Look, even a blind squirrel finds a nut now and then." The idiom got nothing but confused looks and he sighed, pressing on. "I know that Vienna thinks the Kurjaks are of secondary importance to the NSNS's mandate—"

"Secondary at *best*," added de Wit.

"I don't see it that way," Marc continued. "The regular military hardware these guys trade in, the guns and ammo? The connections they have inside the former Soviet Union? That stuff is *not* fake. What we should be worried about is not who they are, but who they know."

Schrader frowned. "Dane, by now you understand that we do things differently here at NSNS from how it may have been for you at Brit-ish Intelligence."

"That's not—"

She kept talking. "You are here because of other people's decisions." She let slip a brief flash of irritation. In the past, Schrader had made it clear that Marc's arrival in Field Office #7 had not been by her choice. "Your analysis skills have proven very useful. You have good insights. But what you lack is the willingness to be a team player. You've spent too long operating on your own."

Marc glanced at de Wit, looking for some glimmer of support, but the other man showed him nothing.

"I don't have to remind you what kind of organization this is," Schrader went on. "We do not carry guns or kick down doors. We gather and collate information. We work with police forces and na-tional law-enforcement entities. We find leaks and we plug them." She tapped a long, elegantly manicured finger on the folder in Marc's hand. "Most importantly, we are here to protect people and this planet's en-vironment. I am interested in clear and present dangers that can be grasped and most of all, dealt with. Not in liars and vague possibilities."

At length, Marc gave a reluctant nod.

"This time, do not lead so much," said the other man. "It's like you're wearing a sign on your chest telegraphing your next move."

"I'll try to remember—"

Marc's attacker didn't let him finish, he came in fast and hard with a roar on his lips. The sweeping strike was coming at his throat, the blur of a black baton registering at the edge of his vision.

Every instinct in Marc's body screamed for him to fall back and ex-tend the distance, but he did the opposite. Bringing up his right arm, he went inside the arc of the assault and slammed his forearm into the other man's collarbone, elbow to the sternum and his fist smacking against the side of his throat. Marc twisted his feet and dug in, absorb-ing the impact of the attacker's advance and stopping him before he could land his blow.

He was leaving himself open to a swinging hit from the baton, if the other man could recover quickly enough, but it was a gamble he was willing to risk, his foul mood getting the better of his good judgment. Marc's free hand came up curled into a tight fist and he fired piston-fast punches into the attacker's head, throwing him off balance.

For a second it looked as though he'd turned the tables, and his assailant staggered, reeling. But the baton was still in play, and Marc saw too late that the opening he had provided was still enough to use against him. The stubby rod cracked hard against his chest, shocking the breath out of his lungs with a wheeze.

A moment before, there had been a sharp, angry focus to his thoughts. Now that evaporated and he lost the edge completely. The attacker followed through, and he blocked far too slowly to prevent the hit that dropped him. Marc felt the world turn around him and he fell backward onto the thick padded mat with a loud smack.

The bright fluorescent lights overhead dazzled him and he blinked, swallowing a jolt of annoyance at his own mistake. An oval, smiling face hove into view, the expression widening into a sardonic grin. "You know what you did wrong."

A hand wrapped in a fingerless training glove reached down and Marc took the boost back up and onto his feet. "Yeah."

Luka Pavic tossed the rubber baton off the mat and gave him a measuring look. "You're not dropping the left anymore, that's an improvement." He pointed to Marc's forearm, where the scar from a bullet graze was visible. "But what happened? You made a bad choice." He pivoted his head on his neck, showing no sign of distress despite the multiple hits he had taken.

"True," agreed Marc, shaking off the sting of the fall. "Sorry, mate. Having a hard time keeping my mind on the game."

Pavic's hands dropped to his sides. "Ah. Schrader said no." His normally affable manner became glum. He was a perceptive type— Marc liked that about him. And while that made Luka a good police officer, it also meant that he tended to find his way to things far quicker than was good for him.

"It's not like the investigation is dead," Marc countered, rolling his shoulders and moving around. "Just circling the drain."

Pavic caught the meaning, straightening the muscle shirt he wore across his broad chest. "Still, not good." The shirt sported the gym's logo and a flash that indicated the wearer was an instructor. Pavic was ten years younger than Marc and aggressively fit, enough that it was a push for Dane every time he stepped in to train with him.

But the skills Pavic was teaching him were worth the effort and the bruises. The stocky police sergeant was into coaching mixed martial arts when he wasn't on the job, and he appeared to regard Marc as an engaging work-in-progress. So far, Pavic had managed to drum a few good Krav Maga moves into him, enough that Marc thought he might hold his own a little better the next time someone tried to kill him. After what had happened in the previous year, he wanted to make sure he had a fighting chance if and when things went awry.

The training was free, except that it really wasn't. Luka Pavic was likeable but he was also ambitious, and somehow he had hit upon the notion that working with someone in the NSNS would give his career a boost. Despite all of Marc's attempts to dissuade him, Pavic couldn't let go of the idea that helping out one of the UN's nuke tracers would be a stepping stone to a promotion—and the truth was that Marc needed all the assistance he could get in tracking down the Kurjaks. But so far their arrangement had paid off little more than helping Marc improve his muscle tone and giving Pavic someone to knock around.

Right now, Pavic's street contacts were the only avenue still open to them. Marc told him so as they went through a few more block-and-riposte combinations. "I'm not going to drop it," he insisted. "Those creeps are close, I know it. We miss this window of opportunity and they'll be gone. It could be months before they surface again."

"The timing is bad. Or good, depending on how you look at it," Pavic told him. "I've got an ear to the ground, *inshallah.*" The two of them fell silent for a moment. Both of them were operating outside of the bounds of their jobs, and they knew it.

Marc saw something of a kindred spirit in the cop, the same drive to do right, the instinct that he had ignored in himself until recent events had forced it to the surface.

Pavic was a Bosniak Muslim, a child of the war in the Balkans, and Marc guessed that had a lot to do with why he was a policeman. He'd grown up in the wake of horrors, and he wanted to make some part of the world better in return. Pavic was the polar opposite to a man like Horvat, as evidenced by the fact that the cop hated the other man's guts. The older man wrapped all that in a cloak of bigotry from his Roman Catholic upbringing, seeing someone like Pavic as just another outsider, putting him in the same category as Marc and the others. Luka's disdain for Horvat and his ingrained corruption was one of the other reasons Marc got on with Pavic.

"You don't like this job, do you?" Pavic's question came from out of nowhere as they finished up, clearing the fighting area for the next sparring pair to step in. "Admit it."

"It's not that." Marc shot him a look. "I don't like spinning my wheels. You know what I think? I reckon that Schrader put me on the Kurjak dossier because she didn't expect me to get any traction with it."

"You were dumped on her," Pavic told him. "Right? See it from her point of view. What would you have done?"

"I don't know . . ." Marc threaded his way into the locker room. "Respected my skills, at least?"

"You've never explained about why you came to Croatia," said the other man. "When I ask you, you say things like *I had a disagreement* or *I needed a change of scenery*. I bet you say even less to Schrader."

"About right," he admitted. Pavic waited for him to say more, and he didn't. Where could he have started? *Hey, man, so I was hired by the NSNS because a friend in the British Secret Service called in a favor at the United Nations. And that's because a year ago my own country declared me a fugitive. After a traitor in MI6 killed everyone in my team. And I ended up running halfway around the world to clear my name and stop a terrorist atrocity.*

After the dust settled, he had dragged the truth into the light, but what Marc Dane had had before was gone forever—and the men who were to blame were still out there. For all he had won back, he had lost much more. Unconsciously, his hand strayed to the place on his chest where the puckered mark of another healed bullet wound lay.

He remembered a cold morning in Washington DC and the sharp bark of gunshots. A basement that stank of stale blood. He remembered fire raining from the sky and a pale face falling away from him into dark water.

"Hey." Pavic patted him on the shoulder. "Did you hear what I said? You faded out for a moment."

"I'm right here," Marc said.

The cop glanced around, making sure they were alone in the room. Then he dug in his sports bag and produced a cheap cell phone, an untraceable burner with prepaid credit that could not be connected back to him. "I asked you to meet me here today because one of my informants has something."

The dial on Marc's mood shifted toward hopeful. "And here I thought you wanted an excuse to slap me about a bit." He peered at a message on the phone's screen, but the mix of text-speak abbreviations and Bosnian Cyrillic was impenetrable to him. "Tell me it's something we can use."

Pavic's grin returned. "You're going to make sure I get the lead on the arrest, right?"

"One step at a time, mate."

The cop nodded. "What if I told you that not only were you right about the Kurjaks being in Split, but also that they're meeting with someone?"

Marc's pulse raced, but he tamped down his immediate reaction. "You're sure about this? The source is good?"

"Vanja, he and I have known each other since we were boys," Pavic insisted, waggling the phone in his hand. "We took different paths. He's wayward, but I trust him not to lie to me."

"What do we know about the meet?" Marc was already running an analysis in his head. This was a break in profile for the Kurjaks. They tended to stick their necks out when there was real money on the line, but only if it was enough to make their greed briefly overcome their desire to keep breathing.

"Just that it is happening tonight. But whoever it is, they came out of nowhere and the targets jumped." Pavic showed him the phone again, indicating a particular sentence. "*Velika Stvar*," he read aloud. "*Big Deal*."

— THREE —

Marc found Schrader up on the fourth floor of the police precinct, in conversation with an officer from the Split Port Authority; de Wit was standing sentinel nearby. Marc made his way from the elevator and out through the overcrowded office space, but the Dutchman saw him coming and stepped in to intercept.

"What is it, Dane?"

"I need to talk to Schrader."

The other man paused and sniffed the air.

"I was at the gym on my lunch break." Marc frowned. "Yeah, I didn't bother to hit the shower on the way out. I thought this was more important."

"If this is about the Kurjaks—"

Marc cut off de Wit before the deputy investigator could get the words out. "I told you I had leads." He lowered his voice. "I think I have an angle on them. I just need some manpower to follow up on something, and hopefully we'll be able to bring these creeps in."

"You *think*?" echoed de Wit. "Where is this actionable intelligence suddenly coming from?"

"A strong source," Marc told him, hedging his bets. "He comes with good form." But the brief pause before he answered was enough to make de Wit shake his head.

Schrader stepped away from the uniformed port officer and shot Marc a warning look. "What is it?"

"Dane says he has information on the whereabouts of the Kurjak brothers."

"I've got good reason to believe they're here in Split for a meeting," Marc added. "In the north of the city, most likely. They've been tracked before up near the port at Sjeverna Luka. I think they have a bolthole in that area."

Schrader released a sigh. "This new data comes to light just hours after I reassigned you to the waste-dumping arrest? Conveniently."

"I was going to say *helpfully*, but whatever," Marc replied.

"While you were out working up a sweat, the driver taken at the border cracked under interview," she told him. "We have the name of the ship he was meeting, and it is in port for another few hours. The Croatians are assembling a unit from the Intervention Police to come in and secure the vessel for examination. Even if I was inclined to provide you with officers to follow up on your sudden discovery, I cannot spare them. We're about to make some major arrests, Dane. I need all my people on this, and that includes you."

"It doesn't have to be one or the other," he insisted.

Her gaze bored into him. "Where is this supposed meeting taking place?"

"I don't have that intel yet, but—"

"Do you at least have the source?" asked de Wit. "You can bring him in. We'll talk to him, see what he has to say after we've dealt with the boat."

"No," said Marc. "This has to be moved on *right bloody now*." His voice rose, earning him sideways looks from several of the police officers working around them. He took a breath and worked to keep his tone even. "I mean, we know how these men operate. By nightfall they'll be somewhere else. By tomorrow morning, out of the country and gone."

"If you have an informant, do as Maarten says. Have the police bring him in for questioning," Schrader said firmly. "If all you have is hearsay and rumor, then you are wasting my time. I am not going to keep repeating this, Dane. We need to work as a team, and that means following orders." She walked away, leaving him to de Wit to dismiss.

"You're not helping yourself," the Dutchman told him. "Every time you open your mouth, you're reminding her of the officer she chose whose position you took instead." He shook his head. "You want to think carefully and decide if your future is working with this office."

"She gave me that fucking case in the first place," Marc hissed, as he turned away. "Now I might actually be on to something, and you're not interested?"

The other man stopped himself from retorting, and waved Marc away. "Go back to your desk and cool off. Goss will need some assistance processing any intelligence we recover from the cargo ship. We'll go over what you have after that."

Marc turned around, his jaw hardening—and found himself staring into Franko Horvat's dark, beady eyes. The police inspector made a mock-sad face. "Arguing with mummy and daddy? Very bad."

"You're like a bad penny, aren't you, pal?" Marc said angrily. "Turn up every place you're not wanted."

Horvat's English wasn't the best, so he missed most of what Marc said, but he got the gist from his body language. "Be friendly," he warned. "This? This is all my place up here."

Marc pushed past him and walked away before he said something he wasn't going to be able to take back, but a question pressed at him. *How long had Horvat been there listening?*

He paused near the edge of the office bull pen. Marc pretended to wait for the lift to arrive, shoving his hands in the pockets of his jacket, angling himself so he could see what Horvat was doing without being obvious about it.

From the corner of his eye, Marc saw the man fish a smartphone from a desk drawer and start walking in his direction, raising the phone to his ear and talking quickly. He glanced at Marc and sneered at him, keeping up the conversation on his way toward the break room.

"*Postoje psi njuškati,*" Horvat said, Marc catching the string of curt, slick words in Croatian as he passed by. "*Su blizu. Budi oprezan.*"

The lift arrived and Marc stepped into the empty elevator car. When the doors shut again and the lift began to move, his left hand came out of his pocket with his own smartphone held there. Marc tapped an icon to stop the recording app he had set running and played back what it had just captured. Above the background noise of the office, Franko Horvat's voice was clearly discernible.

Getting out on the next floor, he found Pavic as quickly as he could and thrust the phone at him. "What's he saying?"

The young cop grimaced as he heard Horvat's voice. "Something about a dog. Play it again."

"He heard me talking to Schrader and de Wit. He looked me right in the eye. Taking the piss out of me to my face, because he thinks I don't understand him."

"You don't," noted Pavic. He frowned and had Marc run the replay a third time. "He's telling someone that there are dogs . . . sniffing around. Getting close. He says they need to be careful."

Marc felt a jolt of cold run though him. Horvat was passing on a warning. For a moment he wondered if it might be connected to Schrader's toxic dumpers, but if it was, the message would have been far more urgent. That left only one other conclusion. "He's got to be talking to the Kurjaks. *Damn*."

Pavic made a face like he was going to retch. "Why am I not surprised? Everyone says Horvat is on the take, so why not from those Serb assholes as well?"

"How would you like to prove it?" Marc studied the other man. "Nothing sticks to him, does it? But if we help each other, we could change that. If the Kurjaks are brought to book, you can bet they'll roll right over on any bent cops they have in their pocket."

"Agreed," said Pavic. "But that greasy bastard could ruin everything. If anyone moves out of this precinct, he'll know about it! He'll tell them."

Marc was shaking his head, thinking through the angles. He ignored the nagging echo of Schrader's words about following orders and concentrated. "Luka, mate. You're seeing this all wrong. This isn't a problem. This is an opportunity."

"When have I ever lied?" Bojan Kurjak leaned forward in the back seat of the S-Class Mercedes, holding the phone to his good right ear, his hand reaching up to flick absently at the deformed lobe of the left with his index finger. It was a tell that he pretended he never had, one that always made itself plain when he was irritated. "To you, I mean?"

Bojan's younger brother, Neven, stood outside on the pavement and spread his hands in an irritated gesture that said, *What are you doing?* Bojan waved him away from the car's open door.

"*You've been light on your expenditures recently,*" said Horvat, his voice echoing down the line. The cop sounded as though he was in a bathroom. "*I take that personally.*"

"It's pay-for-play, you know that." Bojan's hand ran up through his tightly permed hair and he resisted the urge to form a fist. "You tell me something I can use, I weigh you out. You're not on a retainer, Franko."

"*Don't say my fucking name on an open line,*" spat the other man. "*I'm giving you something now. You've got heat on you. Maybe leave town.*"

"I'll take it under advisement." Bojan climbed out of the car and slammed the door, beckoning to Neven and the handful of men standing with him. "You want to make a bonus? Keep an eye on it for me. Run some interference." He rang off and slipped the gold-plated iPhone back into his leather coat.

"What did he want?" Neven demanded immediately, his hands grasping one another. "Do we need to pull out?" He rocked back and forth on skinny legs, the tracksuit top he wore zipped up tight against the chill of the day. Neven nodded toward the apartment block rising up above them. The sides of the building were surrounded by scaffolding and sheathed in plastic sheeting that rippled in the breeze. "Fedorin's not even here yet . . ."

"No," Bojan replied with disdain. "It's too late to reschedule this. Let the pig earn his pay for once. It shouldn't take long anyhow." Neven was always quick to worry, and Bojan was downplaying it for his little brother, but he did have some concerns. The elder Kurjak wandered over to one of his men and told him to be extra watchful. *Just in case*, he reasoned.

Neven and the others entered the vacant apartments first, and Bojan trailed in behind them. The Kurjaks owned the building through a series of shell companies, and the construction agency that was supposed to be renovating it was a front for an allied *bratva* clan out of the Ukraine, part of a scam that kept both groups earning by doing nothing. The block was kept in a state of permanent incompleteness, worth more to the Kurjaks as an off-grid place for illicit storage, or, like now, as somewhere they could hold a meeting without drawing attention.

At least, that was the idea. Bojan scanned the faces of the men around him as they walked up a few floors, wondering about Horvat's call. Was somebody in their group talking when they shouldn't be? If so it might be necessary to make examples of some people.

The fifth floor had largely been gutted, most of the party walls gone so the space was open from one side to another. Neven was already telling the men to spread out and make sure the place was clean, so Bojan wandered to one of the windows. Through the dirty glass and the thick green sheets of polypropylene hanging outside, he looked down on Domovinskog Rata, watching traffic passing back and forth along the wide street. He didn't see anything out there that rang alarm bells.

Neven was another story. "Brother," he began quietly, his eyes intense. "I'm not sure this is worth both of us being here. Maybe—"

"You want to go? You're the one who brought Fedorin in the first place." He spoke from the side of his mouth. It annoyed him that he always had to keep Neven in line, and tamp down his impulses. "He doesn't see you here, he'll walk away and we'll never know what he's got to trade. Waste of time."

Neven shook his head. "I don't like this. He pushed us for this meeting, and I hate being *pushed*. It means someone is up to something."

"Just be patient," Bojan told him, glancing at his watch. There was still a while before the meeting was due to happen. "Like it or not, Fedorin has brought us good commerce in the past. He's earned a little latitude."

"I don't know . . ." Neven began again.

Bojan silenced him with a look. "If things don't go how we want," he told him, gesturing toward a shadowed section of the wall, "there's always other options." In the gloom, it was hard to see the patch of bare concrete that had been sluiced with strong industrial solvents a half-dozen times over, but the pockmarks in the wall from through-and-through bullet hits were more permanent indicators of what had happened there.

* * *

Horvat turned the corner past the doors of the interview rooms and ran straight into a wall of muscle. He recoiled, swearing, and found himself meeting the hard eyes of a younger man in a duty jacket with sergeant's shoulder flashes. "Watch where you're walking, prick!"

"You walked into me," insisted the other policeman. "*Sir.*" He pointed at his face. "Maybe you need to get your eyes tested." He advanced a step, and Horvat automatically backed away.

The sergeant was half his age and twice his size. For a half-second, he was actually intimidated, but then he pushed that aside and pointed a finger right in the man's barrel chest. "Who the hell do you think you are disrespecting me?" Horvat searched his memory for a name, but nothing came to him. He knew most of the senior policemen in the precinct by sight, but these kids in the lower ranks were interchangeable and beneath his interest. He carried on regardless. "Don't you know how to talk to a superior officer?"

The sergeant snorted. "You've got rank on me, old man, but you're not superior." He prodded him back, pushing Horvat toward the door of one of the interview rooms. "Not even a little bit."

On the other side of the door, Marc sat at the metal table bolted to the floor, leaning low over the screen of a bulky Amrel Rocky-series laptop. Clipped to the casing of the customized military-spec computer was a device that resembled a walkie-talkie handset. At one end, a cable snaked into one of the hardened laptop's USB ports and at the other, a thumb-sized antenna was aimed at the door. Marc heard the low thud of something pressing up against it and the sound of raised voices.

The device scanned the immediate area for cellular signals and a grid unfolded on the laptop screen. The closest was an active iPhone pinging less than a meter away—the same one Marc had seen Horvat using, the one he still had in his pocket.

Marc switched to a different window, the display shifting like sheets of paper sliding over one another, and tapped in a command line to launch a spoofing program. The scanner changed modes and began spinning a digital lie to the iPhone, telling Horvat's cell to talk to it, and not to the nearest wireless tower. At so close a range, it was easy to wirelessly intervene in the phone's normal operation.

In the time it took for the heated exchange going on outside to progress to full-blooded cursing, Marc's hack was well and truly under way. Sampling the iPhone's number from the signal, he force-sent it a text message hiding an embedded Trojan virus, and let the malicious code virtually kick open the door to the mobile phone's operating system.

That done, the message self-deleted and left behind no evidence it had ever been there. Marc took his own phone and called Pavic's number, letting it ring just once.

"I will have your badge and I will make you eat it, you thick shit!" Horvat's face was red with anger. He heard a buzz that seemed to come from the other man's jacket, but he was too furious to register it. "Do you know who I am? Who I am connected with?"

"I know who you are," the younger man shot back, launching into another tirade. "And if you keep calling my sister, I'll reach down your throat and pull out your lungs, superior officer or not!"

All the wind went out of Horvat's argument in a flash. "What? Who is doing what?"

"Marta told you to leave her alone, you pervert, *so leave her alone*!"

Horvat pushed himself away from the angry young cop. They were drawing too much attention for his liking. "What are you talking about, boy? I don't know any bitch named Marta!"

"What did you call my sister, Kovac? I'll kick you up and down the room for that!" Other cops were gathering in the corridor, hovering on the edge of intervening.

"Kovac? *Who is Kovac?*" Horvat waved his hands in front of the other man. "Someone tell this stupid prick what my name is!"

"Good grief, Pavic! That's Franko Horvat," said one of the onlookers. "Kovac works with customs out at the airport, you idiot."

"Oh, man." Pavic's face fell, the fire ebbing from him, becoming the picture of contriteness. "Inspector. *Sorry*. I'm very sorry. I . . . I thought you were him, see, he keeps sending pictures of his—"

"*Get the fuck away from me!*" Horvat bellowed at the top of his voice, putting all his weight into shoving the younger man aside. The rest of the police officers watching the argument unfold were laughing at the turn of events, and more than anything that stoked Horvat's rage even higher. "All of you useless morons, get back to work!" He roared at Pavic. "And you! I see your face again and I'll push it in, you understand me?"

Pavic backed off, apologizing profusely, and Horvat stormed away down the corridor.

The commotion died off, and after a moment the door to the interview room opened and Marc looked up as Pavic entered. "I really enjoyed that," the cop grinned. "That arrogant cock. He's given me shit more times than I can count, and still he doesn't remember my name."

"He will now," said Marc, the Englishman's attention snapping straight back to the laptop. "Nice job. Gotta move quickly, though, in case he's smarter than he looks."

"You hacked the phone?"

"As we speak . . ." Marc's fingers danced over the black keys of the portable computer as Pavic sat down across from him in the interviewer's chair.

"So how does this work? You got his password?"

Marc nodded. "Brute-forced it. Horvat knows to use a burner, but he's not technically savvy enough to mess around with the core settings. So I've jailbroken his cell phone and rooted it, got myself logged in as a ghosted super-user and . . ." He paused, and looked up again. "Am I getting too technical?"

"Yes," Pavic admitted. "Just tell me, how illegal is what you are doing?"

"Oh, very," said Marc. "Very, very. You having second thoughts?"

"Not many," Pavic replied, after a moment. "I'm wondering how we will explain this all to the State Attorney." He considered that, then answered his own question. "I'll say my informant got us the intelligence."

"There you go. Moral quandary solved." Marc tapped out another command with a flourish. "I've remotely switched off all the encryption and security." He turned the screen so Pavic could see it. "We now own Franko Horvat's burner phone."

Pavic looked at the clock on the wall. "That was fast."

"Frightening, isn't it?" Marc said.

"Remind me to get you to sort out this 'root' thing for my phone."

"Later, yeah." He tapped the screen. "In the meantime, look here. This string of numbers? That's the call-log data for the last conversation Horvat had."

Pavic licked his lips. He was starting to see the appeal of this clandestine stuff. "And we can track the location of the person he called with that?"

"Well, someone can." Marc picked up his phone and dialed a number. "Jurgen? It's Dane. I'm emailing you something. I need you to do me a find-and-forget, yeah?" The nasal tones of the Austrian muttered in Marc's ear and he frowned. He muted the phone and glanced at the policeman. "Give me a minute. He's going to take some convincing."

Pavic stood up. "I'll get the car."

Marc left it a while and then exited the police station through a different door, his battered Swissgear daypack slung over one shoulder. He was trying his best to look inconspicuous as he looped around the car park to home in on Pavic's black VW Golf, but with every step he took, a phantom pressure built up in the back of his head, coming on like a migraine headache.

It is not too late to turn back. The thought pushed its way forward until it was all he could focus on. *Wipe the data on the laptop. Delete the intrusion software installed on Horvat's phone. Convince Luka to let it go.* Those were the steps he would have to take. There was still time. Marc could turn back from what he was about to do and no one would know.

He grimaced and his hands tightened into fists, the physical act an attempt to banish the traitorous notion before it could take hold and spill doubt. The looming sense of an ominous choice was rising up around him, and in a moment Marc would reach the point where he would have to finally commit to it.

It was one thing to spend weeks working on the Kurjak dossier only to be forced to put it aside on the orders of a supervising officer. It was very much another to willingly disobey that directive and break the law in order to stay on the investigation. Back in the interview room, caught up in the energy of the moment, it was easy for Marc to lose himself in the act. He'd been reactive for too long, doing little more than data mining and pattern matching. It felt *good* to do something risky, to go proactive for a change.

But now the spike of adrenaline was waning and he was thinking about what would happen if it all went wrong. Once before, going off-book was what had kept Marc Dane alive when his world had fallen apart around him, but he could not escape the cold reality of another truth—that over a year ago the same thing had ultimately caused the deaths of his MI6 operations team, among them a woman he had cared deeply for. Samantha Green and everyone else in OpTeam Nomad had paid with their lives for stepping outside the rules, and now here Marc was about to start down that same road again. He caught sight of Pavic sitting in the VW and he slowed.

Luka has a sister living in Dubrovnik, he remembered. *His father is retired, out in the countryside somewhere.* Marc was alone and disconnected, but if something happened to Pavic, the lives of good people would be ruined.

If Marc and Luka were going to do this, it would put not just their careers but also their lives in danger. It was a sobering fact to consider.

Pavic got out of the car and looked across the roof of the Golf. "What is it?"

"Last chance to drop out," Marc offered. "We've got no backup, no one we can call on if things go wrong."

"Who are you trying to convince?" Pavic beckoned him, without an iota of doubt in his eyes. "Come on."

Marc's reply was smothered by the chirp of his smartphone. He held up a hand to Pavic, and pulled the device from his jacket. Thicker than a regular cellular telephone, the S60 was a heavy-duty, waterproof handheld designed for industrial users, but Marc had co-opted it for himself with a few custom modifications—an integrated scrambler and a suite of software that stopped anyone doing to his phone what he had done to Franko Horvat's. The caller ID belonged to Jurgen Goss, and Marc pressed the phone to his ear. "What have you got for me?"

He heard Goss let out a sigh. *"Why are you doing this, Dane? If Schrader finds out what you are up to, if she finds out I helped you—"*

"Schrader is results-oriented," Marc cut in. "I get her proof positive and she'll come around." Both of them knew that part of the reason the woman was pushing hard to bring in solid arrests on the toxic dumpers was because Field Office #7 had made few good contributions to the NSNS's mission in recent months. Schrader and de Wit might be convinced to overlook any irregularities in procedure if he gave them a win in return. And despite whatever the Vienna office had said in the past, dismantling the Kurjaks' operation *would* be a victory. "What have you got?" he repeated.

Goss's voice became low and conspiratorial. *"Don't ask me to do this again. The phone belonging to the recipient of the call log you gave me was last active when it pinged off a cell tower in the north of the city. I ran a back-trace to triangulate and found a probable location."*

The Austrian read out an address and something kicked off a spark of memory in Marc's mind. "The Kurjaks have property all over the place in Split, bought up under shell companies. I'm pretty sure that building is one of them."

"I don't want to know!" Goss shot back. *"I am deleting the phone log and everything you sent me the moment we stop talking!"* He paused, then added, *"I think you should come back. Talk to de Wit. I will come with you. Perhaps together we can convince them to look at this."*

Marc shook his head. "You know what the answer will be. Thanks, Jurgen."

"You owe me," said the other man, and cut the call.

"Well?" said Pavic. "Yes or no?"

"Green for go," said Marc, reaching for the VW's passenger door.

* * *

Horvat pulled a packet of Ronhills from the pocket of his jacket and plucked out a cigarette, clamping it between his lips as he fumbled for his lighter. Ignoring the NO SMOKING signs, he marched over to the windows and lit up. He was still angry about that muscle-bound idiot who had made him look a fool in the corridor, and his mind was whirling with different ways that he could make the young sergeant's life a misery from now on. He had plenty of friends among the uniforms, plenty of knowledge about their misdeeds and secrets to give him leverage. Right now, Horvat was annoyed enough to be willing to trade off something weighty just to see that moron reassigned to some dirty, dangerous duty. He grinned at the idea of the sergeant—*What was his name, Pavic?*—getting puked on by booze-soaked tourists on the seafront, or better still, knifed in the gut by some junkie in the nasty part of town.

Glaring out of the window, a figure crossing the car park caught his eye, and between drags on his cigarette, Horvat squinted. It was another of his least-liked people, the dog-faced English prick who always talked back to him. Horvat gave him the middle finger and willed him to stop and look up, but he never did.

Instead, the Englishman stopped to jabber away on his phone for a few moments, and Horvat saw him gesture toward someone in a car. The other person was the muscle-head sergeant. He'd taken off his uniform jacket, but it was unmistakably the same man.

They know each other? The question sparked a sharp intake of breath and Horvat coughed. He stubbed out the cigarette on reflex and processed this new bit of information.

Franko Horvat was not by any stretch of the imagination a good investigator, but what he did have were cunning instincts and a suspicious nature. He didn't believe in coincidences; he held little faith in the idea of random chance. And now he was replaying every moment of that confrontation in the corridor with Pavic, sifting it for some sort of connection with the Englishman and those meddlers from the UN.

Down in the car park, Dane had ended his phone call and was

walking toward Pavic's car. *They are up to something*, Horvat told himself. He was certain of it.

Acting on the gut feeling he had learned always to trust, the inspector rocked off his feet and made for the elevator as quickly as he could, forcing his way in through the closing doors. Horvat slammed the button to take them to the ground floor.

Bojan Kurjak's words came back to him. *You want to make a bonus? Run some interference.*

Horvat grinned to himself as he found the keys to his old Lada in his coat, and his fingers brushed briefly over the unregistered .38 revolver he habitually carried in a hidden pocket.

When Neven Kurjak had first met Oleg Fedorin, it had been on the pool deck of a rich dilettante's yacht in the shallows of the Caspian Sea. He remembered the weekend clearly. Neven and his brother were at the sharp end of their business in those days, there on the boat under the cover of a three-day party, to meet with a group of Finnish neofascists who were interested in buying guns. The Finns had sadly turned out to be a waste of the Kurjaks' time, believing they could trade on rhetoric rather than hard cash—but a chance meeting with Fedorin had rescued the trip from being a total bust. It became the start of a good financial partnership.

Neven got on with Fedorin, but Bojan thought he was arrogant and haughty, strutting about the place as if he was in charge of everything. Fedorin was used to that back across the border in Russia, where he wore the uniform of a ranking general in the Strategic Rocket Forces, but elsewhere he was just Oleg, scrupulously manicured and well-read Oleg, a man with a taste for the more relaxed entertainments on offer in South East Asia and a gambling habit that was in danger of becoming a serious addiction. Always the student of human frailty, Bojan had been the one to suggest they offer Fedorin a "consultancy" role with the Kurjak International Shipping Company in return for helping him with his debts.

Fedorin was a good Russian, a true son of the *Rodina*, and adamant that he would do nothing to jeopardize the security of motherland. However, his reservations did not extend to fixing the books on arms and ammunition stocks, so that the Kurjaks could buy and resell AKMs to African militias or enterprising gang-bangers in North America. And with Fedorin's connections inside the military, he had been useful in providing materials and documentation that gave the Serbians' nuke scams the ring of truth.

But that had been several years ago, and the general had been promoted to the upper echelons in Moscow, where his past associations with Serbian mobsters were considered *déclassé*. So it had come as something of a surprise when Oleg Fedorin reached out to Neven Kurjak through a back channel with a demand to meet.

The communication had been brisk and to the point. Fedorin had a big-ticket item to sell, and a limited window in which to do so. Neven's greed was constantly warring with his sense of self-preservation, and inevitably the former won out.

The man being patted down by one of the Kurjaks' thugs looked like the Oleg Fedorin that Neven remembered from that weekend on the yacht, but a version of him aged far more than the passing of years would suggest.

He looked smaller, somehow. As if he were carrying an invisible weight that was pushing him down. Neven glanced at Bojan and saw a faint smile on his brother's lips. Bojan saw the Russian's weakness and in it, opportunity.

Fedorin had only one man with him, an athletic type in his twenties with the build of a swimmer, wearing a hiker's rucksack and a big coat that had to be concealing at least one firearm. He didn't introduce him, but the way the two of them kept exchanging looks rang a warning inside Neven's head. If it had been anyone other than the Russian, he would have backed out of the meeting immediately.

"General," Neven began. "It's been a while. We thought you'd forgotten all about your old friends in this part of the world."

"I forget nothing," Fedorin replied, with a tight smile. He scanned the other men in the room. "Are all these people necessary? Don't you trust me?"

Bojan took in the dim space of the open floor with a sweep of his hand. "Security is paramount, general," he told him. "You understand." He jutted his chin at the bodyguard. "Who is this?"

"Vladimir," offered the man with the rucksack, even as Fedorin was raising his hand to tell him not to speak.

Neven considered that. So Vladimir was new to this sort of thing, then. Someone with experience would have kept his mouth shut. "Last time I saw you, you had a dozen of your own troops. One is something of a comedown."

"Consider it a gesture of respect," Fedorin offered, still smiling. "I have that much confidence in you."

"Or is it that you don't have the pull you once did?" Bojan wandered across the room. "We haven't heard your name in a long time, Fedorin. Why is that?"

"My more recent postings have been at top-secret facilities. You understand."

"*Mmm.*" Bojan stopped and sniffed the air. He glanced at Neven. "You smell that, little brother?"

They had played this game before, and Neven knew his lines. "Desperation?" Now that he looked at Fedorin carefully, he *did* see something anxious in the man's manner, confirming his earlier suspicions. He decided to push the thought. "The urgent summons. The offer of something valuable . . . You're on the run, I think." A flash of panic in Fedorin's eyes made him sure of it, and he saw the same moment written on Vladimir's face as well. *Both of them, afraid for each other.*

"I don't like to repeat rumors," said Bojan, "but I have heard people say things about you, Oleg." He deliberately used the man's first name, tossing away his title and any possible play at superiority. "About your tastes." Bojan looked Vladimir up and down, and chuckled.

"Oh." Neven suddenly understood what the actual relationship between Fedorin and his "bodyguard" was, and a dozen trivial comments he had never considered from their years of association suddenly snapped into sharp relief. He was dismayed at himself for missing it, but then the ramifications caught up with him and he nodded. "I think I see. Did someone find you out, general? Someone who decided to use it against you?"

Fedorin drew back, closer to Vladimir. Fatigue grew in his expression. "My choice of . . . lifestyle does not sit well with the current administration of my country."

"We don't care who you fuck," Bojan noted coldly, cementing their hold on the upper hand in this. "What do you want and what have you got to trade for it?"

"I am cashing in my last chip," said Fedorin, with a weak sneer. "And quite frankly, if I could have gone elsewhere, I would have. But everyone else is being watched."

"Charming," muttered Neven, staring at Vladimir. "Seriously? He's young enough to be your son."

"You need an escape hatch," said Bojan, staying on topic. "You're *desperate!*"

Fedorin's lips tightened into a hard line. He nodded to Vladimir, and the other man carefully slipped the rucksack off his back. "What I need is twenty million US dollars paid into my Swiss account, tonight." He met the eyes of the Kurjak brothers, and for a moment the commanding, flinty glare of the old General Fedorin was there once more. "And believe me, when you see what I have, you *are* going to give it to me."

— FOUR —

Pavic stashed the VW in the alley behind a three-story shopping arcade and Marc followed him up a rickety metal staircase until they were scrambling onto the tarpaper roof, ducking low so that they wouldn't be seen by anyone on the street.

The sun was already below the skyline and shadows were growing dark and ink black. Aside from a couple of late-closing shops on the arcade's lower levels, there was no activity around to get in the way of surveilling the apartment block across the street.

"Over here." Marc found a turret-shaped air vent near a low wall and crouched down next to it. He dropped the daypack off his back and drew out a long-lensed Panasonic digital camera, taking aim with it.

Pavic squatted next to him, studying the building. "I see some men down on street level. Standing around, trying not to look suspicious."

Marc found them with the camera's low-light lens and snapped off a dozen shots. "Recognize any faces? Your mate Vanja, is he there?"

"I don't see him."

"How did you find this guy, anyhow?" He didn't need to reiterate what they both knew, that the Kurjaks encouraged silence in their ranks by paying with gold or lead, depending on the relative loyalty of their hired goons. An inability to penetrate their organization was one of the reasons the NSNS had never got close to them.

"I called in a debt," Pavic told him, and he said it in a way that told Marc he wasn't about to offer any more explanation.

Marc filed that away for later and concentrated on the job at hand. He let the camera hang from a strap around his neck and used the thermographic sensor in his smartphone to scan the side of the apartment block. In a few moments, he had found the yellow-orange blobs of human heat imprints on an upper floor and switched back to the camera again. He pointed and handed the phone to Pavic. "There we are. Looks like the meet is already happening." He kept shooting with the camera, filling up the memory card with stills, catching glimpses of faces through tears in the plastic sheathing around the scaffolding. "Shit, I wish I had a parabolic mike."

"I see a face. Is that Bojan?" Pavic pointed, scowling.

"Hello there." Marc zoomed in and got a nice side-profile shot of the elder Kurjak brother. "That's him, in the flesh. And if Bojan's here, so is Neven." He knew the faces of the Serbians on sight, along with the mugs of a handful of their gun-thugs, having studied them over and over from photo captures in Europol files. He caught a glimpse of another man—older, with graying hair and a Slavic face—gesturing to someone else. "New player," he said to himself, taking more shots. "Maybe the client?"

"How do you want to handle this?" Pavic said quietly. His jacket was open, and Marc could see his shoulder holster, and the butt of his HS2000 service pistol glinting in the half-dark. "Without more men, the two of us aren't enough to take them in."

"We do the next best thing. We get proof of whatever it is they're doing in there." Marc scowled as he said it, knowing that the policeman was right. "Something Schrader won't be able to dismiss." He tapped a button on the digital camera's control pad and activated the wireless functionality, automatically syncing it to his phone and a cheap cloud server he was subscribed to. The pictures he shot began silently uploading to the Internet, where they couldn't easily be deleted or lost.

Pavic was looking over Marc's shoulder at the camera's display and his eyes narrowed as the device flicked through the images of the men across the street.

"Something wrong?"

The policeman shook his head and looked away. "It does not matter."

Bojan's patience for the arrogant Russian's performance crumbled and he shook his head, glaring at the general's handsome male companion.

"Your boyfriend here is out of his mind," he spat. "You think we've got that much money to spend on the likes of you?"

Neven was frowning at Bojan. The elder Kurjak knew what his younger sibling was thinking. Twenty million in American dollars represented almost the entire operating capital of the Kurjak operation in Croatia. Although they were fairly resource rich, with stockpiles of guns and bullets hidden in warehouses all over the country, when it came to actual currency they were tight on the margins.

Bojan had come to think of their money as if it was the sea. It washed in and washed out with every deal they made, and most of it belonged to others who used the Kurjaks' shell companies to launder their gains in return for a healthy percentage. People like the Georgians or the Ukrainians, their African connections or the cousins in Canada, funneling that silly-looking toy money of theirs back into Europe.

He snorted at the nerve of the Russian for suggesting such a figure. *Twenty million?* Fedorin might well have asked for the moon, because both were equally unlikely for the Kurjak gang to provide.

"We're not interested in Cold War relics like you," Bojan went on, annoyed at having his time wasted. "You dropped us when we became too vulgar for you to be associated with, but now you're here making insane demands?" He shook his head, and waved his men away, out of earshot. Bojan looked at his brother. "He's taken us for idiots, Neven. You were right, we never should have entertained this fool."

Fedorin gave a wary chuckle. "That is funny, Kurjak. Because a relic from the Cold War is exactly what I want to offer you." He made a *go ahead* gesture to Vladimir.

The Russian's companion opened up the neck of his rucksack and removed a large, heavy suitcase made of metal, the kind that were usually lined with thick foam for carrying antiques or fragile pieces of equipment. Vladimir held it like it was poisonous, carefully laying it atop a collapsible metal workbench. He backed away, sweating, as Fedorin unlocked the case's heavy latches.

As he worked the locks, he started to lecture them. "Your bullshit business with the Red Mercury. Did you ever stop to wonder who it was that first invented the story?" He didn't wait for them to answer. "It was *us*. The KGB liked to play the long game when it came to disinformation strategies. We seeded the idea of it out in the world, used the myth to blind our enemies in the West to the truth. We were less powerful, less advanced than they thought. But we had to make sure they never knew that. America has always been brute force and no subtlety, so we used that against them. After all, a lie is so much cheaper to make than something material, don't you think?" He flipped open the last latch on the case, and the snap of metal on metal made Bojan's hand reflexively slip toward the Glock semi-automatic stuffed in his belt.

He hesitated, but the tension was suddenly hard and sharp in the air. He glanced at his men, warning them to hold off with a narrow shake of the head.

"What's in there?" Neven was asking, his curiosity getting the better of him.

"Another kind of lie," said Fedorin. He lifted the lid and turned the case so everyone could see inside.

A fat steel cylinder lay across the longest axis of the case, webs of connectors threading out from both ends to a complex control panel made up of clunky electronics that were thirty years out of date. The Russian produced a key from his pocket and inserted it into a lockswitch. With a twist, the device came to life, a string of numbers spinning up along thick red LEDs. He tapped in a code on a small keypad next to it.

"A bomb," said Neven, backing away.

"Not just *a* bomb," Fedorin corrected. "*The* bomb. Say hello to a toy from the bad old days, gentlemen. This is Item Three from the Exile program. I imagine you've heard of it. One of five portable tactical nuclear devices developed as first-strike weapons for a war with the United States of America."

A nervous burst of laughter spilled out of Bojan's mouth. "You are joking, of course. No such weapons exist. It's a fake, like Red Mercury!" He snorted. "You can't con a conman."

Fedorin met his gaze, and at his side Vladimir had gone as white as a sheet. "Six kiloton yield. A masterpiece of Soviet science and engineering. If this was detonated here, the city of Split would become a radioactive wasteland for hundreds of years."

Neven was shaking his head. "No, no, no. The Russians dismantled the Exile program in 1991, when Gorbachev was president. The
Americans strong-armed him into it, that's what I heard!"

"Partly true," Fedorin countered. "Two devices were rendered inert and retained. I acquired one of them as . . . an insurance policy, and
had it reactivated." He studied the other men, now fully aware that
he was in total control of the narrative. "You know me, Neven. You've
seen me play cards. Seen me win a million dollars in a Macau casino
and then lose it all again the same night. Think, now. Am I bluffing?"

"No." Bojan's brother said woodenly. Vladimir handed him a particle detector from the rucksack, and after checking it to make sure it
hadn't been tampered with, Neven ran it over the device. The insect-
like clicking of the counter rose alarmingly as he waved it at the case.
"Oh, mother. This is . . . *This is* . . ." He couldn't finish his sentence.

"The last of the USSR's ghost weapons," Fedorin completed his
sentence for him. "You boys have sold enough fakes in your time to
know when you are looking at the real thing, I believe. I'm offering
you the chance to trade up."

Bojan took a wary step closer. He was familiar with the stories of
so-called "suitcase nukes," compact weapons that were designed to be
smuggled across the borders of enemy powers and left in place, there
to be triggered close to the seats of government or key military instal-
lations if the Cold War turned hot. He glanced at his men, wondering if any of them understood what they were standing next to.

The general retrieved a thick file from the rucksack and tossed it
on the workbench next to the device. Bojan blinked, barely registering it. It was hard not to be drawn to the crimson glow of the bomb's
digital display. "The asking price gets you all the technical specifica-
tions and blueprints of the devices as a bonus. Act quickly. This is a
limited-time offer." Fedorin gave a grim snort at his own gallows
humor.

Bojan drew his pistol. "Suppose we kill you and the handsome one
here, and we take this thing? Why should we pay so much?"

"I've set the weapon's anti-tremor trigger," Fedorin told him. "Only
I have the deactivation code. Hurt Vladimir or myself and we all die.
The city out there along with us." The general's companion turned to

him, a pleading look on his face, but Fedorin waved him away, becoming hard and cold. "This is how it will be. If you prefer, consider the money as an 'unlocking fee.' But don't take too long about it."

"Why are you doing this?" Neven demanded. "If this explodes . . . !"

"I am desperate, remember?" Fedorin told him. "You do not know how much! Tomorrow, in Moscow, news will be released that will accuse me of . . . terrible things. I have no time. I must disappear. I have been forced to this extreme." His mood shifted into sudden anger. "I know you have the money! Don't lie to me! I've seen the details of your accounts in the Caymans. You have it!"

"That isn't ours to—" Bojan snapped, but Neven put a hand on his arm to stop him, pulling his brother to one side.

"It is real," Neven whispered. "*It is*. We know Fedorin had access to these kinds of devices. We know he could do what he says he has done. Brother, he's brought us the prize of a lifetime."

"*A nuclear weapon?*" Bojan shook his head, cold fear gripping his chest as he accepted the fact. "This is much more than rifles and shells, Neven. It's too much, we can't . . ." He stopped, shaking his head. Fear was not something that often came upon him, but it did now. "Tell him to disarm it. Take it away."

Then Neven asked the question that made the panic ebb. "How much do you think it is worth? We could sell it for *five times* what Fedorin wants, at the very least. You know I'm right."

"Yes." Bojan's throat went dry and he fought off a moment of light-headedness. "*Yes*. But there's just one problem."

"The money." Neven nodded. What Fedorin had seen in the Kurjaks' secret bank accounts was laundered cash being held for their clients. Not a penny of it was theirs to spend, not unless they wanted to embezzle from violent men with short tempers. Men who, unlike the terrorist marks the Kurjaks had defrauded in the past, knew *exactly* where to find them. "You are thinking short term, big brother. We spend that money now, tonight. Then we replace it later with interest. And still we would retire from this life as rich, rich men with what remains."

Unbidden, a grin began to force its way across Bojan's face. He felt the same rush of adrenaline and daring that had always accompanied the most dangerous of their con games. He looked at the silver case with new eyes, and found he wanted what was in it. Wanted what it represented.

"I'm losing patience," said Fedorin. "What is your answer?"

Neven and Bojan shared a knowing look, each of them feeling the same thrill in that moment.

"Pay the man," said the elder brother. *In the end, greed always wins out*, he told himself.

"I don't know," said Marc. "Maybe they've got a sewing circle going on up there." He panned the camera along the length of the building.

"Movement," said Pavic, with a jut of his chin.

Marc leaned in and laid the camera lens across the edge of the roof, quickly finding and then framing the men emerging from the ground floor of the apartment block. Bojan Kurjak was among them, lighting a cigarette, and his body language was all tension and edges. The older man with the Slavic look Marc had glimpsed earlier was with him, as was his athletic companion. Both of them were drawn and tired.

The camera's artificial shutter whirred as Marc captured more stills of the men. They walked to the curb where a silver Skoda was parked, and the younger man scrambled into the driver's seat as though anxious to get out of there. Marc snapped his face and then zoomed in as closely as he could to get Bojan and what had to be their client.

"You can see what they are doing?" asked Pavic.

"Yeah." The client was looking intently at his phone. He saw something that agreed with him, because he nodded with relief and offered the Kurjak brother a folded piece of paper.

Bojan snatched it out of his hand and was immediately making a call of his own. As the client climbed into the Skoda and the car peeled out, Marc dithered, finally deciding to hold the image on the Serbian. He watched Bojan look up at the higher floors of the apartment building as he read something aloud from the paper he had been given. *One of these days I've got to learn how to lip-read*, Marc told himself.

"He's talking to someone up there," said Pavic. "Neven, probably."

Marc nodded as Bojan ended his call. Then, very deliberately, the Serbian took the lit cigarette from his mouth and used it to set fire to the slip of paper.

As he flicked the ashen remains away, a pair of vehicles—a sleek Mercedes town car and a dark blue Renault van—emerged from the concealed entrance of an underground car park beneath the apartment block, and swung around to where Bojan was waiting. Marc swore. The meeting was done and dusted, and now the Kurjaks were moving out.

He slipped back from the edge. "Come on, we've got to go!"

Pavic followed him down the rattling metal staircase at a run, the rusted frame shaking alarmingly as they descended. Marc reached the VW, but his heart sank as he saw a blur of taillights up beyond the far end of the alleyway. He sprinted to the street in time to see the Renault and the Merc vanishing around the corner and into the flow of evening traffic. Acting on reflex, he aimed the digital camera in the direction of the vehicles and hit the shutter button. "*Bollocks!*" He spat out the word. "We'll never catch them now."

"Did you get a shot of the plates?" Pavic asked, jogging up to his side.

Marc handed him the camera. "Should be enough to read." He shook his head, angry at himself. "Maybe we can get something from it, but I don't know . . . This is what happens when we don't have backup."

This is what happens when you go off-book, said a voice in his thoughts. It sounded unpleasantly like Samantha Green.

"We're not done yet," said Pavic, glancing right and left as he watched for a break in the traffic. "Come on." He dashed out across the street and made a beeline for the silent apartment building.

Marc grimaced and went after him.

Horvat was sneering as he watched the Englishman sprint across the lanes of traffic, and for a moment he entertained the fantasy of running him down with the Lada. Parked beneath a dead street light, the car and Horvat were lost in a puddle of shadow, free to observe what had happened and remain unseen.

His instincts had been good, as they always were. He found the gaudy gold iPhone Bojan had given him and dialed a number. He hated the thing. It looked as if it belonged to some vapid streetwalker, and Horvat suspected that was part of the reason that Bojan had forced him to keep it on him. The Kurjak brothers liked to have their little jokes at the expense of others. *Well, tonight the joke is on them.*

Bojan picked up on the second ring. *"Got something useful for me this time?"* he sniffed. The background noise told the cop that the Kurjaks were still inside the Mercedes he had seen pull away moments earlier.

"What were you doing at the Dolphin Apartments just now?" said Horvat, recalling the name for the shuttered building.

"What?" He heard anger in the other man's voice. *"You snooping on me?"*

Horvat ignored the question. "I ask because I guess you didn't know you were being followed by some dog working for Europol."

There was a long silence. *"How do you know this?"*

"Because I'm outside the apartment block right now. And the dog and his pal are sniffing around in there. I did warn you before."

There was a rattle as Bojan put his hand over the phone's pickup in an attempt to muffle it, but Horvat still heard him giving angry orders. He heard the screech of brakes and the distant complaint of car horns. A door slammed and he caught something about *the van, get them back there, hurry up.*

After a moment, the elder Kurjak was talking to him again. *"Listen to me,"* Bojan said carefully. *"You go up to the door and you wait there, out of sight. My men are coming. You tell them what you know and clean this up for us."*

Horvat gave an airy sigh, reaching for a ski mask in the glove compartment. "What about my fee?" He shifted his jacket, feeling the weight of the unregistered revolver in his pocket.

"Earn it," Bojan told him, and cut the line.

Pavic took point, drawing his semi-automatic and holding it close to his body as they advanced up the stairs. He threw Marc a quick look and frowned. "You didn't bring a weapon?"

Marc shook his head. Back in the rooming house where he lived, there was a stun gun hidden in the nightstand, but it did little good for him there. "I never was someone who shot people for a living, Luka." He grimaced at the smell of paint fumes that lingered all around them in the stairwell.

Pavic gave a vague shrug and continued on and up. "That won't give bad men any pause." He was matter-of-fact about it in a way that didn't make Marc feel any less vulnerable.

As they emerged on the fourth floor, the wind was starting to pick up. The cold breeze coming in across the city off the Dalmatian Coast was bringing in rain clouds, and the air was growing chilly. Around them, the plastic sheath over the scaffold supports was rippling, cracking against the steel poles. Marc held his breath and strained to listen, but all he heard was the rush of traffic out on the street below.

"Look around," he told Pavic. "You see any clues, sing out."

"Don't get into trouble without me," grinned the younger man, and he made his way up the central corridor that bisected the layout of the floor.

Each level of the Dolphin Apartments had eight flats, four on either side—but the Kurjaks' workers had hammered their way through all the partitioning walls from one side to the other, making the spaces into large open voids supported by thick concrete pillars. Similarly, there were square holes cut in the floor and ceiling that might have accommodated a new elevator shaft or service trunk, but for now were gaping pits that went all the way down to the basement-level parking garage. Marc gave them a wide berth and ventured in the direction of the balconies, making his way past pallets loaded with sheetrock panels and breeze blocks. Inert gas-powered work lamps were set up here and there, all covered in a layer of brick dust.

Marc paused in the middle of the open area and drew the S60 smartphone from his jacket's inside pocket. He took a few shots of the space, switching to thermal mode in the vain hope of spotting something that might stand out. Turning in a slow circle, he peered at the ill-defined images of cool sea greens and cobalt blues, the objects all around him rendered into visual representations of their surface temperature.

Something nearby flickered and registered with the digital camera: a faint pool of fading yellow atop a metal bench. Uncertain of what he was seeing, Marc moved closer.

He heard Pavic's footsteps as the police officer came in from the far end of the open area. "What have you got?" he called.

"Heat." Marc put his fingertips in the hot-spot. By touch, it didn't feel that much warmer to him, but the camera didn't lie. "Something was here, all right."

A distant metallic clank sounded several floors below them, the sound carrying up the concrete stairwell. Both men exchanged a look. "The wind," offered Pavic. He was more interested in the thermal image the phone was showing him.

An unpleasant thought pushed its way to the front of Marc's mind, and he switched modes on the device, activating a different application. "We know what games the Kurjaks like to play, yeah?" he said, asking the question without really needing an answer. "I've got a bad feeling about this."

"What is that you are doing?" said Pavic.

"The thing about digital cameras," Marc told him, "is that they don't work like film cameras do. Light particles bounce off a circuit, not film. Computer turns that into an image. But light isn't the only thing they can pick up." He set a program called CellRAD running. "See, gamma rays are just a different kind of high-energy photons, after all . . ."

"You're talking about radiation." Pavic's enthusiasm slipped a little. "Up here?"

The smartphone let out a low warning tone, and showed Marc a pop-up window with the words RADIOLOGICAL DETECTION EVENT in large and unfriendly letters. His blood chilled and he backed away a few steps without even realizing he had done so.

"*Shit*." He told Pavic what it meant—that someone had placed a powerful radioactive source on the workbench within the past few hours. "Reckon we can guess the rest."

The policeman nodded grimly. "So the Kurjaks are up to their old tricks again? Selling counterfeits to murderous idiots?"

Marc shook his head and slipped the phone back into his pocket, his throat suddenly desert dry. Pavic wasn't quite getting it. "Luka, mate, it's more than that. This reading? Its way higher than anything some fake-bake would put out. This is like *dirty bomb* levels of nasty."

Pavic looked around, weighing the seriousness of Marc's words. "Call it in. This is more than we can handle—"

This time the sound from the stairwell was clearer, closer and followed by a scrape that could only be a boot catching on the bare concrete floor of the corridor.

"Bojan says you tell us what to do," whispered the thug with the heavy shotgun. He didn't appear to like the idea.

Horvat had seen big full-auto weapons like the man's gun before, resembling the bulked-up silhouette of an assault rifle. He knew from experience how lethal they could be. He pulled down the ski mask over his face and smiled. "Kill them both."

"I thought we're supposed to take them back?" said the other man, a thin-faced Serb who carried a dented aluminum baseball bat.

"Bojan told you to listen," Horvat hissed. "Don't tell me how to do my job. Waste those fools and destroy the evidence."

"Okay." The one with the gun seemed like the simple type, and he didn't wait for any further instructions. Coming up out of the stairwell, he went for one of the apartment doors that was still set on its frame and let the auto-shotgun reduce it to matchwood with three blasts of double-aught buckshot.

Horvat had his revolver drawn and he followed the thug with the bat into the open area beyond the corridor. Two figures were caught framed against the light bleeding in from the city outside, and Horvat's grin widened. The fates had to be smiling on him, to grant him the chance to cross off the dog-faced Englishman and that muscle-bound sergeant at the same time. Even better that the Kurjaks would be paying him to do so.

The gun blasts were peals of low thunder that echoed off the bare walls of the building, and Marc flinched back in shock as a man in a dark

red tracksuit came charging in over the ruined door blown off its
hinges. He held a USAS-12 combat shotgun at his hip, sweeping the
room for targets, and behind him were two more men coming in to
back up the shooter.

Pavic spun and aimed his service pistol, throwing up his badge with
his other hand. *"Policija!"* He bellowed the words across the room.
"Baci oružje!"

The command had absolutely no effect. The shotgunner fired in
their direction in another booming three-round burst, and Marc instinctively dove for cover behind a crate of building supplies. He heard
lead pellets whistle and clatter off the concrete supports around him
as he hit the floor in an awkward scramble.

Pavic wasn't with him. His breath caught and he twisted back in
the direction he had come, fearing the worst—but the police officer
had leaped the other way, running between cube-shaped piles of bricks
a few meters away.

There was another shout, and more words in Croatian that Marc
couldn't follow. The intention was clear enough, however, and it ended
with them dead. These men had to be Kurjak muscle sent in to silence them, and they were blocking the path down the stairs.

Need a weapon. The impulse flashed through Marc's mind and he
grabbed at the first offensive-looking thing within reach, a two-meter
length of scaffold pole. He barely got a grip on it before one of the Kurjak thugs was rushing him.

The fact that it wasn't the shotgunner saved his life. The thug committed to a looping swing with the metal baseball bat in his hand,
and Marc inelegantly deflected it with the edge of the pole.

He tried to bring the pole around again, but it was heavier than it
looked and the momentum was all off. The man with the bat used
his weapon in a forward stabbing motion that put it squarely in Marc's
sternum.

Winded, he stumbled over a pallet. The thug rolled the baseball bat
around in a showy loop and brought it down in a plunging arc, aiming for a point in the middle of Marc's face.

Marc still had a grip on the length of scaffold and brought it up
across his chest to block the falling blow before it could connect. The

impact juddered through his wrists and, belatedly, it shocked his muscle memory into action. Adapting one of the Krav Maga moves Pavic had taught him, Marc pushed up and angled the pole into a sliding strike that cracked the thug's shins. He went down, losing the bat along the way.

Marc let the pole drop, ignoring the stress it had put on his grip, and followed up with a savage one-two punch to keep the Kurjak thug down on the floor. He landed the blows, but the third man in the shadows was already drawing a bead on him, and a heavy-caliber shot rang out. Marc heard the wasp hum of the round as it narrowly missed him and he reacted without thinking, going for cover once again, putting distance between them.

He dared to glance over his shoulder and saw a masked face and the glint of light off a gun. The outline of the man, and a familiar shit-eating grin on his lips, betrayed him. *Horvat. That son of a bitch!*

The crooked cop gave him little time to react. Another round cracked into the floor near Marc's feet and he was forced to run on, toward the far end where Pavic was exchanging fire with the shotgunner.

Marc saw the young policeman telegraph his next action and pop up from behind his meager cover. He shouted a warning, but Pavic was already moving.

The thug with the shotgun was waiting for him, and he fired off the last shells in the USAS-12's magazine in a single roaring discharge. Pavic squeezed the trigger of his HS2000 pistol in the same instant, and Marc saw the moment unfold through a lens of adrenaline-distorted perception.

Pavic's snap shot went straight through the soft tissues of the shotgunner's throat and the shooter reeled back, slumping over into one of the access holes cut through the floor. Man and gun disappeared into the building's lower levels.

But the rounds he had fired hit home. Pavic's right side was raked by a cloud of buckshot, shredding his jacket and the flesh beneath, clawing his face into a red mess. The policeman crashed to the floor and Marc sprinted toward him, his heart pounding.

Blood oozed from Pavic's cheek and shoulder, from the ruin of his right ear, and Marc fought down a jolt of terror as he clamped his hand around the other man's throat. Mercifully, the buckshot had not opened a major artery, but the policeman was twitchy with shock, and blood loss could still end him easily enough if he remained here.

Pavic tried to speak as Marc dragged him back behind a low work-bench. He ignored him, snatching up the pistol Pavic had dropped when he was hit, and blind-firing in the direction of the other Kurjak thugs. Shots came back at him in answer, and he ducked again. Less than a minute had passed since the first round had been fired, and already it felt like an eternity.

Horvat drew back into cover and swung out the cylinder on his re-volver, letting the spent shells within fall into his open palm. He snapped in fresh reloads as the thin-faced Serb limped painfully to-ward him. "You're what Bojan considers good?" He looked the thug up and down and gave a snort. "Pissants."

"Fuck you, old man," growled the Serb. "How many bullets did you waste missing him?"

Horvat tensed, momentarily on the verge of cracking the other man across the face with his pistol. He reigned in the violent urge and grew a sneer. "Your playmate is dead, and I'm getting bored with this shit." He strode back out into the corridor, searching the shadowed corners.

"The cop is hit, probably dying," said the Serb, grimacing with each step he took. "What are you doing?" He jerked his thumb at the room behind them. "They're back there. We have to finish them off!"

"I intend to." Horvat found what he was looking for among dozens of drums of weatherproof paint, and dragged a container into the middle of the corridor.

The can stank of solvents, and he kicked it over, sending a gush of oily paint thinners out across the floor. The fluid pooled around the foot of the inert elevator banks and dripped down into the stairwell.

Horvat found his cigarette lighter and thumbed it to life. "Get mov-ing, unless you want to burn with them."

The thug's eyes widened and his injured leg suddenly became the least of his concerns. Horvat followed him down the stairs, pausing only to toss the lighter up, into the puddle of liquid.

* * *

A bright yellow flash of ignition washed out from the corridor and through the open doors, and Marc held up a hand to his face as pungent chemical fumes filled the building. Cans of cheap, solvent-heavy paint popped and cracked with the surge of heat, and the fire took hold in seconds, reaching out to consume whatever fuel it could find.

"What . . . is happening?" Pavic coughed up a mouthful of pink foam. "I can't . . . see . . . ." His eyes were losing focus.

"Never mind that." Marc shouldered him up to his feet. "Can you walk?"

"Have to," Pavic told him, gasping at the pain. There was a wet rattle to his words that made Marc fear for the damage that had been done to his friend.

The fire churned in the corridor, spewing acrid smoke that drifted past them and out into the air through the open balconies. "Can't get down that way," said Marc, nodding toward the stairwell. He looked around. The access chutes in the floor would be a straight fall to a broken neck. That left the scaffolding surrounding the building. "You're not going to like this, mate. We have to climb down the outside. You up for it?"

Pavic wheezed and managed a nod. "This is not . . . like those American films where the man . . . He says, *Leave me behind, I'll slow you down*. I'm not going to die in here!"

"Yeah, me neither. Come on then."

Together, they lurched out onto the balcony. Below, some of the evening traffic had halted so passing rubberneckers could watch what was going on, but no one was racing to their rescue. Marc thought he heard the distant skirl of sirens, but the wind was blowing in the wrong direction, feeding oxygen to the fire and smothering them in black haze. Pavic slipped off his shoulder and fumbled at ropes dangling down the side of the apartment block, wrapping them around his uninjured arm.

Each new gust made the growing blaze rumble and pulse, and Marc couldn't stop himself from taking in a lungful of fouled, smoky air. The heat and the fire smell triggered a powerful memory that he had worked very hard to bury deep, and without warning it was upon him in full force.

On a dockside in France, he had been soaked in that same ashen stench, the reek of it filling his throat and his nostrils. The mix of burning fuel, scorched metal and seared flesh, so strong it soaked into his pores. For months, that burned stink had followed him around, and he couldn't tell if it was real or his mind playing tricks on him. He read somewhere that scent-triggered memories were the most powerful of all recollections, and for Marc Dane the smoke dragged him back to that brutal night when his team had perished.

He staggered and shook it away with a violent tremor that ran through his whole body. "*Piss off!*" he growled, angrily dispelling the memory with a snarl.

"What . . ." Pavic was trying to form the question when the next blast came.

Marc felt it rather than saw it. Some questing, writhing stream of fire found another cluster of paint-thinner cans and they exploded with a concussive chug of detonation. A shock front of new combustion found the path of least resistance and blew out through the balcony, slamming into Marc and Pavic.

The policeman lost his shaky footing and went over the edge of the scaffolding, falling toward the street, his arm still tangled up in the safety ropes. His descent was slowed, but still he landed with a crash atop a parked car four stories below, the shock of it knocking him unconscious.

With nothing in the way of the flames, the discharge swept over Marc and he caught fire. The material of his jacket ignited instantly and the ends of his hair crackled and burned, tearing an agonized howl from his lips.

He tore madly at the jacket, shrugging it off before the flames could eat through and burn him alive. The fire was everywhere, consuming his world, and in the moment Marc could have sworn it was alive— that it wanted to take him, destroy him, make him cinders and ash.

"*No!*" His breath dying in his throat, Marc made a wild leap at the dangling ropes and snatched at them. Gravity took hold and he tumbled through the smoke, falling and falling.

— FIVE —

The cold, steady feed of oxygen through the mask was painful and soothing all at once. Marc took it in shallow breaths, hunched forward on the edge of the hospital bed, blinking back the ache in his lungs. His chest felt as though it had been hollowed out and re-packed with needles, and the strong chemical smell of anti-infectives hung around him, soaked into the burn dressings on his neck and hands.

Outside the windows of the hospital ward it was overcast. He had lost track of time. For a long while, it was hard to do anything more than concentrate on breathing, but gradually he began to sort out his thoughts and get his head straight.

Emergency vehicles had come for them, fire trucks and paramedics crowding the street as the apartment block surrendered itself to the flames. Marc managed to get Pavic off the car he had landed on and down to the pavement before others came in to take the policeman away. Someone led him into the back of an ambulance and then things went blurry for a while.

He searched his recollection, looking for specific memories—a masked face, a sneering grin. Franko Horvat had been at the building, Marc was certain of it. The corrupt cop had tried to kill them both, doubtless on the orders of the Kurjaks. And he was still out there.

Other memories, old and laced with pain, threatened to resurface, but he ruthlessly smothered them.

A nurse with a curt but motherly smile came and gently took the oxygen cylinder away, offering Marc a bottle of water in exchange. He accepted it, but he wanted more.

"The man brought in with me . . ." He started to speak, and the cracked sound of his own voice startled him. He pressed on. "The policeman. Luka Pavic. *Policija*. Where is he?"

The nurse's smiled faded and she made a gesture across her shoulder, like the cutting action of a pair of scissors. "In surgery," she told him. "Is alive."

He wanted to feel relief, but the look in the nurse's eyes communicated more than her limited English could convey. Pavic was still a long way from safety.

Marc slid off the end of the bed and the nurse held up a hand to stop him, but someone else was approaching, and the official Europol identity card in the man's hand was enough to warn the woman away.

Maarten de Wit looked tired and angry. "What were you thinking?" He spoke in a quiet, intense growl. "I was right there when Schrader gave you your orders. There was nothing in them about cowboy tactics with the local cops!"

"I told you something was going down today," Marc managed, rasping out each word. "You didn't want to hear it. I had a time-sensitive lead on the Kurjaks—I followed it on my own initiative."

"You convinced Sergeant Pavic to go with you? Or was it the other way around?" De Wit went on before Marc could take a breath and reply. "It doesn't matter. That detail is moot at this point. The fact is, both of you were operating outside your authority tonight, and this is the result! Reports of shootings, a serious fire in a residential district. And I have learned there is a corpse in the building yet to be identified by the police."

"One of the Kurjaks' trigger men. They were there to make sure we didn't get out alive," Marc explained. He had already given a statement to one of Pavic's fellow officers. "Came off the worst in it, though."

"Do not be glib with me, Dane." De Wit shook his head. "This is a very serious breach of protocol. NSNS is in Split at the invitation of the Croatian government and in partnership with local law enforcement. We have a well-defined mandate, and you exceeded it!" He turned away, scowling. "We are investigators, not operational agents, not police officers! You have jeopardized the entire presence of our unit in this country, do you understand? This will reflect badly on Europol and the IAEA."

"What about the fact that I was right?" Marc shot back, wincing in pain, his words coming out like a tiger snarl. "The Kurjaks were making a deal with somebody. I got photos of all the players."

"Pictures are not enough." De Wit dropped Marc's backpack on the bed, and inside was the digital camera he had used on the rooftop. "Your property, I believe? This was recovered from the sergeant's car. The images captured by your camera have already been turned over to the Croatian Special Police directorate." He paused. "Is that all you have? Show me some physical proof. Convince me this wasn't just some reckless idiocy on your part."

"They had nuclear material *on site*." Marc's tone hardened. "I saw trace evidence." He told de Wit about the CellRAD readings, and for a moment he thought that might be enough to take him seriously. But when the other man asked to see the smartphone, Marc's shoulders fell. "It's gone. Lost it in the fire along with my jacket."

"Then once more you have nothing but circumstantial evidence. What you say you saw could have been anything, just another of the Kurjaks' signature fakes. I can't go to Schrader with that." He leaned in. "The Serbs sell weapons and that makes them common criminals, and the remit of the police force. But we don't hunt *common criminals*."

"You're wrong about them," Marc insisted. His voice cracked and he had to gulp down a mouthful of water. "They're more of a threat than you realize—they're dialed in. The Kurjaks have got their hands on something deadly, for real this time, and I think Franko Horvat is working with them. He was there tonight."

"Again, a meaningless statement without solid proof. Given what I know of the man, I imagine Horvat has an alibi for his whereabouts this evening," de Wit said blankly.

"He always has an alibi." Marc remembered something Pavic had told him a few weeks ago. "That's because he has something on everyone. But Horvat is a part of this. If we can put pressure on him—"

"Stop." De Wit held up a hand. "Just stop talking, Dane. You need to consider your own circumstances. Schrader is going to review your conduct once we have dealt with our current operation. Until then, you are suspended pending further action."

Marc tried to reply, but all that came out was an exasperated choke.

"There will be an investigation. A man is dead. Sergeant Pavic is seriously wounded. You are in danger of facing criminal charges," continued de Wit. He frowned, pausing for a moment. "The pictures . . . I will have someone in analysis take a look at them. But right now, the focus of our field office is on the disruption of the toxic-waste trafficking network."

"So how did the thing at the docks pan out?" Marc asked.

"Small fish only," said de Wit after a moment, reluctant to admit that the operation had not been a success. He walked away, halting at the doorway. "Some advice for you, Dane? You do not have many friends here. I suggest you be careful about what you do next."

"You burned down our building," Bojan growled into the cell phone. "And now you have the balls to ask me to pay you?" He prowled the length of the big Turkish rug in the middle of the office floor, moving back and forth as his brother watched from the sidelines. The room was over-decorated with heavy, dark wood and leaded-light panels on the walls. Through the floor, the steady thrum of music and slot machines underscored the tense conversation.

"You said get rid of the evidence. I did that. And don't pretend you're not insured." Horvat snorted at the other end of the line, his voice loud over the speaker. *"I probably made you a profit by doing it."*

"Except that you didn't get rid of anything. The cops snooping around there got out alive." Bojan tried to stay in control of his temper, and he moved to a bank of television monitors showing various camera-eye views of the casino below them. Tourist retirees were visible at the neon-drenched bar or lining the slots and video-poker machines, slowly gambling away their children's inheritances. At the tables in the center of the big room, the more serious players surrounded games of punto banco, American-style roulette or Texas hold 'em, humorlessly pushing cards or folds of euros back and forth across the green baize.

"The police don't have anything on you. I would know if they did."

Bojan ignored the reply. "And the man we lost? Who pays his widow?"

"Next time, employ better men."

Neven grimaced and made a throat-cutting gesture, then turned away to help himself to a bottle of Jack Daniel's and a clean glass.

Bojan's hand tightened around the phone so hard it made the plastic casing crack. "You're testing my patience."

Horvat laughed. *"You don't have to like me, Kurjak. You just have to accept that I am useful to you. My advice is the same as before. Lay low."*

"We're at the Queen's High," Bojan told him. "No one is getting in here without us knowing it."

"Good choice. Now let me tell you where I am." He heard Horvat moving around. *"I'm standing in the shitty little rooms where a certain nosy Europol analyst is living. I've searched it for you, in case he had something that could connect back to your . . . dealings."*

"And?" Bojan's tone quieted. He glanced back at Neven. Both men waited for the reply.

"Nothing. I'll go back to the precinct house later. Poke around. Make sure everything is fine." He paused. *"Unless you'd rather I stopped providing my assistance to your organization?"*

Neven silently mouthed a particularly unpleasant curse that had to do with Horvat and a farm animal, and wandered back across the room, toward the large metal case on a far table. He circled it warily, sipping his drink.

"Keep it up," Bojan said, at length. "Just don't set fire to anything else that belongs to us."

"I'll try. I can't get to the hospital right now, too much heat there. But don't worry. I'll catch the dogs for you." He cut the line, and Bojan's annoyance boiled over. He hurled the phone at the wall and it shattered into pieces.

"Son of a whore!" Bojan spat. "Let's pay someone to put a bullet in his face. The whole city would have a fucking party if that shit was dead!"

"We could afford to," Neven said quietly, his eyes never straying from the steel case. "We could afford to do a lot, if we make the right deal here."

The elder Kurjak took the bottle and gave himself a generous measure of the liquor, downing it in one to hide the nervous twitch in his fingers. "We've shaken hands with the Devil, little brother," he said. "How do we do this? I can't imagine any way to sell it on that doesn't open us up to risk . . . The biggest risk."

Neven gave a snorting laugh. "This from the man who helped me dupe the Aum Shinrikyo into thinking they were buying uranium rods? Everything we do is risk, brother. That's why the reward is so great!" He opened his arms and cast around. "Look at this place. For all we've done, it is still a trashy little hole in a town that hates us. Don't you think we deserve better?" He prodded his brother in the chest and topped up his glass. "Don't you want to be richer than you've ever thought possible? Don't you want to *retire*?"

"Yes," he agreed. "But retire *alive*." Bojan aimed a finger at the steel case. "Selling lies and weapons is one thing. The big players out there, they don't give a shit if we peddle machine guns to people who are going to kill each other anyway. But *that thing*? We put it on the market and we will draw some real heat."

"So we sell it quick," Neven retorted. "Believe me, I don't want it around any longer than you do." He cupped his crotch and grinned weakly. "I want kids one day!"

Bojan made a sour face. "So who do we sell it to, genius? The family over in Canada?" He shook his head and answered his own question. "No. They'll horn in and we'll never see a penny."

"So we talk to the Ukrainians or the Georgians," insisted Neven. "Cut them in as brokers for a fair percentage. They can peddle it to the North Koreans, the Chinese, back to the Russian Army, for all we care!"

"They would laugh at us," Bojan said, his jaw stiffening. "Then come in the middle of the night to kill us and take it for free." He shook his head. "Think, you skinny little prick! Where can we offload this where it won't come back to bite us in the ass?"

Neven scowled as someone knocked twice on the door. Bojan called them in, and Big Mislav entered. The stocky man was one of the gun hands from the counting room, and he had a searching look on his face. "Boss," he began. "We just got a message, through the blinds. From a client."

The "blinds" were shorthand for a shell of low-security computer bulletin boards that the Kurjaks and their criminal associates used for coded communications. Hiding in plain sight, they could post seemingly innocuous messages that were really requests for meetings and the like. The Kurjaks mostly employed them in their money-laundering business, rinsing dirty dollars and euros through the Queen's High casino downstairs and their various other legit business interests.

A sudden cold feeling crept up Bojan's spine, like a precursor to something terrible. "Which client?" he heard Neven asking, even as his mind went straight to the absolute worst answer he could hear.

Fate gave him exactly what he was afraid of. "The pirate."

The color drained from Bojan's face and he sat heavily on the edge of his desk. *How was it possible? How could he know?*

Neven licked his lips and kept talking. "What does he want?"

"He's coming. He wants a meeting. Didn't say why."

"Get the fuck out." Bojan found his voice again and snapped this at Mislav, who hesitated, uncertain of what he had done wrong. "I said, *Get out!*" He raised his fist and the other man got the message, slipping back through the door.

"The Somalian . . ." Neven sounded it out, as if he was uncertain of the reality of it. "He's on his way *here*?"

"Is . . . is that scar-faced bastard a fucking mind reader?" Bojan shook his head. "He can't know that we spent his money on the bomb, he can't know that yet!" His gut churned and the whiskey burned in his throat. Panic threatened to bloom and he forced it down hard.

"*He doesn't,*" Neven insisted. "This is just . . . it has to be . . . bad timing." He blew out a shaky breath. "No reason to get worked up. He's come to us before to make deposits in person. You know that. He likes to look us in the eye from time to time, remind us who is working for whom." Neven nodded to himself and wiped away a bead of sweat. "Yes."

Bojan unconsciously mirrored the gesture. "Right. That's it. We can handle him." He poured one more drink and used the burn of it to sear away his moment of secret fear, erasing the little weakness as if it had never happened. "We'll see him. And we'll do what we always do."

Neven's grin returned. "We bullshit our way out of it . . . or we shoot our way out of it."

A harried junior doctor gave Marc a bottle of painkillers and told him he was discharged, but he couldn't find the impetus to leave the hospital yet. Taking the bag de Wit had left behind, Marc found his way to an upper floor where Luka Pavic was in post-operative recovery.

He spent a few blank hours in a chair down the corridor from the injured policeman's room, alternating between a fitful doze and an endless cycle of poring over the photos in the camera's memory.

"Dane?" He looked up and saw Jurgen Goss standing over him. The analyst looked flushed and nervous. "You look terrible."

"Thank you," Marc retorted sarcastically. "You got my message, then?" He had called Goss's number the first chance he had and left a voicemail asking for help, half expecting that it would be in vain. He was heartened to see that he'd been wrong.

Goss handed him a plastic sling bag with some clean clothes and other stuff for use in emergencies. But as soon as he opened it, he knew something was off. "Did you go through this?"

"No," Goss said glumly, "but someone has. I went to your flat, but the door had been kicked in. It was all turned over in there. You've been robbed."

No, I haven't, he thought. "Coincidence, that happening the same night? I bet you measure the boot-print and they'd match Horvat's feet . . ." He blew out a breath and began a quick inventory of the contents. "Thanks for doing this. I know you didn't have to."

Goss looked around, his hands finding each other. "Okay, look, I have to go. Schrader has called everyone in early to do post-raid work on the trafficker arrests. She is very pissed off that the dock operation pulled up next to nothing."

Marc resisted the urge to say something cutting. The Austrian stepped away, but Marc grabbed his arm. "I need you to do something else for me." He scribbled down a URL and a nine-character password on a piece of paper, then pressed it into Goss's palm. "This is a cloud server where I sent some pictures I took tonight, of the Kurjaks and their latest playmate."

"Dane . . ." Goss started to object.

Marc went on. "I want to run his mug through the facial-recognition database, but de Wit has benched me, so I need you to isolate an image of this guy, put it in the system and see what pops." He held up the camera, zooming in on a shot of the Slavic man from the meeting. "Get me a name. And don't talk to anyone else about it."

"I don't know if—"

Marc shot the other man a severe look that silenced him. "I'm not kidding here, Jurgen. This is the real deal, and that man is in the middle of it. I am not going to sit on my hands until some mouse monkey in The Hague gets around to looking at those images. By then, it'll be too late!"

"Schrader knows I helped you with the phone trace!" Goss blurted out, and he blinked. "She didn't say as much but . . . she knows. She warned me not to follow your example."

"Oh." Marc felt a jolt of guilt that stopped him dead. It was one thing to risk his own future over this, but could he jeopardize the Austrian's as well? Luka Pavic had worked with Marc knowing full well what the risk was, but Goss . . . The honest truth was that Marc had been using his friendship with the other man to get what he needed. "Right. I'm sorry. But I wouldn't be asking you if this wasn't important, Jurgen." Even as he said the words, he hated himself a little for doing so.

Goss swallowed and looked at his shoes. "Okay. Sure. I will see what I can find." He set off quickly, as if he wanted to get away before Marc pressed him to do more.

Glumly, Marc opened his weather-beaten backpack, stuffing the camera and the other gear from the sling bag inside. If Horvat or some Kurjak goon had decided to toss his place, they would have found nothing worth taking. Everything Marc needed in an emergency was in a custom-hidden compartment in the base of the Swissgear backpack, concealed behind layers of lightweight frequency-scattering materials designed to confuse metal detectors and T-wave security scanners. There was some money and two snap cover passports in there, parting gifts from his old friend John Farrier at MI6. Enough to get him out of the city, if he needed it. But *cut and run* wasn't on his mind at the moment.

Marc slipped into a public restroom down the hall and cleaned himself up as best he could. Changing into the fresh clothes, he carefully put a heavy shirt on over his dressings, as others came and went around him.

He was in the process of zipping up the backpack when a man stepped up to a nearby sink to wash his hands. Glancing over, Marc found himself looking at a face he had seen before, reflected in the neighboring mirror.

A guy a few years younger than him, with a distracted expression on a gaunt aspect, he wore black jeans and a dark brown leather jacket over a baggy hoodie. The jacket was cut large, in the way that a lot of *bratva* types liked, all the better to conceal the shape of a holster hidden beneath.

Marc looked away as the man left the room, placing him a moment later. *I have his picture. He was at the apartment block.*

Going through the stills over and over again, Marc had committed the faces to memory, searching them for something, for any detail that might be useful. And now one of them was here.

But he hadn't recognized Dane. Which could only mean one other thing.

Luka Pavic was a sketch of himself, drawn out and pallid against the starched sheets of the hospital bed in the corner of the recovery room. An IV drip reached down to his uninjured arm. Part of his face was concealed behind a half-mask of bandages, and more dressings covered his right shoulder and arm. The trauma team had done their best to dig out every piece of shot that had lodged in his flesh, and to close up the myriad of wounds which clawed across him. The damage had gone through to bone and muscle, some random fragments even scoring the edges of his lungs—but Pavic was strong and fit, and if he could pull himself through the first few days, he would survive this. The soft pulse of a heart monitor chimed steadily to itself, watching over him.

The man in the leather jacket stood at the foot of Pavic's bed, studying him silently. Outside in the corridor, there were few people to notice the intruder and he had crept into the room easily, without alerting anyone. Now the question was whether he could manage what he had come here to do without being discovered. There were policemen in the building; he had seen them as he had entered, being careful to avoid their glances. If they got him, if he was arrested . . . It would all be over.

He moved until the bed was between him and the door, and looked around, finding a locker that contained Pavic's clothes and personal effects, sealed in a plastic packet.

He was reaching for it when he heard the door behind him click shut.

"Get away from him." Marc dropped the backpack onto the floor and spoke in low, clear tones. He kept his hands at his sides, shifting his feet so he could move fast to block the other man if he tried something. Other than deciding to take a dive through the third-story window behind him, there was no way out of the recovery room except via the door that Marc was now blocking.

The guy in the leather jacket glanced at Pavic, who lay there unconscious and unaware, his breathing shallow beneath the oxygen mask over his mouth and nose. The bag of fire-damaged clothes in the man's hand didn't move. Marc could see him weighing his options, and knew that he could understand his words.

"I'm not going to tell you again."

That got him a wary nod, and the man moved around the bed, still holding the bag, slowly raising one hand in a conciliatory gesture.

There has to be an alarm button in here, Marc thought, and for a second he broke eye contact, searching for it.

The man in the leather jacket took the opportunity and threw the bundle of clothes at Marc's chest in a sudden flurry of motion.

Marc instinctively put up his hands to deflect it, and in the same moment the other man was drawing a gun.

The first move caught him off guard, but now he was reacting with the intruder, and as the pistol came around he dashed forward and closed the distance between them. His arms came up in a motion that caught the other man's forearm between them in a crossing blow. Done right and with enough force behind it, the move could snap bone, but Marc was still inexpert with the tactic and the block was only good enough to disarm the other man.

The intruder grunted in pain and lost the grip on his pistol. Marc immediately kicked it away, under the bed where neither of them could reach it, and then put his shoulders into forcing the intruder away from Pavic's sleeping form.

They pivoted, trading short jabbing punches and dragging against one another. Marc fought to keep the other man close in and off balance, while the intruder desperately tried to disengage and get some distance. When that didn't work, the man in the leather jacket tried a different tack, aiming hard, sharp kicks at Marc's lower legs.

One blow landed and Marc swallowed a snarl of pain. A second and third kick in the same spot came straight after and Marc felt his knee suddenly bend. The intruder was trying to put him on the ground.

Marc relented and staggered back before he lost his footing, and there was a split second when the man's eyes flicked away from him to the bag of clothing lying on the floor. This time, Marc turned on the intruder's moment of inattention and lashed out in a wide swing that caught a ceramic vase full of decorative origami flowers sitting on the top of a nearby dresser. With an artless half-throw, half-shove, Marc sent the vase through the air and the man in the jacket hit back by reflex, striking out with his hand. The cheap vase shattered as he connected with it, and Marc was already coming back at him.

Snatching at a fistful of a loose blanket at the end of the bed, Marc dragged it up with him. Clumsy but fast, he swiped it toward the intruder, forcing him back.

The man cursed and flailed, throwing a blind punch. Marc hissed in return as a falling blow clipped his forearm where the old bullet graze was, and a surge of agony shuddered along his nerves, deadening the flesh where the blow landed.

Marc punched at the shrouded, thrashing figure and the pair of them overbalanced, tumbling against a threadbare armchair beside the bed. His opponent shrugged out of the confines of the blanket and his face emerged, eyes wide and cheeks flushing a furious crimson. Another vicious blow landed in Marc's gut and all the air gushed out of his chest in a strangled wheeze. Fighting past the moment, he grabbed for his opponent's throat.

"What are you two doing?" The strained voice from the bed made both combatants stop dead. Pavic tried to raise his head, pulling the oxygen mask down from his mouth. "Stop . . . stop that." The effort of talking was hard for him. "Vanja," he said to the intruder. "You should . . . not be here."

"*You're* Vanja?" Marc let go of him. "The informant?"

The other man managed a nod.

"Marc," said Pavic thickly, his eyes fluttering as he started to fade back into unconsciousness. "Stop hitting my cousin."

They sat down opposite one another, Vanja in the old armchair and Marc on a stool he found in the corner of the room. Two plastic cups of bad machine-brewed coffee were between them on a moveable table, a kind of mutual peace offering that both men sipped once and then left untouched.

Together, they had silently cleaned up the debris from the broken vase and Marc had recovered the Czech-made CZ 75 semi-automatic from beneath the bed. Unloaded now, it sat out of reach of both of them on the dresser, on top of the bag of clothing.

"Cousin," said Marc, turning this new piece of information over in his thoughts. "Huh. That explains a lot." Something Pavic had said before came back to him. *He and I have known each other since we were boys. He's wayward, but I trust him not to lie to me.*

"I was afraid you were here to kill Luka," said Vanja.

"Ditto," said Marc. Vanja didn't get what he meant, so he pressed on. "You work for the Kurjaks. I saw you at the Dolphin Apartments tonight."

Vanja nodded. "They don't usually bring me along. But Neven wanted more men there . . ." He trailed off.

Another memory snapped into place for Marc. Pavic had reacted to something when they were up on the roof across from the apartment block. He had seen his cousin there among the Kurjak gunthugs, and said nothing.

"You know they're scumbags, right?" Marc told him.

"Don't judge me," Vanja snapped back, keeping his voice down. "You're not from this place. You don't know how it is for us. You take any chance to make money that comes to you."

"Fair enough," Marc said. On the South London council estate where he had grown up, a few of his contemporaries had been sucked into gangs and the lower ranks of organized crime. Marc had broken away from all that by joining the Royal Navy, and he wondered if similar paths had been put before Pavic and his cousin—the good road or the bad.

"Luka's family always treated me well," Vanja offered, without prompting. "I owe him." He left it at that.

"So why are you here?"

Vanja looked away. "I heard he was hurt. I wanted to make sure he was still . . . that he was okay." He shook his head. "If the Kurjaks know Luka and I have been talking, we are both dead men."

"You're afraid someone in the police force will find out you were giving information to Pavic, if something happened to him?"

"The cops have rats in their house," Vanja replied.

"Yeah," said Marc. "I've met Franko Horvat."

The other man looked as though he wanted to spit. "He does their dirty work for them, and no one can touch him." He leaned in. "I have to make sure Horvat can't connect anything to me, you get it?"

All at once, Marc knew the reason why Vanja was sneaking around in Pavic's recovery room, why he was so interested in the injured man's personal effects. Marc snatched up the bag of clothes and stepped away. He reached inside, feeling around. *Shoes, wallet, keys, cell phone . . . Two cell phones.*

He pulled out the cheap burner phone that Pavic had shown him in the locker room of the gym. "Looking for this?"

"Give it to me!" Vanja went to stand up but Marc waved him away.

"All the messages you sent him are in the memory of this thing, yeah? If the Kurjaks had it, they'd be able to figure out who was talking out of school."

Vanja's face fell. "Please, just let me have it. I'm sorry about what happened to you and Luka, but I have to be thinking about myself now. Give me the phone!"

Annoyance flared in Marc's chest. "What, so you can walk away and pretend this didn't happen?" But even as he said the words, he could see it from Vanja's perspective. Europol's files on the Kurjaks had plenty of grisly data proving their reputation for coming up with creative punishments for the disloyal.

Marc's instinct was that Vanja was on the level, and backed up by Pavic's faith in the man, he guessed he was hearing the truth from him. Pavic was eager, but he wasn't a fool, and if the policeman trusted Vanja, then Marc reckoned he could too. But that didn't go both ways. Marc didn't have twenty-plus years of familial relationship to secure Vanja's trust.

What he did have was leverage, and he was holding it in the palm of his hand. "You want this?" Marc heard himself saying. "It's yours . . ."

"*If* I help you?" Vanja said bitterly, seeing it coming.

Marc hesitated. During his basic training at British Intelligence, he and his fellow inductees had been briefed on the complexities of acting as a handler for a confidential source—an "asset" as they were typically known. And while he understood that manipulation and coercion were a part of that process, vital to intelligence gathering, it wasn't something that sat right with him. Finding someone's psychological weakness, locating their pressure points and squeezing, did not come easily to him. *At least, it didn't before today.* Marc recalled his earlier conversation with Goss and frowned.

He took the direct approach instead. "You were there when the Kurjaks had the meeting. Do you know who they were dealing with?"

Vanja shook his head again. "A Russian. But they kept us away.

Never heard anything. The Kurjaks don't like anyone listening in on their deals."

"The case," Marc said, pushing hard. "There's radioactive material inside it. And not just some glow-in-the-dark paint. *Weapons-grade*. You understand how serious that is, yeah?"

The other man paled, and Marc knew this was news to him. "*O moj Bože . . .*"

"Listen, you tell me where the Kurjaks took that case, the phone is yours. Deal?"

Vanja leaned forward in his chair, breathing hard. "I . . . I can't. I don't know. The brothers are paranoid about their security. Always moving around."

Marc pocketed the burner. "So how do you get your orders?"

"I am told. The men who tell me get texts. Neven has phones for them, with software that makes the words all *slučajan . . .*" He waved at the air. "Random."

"Encrypted messaging."

"I can't go against them . . ." Vanja nodded, got up and went to his cousin's side. "I didn't mean for Luka to get hurt. But he's impulsive. Always has been."

"If it's immunity you want, I can talk to Europol. You help us bring in the Kurjaks, that can happen." Marc made the promise even though he had no guarantee that he could fulfill it. Vanja was the only lead he had right now, and he couldn't afford to let him slip away. "Tell me what you know."

"Something is going on," Vanja admitted, after a long silence. "I heard a couple of the other men talking about a meeting. Not with the Russian. Another foreigner. Today. That's all I have."

"Another big deal? Where?" Marc demanded. "Think, man. There's a dozen places in Split and out of town where the Kurjaks have their boltholes. I only need to know *which one*."

"I told you, *I don't know!*" Vanja snapped, his voice rising. On the hospital bed, Pavic stirred and groaned. "I do not see the messages," he added. "I am just muscle. Not *important* enough."

"Maybe so," said Marc, as the spark of an idea formed. "But I reckon I know a guy who thinks he *is*."

— SIX —

The commuter jet from Zagreb was the first arrival at Split's airport that morning, touching down on the runway just after dawn. Ramaas appeared to be asleep for the entire flight, but it was a mask he wore to avoid having to converse with any of the aircraft's crew or passengers. His eyes closed behind a pair of large Oakley sunglasses, the warlord allowed himself to drift with the passing of the journey, but he could not rest.

He did not like to fly. Being confined inside a pressurized metal tube thousands of feet up, breathing in processed air, all while someone else was deciding where they would go . . . That made him tense and irritable. Ramaas was unwilling to give up control of life to any living being. He granted that trust to *Waaq*, and he was willing to give it briefly to the oceans when he sailed upon them, but those were both forces of nature that all men had to respect. Putting his life in the hands of a mere pilot was anathema to him. Still, he took some small comfort in the knowledge that, if he were to perish because of some error made by the captain of the airliner, the man's entire family would be murdered in forfeit by Ramaas's clan. *Perhaps it is best for the man's concentration,* he reflected, *that he does not know this.*

The flight was the last leg of an endless parade of identical passenger cabins and airport departure lounges, from Mogadishu out to Istanbul and then to Croatia. Ramaas imagined that the men who feared him back in Somalia were aware by now that he had left the country. They had spies at the airport, the docks, and every border crossing. But they would not know the reasons why, and that would worry them.

He smiled slightly as the jet rolled to a stop by the gate and the passengers began to disembark. After the killing of Welldone Amadayo, the warlord's enemies and allies alike were caught in a cycle of indecision, afraid to make an overt move in any direction for fear it would be the wrong one. In this moment, Ramaas would take the next step, advancing his cause while theirs stagnated.

The men at immigration control waved him through without comment. He carried little in the way of baggage, and nothing on him that was illegal. The Republic of Kenya passport he traveled under was a very expensive forgery sourced for him out of Hong Kong, one that had never been challenged. Ramaas strode across the black-and-white grid of the airport terminal's tiled floor, finding a spiral staircase to take him to the upper terrace.

The airport was relatively small and there was no multi-faith prayer room here, which irritated him. It had been far too long since he had spoken with God, and he wanted the clarity that gave him. It was not something he could do out in the open, among foreigners. It was a private act, for Ramaas and his deity alone to share.

Finding a quiet corner, he switched on his smartphone and the device awoke with two messages waiting for him. An ordinary iPhone he had taken from a plundered cargo, it sat inside a form-fitting case that doubled its thickness and transformed it into a satellite-capable device. Ramaas entered his user code to activate the phone's encryption software and a moment later he heard Zayd's voice on the other end of the line as an Internet connection was made.

"*Boss. I'm here.*" Ramaas smiled at the man's terse report and listened to him name a time a few hours hence. "*Meet is set. What do you want me to do?*"

Here meant Western Italy. *Meet* meant a face-to-face audience with the *gaal,* Brett. What would happen there, what orders the warlord would give to Zayd, would very much depend on the conversation Ramaas was going to have with the Serbians. "Be ready, brother," he said, at length. "In the days to come, we will free ourselves from the last of the shackles."

Ramaas cut the line and then frowned at the second message. A string of text from Guhaad brought troubling news.

One of Ramaas's men was an educated youth named Jonas, who had lived in America for years but returned to Somalia to flee police authorities. His dalliances with computers had been his undoing, but he was from a brother clan, and Ramaas had found good uses for him and his skills.

Ramaas likened Jonas to a spider in the middle of a web, sitting patiently and feeling for vibrations from across the world. He had set up their paths of digital communication and his lines reached out to many places, from monitoring the cargo manifests of passing ships to be targeted by the clan's raiders, to watching the poorly shielded bank balances of the Serbian money launderers.

The warlord's expression became stony as he read Guhaad's clumsy words. The Serbs had moved a lot of money in the past twenty-four hours, and there was no sign of where it had gone to. Ramaas read the message a second time to make sure he had missed no nuance of it, then cleared the phone's memory and walked outside. He needed the air.

On the airport terminal forecourt, taxis and tour buses were arriving, sliding in beneath a wide white pergola held up by sculptured pillars that resembled metal palm trees. Wind off the sea made the fabric crackle and Ramaas walked on, considering his next move.

He had never expected his path to be a simple one. With each step forward he took, there were always obstacles. Amadayo and his so-called influence had been the most recent of them, and the Serbians would be the next.

But the *money* . . . If there was a problem, then it could jeopardize everything. He had come here to take what the Serbians owed him, but if they suddenly reneged on that agreement, the results would be unacceptable.

Bold action was measured in bullets, blood and dollars. Ramaas had much of the first two on hand, but the last he still needed to control.

He halted, alone in a stand of trees, and bowed his head reverently. *A sign,* he decided. *It is said that the world is forever balanced upon the horns of the bull, so I will know if that balance favors me. I will ask for a sign, and if it comes I will know I am just in this.*

Wheels crunched on tarmac nearby and he heard the slam of a car door. Ramaas looked up, irritated by the intrusion upon his private introspection.

Three men, all wearing tracksuit jackets that did nothing to conceal the guns they carried, stood in front of an idling Mercedes. "I am Mislav," said one of them, in heavily accented English. "You are Mr. Ramaas?"

"Just Ramaas," he corrected.

"Car is for you," Mislav told him, indicating it with a sweep of the hand. "Please come."

"You are all alone?" said one of the others, looking around to see if he had arrived with an entourage. There was judgment in the words, and Ramaas found that objectionable.

He walked toward the Mercedes, pausing to loom over the man who had asked the question. "I have never needed anyone else to handle my business." Ramaas pulled down the sunglasses so his dark shark's eye could get a good look at him. "Take me to the Kurjaks."

"Bojan, he has a nice hotel room booked for you," Mislav began. "We go there first."

"This is not a discussion," Ramaas corrected him once again, and climbed into the town car's back seat.

Marc stifled a yawn and pulled his laptop from the bag on the seat beside him, sliding down a little below the level of the windows. From the inside of Vanja's battered Fiat Punto, they could both watch the police station across the street, but Marc knew their time was limited. Sooner or later, someone on the front desk would notice them parked out here and send a patrol officer to come and take a look.

Up in the front, Vanja leaned across the steering wheel and set to work lighting a cigarette. "How long will this take?"

"You in a hurry?" The laptop ran through its boot sequence and Marc activated the Wi-Fi sniffer, quickly locating the secured network inside the precinct.

"If I am missed, people will get suspicious," Vanja went on. "Why do you need me? I can't help you with that . . ." He nodded at the computer.

"You're here because I need a ride, among other things," Marc said absently, his hands moving back and forth over the keyboard. The confidence that had been blown out of him in the apartment fire, the impetus that had pushed him into these actions in the first place, had returned to him now. The laptop was a tool he could understand, a system that Marc had full control over. Through it, his skills were at their strongest, and for the first time in hours he didn't feel battered, strung out or bleak.

He pulled up the command panel of the root control program he had installed on Franko Horvat's phone and asked it to report in. A heartbeat later, a rich stream of co-opted data told him exactly what he wanted to know. The phone's GPS showed Marc it was two hundred meters from where he was sitting, turned on but not currently in use. He toyed with the idea of using the control program to remotely activate the microphone, then dismissed the thought. Doing so too soon would risk exposing his intrusion to the user, and if Horvat suspected for one moment that his phone was compromised, he would dump it.

"We're going to have to be subtle about this," Marc said aloud.

"How are you going to get Horvat to tell you where the Kurjaks are?" Vanja took a long drag on his cigarette and blew smoke, filling the car's stale interior. "He won't sell them out unless his life depends on it."

"He's not going to tell us," said Marc. "He's going to show us."

Horvat's burner phone had only one number in its memory, and the text-messaging subroutine was set to self-delete every communication it got after one reading. But what was visible to the user and what was actually still stored on the phone were two different things. In the time it took Vanja to finish his cigarette, Marc had descended into the phone's redundant memory and reconstructed the last text message it had received.

He turned the laptop so Vanja could see it. "I don't read Croatian. What does that say?"

Vanja leaned closer, squinting. "It's from last week. From Bojan. Telling him he's going to be in town. Like, a warning. Bojan saying he doesn't want anyone to bother him."

Marc offered the computer to him. "Write another message. Pretend you're Bojan, tell Horvat to come and see him. Don't put in a lot of detail. *Get over here now,* that kind of thing."

"What is the point of that?" Vanja didn't reach for the laptop.

"We're taking a gamble, see," Marc explained. "If Horvat knows where the Kurjaks are right now—"

"You can tail him." The other man nodded. "Okay, I get it." He started to hunt and peck at the keys. "I should insult him," he added. "Bojan does that all the time."

"Whatever is authentic," Marc agreed. "Just don't bury yourself in the part." While the other man typed laboriously, Marc found the digital camera and carefully aimed it in the direction of the police station's entrance.

"Done," Vanja said eventually, with a crooked smile. "I say, *Hey, asshole. We want you here, right now. Don't make us wait.*" He handed back the laptop, and Marc hit the key that would send the message to the phone, as if it had just received it from Bojan's number. "We are done?" added the other man hopefully. "You give me the burner now?"

"You get the phone, you're safe," Marc replied. "What about Luka? If the Kurjaks get to him, what then? What about his family, if Luka winds up dead?" He pressed on Vanja's loyalty to his cousin, pushing away the momentary antipathy he felt for his own actions. It was easier to silence than he'd expected, and if anything, that troubled him even more. "You want that to happen?"

Through the lens of the camera, Marc saw Horvat emerge from the police precinct, scowling up at the gloomy morning sky and the implied threat of rain. The corrupt cop walked to his car and climbed in. Horvat had tailed Pavic's VW the night before and turnabout would be fair play.

"The green Lada over there." Marc pointed out the car before Vanja could reply to his earlier comments. "Follow it, and don't be obvious. We screw this up and that's the end of it."

Vanja said something under his breath that was clearly some kind of curse, and started the engine.

"I'll do the talking," said Bojan, taking up a spot near the big oak desk in the back of the office. "Africans respect strength."

Neven made a sour face and dragged a dust cloth over the steel case on the opposite side of the room. "I can show strength when I need to," he insisted. He tapped his head. "Mine is all up here, not in my dick like yours, brother."

Bojan scowled back at him. "Just shut up and let me deal with this. We want him out of here as quickly as we can." He shook his head. "Too much is happening all at once. He's the last thing we need right now. We have to get rid of him and find a safe place for *that*." He jerked a thumb at the concealed case.

"There's the warehouse out by the railyards—" Neven began a reply, but then there was a knock at the office door. Big Mislav entered with Erno, another of the Kurjaks' drivers, and the pirate warlord himself.

Ramaas took in the room with an imperious glance and removed his sunglasses, folding them into one of his thick-fingered hands. That strange, half-blank gaze of his raked over Neven and he did his best to give a nonchalant nod in return—but the African's presence unsettled him and he wanted to be far away from here. Ramaas made Neven think of the bomb, hidden there in the room with them. Both contained destructive forces he didn't want to be witness to.

Bojan mouthed a few pleasantries, offering his hand to the warlord. Ramaas gave it a cursory shake. "We have business to discuss," he said.

"I will tell you now, you have come at a bad time." Bojan made it sound as though he was bringing the man into a confidence. "We have a problem with the local police force. *Spies.*" He put hard emphasis on the word. "Perhaps if you could come back in the evening?" Bojan threw a glance at Mislav and Erno. "We'll get you a good meal after that airline garbage food, a drink? A bed, a woman if you want one."

"I am not here for pleasure. I am here for vital reasons." Ramaas walked slowly into the middle of the room, and Neven watched as Mislav moved with him. The bigger man was waiting for something bad to happen.

Neven dropped into a chair and did his best to simulate an air of aloof disinterest. He didn't like admitting that the African made him uneasy. He countered the thought by reminding himself that for all his dangerous manner, Ramaas was just a pirate, a crude bandit with little sophistication. He had ideas above his station, that was clear, but Neven doubted he would ever have the intelligence to achieve them.

He decided at their very first meeting that Ramaas was all animal cunning but with no real education. Coming from that backwater shambles of a country he called home, how *could* the man be any more than that? The Kurjaks were worldlier than Ramaas would ever be, and Neven smiled a little at that, convincing himself of his superiority.

"Of course," said Bojan, returning to the desk where he took a seat. He offered one to Ramaas, but the African didn't take it. "Business comes first. After all, our association has been profitable for everyone involved."

Over the years, a lot of money had flowed up from the wilds of Somalia and into the coffers of the Serbians, thanks to the careful laundering of cash ransoms between the pirate clans under Ramaas's control and the shipping concerns who paid up rather than lose their vessels, cargos and crews to his gunmen. That flow had tailed off in more recent times as UN coalition naval forces had made it harder for the pirates to operate in the Gulf of Aden, but the clans were nothing if not adaptable. Trafficking in drugs, weapons and people made up the shortfall for a while, and then some. There were stories that piracy was on the upswing again, but it had been months since the arrival of any new deposits.

Now that Ramaas was here on a surprise personal visit, Neven expected that drought was going to end.

"Do you believe in fate?" Ramaas asked them. "As a God, a force or power, it does not matter what form. Do you believe in it?"

Neven couldn't stop himself from giving a snort of derision. "In my experience, you make your own luck."

The African ignored him completely. "Something has come to me in recent times. I will tell you about it. At sea one morning, I came to an understanding."

Neven shot his brother a quizzical look. *What the hell is he talking about?* Bojan gave the smallest of shrugs in return.

"I have done much," Ramaas went on, as if he was teaching them a lesson. "But nothing changes for me, for my clan. Poverty. Oppression. Ruin. They stay. So I will change things. I have already begun."

Bojan leaned forward over the desk. "That's a lot of insight for one man to have. You say you learned all that at sea?" He nodded, keeping his tone just on the right side of patronizing. "I've never liked boats myself."

Ramaas sensed he was being insulted, and showed a flash of teeth. "This is for you." He reached into his jacket pocket, showing no concern when Mislav's hand moved toward the butt of his gun in reaction. Ramaas drew out a piece of paper and put it on Bojan's desk. "Details are here. Bank transfer codes. Routing information."

"What do you want me to do with it?" Bojan said firmly, keeping up his pretense of superiority.

"I have come here for my money," replied Ramaas. "Every single dollar. I am . . . *cashing out*."

Neven's faked calm melted. Bojan's gaze flicked to Mislav and Erno as the tension in the room jumped tenfold. "We had an agreement, Ramaas . . ."

"It ends now," said the pirate. "Our association is over. I have shown you respect by coming here in person to tell you so."

"Coming here *alone*," Neven added with a sneer, grasping for a vague threat.

"Unless you cannot pay me." Again, Ramaas ignored every word Neven uttered, as if he was beneath his notice. "Because you do not have my money."

"Of course we do," Bojan lied smoothly. "But there is a certain way things are done in this part of the world. This is not Africa—we do not give ultimatums out of thin air and expect them to be immediately met. That is not how business happens!"

"You do not have my money," Ramaas repeated, with chilling certainty. "Until this moment, I was unsure. But now I know."

Bojan stood up, his body language dismissive. "Look, we're all tired. You've had a long trip, we've had a busy night . . ."

Neven saw Big Mislav take his cue and step toward Ramaas, reaching for his arm.

"Come back tomorrow," Bojan continued, "and we'll talk about this properly when everyone is rested—"

Mislav touched the pirate's arm and made the biggest mistake of his life. Ramaas did something with the sunglasses in his hand, flicking them so that one of the carbon-fiber arms snapped out. In the same motion, Ramaas stabbed it into Mislav's right eye and sent him staggering back, squealing in pain.

Neven bolted up from his chair in fright as Ramaas tore the Taurus semi-automatic from Mislav's belt and used it to pistol-whip him to the floor. Erno was fumbling for his own gun, but the pirate was on him in two quick, fluid strides, and he got the same treatment, cracked three times on the brow in rapid succession.

Bojan had a bulky Python revolver in a desk drawer, and he went for it; but again, he was too slow. By the time Neven's brother had the gun in his hands, Ramaas was back across the room with the Taurus pressed into the small of Neven's back.

He was hauled around as though he weighed nothing and shoved into the firing line between the two men. "I am not coming back later," said Ramaas. "Where is my money?"

Neven whimpered, struggling in the man's unbreakable grip.

"We can't just give it to you now!" snapped Bojan. "Be reasonable!"

"I have no interest in reason," Ramaas replied, then changed tack. "Do you know why I have used your services for so long, Kurjak?" He went on without waiting for an answer. "Because you place value on family. I understand this. My clan is important to me. Those bonds make a man strong." He glanced at Neven. "Also they provide a point of leverage, when it is required. I will shoot him through the throat. He will drown in his own blood. You will watch it happen."

There was no equivocation in the pirate's words, and Neven blinked, his vision blurring. "Brother, please . . ."

"Give us time," Bojan insisted, a rare expression of helplessness on his face. "I'll do what you ask. Just don't do anything you might regret . . . There's no need for that!"

"You think I will regret killing a man?" Ramaas shook his head.

"We can make a deal!" Neven spluttered. "Nuh-negotiate a . . . a bonus fee for the delay!" *The Somalians are always greedy,* he told himself. *I can sell him the lie.*

Ramaas moved the gun until the barrel was jammed into the soft flesh of his neck. "No delay."

Panic broke its banks as Neven abruptly understood how wrong he was. Words gushed out of his mouth. "We don't have it, *we don't have the money anymore!* We used it, spent it, we got something *better*!"

"Better?" He felt Ramaas's hot breath on the back of his neck. "Show me."

"All right . . ." Bojan put down the revolver and gingerly moved to the dust cloth, pulling it away to reveal the metal case beneath. He opened the lid and stepped away so that Ramaas could see the workings of the nuclear device within, and the unmistakable icon of a radiation warning trefoil.

"It is false," sneered Ramaas, and he cocked the pistol's hammer. "I think I will kill you both now."

Neven heard the fatal click of the gun's mechanism and voided his bladder, his will breaking. "It's real!" he screamed. "Please don't kill me it's real *it's real* . . ." Tears streamed down his face.

"This can make us all rich," said Bojan desperately.

Then Neven realized that Ramaas had let him go, and the sound he was hearing like a chugging snarl was the pirate's laughter.

"I have my sign," he told them.

Horvat pushed open the glass doors and walked into the entrance hall of the Queen's High casino, glancing around with an air of indifference. The place wouldn't officially be open for hours, but as with most of the businesses belonging to the Kurjak brothers, there was always something suspicious going on there.

A stringy-haired blonde with her attention buried in a magazine looked up as he crossed toward the casino proper and she called out to him. "We are closed now!"

"I'm not here to lose money," Horvat said, out of the side of his mouth.

The main room was empty except for a couple of old mamas running droning vacuum cleaners over the threadbare carpet, and a stocky youth in a muscle shirt and jeans standing near the roulette wheel. He saw Horvat and moved to intercept him as the blonde came in, still complaining.

The youth waved her away and blocked Horvat's path. "What do you want? Too early for Senior Citizens' Night, old man."

"Stupid little boy." Horvat opened his coat so the idiot could see the holstered gun and the black wallet holding his Policija badge. "I've got an appointment."

"No, you don't," insisted the thug. "Cops don't mean shit to me."

Horvat's patience was running thin. He hadn't got much sleep over the past twenty-four hours with all that was happening, and he was running on nicotine and irritability. "Look, stupid. Bojan called me in. So go and get your boss and tell him Franko is here like he asked, or else your two girlfriends over there are going to watch me put your face through one of those slot machines."

"Bojan isn't here—"

Horvat growled and put his hand on his gun. "Do I look like a fool to you? *Go and get him.*"

The youth paused, processing the risk. Horvat was old enough to be his father, but he had the weight and the reach to make good on any threat. "Bojan is in a meeting," he said, at length. "He told me not to admit anyone."

"The fuck?" Horvat spat on the carpet and found the gaudy iPhone. "He better not be wasting my time." He tried to dial the single number in the memory, but the phone didn't work properly, taking twice as long as usual to respond to every tab he pressed. He shook it angrily. "*Shit!* Is everything going to piss me off today?"

"Okay," Marc said to himself, glancing up to look at the casino and then back to the laptop. "Can you park around the back?"

"Yeah." Vanja's reply was sullen. "What for?"

"We're going to find out if the Kurjaks really are playing with fire." With root access to Horvat's phone, Marc began the work of turning the device into his inside man. First, he remoted-loaded a copy of the CellRAD app on to the phone and set it running; the moment the crooked cop went anywhere near a radioactive source, Marc would know about it. Next, he activated the phone's mike and turned up the laptop's audio output so Vanja could listen in. "Pay attention to this," he told him. "I need to know what's going on in there."

Vanja parked the car and scowled as Horvat's voice issued out of the laptop's tinny internal speaker. "He's angry about something."

"Isn't he always?" Marc scanned the back of the casino. A fire escape door was propped open with an empty beer crate. He could see nothing but shadows inside.

An old, familiar tingle of anticipation gathered in him—the sense of a point of no return coming up fast, the *go/no-go* decision bearing down like an oncoming train. If he got out of the car, where would this end? Men in that building across the way had tried to kill him once already, and if he gave them another opportunity . . . Marc shook off the thought and turned his attention back to the laptop screen.

In the program window for the CellRAD app, the detector alert display suddenly flicked from green to yellow.

Ramaas smiled widely as he watched the Kurjak thug with the bloodied face shoot him a murderous look and gather up the man he had blinded on his shoulder. That one wanted to tear his heart out, and Ramaas might have been willing to let him try, if the older of the Serbian brothers had not ordered him out of the room.

At this moment, Ramaas felt *invulnerable*. Only a short time ago, his mood had been troubled by the news from Guhaad and the very real possibility that the Serbs had robbed him at this most critical of moments. But now he understood what had happened, and why it had occurred.

A final test of my resolve from the hand of Waaq, *a challenge*, he told himself. *To see if I would court despair or cut through it and remain true.* Here in this stale, cheerless room, a moment of transcendent truth unfolded, and as Ramaas processed it, he saw ever more clearly how it had been fated to happen from the start.

He believed that he would need money for the mission before him, but his thinking had been too limited. God showed him that with this gift, this *blessing*.

Ramaas ran his hand over the surface of the device. The cylindrical chambers inside it were faintly warm to the touch. "How does it feel?" He directed the question toward the younger of the Kurjak brothers. "To finally see truth where before all you held on to were lies?"

"It's worth more than we paid for it," said Bojan, from across the room. "Much more. And with you as our partner, we can come out of this as wealthy men."

Ramaas turned to look at him, closing the lid of the case with his free hand. The Kurjaks suddenly seemed very small to him, with all their fixation on treasure. "You think you know why I came here today, don't you? For greed's sake?" He shook his head. "No. I do not want wealth. I want *power*."

He took the digital phone from his pocket and dialed Zayd's contact number. As always, his man answered after a single ring. "*I am ready. What are your orders?*"

"We do not need them now," he said in Somali. "Cut all our ties to the *gaal*."

"*I will contact you when it is done.*" Zayd ended the call and Ramaas took a breath, filled with a sense of how *right* this all was.

At the door to the office, another of the Kurjaks' men stood on the threshold, unwilling to enter without explicit permission. Bojan turned his annoyance on him. "What the fuck do you want?"

"Franko Horvat is on the floor," said the thug. "He wants to talk to you."

Bojan swore violently and glared at the monitor screens behind his desk. Ramaas saw a lone figure on one of the displays, standing by a poker table. "Get rid of the pig," said the elder Kurjak. "I am having the worst fucking day of my life and I don't want him in it!"

"He's not going to take no for an answer," complained the thug.

Before Bojan could reply, Ramaas made an expansive, sweeping motion with his hand. "Deal with your friend," he said, and with the order it was made clear who was now in charge here. "Your brother and I can have a conversation while you are gone."

He rested on the edge of the desk, across from where Neven sat uncomfortably. As the office door closed behind him, he searched the other man's face for any signs of further duplicity.

"Tell me about this prize," said Ramaas, gesturing at the steel case with the Taurus pistol still in his hand. "I want to know everything."

The indicator changed from yellow to orange and the RADIOLOGICAL DETECTION EVENT banner cut across the middle of the laptop screen.

"Oh, shit. It's in there." Marc's mouth went dry and a flood of cold washed through him.

"This is bad, isn't it?" said Vanja.

Marc managed a wooden nod and grabbed his phone, hitting the speed dial. *"Jurgen Goss,"* said the voice on the other end.

"Remember what I said to you in the hospital?" He didn't bother with any preamble. "Look, man, I'm sorry about this, but I didn't give you the full story."

"Marc? Schiesse, where are you? De Wit is on the war path, he's—"

"Listen to me." Marc spoke over the other man. "I wasn't certain about it before, but I am now. The Kurjaks have nuclear material inside the city limits. I'm outside the Queen's High casino, one of their fronts, and CellRAD is lighting up like a bloody Christmas tree. You need to get Schrader, tell her to come down here mob-handed with the local SWAT, a Hazmat team, the whole thing . . ." He ran out of breath and started again. "Are you hearing me?"

"Marc . . ." Goss trailed off, and for an unpleasant moment it was as though the line had gone dead.

"Jurgen, I am deadly serious. Let me send you the readings, the signatures are the same as before—"

"I believe you." Goss cut him off. *"Oh, I wish I didn't."* Marc heard movement as the other man stepped away from his desk to somewhere where he couldn't be overheard. *"I did what you asked, I ran the face you gave me. Nothing came up on the European criminal database, so I widened the search. Eventually I found him on the threat book of a NATO military intelligence server."*

"Military?" Marc echoed.

"His name is Oleg Fedorin. Until recently, a general in the Russian Federation's Strategic Rocket Corps." Marc listened as Goss explained how a story was circulating on the *Russia Today* news stream, a bulletin

released out of Moscow this morning about Fedorin's dismissal from the army because of "gross misconduct and sexual impropriety."

"What do NATO have on this guy?" he asked, in a dead voice.

"*It is as scary as it is vague,*" Goss replied. "*Fedorin is . . . I mean, he was flagged as having a connection to something with the codename 'Exile,' but that's all I could get with my security clearance.*" He fell silent for a moment. "*Marc, this man is a real Cold Warrior from the bad old days. If he's trading radioactives with the Kurjaks, they could have an ICBM in there for all we know!*"

"Tell Schrader to get here," Marc repeated, as Goss's report echoed back and forth in his head. "I don't care what excuse you give. Make it happen!" He cut the line and looked at Vanja.

"This is *very* bad, isn't it?" said the other man.

"Your employers have just jumped into the premier league of global arms-dealing scumbags," Marc told him. "If I was you, I would get as far away from here as you can." He paused, then dug in his backpack for Pavic's burner phone and tossed it to him. "There. You're off the hook."

Vanja shook his head. "The look on your face says something different."

"Yeah." Marc still had Vanja's CZ 75 pistol, and he pulled it from the bag, checking the magazine and the presence of a round in the chamber.

What are you doing, Marc? The ghost voice, the Sam voice, was pushing back into his thoughts. *You go in there, you're on your own.*

"Yeah," he repeated. "Vanja, listen. Do one last thing for me. Call the police." Marc stuffed the laptop into the backpack and pulled the straps over his shoulders. "Tell them you saw a man with a gun walking into the Queen's High. Tell them you heard gunshots and someone shouting about a dirty bomb. That last bit is really important. *Dirty bomb*, okay?"

"What?" Vanja threw a look toward the casino. "Why?"

Marc opened the door of the Fiat and stepped out, the pistol held low to his thigh and out of sight. "Because in a minute or two that's what's going to happen."

SEVEN

W henever I hear your name, my life takes a turn for the worse." Bojan snarled the words at Horvat as he slammed through the door and onto the casino floor. "You bring me nothing but *shit*!"

Horvat looked up from the poker table where he was leaning, tossing the gold iPhone on the green baize. "The problem," he began, "is that you believe I am the same as these imbeciles you surround yourself with." He nodded toward the youth in the muscle shirt. "I'm not your damned employee, Kurjak! We have an *agreement*. That doesn't mean you get to order me around whenever you want!"

Bojan stopped in front of him and fixed Horvat with a look that was part exasperation, part fury. "What. The fuck. Are you talking about?" He sounded out the words as if he was talking to a dim child. "Why are you even here? What's wrong *now*?"

The first inkling of something awry trickled down into Horvat's thoughts. "That's what I came here to ask you! I'm right in the middle of trying to clean up this mess, and you tell me to stop what I'm doing and come out to this rathole?" He picked up the iPhone and waved it at Bojan. "'*Don't make us wait?*' I'm not at your beck and call!"

He watched as his words got through to the other man. Bojan's gaze fixed on the gold smartphone. "I haven't contacted you. Neven hasn't contacted you . . ." He surged forward and snatched the phone from his hand. "What have you done?"

"I got a text message." Suddenly Horvat was thinking about how the phone was working slowly. "It came from your number."

Bojan held up the device and shouted at him. "You fucking dinosaur! We didn't send you anything! This has been tapped, someone is . . ." His words caught up with him and he turned pale. "Were you followed? Horvat, did you lead them right to us?"

Horvat blinked, all his usual bluster gone in an instant.

Bojan rounded on the thug in the shirt. "This idiot has blown our location. Get everyone out!"

"I never told anybody—" Horvat tried to regain some of his poise. He wasn't about to let the Kurjaks put the blame on him.

"Shut up!" Bojan dropped the iPhone on the floor and stamped on it. "You stay right there. I'll deal with you in a moment!"

Marc pressed himself against the outside of the casino and peeked in through the open fire exit. A dark corridor clogged with piles of crates extended away into the building and he slipped in, holding the Czech semi-automatic in one hand and gripping his clip-on Europol identity card in the other.

He was halfway to the door at the far end when it opened and two older ladies in cleaners' smocks pushed through, both of them agitated and fearful. They saw the gun and froze.

"Police," he hissed, holding up the card as though it was actually a badge of authority, and not the thing that got him past the precinct security desk. "I mean, uh, *Policija*." He sighed and gave up, jerking his head at the exit door. "Ah, whatever. Just get out."

They didn't need to understand English to get the message, and they fled past him. Marc watched them go, and then crept up to the other door. He held his breath, listening for voices or sounds of movement.

He heard someone shouting, and then a snarled reply. The second voice he had heard only moments ago in the back of Vanja's car. Horvat was still in the building.

Marc took a few deep breaths to even out his racing pulse and started forward again.

Ramaas listened to Neven Kurjak as the criminal talked in broken, halting sentences. English was not the mother tongue to either of them, but each knew it well enough to sift the words for nuance and intent.

Neven knew that Ramaas held his life in his hands, and Ramaas knew that Neven was petrified of him.

He smiled wolfishly, considering the situation. The younger Kurjak brother talked about the device, hinting at its horrific destructive capabilities and once again returning to the matter of its material worth. He showed Ramaas a folder full of blueprints and technical schematics, and as the warlord pored over the inconceivably complex diagrams, a cunning idea began to gather in the back of his mind. He pushed it aside for the moment to let it mature. There were more pressing concerns to be dealt with at hand.

Neven told him the weapon could be remotely activated, rendered inert or detonated with a series of commands transmitted on ultra-low-frequency radio bands. Those commands were strings of seven letters. "I've memorized the code the Russian gave us," Neven insisted. "For safety's sake."

"Good." Ramaas granted him a magnanimous nod. "God has given you a purpose."

Neven shifted uncomfortably, uncertain what to make of his statement. "Okay," he managed, after a pause.

"I think I will need a man like you," Ramaas went on, wandering to Bojan's desk. The elder brother's heavy-caliber Python revolver was still where he had left it, and Ramaas studied the weapon before exchanging it for the smaller Taurus pistol he had taken earlier. The big gun sat comfortably in his hand, and he decided he would keep it for his collection.

On the bank of security monitors he saw Bojan arguing with the interloper, and their voices were raised so much that in the echoing space of the empty casino, he could faintly hear them through the walls. He watched Bojan stride away and vanish from the sight of the camera. "Your brother is upset." Ramaas turned on Neven and he flinched as he saw the Python in his grip.

"Horvat . . ." Neven said the name, then took a weak breath. "He's police. We pay him but . . ."

"He always wants more?" Ramaas cocked his head. "I know that kind. Men who think everything belongs to them."

"I'm not like that," blurted Neven.

Ramaas gave him a disappointed glance. "You are telling me a lie."

The office door slammed open and Bojan entered at a rush, red-faced and sweating. "We have to get out of here right now," he insisted. "This place isn't safe anymore. Horvat screwed up!" His gaze shifted to his brother, then to Ramaas. "You need to go."

"I agree with that," said Ramaas, and shot Bojan through the head. The heavy revolver let off a deep peal of sound as it discharged, and the back of the elder Kurjak's skull blew out in an aerosol of pinkish-gray matter. His body collapsed against a chair and slid to the floor.

Neven howled like a wounded dog and his shaking hands went to his face. He started stuttering in his native language, so Ramaas crossed to him and put the searing hot metal of the gun muzzle against his temple. He cried out and shied away, but Ramaas held him in place. "I did not like the way your brother spoke to me. I do not need him." He used the revolver to point at the steel case. "Pick it up."

Neven got to his feet and hauled the case up from the floor. "Bojan . . . He's dead?" he managed, as if the reality of it was not quite clear to him.

Ramaas saw no point in addressing the meaningless question. "Where is the car that brought me here?"

"Out . . . Outside . . ."

Ramaas nodded once. "Take me to it, or you will join your brother."

Horvat crouched next to the mess of broken glass and smashed circuitry that was all that remained of the iPhone, and he prodded it with a thick finger.

Was it possible? Had some kind of computer virus been inserted into the device without him being aware of it? He scowled. Horvat had a distrusting relationship with technology that didn't go much further than the cable TV box he used to watch pornography and the decades-old computer he was forced to write his police reports on. Immediately, he was thinking of the doughy Austrian in the Europol office. *Did he have the balls to do something like this?*

Horvat decided he wasn't going to wait around to see if Bojan's paranoia was justified, and he set off toward the rear of the building at a swift pace. He knew his instinct was on the money when he found the dour-faced Englishman blocking his path.

"Well, shit." Horvat kept his hands at his sides. The other man had a gun aimed in his direction. "What do you think you will do here?"

"Hello, ugly," said Dane, venom dripping from the words. "Nice try with the fire. Didn't take, though. You want to go again?"

"Let me tell you a thing," Horvat said in a languid tone. "You are in trouble, English. I say you are out of your depth."

"Yeah," Dane admitted. "I get that a lot." He advanced on him, raising the pistol. "Back up! I don't care who or what you know, you're not going to slither your way out this time."

"I am a policeman, not you," Horvat insisted. He looked around and caught sight of one of the Kurjaks' men, the idiot he had met earlier. The youth was showing at least some intelligence by keeping low behind the punto banco table, sneaking around to where the foreigner wouldn't be able to see him. "You don't arrest anyone. You don't shoot anyone."

"You reckon?" The muzzle of the pistol dipped to aim directly at Horvat's right knee. "We'll see what—"

The heavy report of a large-bore weapon sounded from elsewhere in the building and both men flinched at the unexpected noise. The idiot in the muscle shirt took it as the cue for his attack and burst out of cover, rushing at the Englishman. Horvat spun away, grabbing at a tray of poker chips and throwing them in their direction. Another shot rang out, closer to hand, and the bullet shrieked as it deflected off a marble support column.

Grabbing for his own weapon, Horvat ducked behind a row of slot machines as a third shot cracked through the air.

Luka's burner phone was an older model, the flip-open kind with a black plastic shell that snapped easily when Vanja bent it the wrong way. He twisted it apart and then threw the pieces into the gutter, kicking them through the mouth of a storm drain.

His obligation to his cousin's comrade fulfilled, the emergency 1-9-2 call to the cops over and done, he dashed back to his car and wrenched open the door. Vanja's mind was still reeling with everything this man Dane had told him. All this talk about *radiation* and *bombs* . . . He shivered at the possibility.

He was little more than a petty crook, if he was honest with himself, a driver for the Kurjaks and occasional muscle when it was needed. Vanja knew enough to be truthful about the men he worked for—but what Dane was talking about was way beyond their normal crimes. He thought about his cousin, Luka, back there in the hospital, worn out and pale. He thought about why someone would do that to him, and what else people like that could do.

In an hour, Vanja could be a long way from Split. In a day, across the border, maybe looking to lie low with a pretty Slovenian girl he knew in Trieste.

A gunshot rang out, then more a moment later. Vanja held his breath to listen for the approaching skirl of police sirens, but there was nothing.

The man collided with Marc in a rush and they started to wrestle for the pistol. Shots cracked wildly as he attempted to force the Kurjak thug away, but the other man was nimble and they moved into a kind of violent pirouette around one another, trading blows with neither of them getting the upper hand.

That balance lasted only a moment and air gushed out of Marc's lungs in a whoosh as he took a hard punch to the chest. Gasping, he dropped his head forward and tried to headbutt the criminal, but the blow was poorly timed and he only got in a glancing hit that shared the pain equally between them.

Things started to slip away from him. The Croatian got behind and caught Marc's swinging gun arm, pulling him into a clumsy grapple, reaching up for a choke hold with the other. Marc struggled for a second, unable to bring the weapon to bear. Pain spread across his throat.

Leaning forward as far as he could manage, Marc pointed the CZ 75 up and backward over his shoulder, turning the gun's ejection port in the rough direction of his assailant's head. He pulled the trigger as fast as he could, shots cracking uselessly into the mirrored ceiling over-head. Hot exhaust gas seared the back of his neck and he recoiled, but the fumes and spent 9mm shell casings hit the Kurjak thug in the face and he cried out in pain. He let go, clawing at his eyes.

Marc spun around and hit him in the throat with the butt of the gun, sending the man down to the carpet in a heap.

Another shot cracked across the casino, and a neon display in the shape of a fan of aces exploded as the bullet narrowly missed Marc. He ducked, glimpsing Horvat flee into a corridor across the room. The corrupt cop halted at the threshold, firing again to discourage pursuit, before he vanished from sight.

Marc checked the CZ 75's magazine and dashed after him. He grabbed a metal stool from in front of a slot machine and hurled it at the door, the weight of it slamming it open. He expected Horvat to be lying in wait on the other side, but no shots came back at him, and he shouldered through.

Ahead of him were store rooms and offices. One door was already open.

Coming in low, the pistol raised to eye level, Marc edged around the corner and pivoted so he could see the room beyond in glimpses without stepping out from cover. It had to be the boss's office—the big power-player desk was a dead giveaway. A moment later, he knew for sure. Bojan Kurjak's corpse lay on the floor, with most of his head missing.

Horvat was standing in front of a dozen video monitors, swearing and pulling at the CCTV control unit jammed underneath the screens. He was attempting to remove it by force, but he looked like a pissed-off bear tearing at a box of food and unable to get it open. *Sharper than he looks,* Marc thought. *He's trying to get rid of any evidence that he was here.*

He entered the room and took aim at Horvat's back. "You could just disconnect the hard drive, you dope. No need to wreck the thing. Turn around and put your hands up."

"*Fuck off!*" Horvat spun with more speed than Marc believed him capable of, blindly firing off the last two rounds in his revolver as he came about. Marc shot back, diving behind a heavy leather chaise longue as the slide on his own gun locked open.

Horvat didn't waste time reloading and bellowed as he rushed him, turning the revolver to use it like a knuckleduster.

Marc burst from cover and snatched at the first thing he could turn into a weapon—a free-standing bowl ashtray on a metal pole. He got a hand on it and swung the pole in an upward arc that made the tray connect with Horvat's chin. Tobacco ash and the stubs of cigars scattered in the air, and the corrupt cop stumbled backward. Marc dropped the improvised weapon and went in after him, not thinking, just reacting.

Horvat landed on a low coffee table with a cry of pain and Marc punched him hard across the face. He kept hitting him, over and over, as something broke loose inside; anger that had been buried and left to fester, now rising back to the surface in a red rush. Marc's knuckles rang with the pain and then he gasped, abruptly releasing his grip on Horvat's jacket.

He put distance between the two of them, uncertain where the moment of unexpected violence had come from.

Movement on one of the security monitors drew his attention. Marc saw two figures on the screen. One was a large, dark-skinned man with a big pistol in his grip, and the other could only be Neven Kurjak, pale and frightened, trailing close behind. In Neven's hand was the heavy steel case Marc had seen at the Dolphin Apartments. *Fedorin's asset. Right there.*

He glanced back at Bojan's body and thought about the shot he had heard. It wasn't hard to piece together what had happened in the room.

Now the big man and the surviving Kurjak brother were threading through the back of the casino, disappearing from one screen to return on another as they passed into the kitchens. An exit door from there would put them next to the parking lot.

Marc slotted a fresh magazine into the CZ 75 and threw an angry look at Horvat, who still lay moaning where he had fallen. After everything the corrupt policeman had done, Marc wanted him to pay for it, to suffer the indignity of being stripped of his rank, to face a severe prison sentence. But what was inside that steel case was far more dangerous than a single bent copper, and it could not be allowed to slip away.

His jaw set, Marc sprinted out of the office and down toward the kitchens.

Inside Neven's head there was nothing but a constant roll of thunder, as if the sound of the shot that had taken his brother's life was trapped in an endless roaring cycle. The rushing in his ears and the shortness of his breath were making it hard for Neven to keep up with the pirate, but he did not dare to slow down in case Ramaas decided his usefulness was over as well.

All the arrogance and superiority he assumed he had over the Somalian crumbled. In a single instant, Ramaas showed Neven who it was that wielded real power here, snuffing out Bojan's life as easily as dousing a candle. And now Neven's fate was tied to this psychopath. He kept looking around, hoping that they would stumble upon some of the men who were supposed to be guarding the Kurjak brothers, but the casino was empty. Too paranoid to bring in more muscle after taking the case from Fedorin, Bojan had insisted they keep a low profile. Now that decision was going to ruin them. Big Mislav, Erno and whoever was left had most likely abandoned him.

He swallowed a gasp of fear and hauled on the steel case. It was heavy and the weight was uneven, so it swung back and forth as he carried it with him. Ahead, Ramaas reached a fire exit and kicked it open. Somewhere behind them an alarm began to sound.

Ramaas looked at him, that dark and distorted eye glittering. "This is no time to be a brave man or a foolish man," he intoned. "Do as I tell you and you live another day."

"Yes . . ." Neven nodded, but Ramaas was already moving, breaking into a run across the car park, weaving around other vehicles toward the waiting Mercedes. He vanished out of sight and Neven released a panting breath, adjusting his grip on the case, now dragging it with both hands. Every step he took it seemed to weigh more, and all Neven wanted was to drop it and run. *Bojan is gone.* Nothing else mattered. He felt lost without his brother there to balance him.

Another revolver shot sounded from the far side of the car park, and Neven guessed that someone—his driver—*had* stayed behind, stayed loyal. Now that man was dead too.

"Neven Kurjak!" The shout came from behind him, and it was such a shock that he half-turned and fell over the case, dropping it to the asphalt. A white guy with a ragged growth of beard and a mess of dark blond hair advanced toward him, a pistol in one hand and some kind of ID badge in the other. "Keep your hands where I can see them and step away from the case!" he called out in English. "You're under arrest!"

"Who . . . ?" Neven slipped back on his haunches. "You are not a cop . . ."

"Europol, Division of Nuclear Security," snapped the man, brandishing the badge. "You know what that means?"

Neven did. He slowly stood up, and he couldn't deny how *grateful* he felt. Europol, the police . . . They would only take him into custody and send him to prison. And with what he knew, with the information he could trade for an easy ride, it was a far better option than being forced to serve as the pirate's hostage and pack animal.

"Where's the big guy?"

"He's gone?" Neven looked around wildly. He wanted that to be true more than anything else, but then he remembered the device in the case and he knew that Ramaas would never leave it behind. He reached out. "Please, you have to help me . . ."

"Watch those hands!" repeated the foreigner, and he edged toward the case. Where Neven had dropped it, the poorly secured latches on the lid had jolted free and now hung askew. The other man's face shifted, an unreadable expression crossing it. "Open it. *Carefully*."

His fingers were shaking so much, Neven found it hard to obey, but then he got a grip and did as he was told. The man with the gun saw the workings inside the case and Neven wondered if he understood what he was looking at; then the man turned deathly white and that was answer enough.

"Close it!" he shouted back. "Lock that fucking thing up. *Shit!*"

The innards of a nuclear bomb tended to follow one of two designs. The implosion-assembly types were spherical in shape, made up of curved polygonal panels like the surface of a football. Each panel was an explosive matrix that would go off at once, creating a wave of inward-directed force that would compact a plutonium core in on itself, unleashing the monstrous power of nuclear fission. The other kind was something called a gun assembly, which used a chemical charge to shoot two slugs of sub-critical uranium 235 into each other, with the same effect. Gun types were cylindrical and more mass efficient, or at least that was what Marc recalled from all the briefer files and Discovery Channel documentaries he'd seen.

Neven Kurjak slammed the case shut as if he was closing the lid on Pandora's Box, and it occurred to Marc that if the device inside it *was* another of their fakes, then Neven deserved an Oscar for the authenticity of his shit-scared performance.

Marc expected to find something nasty in there—spent fuel rods from a nuclear reactor, maybe, industrial-grade polonium or caesium for a radiological dispersion device—but somehow the possibility of *an actual weapon* seemed too big to be credible. Now he found himself shocked at thinking that small.

Then reality came crashing back with the roar of a V8 engine, as the glossy black shape of a Mercedes skidded around the far end of the car park and hurtled toward him.

Marc glimpsed an intent, expressionless face behind the steering wheel, as the driver turned the car into the weapon he would run Marc down with. Had he thought and not just reacted, Marc would have brought up both hands to guide his pistol toward the target, but a cocktail of adrenaline and fear was racing through his bloodstream and he acted on instinct.

Fire blazed from the muzzle of his CZ 75, sparking off the grille and the bonnet of the Mercedes as the rounds raced up toward the windscreen. White craters appeared in the glass as shots hit home, but the car's bullet-resistant windows shrugged off each impact as though they were hailstones.

The vehicle screamed toward Marc and he vaulted aside before it could plow over him, but not quickly enough to get away untouched. He didn't see the Mercedes clip his leg, only felt the sudden pain of the glancing impact as the energy of it shocked through his bones, spun him into the air and down again. Dazed and shaky, he felt blood through his bandages as the wounds from the fire reopened.

Marc tried to rise, but his body defied him and he collapsed to the ground. Blinking through blurred vision, he saw the Mercedes lurch to a halt and the towering dark-skinned man climb out. He was saying something to Neven, giving him orders.

It was hard to grasp the words through the tinny ringing in Marc's ears. He snarled with effort and rolled over, levering himself up on one hand. Grit and loose chips of asphalt ground into the oozing cuts on his palm. When he looked back toward the car, Neven was in the back seat staring fixedly at the steel case, and everything else about him seemed dead to the world.

A shadow blotted out the morning sun and Marc got his first clear look at the big man. He was aiming the large-frame revolver at Marc's head, and in his other hand was Marc's Europol ID badge, which he considered briefly, then tossed away.

The man pulled the pistol's trigger, and the hammer clacked harmlessly on a spent bullet. Marc couldn't help but flinch, frozen in place as he waited for the sound of thunder. It never came. The man grinned and said something Marc didn't catch. There were sirens now, getting louder, coming closer.

Then the shadow was gone and the car melted out of Marc's sight. He felt sick with dread and frustration, but it was all he could do to direct himself to the painstaking business of getting up off the asphalt, inch by aching inch.

Hands came in from behind him and took some of the weight, helping Marc up the last of the distance. He sagged and heard Vanja's voice. "It is okay. I have got you."

"Can't let them go," Marc wheezed. "Stop them . . ."

He pushed off from Vanja with as much effort as he could muster and staggered away, shaking off the pain, but around him there were only the shapes of white-and-blue patrol cars. The black Mercedes and the cargo it carried were gone.

*   *   *

Marc knew it wasn't going to go well for him when the paramedics patched him up for the second time in twenty-four hours and turned him over to a pair of solemn, unsmiling cops. If they spoke any English, they didn't acknowledge it, and Marc's poor grasp of the basics of Croatian got no replies.

They put him in the same interview room where he had hidden in order to spy on Franko Horvat's smartphone, and he waited, anxious with every minute that passed, knowing that it was giving Neven Kurjak and the man holding his lead more time to get away.

Marc put his thoughts in order and mapped out all the places where he had been injured over the past day, feeling the patched cuts and stiffening bruises. He was dog tired, propelled only by a fading wave of adrenaline and the need to get the warning out. There was a pencil and a legal pad on the table in the middle of the room, and he set about scribbling down as much as he could remember before the impressions grew hazy. Within a minute, Marc had generated a page of disconnected notes in his spidery, undisciplined handwriting.

His fears about the risk presented by the Kurjak clan were now fact, but he took little comfort in being right. All that mattered was that the weapon Oleg Fedorin had brought into Europe was found and defanged.

The door banged open and Gesa Schrader paused at the threshold. As impeccably pressed and poised as usual, her hard eyes met his and she gave the slightest shake of the head. Schrader came in, and he saw a glimpse of Maarten de Wit outside, arms folded in front of him with a frosty expression on his face.

She pulled out the chair on the other side of the table and sat down. Schrader produced a cigarette and put a slimline lighter to it. It was the first time Marc had seen her smoking.

"Talk," she ordered. "I want you to explain this to me. What you have done."

He slid the pad across the table toward her. "We need to get the locals to put up roadblocks outside the city with radiation detectors, stick people at train stations and the sea port. I've written out a description of a man who was with Neven Kurjak—he's the one pulling the strings." Marc flipped over the page to where he had sketched a rough image of what he had seen inside the steel case. "They're in possession of a weapon of mass destruction, live or not, I don't know . . ." He ran out of breath.

Schrader blew smoke. "This is the choice you are going to make?"

Marc blinked. For a moment, he genuinely didn't understand what she was saying to him. "Are you not getting this? There's a rogue nuke out there!"

She studied the sketch. "A suitcase nuclear weapon? That is an idea from the realm of trashy action movies and hyperbolic television, Dane. The International Atomic Energy Agency works in the real world." Schrader's tone veered toward patronizing. "You are describing a fairy story for conspiracy theorists."

"No." Marc punctuated the word by dropping his fist on the metal table. "That technology exists. The Yanks said they couldn't make it work, but if the Russians did . . ." He broke off suddenly, shaking his head. "Bloody hell, why are we even debating this? Even if it's a dud, it's still a nuclear fucking bomb! Get Goss to look at my laptop—he can show you the CellRAD readings I got from inside the Kurjaks' casino!"

"Jurgen Goss has been suspended from duty," Schrader said coldly. "Pending an investigation into his access of a secure NATO database without proper authorization."

Marc's gut twisted. "I made him do that," he insisted. "It's not his fault—"

"*Ja.* You took advantage of a good man and ruined his career to further your own unsanctioned investigation. Now he's going to take the fall with you." She pressed on before he could reply. "As for the Queen's High, we have people sweeping the building. We did locate a hot-spot in the office where Bojan Kurjak's body was found . . ." Schrader eyed him briefly, as if she was considering adding that particular crime to his misdeeds, then dismissed the idea. "But considering what was found in the basement, that is not a surprise."

"What?" Marc hadn't considered what might be lurking in the casino's underground level.

Schrader pulled out her phone and showed him photos of a dingy, dimly lit space filled with piles of boxes. Some of them had been opened, and he could see blister packs inside filled with bowl-shaped plastic objects. "Those are commercially manufactured household smoke detectors," she told him, "which each contain a tiny amount of strontium-90 isotope inside their sensing components. The Kurjaks secretly bought them in bulk from suppliers in the Far East and the Indian subcontinent. Most of the ones in this picture have already been opened and that material removed." She put the phone away again and took another drag. "Even if they harvested all of it, it wouldn't be enough to do serious damage, but the radiation signature would be sufficient to convince someone credulous."

Marc shook his head. "No," he said again, seeing the path Schrader was already taking them down. "This is not the Kurjaks up to their usual tricks!" He jabbed at the pad with a finger. "General Oleg Fedorin of the Russian Strategic Rocket Corps was in this city last night, and he was here to sell off this weapon!"

"How do you know this?"

He faltered. Marc understood now that he was on very thin ice, and the last thing he wanted was to drag Luka Pavic out there with him. "A confidential informant," he went on. "From my time at MI6. They reached out to me."

Schrader's cold expression grew into a distant sneer. "Was it the same man who helped you into the ambulance outside the casino? The police officers who were on the scene say he disappeared while you were being attended to."

Marc said nothing. Vanja was another person he didn't want to see caught up in his problems. Marc had leaned on him more than he wanted to, and even after he had been cut loose, the man had come back to make sure he was all right. Pavic's cousin might have been a small-time hood, but he had at least some good intentions.

"It doesn't matter," Schrader continued. "I will have that looked into. But you know as well as I do that the Serbs have dealt with the Russians before, largely to help them bolster the veracity of their lies. Fedorin's presence, if it was him, proves nothing."

Marc could not believe what he was hearing. "But if there is the *smallest* chance that I am right, can we afford to take the risk? Do you want to be the one who tells the agency director that you had a line on this and did nothing, after some city gets a smoking radioactive hole put in it?"

"Watch your fucking tone," Schrader snapped.

Another first, he thought. The woman had never cursed in front of him before.

"Have you forgotten who you are talking about?" she went on. "The Kurjaks founded their entire criminal enterprise on the sale of counterfeit nuclear materials! They have cheated terrorist groups and smarter men than you all over the world, Dane. What makes you think that suddenly, inexplicably, they have put their hands on the real thing?"

If he told her the truth, if he said *gut instinct* and *reasoned guesswork,* Schrader would laugh him out of there. As investigator-in-charge of the field office, she had made her reputation as a stickler for absolute factual certainty. And what Marc had were phantoms, nothing but suppositions that were impossible to prove.

She looked away. "I follow the rules and I act in a professional fashion, Dane . . . The evidence you provided *will* be investigated, because we have an obligation to check every lead, no matter how slight my personal confidence in it may be. But you won't be part of it. You've spent whatever amount of trust you have with this office. You are done here."

There was one other approach Marc could try. "Franko Horvat," he began. "He's dirty. He's been taking bribes from the Kurjaks for who knows how long. He tried to kill me, *twice*—he will have at least some idea of what the Serbs are up to . . . Bring him in, sweat him, offer him immunity, whatever works—"

"Horvat hasn't been seen since this morning," interrupted Schrader. "He's not answering calls and no one knows where he is."

"He was at the Queen's High!" Marc insisted, his knuckles tensing with the memory. "Pull the CCTV footage from their system, you'll see . . ." He trailed off and his gut twisted as he realized what Schrader would say next. *If Horvat was gone by the time the police got to the casino, then . . .*

"The officers on the scene reported that the security camera hard drives were missing," she explained.

Bravo, said a voice in Marc's thoughts. *And you were the one that told the little shit how to do it.*

Schrader stubbed out her cigarette on the metal table and pushed back on the chair, putting distance between them. "De Wit warned you that you were already in trouble and you carried on without pause. What is that phrase you British have? You took the rope you were given and you hanged yourself with it. You exposed Pavic and Goss to the same." She shook her head. "And this is partly my fault. I should not have given you the Kurjak dossier. You were the wrong person for the job. You allowed the fiction in it to overtake any facts there were."

"That's not how it is," Marc insisted, but Schrader spoke over him.

"I gave you that case to work on because I did not want you here!" Her voice rose as she slowly lost her temper. "Your friends in high places at British Intelligence, they made sure you were pushed on to me and because of that, an agent I actually *did* want in my division was tasked elsewhere. I had plans for operations that your presence disrupted. You don't have the temperament this office needs!" She aimed a finger at his face. "*You are not a field agent, Dane.* You are not a team player! And this chaos you've created proves it!"

"That's what this is all about?" he retorted. "I knew I wasn't your choice for this gig, but you and de Wit did—what? Throw the Kurjak case at me because it was a bloody makeweight assignment? And now you refuse to accept that I may have actually got something!"

She was shaking her head. "You were given that case to keep you as far from this office's main focus as possible. Understand, you are not the only one with MI6 contacts and confidential informants. Do you believe I would take you on and not look into your background? I know what happened last year." Schrader held his gaze, her eyes unsympathetic. "You alone survived the killing of your entire operations team during a covert mission. Your own country's security services had a global warrant put out for your arrest."

A shadow passed over Marc's face. "You don't know what you're talking about," he snarled. "I was cleared of all that. I did . . . I did my duty."

"But now you think the rules don't apply to you anymore. Whatever the truth is about your departure from MI6, you are not fit for purpose, Dane. You never should have been sent into the field." She sighed. "At least now I have a reason to be rid of you."

A rush of ice ran through Marc's veins as he felt the moment turning against him. It was horribly familiar, the same sense of powerlessness that had threatened to engulf him after fire and death had reached out all those months ago. "You're making a serious mistake," he told her. "I'll take this up the chain of command—"

"No." Schrader's manner became stiff and formal once again. "Marc Dane, as of now I am legally terminating your position as an operations consultant with the Division of Nuclear Security, and revoking all access to Europol agencies and authority." She stood up and crossed the room. "You're not under arrest . . . yet. But I advise you to talk to a lawyer, as you may face criminal charges when this mess is sorted through."

Marc rose as she opened the door, and when he spoke he was almost pleading with her. "Schrader, listen to me! I saw the bomb!"

She didn't look back as she walked away. "I think you saw what you wanted to see."

EIGHT

Zayd was made to wait for at least half an hour beyond the time the meeting was supposed to take place, and he imagined that it was a rich man's way of showing him who was in control.

The calculated slight rolled off him without real impact. Perhaps the *gaal* assumed that Zayd would be impressed by everything he saw around him, cowed by the opulence and majesty of the expensive hotel suite. If that was the intent, then it was a wasted effort.

The gunman saw little difference in this place from the overblown mansion where Welldone Amadayo had been killed, the man whose clothes he now wore. The taxi driver who drove Zayd across Naples—a well-fed Kenyan immigrant who called himself Dahable—had spoken at length and in great detail about the Grand Hotel Vesuvio, named after the volcano that loomed in the distance and renowned as the most luxurious place in the city. Dahable had not concealed his admiration for Zayd, insisting that he had to be an important man in order to be meeting someone in such a place, and the Somalian had let him prattle. He wasn't interested in correcting the driver's misapprehension. He was here to communicate a message, nothing more, and for all the pretense the *gaal* was putting on, the pale man he was here to see was as much an errand boy as he was.

The room had a high ceiling, made to look even higher by striped walls in silky black and gold. Windows open to the sea breeze across the bay let in the sound of traffic along the waterfront. The chair Zayd sat in faced another, and aside from some cabinets and a low table the room was sparsely furnished. Two men stood by the only door, each of them tanned, muscular and expressionless. Dressed in immaculate black suits over white shirts, they each wore the silver rectangle of a high-tech Bluetooth earpiece and kept their arms at their sides.

Zayd had seen the glimpse of a handgun in a shoulder holster when one of the men had patted him down. The results of that search lay on the low coffee table out of his reach; a pair of Japanese-style kunai throwing knives and a small Colt 1908 palm pistol. Comfortable that they had effectively disarmed him, the two guards had done nothing to interact with the Somalian from that point on.

For a while, Zayd amused himself by staring blankly at one of the men, trying to goad him into a reaction, but the guard did not respond and eventually he grew bored. He was about to speak when the suite's door opened suddenly and a woman dressed in a servant's uniform entered. She rolled in a trolley upon which was a teapot, cups, spoons and sugar bowl. If she noticed the weapons, she didn't react to them, and in a moment she had poured two cups, one of which she offered to Zayd with a careful bow.

The smell of the brew sparked memories of home and Zayd took the proffered cup. "Apple tea," said a voice. "I thought you might like something familiar." The woman exited silently as the white man called Brett finally arrived. He flashed a fake smile and took the other seat. "Do you approve?"

Zayd didn't drink it at first. "You have been to Somalia?"

Brett shook his head, "Heavens, no. But I make an effort to learn about other cultures. This is a common courtesy in your country, is it not?" He waved at the trolley. "Tea and polite conversation before one gets down to business. Or am I wrong?" He sipped from his cup and made a face at the flavor. "Hmm. Quite . . . Perhaps it's an acquired taste."

Zayd took a drink from his own. "This is weak. It needs to steep." He put down the cup. "You do business in Italy?" He nodded in the direction of the windows. "You are not from here."

"That was brief," said Brett, with a smirk. "Well, yes. My employers send me where I am needed."

"The Com-bine." Zayd sounded out the name. "You are their messenger."

Brett's nonchalant manner faded. "There's rather more to it than that." He leaned back in the chair, his gaze flicking toward the weapons. "Your leader, Mr. Ramaas. He's making a lot of people very worried. He's unpredictable. That is bad for business."

"What people?" Zayd eyed Brett. "The ones who came in giant ships and took all our fish? The ones who dumped poison in our sea?" He was old enough to remember when the foreign factory vessels first came to the waters off the Somalian coast and trawled them clean, practically destroying the local subsistence economy overnight. And later, the decrepit hulks carrying toxic waste, scuttled in the shallows.

"Your pirates chased them all off," said the other man, and then he corrected himself. "I'm sorry, you don't call them pirates, do you? They are your *coast guard*."

"We did what we needed to," countered Zayd. "Just as Ramaas does what he must."

Now the *gaal* frowned and he began to talk to Zayd in the way that he had often heard Westerners speak, as if they believed he was a primitive unable to grasp the higher meaning of things. "Your country has great potential, if only it can be tapped. I'm sure Ramaas sees that. There are riches buried in the earth and out at sea. Iron ore. Gas and oil. My organization can supply the means to exploit that potential. The men who open up Somalia will reap the rewards. You can be one of them. You could live in places like this one, drink all the apple tea you want . . ." He eyed the jacket on Zayd's back. "Get yourself a much better wardrobe . . ."

"Ramaas does not want wealth for himself," said Zayd. "He understands *shahaad*. Do you know what that is?"

"Do tell."

Zayd paused, fishing for the right word. "*Obligation*. To family, to clan. To the nation. It is tradition to share good fortune with the people."

"Is it? Welldone Amadayo was one of your people, wasn't he? And he didn't share much." Brett's smile returned, as if he had scored a point in some game. "But that's by the by. Ramaas can do whatever he likes with his percentage. The important thing is that we find . . . *stability*. Do you see?"

"I see." He reached for the teacups. "We drink to it, yes?"

"If you wish." Brett's lips compressed to a fine line.

Zayd poured for both of them, but stopped Brett before he could take his. "No, this is not sweet enough. It must be right." He spooned in several more measures of sugar before finally filling the cup and handing it over.

The syrupy liquid still tasted insipid to Zayd, a poor imitation of what he was used to, but he drank it down, watching the *gaal* do the same. Ten seconds elapsed before the pale man started to cough.

"It is an acquired taste," Zayd echoed. Brett's face finally took on some color as he flushed crimson and began to splutter. His cup and saucer fell to the carpet and he clutched at his chest, fighting for breath.

Zayd palmed the packet of powered oleander he had emptied into Brett's cup. The poison extracted from the flower was the last weapon he carried, and the one the guards had missed. The white man began to die as his heart seized in his chest.

The men in suits reacted. One drew his gun and remained by the door, tapping his earpiece. The other rushed to Brett's side as the *gaal* pitched off the chair and onto the floor. "What did you do?" demanded the guard, shoving Zayd aside as he pretended to give support.

"I have delivered a message," he offered.

"Saito!" said the first guard, addressing someone elsewhere in the building. "Get up here! Code Red!"

Zayd shifted and took the next step. Grabbing the metal teapot, he smashed it into the head of the closest guard, a gush of searing sweet liquid splashing across his face and neck. Then, kicking the man away with a hard blow in the back, Zayd snatched up the kunai blades and threw them at the other man. One blade missed and buried itself in the door, but the second cut into the guard's belly. Crimson bloomed on his white shirt and Zayd leaped at him. Fast and agile, he was on the man with the gun before the guard could get a shot off. Zayd slipped his finger into the metal loop at the end of the kunai's hilt and pulled it out— then went back at the guard with the blade held like a push-dagger, stabbing him a dozen more times within the span of a few seconds.

Blood spattered over his stolen jacket and Zayd let the man slump back against the door, his weight slamming it shut. He recovered his other throwing knife before returning to the guard he had scalded, who was fumbling for his own firearm. With a blade in either hand, Zayd jammed them both into the sides of the guard's head with enough force to penetrate the skull. The second one dealt with, he turned his attention back to the white man, who was still clinging to life.

Zayd shrugged off Amadayo's crimson-stained suit jacket and the shirt beneath, stealing the black jacket from the man he had killed. The replacement was dark, all the better to hide the blood on him. He gathered up his weapons, watching the life fade from Brett's eyes.

Some of the others—Guhaad and his men—they said that Zayd was squeamish about killing close at hand. But that wasn't so. What he liked about the act of taking a life with a sniper rifle was the purity of it. The moment of death was untainted—not like now, clouded by fear and panic. When Zayd watched that last moment of life before he pulled the trigger, he was seeing into the world beyond death. It felt *holy* to him.

Only those who did not see it coming could truly be that gateway. Men like this one, their own flesh corrupted by poison, would hang on and fight to live even when reality told them it was already over. It was pathetic and impure.

He heard voices outside, the rush of feet coming closer. Zayd left Brett to breathe his last and climbed out onto the hotel's balcony, scrambling up over the exterior toward the roof.

Crossing the tiles, low and fast like a cat, he came to the back of the Vesuvio and jumped down to the top level of the hotel's metal fire escape. Zayd descended in bounds before scrambling over a service gate to the narrow cobbles of the Via Chiatamone.

A few hundred meters distant, Dahable sat listening to tinny dance music in his cab with the window down, drumming his fingers on the outside of the door. He caught sight of Zayd coming his way and reversed off the taxi rank, swinging the vehicle around in a wide turn. Zayd climbed in and they were off before he closed the door behind him. The cab shot away into the backstreets, taking seemingly random turns at every intersection without slowing down. Dahable appeared to drive with the horn as much as the steering wheel.

"All done?" asked the Kenyan, flicking a look into the rear-view mirror. He held out a digital phone. "This one is fresh," he added.

"Take me somewhere I can clean up," said Zayd, as he set about inputting a lengthy code number from memory.

The Mercedes rolled slowly at first, then picked up speed as it bit into the incline and gravity took hold. In moments, it was racing toward the slipway, and then there was a sudden crunch of splintering wood as the vehicle smashed through the safety barrier.

Ramaas watched the car skid and wandered after it, hearing the grinding noises as it flipped over and rolled. The battered bulk of the Mercedes landed in the shallow channel on its roof and sank quickly. When it was fully submerged, he turned and found Neven Kurjak nearby. He was staring fixedly at the steel case by his feet.

"What now?" said the Serbian.

Ramaas pointed in the direction of the docks. "That way. Start walking." He was going to say more, but the trilling of his phone demanded his attention. He pulled out the device and glared at it. "Speak to me," he demanded.

"*The work is done,*" said Zayd. He sounded out of breath. "*The message was sent.*"

He considered asking if there had been any complications, but the sniper did not volunteer any more information and for Ramaas that was an answer in itself. He paused, thinking of all the things he wanted to tell his comrade, of the incredible bounty that had fallen to them. Watching the surviving Kurjak brother haul the case down the dusty pathway ahead of him, he found himself grinning widely. "Good," he said. "Now listen to me carefully. You are not going to return home. Things have changed. I have another task for you, one more important than any other mission."

Zayd took a while to reply. "*Okay.*"

"I will explain it you," he went on. "We will have a conversation, very soon. But for now, I want you to call upon some captains who owe us favors."

"*Okay,*" Zayd repeated. "*Send me the names.*"

It was foolish of him to do so, but caught up in the moment and emboldened by his gift from God, Ramaas said something more. "We

have a blessing, brother," he said. "I promised you *Waaq* would provide. And he has, beyond anything I ever hoped for."

Luka Pavic had a visitor sitting across from him when Marc returned
to the hospital. Vanja tensed in his chair and there was a moment of
odd déjà vu as the two men met each other's gaze.

"It's okay," Marc assured him. "We don't have to fight this time,
yeah?"

"I thought I had dreamed that," said Pavic, from his bed. "They
have given me a lot of medication."

Marc found a stool to sit on and angled himself so he could see the
door. "Your cousin helped me out," he told Pavic. "He's a good lad."
Marc looked toward Vanja. "You need to be careful. The police have
your description. Coming here wasn't the smartest move. If someone
spots you, calls it in . . ." He trailed off.

"He came here to make sure I was all right," said Pavic.

"He's family," Vanja said simply.

Marc frowned. "I wouldn't blame you if you did a runner."

"This is not over." Pavic's voice hardened. "Not until that maggot
Horvat is rotting in a prison cell. I'm going to take him down. Once I
get out of here, he won't be able to hide from me."

"Easier said than done," Marc replied. "Horvat's gone dark. Apparently, there's no sign of him in any of his usual haunts and he's covering his tracks well." He explained about the missing hard drive from
the Queen's High casino's security system. "Without that, it's only our
word and circumstantial evidence linking him to the Kurjaks."

"I'll be a witness," said Vanja, but then he looked away. "It won't
count for much, though. Not against a cop, even a corrupt one."

Pavic grimaced. "Horvat has been getting away with this shit for
years. Protecting those Serbian pricks while they buy and sell weapons in our backyard. And now this . . . This *thing* they have . . ."

"I told him what you told me," Vanja explained. "About the dirty
bomb."

"Yeah." Marc's gaze dropped to the floor.

"It is worse, isn't it?" Pavic leaned toward him, seeing the change in his expression before he could mask it. "Marc. Don't bullshit me. I can tell when you are telegraphing and when you are holding back. You don't get in the ring a dozen times with someone and not know that."

He let out a long breath. "Yeah, it's worse. Long story short, I think the Kurjaks brokered the sale of an authentic 1980s vintage nuke to a third party, but things went sideways . . ." Marc described the dark-skinned man who had tried to turn him into a hood ornament. "And now that guy has it. He most likely killed Bojan Kurjak and took his brother hostage along with the device. But I've been given the sack from the NSNS, so there's sod all I can do about it. Who this big bugger is and what he plans to do with the thing is unknown, so we're back to square one."

"I know," said Vanja, licking his lips. "His name, I mean."

"*What?*" Marc turned on him. "You never mentioned that!"

"You never asked me," Vanja retorted, becoming defensive. "When we were in the car outside the casino, you told me to listen to Horvat talking. I did! He was yelling at the other guy there, kicking off because the Kurjaks were meeting with someone and they had no time for him."

"They were meeting the big black guy," suggested Pavic.

Vanja went on. "You told me to pay attention to what Horvat was saying, not the other—"

Marc stopped him with a wave of the hand. "Doesn't matter. Just tell me the name you heard."

"*Ram*-something." Vanja's eyes narrowed as he thought about it. "Sounded like *Ram-Az*."

"Could be Arab or African?" offered Pavic. "The Kurjaks have always been generous with who they will trade cash and guns to."

"I really could have used this intel when I was in Schrader's office, before she fired me . . ." Marc muttered, turning it over in his mind. *But then again, she was going to can me whatever happened.* He reached for the backpack at his feet that currently contained all his worldly possessions, and rooted through it for his laptop. "Okay, better late than never." He booted up the computer and started typing a rough search macro.

"I'm going to make them discharge me from the hospital," said Pavic. "Franko Horvat has a lot of enemies in this town, so you can be sure that when I get back to the station, they'll be very interested in seeing him in handcuffs. If we can get him, he might be able to lead us to this buyer. He will sing like a bird if he thinks it will save him."

"No doubt," agreed Marc. "But while we wait for that to happen, the bomb is still out there."

"It couldn't still work after more than thirty years," said Vanja. "Right?"

Marc glanced up from the laptop's screen. "You want to roll those dice? It's not like the world has a shortage of psychos mad enough to try it out."

"True." Pavic nodded to himself. "Can't you convince Schrader this is a real threat? I mean, this is what NSNS is for!"

"I've already tried. She's decided that everything coming out of my mouth is wrong," Marc snapped, irritated by the fact. "She looks at me and sees a burn-out, a liability she's been saddled with." Saying the words twisted a knife in his chest, and a doubt formed at the back of his mind. *What if she is right?*

He pushed it away before it could take hold. "It comes down to one thing; Schrader doesn't trust me. She never did, and she was never going to let me earn it. So I need to find another way . . . Because I'm not going to sit on my arse until some nutter tries to detonate a suitcase nuke!"

"You told me you once worked for the British government," said Pavic. "Isn't there someone there you could contact?"

Marc let out a bitter laugh. "If anything, my rep at MI6 is probably worse than it is with Europol right now. Without any proof? There's no one I can call, no one *I* could trust." But even as he said the words, he knew that wasn't strictly true. Marc put the laptop aside and started pulling other items out of the backpack—a careworn notebook secured by elastic bands, folded maps, and pieces of a camper's first aid kit.

Presently, he found what he was looking for. The gray business card was crumpled where it had been sitting in the bottom of the pack for over a year, deliberately ignored but not discarded. It bore a couple of lines of text in a crisp, minimalist font. A name—RUBICON— and an unlisted international telephone number.

"What is that?" said Vanja.

"A question I haven't answered," said Marc.

* * *

The deck beneath Neven's feet creaked in a rising and falling rhythm that he found difficult to ignore, and for what felt like the hundredth time in the past hour, he fidgeted and tried to find a place on the threadbare chair that approached being comfortable.

The communal space on the upper deck of the little tramp freighter was a mix of dining room and recreation area, with seats bolted to the floor arranged around similarly fixed tables and an old TV and DVD player in a cabinet. Books and magazines with Greek text were scattered about, and there was a pungent smell of strong, tarry coffee in the air, emanating from an ancient heater flask in the corner of the room.

Neven had expected to be locked in a cabin somewhere, or worse, some damp and rusting compartment on the lower decks. But instead, Ramaas had spoken with the men crewing the ship and one of them had brought him here. Hours had passed since they cast off, and he could see the colors of sunset coming in through the portholes.

Neven wondered how he was going to be able to keep Ramaas from killing him. Now he was alone, without any organization to call upon and his brother dead, Neven only had what he brought with him.

Accepting that reality was almost enough to make him weep. He had no idea what was going on around him. He could only guess at the ship's heading—south, into the Mediterranean—and wonder what the pirate warlord had planned for him and Fedorin's bomb. He had not seen the steel case since they boarded the ship, hours before setting sail.

Panic spiraled around in his mind, feeding off itself and growing stronger with each hour that passed. Neven was not accustomed to feeling powerless. Not since he had been a boy, on the nights his father had come home drunk and violent, turning the rage at his own failures on his young sons. He and Bojan had come through it together then, one supporting the other. Now for the first time he was truly alone, and that terrified him.

The padlock on the other side of the common room door rattled abruptly and Neven was startled, gripping the sides of the fixed chair. Ramaas entered and gave his prisoner a sly smile. He had changed his clothes to something better suited to a ship-hand, and he dumped a greasy boiler suit on the table next to Neven.

"You stink of stale piss," he told him. "In a moment, you can go below and use the washroom. Put that on when you are done."

"All right," Neven agreed. "Can I ask where we are heading? Or whose ship this is?"

"Our destination, it is fluid," Ramaas replied. "And for now, this ship is mine. The captain will follow any commands I give him."

Neven could not square that with what he knew. Sea traffic in and out of Split and the surrounding ports was watched over by the factions of the *bratva*, and just as the Kurjaks and their dealings were tolerated by the larger predators in Eastern Europe's criminal ecosystem, any smuggler ships were forced to pay a tribute to the bigger network in order to operate.

The warlord saw the question in his eyes. "You are surprised I can do this? It is simple for me. The company that owns this ship owns many more, and other men own other ships that pass around the Horn of Africa. Many vessels can be so influenced. I can have those ships raided, the crews put to death, all with a snap of my fingers." He did so, his smile widening into a grin. "So we make a deal. I grant them safe passage and they provide me with services." Ramaas took in the boat with a nod of his head. "Today, that is transportation and communication. I have had much to say to my men. It has been an eventful day, no?"

"Why am I still alive?" The words came out small and quiet.

"I saw a sign from God," said Ramaas. His dark eye glittered as it turned toward Neven, lit with a kind of passion that was frightening. "At first I believed it was a trial, do you see? That in this moment, as I reached for greatness, He would drag me down into the dust for my pride. To teach me a lesson." He shook his head. "I was mistaken, Kurjak. You must understand this. After all, you were the vehicle for *Waaq* to reach out to me."

"I do not want to die," Neven managed, but Ramaas seemed to be speaking not to him, but to an invisible audience. *His God, perhaps.*

"My life has been about finding strength," he went on. "Taking it from the venal. All I ever wanted was to find a way to make my clan and my people proud again. To take our nation back from the weaklings who try to rule us. But now . . . This is more than I could have dreamed of." Ramaas spoke like a man who had seen heaven. "We have so many enemies. They have held us down for the longest time. But only a few are the most deserving. Now I can pay them back, my friend. They can learn what vengeance costs."

Neven tried to speak, but he could find no words. His gut was hollow with dread, worse than before at the casino, worse than when the warlord had executed Bojan without a moment's hesitation.

The reason was in the truth of the moment. Neven felt as though he was seeing beyond the mask that Ramaas had always worn whenever they had met. He had never known it was there until now.

This man, whom he assumed to be a talented but uneducated thug, a vicious killer who was content to be king of his own distant wasteland, was fully revealed to him. And now Neven Kurjak was cursed with clarity, as his own shortsightedness rolled out before him. Far too late to escape, he was understanding exactly what kind of man Ramaas was, and it terrified him to his core.

If God is real, Neven thought, *is this His way of paying me back for all the wrongs I have done?*

"I have a plan," intoned Ramaas. "It will come to be. You will give me the code. You will help me, Kurjak. *That* is why you are still alive."

"I can't . . ." Fear flooded through him. Even the inkling of the warlord's scheme was enough to set Neven's heart pounding in his chest, and make him desperate to flee. "I won't do it . . . !"

"No?" Ramaas cocked his head, as if this were only a minor inconvenience to him. "It is your choice. But if you are no use to me—"

"You are going to kill me no matter what I do!" Neven blurted out, shouting the words. He shrank back against the chair, as if he could disappear into it.

"I will not kill you," Ramaas corrected. "And neither will the men I sell you to. Not at first. Not for a very long time."

"Suh-sell me?" Neven had expected to meet the same fate as Bojan had, in the roar of a bullet. But there were worse ways.

Ramaas nodded. "How many terrorists did you and your brother make fools of? They will be angry their money is gone but still they will pay to take that cost back from you in blood. Who will offer me the most, do you think? I will *auction* you." He grinned. "Like an animal to be slaughtered."

Neven felt giddy, and the deck at his feet briefly became an abyss that yawned open and swallowed him up. He screwed his eyes shut and fought down tremors in his hands. All the weaknesses and frailty that Neven had been able to hide with his brother at his side were stripped bare. Inevitably, inexorably, he was drawn toward the person with the power, giving himself to Ramaas with a feeble nod before he was even fully aware of it. "What do you want from me?"

Ramaas sat down across from him and began to outline a plan of action to Neven. Slowly at first, building up momentum and passion with each reveal. It was audacious, risky, and there were a hundred ways in which it could go wrong—but it was the strategy of a brigand, a predator. Cunning, callous, *brutal*.

When at last Ramaas fell silent, Neven reflected that it was exactly what he expected of the warlord. "There is someone," he began, trying to think a few steps ahead, grasping for a way to use the situation to his advantage. "There is a man who can give you what you're asking for. I know him personally. We worked together, in the past . . ."

"Good." Ramaas's head bobbed. "I knew it was right to let you live. Go on. Tell me about this man."

"We call him 'the Baker.' A genius, certainly. I know where to look for him, but I must warn you . . . He is no longer part of the business. He retired as a very wealthy man. He has little interest in causes or money."

"Let me worry about that," said Ramaas, getting up to cross to a porthole. "God will provide a way." It was dark outside now, and Neven saw the faint flicker of distant lightning reflected off the warlord's face. The ship was sailing into a storm out across the Adriatic Sea. "You will mark the path, Kurjak."

"And then you'll let me go?" Neven asked the question, more afraid than he had ever been in his life of the answer he would get.

Ramaas didn't look at him. "I won't kill you," he repeated.

── NINE ──

*P*hobie de l'avion?" said the man in the next seat.

Marc shook his head, raising his voice to be heard over the sound of the helicopter's rotors. "No. It's more like I have a professional sense of concern . . ."

Beneath them, cerulean-blue waters flashed past as the red-and-white EC130 followed the French coastline north toward the Ligurian Sea. The journey from the airport in Nice was a short one, but flying over the water was always enough to dredge up some of Marc's more unpleasant memories. He had hoped it wouldn't show on his face, but that clearly wasn't the case.

"I used to fly these things myself," he added, feeling compelled to explain away his reaction. "I don't like it when someone else is the pilot." For a giddy second, he feared the sea was rising up to reach for them—it could be deceptive that way, easy to gauge your height wrongly if you weren't paying attention—and he closed his eyes to banish the thought.

It didn't work. He remembered a stretch of ocean half a world away, and the heart-stopping impact of a Royal Navy Lynx's canopy hitting the water. He took a deep breath before the recall could take hold and pull him under.

"Backseat driver?" Somewhere in his late fifties, deeply bronzed beneath a panama hat and an expensive safari suit, the man next to him studied Marc's face.

Marc gave a wry nod. "Yeah, you could say that." It was hard for him not to drop back into a kind of muscle-memory, placing his feet just so where the pedals for the tail rotor would be, his hands automatically reaching for the cyclic and collective control sticks. He made a conscious effort to shake off the sensation and looked away.

Ahead of them, the dense sprawl of Monaco filled the view, sand-colored buildings with orange tiled roofs compressed into some of the world's most expensive real estate. Here and there, residential towers and office blocks rose up from the mass, mirrored windows reflecting sunlight back at the cloudless sky above.

Marc caught sight of the landmark Louis II football stadium as the pilot executed a clean turn and they descended quickly, dropping onto a broad concrete apron jutting out over the water. As the engine spooled down, Marc felt a tension he didn't know he had been holding in dissipate like vapor. He climbed out, dragging his weather-beaten backpack over one shoulder, and blinked through his aviator sunglasses at the city-state laid out before him.

As the helicopter fell silent, the first sounds carried to him on the wind were the rattle of ropes on the masts of yachts and the clinking of champagne glasses from a nearby restaurant. The sun gave everything a crisp, bright sheen and for a moment, it was as if Marc could smell the money in the air.

It didn't come as a surprise that here was where Ekko Solomon wanted to meet with him. After all, the man *was* a billionaire.

A black Bentley Mulsanne sat waiting for Marc when he exited the heliport. Standing by the driver-side door was a pale man with sandy hair and a watchful, unsmiling face. He wore a casual suit that did little to soften his hard edges. Malte Riis was probably Finnish, and probably ex-special forces, but that was about all Marc had ever been able to glean about Solomon's taciturn driver. Malte saw him approaching and directed a nod toward the rear passenger door.

"Hey, man." Marc felt a little awkward. Malte had never said more than a half-dozen words in his presence, and he was never really sure how to take the guy. On an impulse that he would swiftly regret, Marc tossed his pack into the back of the Bentley and slipped into the front passenger seat instead.

Malte gave him a withering look and the car vaulted away from the curb. The driver took turns down the tight streets with speed, threading them through underpasses and down narrow avenues choked with clumps of parked mopeds.

"So . . ." Marc began, unable to fight the urge to fill the silence. "Where are we going?"

"Rubicon," Malte told him. "Making a stop first," he added, in a tone of voice that made it clear they had covered the full scope of their conversation.

Marc leaned into the turn as the Bentley shot across a roundabout and down the Avenue du Port, heading back around to follow the line of the waterfront. The car emerged from another boxy tunnel and he saw the massive flotilla of yachts and other watercraft filling the moorings of Port Hercule.

Malte accelerated and Marc realized with a jerk that they had crossed the Antony Noghès corner, the turn at the bottom end of the Circuit de Monaco route used in the city's Formula One races. They sped up past the point of the starting grid and the Sainte Devote turn, and for a moment Marc felt a smile pull at his mouth. If things had been different, he would have loved the chance to drive the F1 route himself.

The moment faded. *You're not here on holiday, Dane,* he told himself. *Focus.* They were heading for the business end of the principality. Ekko Solomon's globe-spanning corporation had a building on the Avenue de Grande Bretagne, one of many such offices that the African industrialist maintained in cities all over the world.

A conglomerate that dealt in mining, aviation, biotechnology and a dozen other lucrative fields, the Rubicon Group was also the parent entity for a small but well-funded private military contractor. Operated under Solomon's direct supervision and empowered by a mandate that put justice over profit, the so-called "Special Conditions Division" was a micro-scale version of a national intelligence-gathering and covert-actions agency operating on the blurry edges of legality.

A year ago, Marc Dane had crossed paths with them in Rome while on the run from his own side, and that had marked the beginning of an ad hoc association with the billionaire and his team, one that led to the thwarting of a terrorist conspiracy to murder the President of the United States and hundreds of civilians on the streets of Washington.

Together, they saved a lot of lives and—more importantly for Dane—they uncovered the conspirators in MI6 responsible for the deaths of his team, the men who had tried to frame Marc for that crime. But for all they achieved, the power-brokers behind the traitors and terrorists, the ones who set the plans for atrocity in motion, were still at liberty.

That single fact gnawed at Marc every day, and in part it had been the reason why he walked away from both MI6 and the offer of a job with Solomon's PMC. Taking the analyst assignment with the United Nations Division of Nuclear Security had been an attempt to find some clarity, some *distance*. But now here he was, propelled forward by his inability to leave well enough alone, by an undeniable sense of *what had to be done*. Despite everything, he was falling back into the orbit of the same circumstances that had almost killed him.

In his hand, out of sight from anyone else, Marc held the gray Rubicon business card that had been consigned to the bottom of his backpack for the last few months. He turned it over in his fingers, weighing the implications it represented, before finally stuffing the card in his jacket pocket.

The Bentley left the path of the F1 track at the Portier turn and followed the line of the beaches along Larvotto. Then without warning Malte turned it sharply and parked at the entrance to an unmarked private pavilion on the seafront. Beyond it, a whole slice of the exclusive shoreline had been partitioned off with tasteful but very definite barriers to screen anyone in the more public areas from seeing within.

Marc felt distinctly shabby in his nondescript clothes as he left the car and crossed through an expansive wet bar, and onto a terrace dotted with tables and chairs. Good-looking people in thousand-euro shirts and equally pricey swimwear enjoyed the sea and the sun. As Marc stepped onto the golden sand he noticed the discreet shape of the Rubicon Group logo on the tablecloths and glassware.

Two children, a boy and a girl who couldn't have been older than ten, ran past him laughing and calling out to one another. They dove onto the sand at the feet of their parents, a willowy woman with long auburn hair and a broad-shouldered man who Marc recognized.

It took a second to place him in this context, but then he had it— *Silber, from the plane* . . . The Israeli was Solomon's personal pilot, who captained the billionaire's private Airbus A350 jetliner. He met Marc's gaze and gave him a neutral nod of greeting before going back to his wife and kids.

Marc looked around, questions rising. If Malte the driver and Silber the pilot were here, then how many other members of the Special Conditions Division were also in Monaco?

A figure wading in from the shallows caught his eye and he got his answer. The woman was sinuous and ochre-toned, wearing a russet bandeau bikini with a thin wrap draped about her waist. Her face was half-hidden behind oversized Dolce & Gabbana sunglasses, and she had a large sun hat cocked at a breezy angle. Lucy Keyes pulled the glasses down her nose to look over their frames in Marc's direction and she grinned a little, coming his way.

"Close your mouth," said Malte, from behind him.

Marc coughed politely and managed a smile. The truth was, he was genuinely pleased to see her again. "Hey, Lucy. You seem, uh, well."

"Marc Dane." She made a show of looking him up and down. "Here you are. I like the scraggy beard thing you got going on. It adds character."

He snorted self-consciously. "It's not so much a beard, more like a lack of shaving."

"Right. Still got that monitor-screen tan, though . . ." Lucy reached out and poked him in the shoulder with a long finger. "You been working out?"

"Little bit," he explained. "I got tired of having my arse kicked by strangers."

"*Huh.* Fits you good." She took off the hat and tossed it onto a table, revealing her short, cropped hair beneath. "But you don't call, you don't write. We were starting to think you'd forgotten all about us."

"That would not be easy," he admitted. "How is . . . work?"

She shared a loaded look with Malte and for a brief instant Lucy's playful mask dropped. Her expression shifted, from looking like a model who could have walked in from the pages of a fashion magazine to the cool-eyed, lethal sniper he knew she really was. Then the moment passed and that sleepy, boyish smile of hers was back in place. "You know how it goes." They started back toward the pavilion. "So why do I get the feeling that our generously paid-for down time is about to be interrupted?"

On the flight in from Croatia, Marc had rehearsed and reviewed how he was going to present his discoveries, but each time it felt forced. His lips thinned and he went for what he knew was undeniable. "I've tripped over something very dangerous," he told her. "And I'm smart enough to know when I'm out of my league. I need some help from people I can trust."

She saw the seriousness in his eyes and all the gentle mocking in her tone faded away. "All right. I guess vacation is over. Let's go see Solomon."

The Pakistani driving the truck from Muscat was far more talkative than Guhaad liked, and finally there was a moment as they stopped on the side of the road to take a piss when he had Macanay and Bidar rough him up. Not too much, of course, because he still had to be able to drive, but enough to convince him to stop running his mouth or playing the same *filmi pop* CD over and over.

The rest of the journey passed much more to Guhaad's liking, and they crossed the border between Oman and the Emirates without further incident. The guards checking their papers didn't notice the driver's black eye and mournful expression.

Guhaad spent most of the time in the back of the truck with the suitcases of good clothes Ramaas had ordered him to bring, watching the digital satellite phone he had been given like a mother hen waiting for an egg to hatch. He did not allow the stale, searing air or the smell of cramped male bodies to bother him. It was important to make sure that this mission went well for the warlord. Guhaad knew that Zayd was favored over him for doing jobs in other places, and he wanted to prove to Ramaas that he was more than capable of the same thing. Bringing along the other two men was insurance. They were both afraid of him, and he trusted that to keep them in line.

Guhaad kept thinking back to the conversation a day or so ago. He did not really understand what this machine was that Ramaas had been given, but he could grasp the idea of a bomb powerful enough to destroy a city. He had seen the airstrikes the Americans sent from the skies to blow up the hideouts of the Al Shabaab, and in his mind's eye, he imagined Ramaas's new weapon to be something like that on a far greater scale.

God had given it to him, the warlord said. Guhaad wasn't sure if that could be true, but he didn't care. Weapons made you stronger, that was something he certainly believed in, and if this bomb was enough to make foreigners tremble, then he was all for it.

Macanay called out from the cab and told him that he could see the needle tower in the distance, the one that pierced the sky from the middle of the Arab city. Guhaad stepped over Bidar's sleeping form on the truck's flatbed and stared out through the windscreen, but then the phone began to chirp and he scrambled back to it, desperate to be quick to reply.

He made the driver stop and scrambled out into the shade of the halted vehicle. There was a set of headphone beads he could use and he stuffed them into his ears. "Yes, boss?" he began. "I am here."

"*Where is that?*"

"The highway. A few hours' drive from the city."

Ramaas's voice had a strange mechanical echo on it that made the warlord sound like a ghostly revenant reaching out from beyond the grave. "*Good. Have there been any problems? Be honest and tell me, brother.*"

"None," Guhaad insisted. "Everything is good. I won't fail."

"*I know that.*" There was a smile in the reply. "*Listen now. I have things to tell you.*"

"I am ready." He dropped into a crouch by the wheel well of the truck, hearing the creaking and ticking of the vehicle's metal body-work. The vague orders Ramaas had given him might have troubled another man, but Guhaad had total trust in his leader. He was impatient to know everything, that was true, but he also understood that some things had to be kept secret for reasons of safety. The only thing that irritated him was that Zayd would often know things before he did. Guhaad told himself that would change once this mission was complete. Ramaas would bring him fully into his inner circle. He knew it.

"*First. The Combine man, the one who was holding Amadayo's chain. He is gone. Zayd killed him for us.*"

Guhaad frowned. "I could have done that for you." Then he quickly moderated his reply. "It does not matter. The *gaal* is dead. Good." He spat into the dust, cursing the pale man's soul. "Fuck the Combine."

"*Yes. We have sent a strong message, brother. There will be no turning back now. In time, we will send another.*"

He licked his dry lips. "What about the . . . gift? Are you bringing it with you?"

Ramaas's tone shifted. "*I have everything in hand, do not fear. I will be with you in a few days, and then we will take the next step forward.*"

Guhaad nodded, even though he knew the warlord couldn't see him. "What do you want us to do once we are in the city?" He began to hope that Ramaas had chosen a man for him to murder as well. He liked the idea of showing he could do that job better than Zayd.

"*Someone will be waiting for you,*" Ramaas explained. "*They will give you food and shelter. You will find someone for me. This is important, brother. I need this man alive and well. He is going to help us.*"

"All right, boss." Guhaad frowned, unable to cover his disappointment. "Who is this person?"

"*A rich, spoiled child,*" said the warlord, with open disdain. "*It will not be hard to hunt him down. He posts pictures of himself and his exploits all over the Internet. The cars he drives, the places he goes to and the women he lies with. Little Jonas will send you details of how to look at them.*"

"What is his name?"

"*He calls himself Kawal Daan. But that is a lie. You are going to use the truth in our favor. God is helping us, Guhaad. You will see it.*"

Ramaas talked for a while longer, explaining Guhaad's part in the larger plan. And while at first he had been frustrated to learn that he would not have the chance to better Zayd's execution of the pale man, he gradually came to see that the task the warlord had for him would be better. After all, anyone could do a killing, but it took someone with cunning and strength to make a man into his servant.

The Bentley pulled into an underground car park and Lucy led Marc to an isolated private elevator with no call button, just a coin-sized camera lens placed at eye level. The doors opened automatically and he followed her inside.

As the glass-and-steel box rose swiftly, Marc glanced around. Rubicon had the kind of security systems that were so discreet as to be practically invisible, and the hacker in him couldn't help but wonder what kind of hardware lurked behind the walls of the elevator car.

"Biometric scanner," offered Lucy, intuiting his thoughts. "Got a dedicated facial-recognition system, gait analysis, the works."

"What happens if it doesn't recognize you?" He pointed at the floor. "Trapdoor and a shark tank?"

"If we didn't know you," she replied, "you wouldn't get this far."

Honey-gold light abruptly flooded the lift as it slowed to a halt in the middle of an open atrium level, and Marc was treated to his first view of Solomon's private Monaco headquarters. The entire floor was a space wider than a football pitch, with staggered balcony half-levels stacked above it. He trailed after Lucy, out across a wood-deck floor, and couldn't help but crane his neck around to take it all in.

Frosted glass walls blocked off sections for office spaces and meeting rooms, and a wide diamond-shaped area filled with soft furnishings was set low at the eastern face of the building, toward the sea. The city rolled out around them, and through the smoky floor-to-ceiling windows it took on an oddly toy-like appearance.

Marc circled around a piece of modern art made from aged spars of driftwood and caught sight of the man himself, across the atrium inside a glass-walled boardroom.

Ekko Solomon was in his early fifties, although you might be forgiven for thinking he was ten years younger. Tall and angular when he was at rest, he wore an unpretentious linen suit in pale cream and a white silk shirt that accentuated the dark teak tones of his face and his hands steepled before him on the table. The boardroom was sound-proofed, so Marc couldn't hear what he was saying, but his body language was clear enough. Solomon had the air of a man at ease in the world he had made for himself, moving through it with an urbane confidence that Marc couldn't help but admire. If he had to hang one single word on Solomon, it would have been *suave*.

But there was more to him than that, even if Marc had only glimpsed the edges of it. Here and now, Ekko Solomon was one of the world's richest people, with a corporate empire at his fingertips and a personal philosophy that was, if Marc understood him well enough, somewhere on the spectrum between philanthropy and vigilantism. But he hadn't always been that man. Secrets trailed after him like shadows, and buried in Solomon's past there were threads leading back to a troubled youth among Africa's brush-fire wars and child soldiers. Seeing him for the first time in a long while, Marc found himself wondering if he would ever know the full story about the enigmatic billionaire. *Is that a thread I want to pull on?*

Solomon glanced up and caught his eye. He gave Marc a nod of greeting and then went back to his business at hand.

"He's got a thing with the board of directors," Lucy explained. "I guess we'll see him when he's done."

"You brought Dane to the office?" said a voice, and Marc turned to see Henri Delancort crossing the room toward them. Solomon's Québécois assistant was, as always, impeccably groomed and expensively attired—although Marc always found him to be a little *too* perfectly presented, as though it was a kind of protective coloration for him. The rakish man's standoffish attitude toward Marc clearly hadn't thawed at all since last they met.

"Figured it was the practical choice," said Lucy, with a frown.

"I'm standing right here," Marc insisted. "Nice to see you too, Delancort."

"I won't insult your intelligence by returning the compliment." The other man pushed his rimless spectacles up his nose.

"Ignore him," said Lucy. "He's still pissy that you turned down Solomon's job offer back in London."

"I didn't turn it down," Marc replied, quicker than he would have liked. "I just didn't . . ." He sighed. "It's complicated."

"In my experience, that's usually what people say when they've run out of convincing explanations." Before Marc could reply, Delancort went on. "The Special Conditions Division operated perfectly well before you crossed our path, Mr. Dane. It continued to do so after you moved on."

Marc glanced at Lucy. "Is that right?"

She gave a deliberately vague shrug. "It hasn't all been a vacation," she allowed.

Delancort extended a hand. "Why don't we make a start? Let's see what you have for us."

Marc made no move to pull his laptop from his backpack. "I'd prefer to lay it out in my own time, if you don't mind. Just give me somewhere to set up—"

"This way." Delancort was already walking away, up a shallow flight of stairs toward one of the other meeting rooms.

Lucy started after him, and belatedly, it had occurred to Marc that Delancort might not be the only one he had pissed off. These people had put themselves on the line for him while he had been on the run from MI6, and he had repaid that by cutting them off once the dust had settled. Now he was at their front door again, and only because he needed something from them. *Of course they're going to be wary. I would be.*

The last familiar face from Rubicon's staff was seated at the meeting room's white glass table, working at a chrome-skinned Macbook with sharp-eyed intensity. Kara Wei gave him a quick look and flashed a cat-like smirk before she turned back to her computer without losing pace in her typing. "Hey. Welcome back. What rig do you have? We've got wireless induction links built into the table."

She went straight to business, and that was fine. The information churning in Marc's thoughts was weighing him down like lead and he wanted to get it out in short order. "I'll manage." His battered military-spec laptop looked completely out of place among the room's clean, shiny lines, a grimy chunk of machinery in the middle of a modern art gallery.

Marc found a projector connection and suddenly the laptop's screen was being mirrored on one of the frosted-glass walls. Kara had not been exaggerating about the office's embedded tech. He made sure that his machine was isolated from the Rubicon network as a matter of course—*to be on the safe side,* he told himself—and brought up a set of data panels. Each one was a scan of a partly redacted document from the Russian central military archive in Moscow, data that Marc had stealthily duplicated from a poorly protected NATO database the day before.

Lucy immediately recognized it for what it was. "That is all kinds of illegal," she said, her native New York drawl coming through the words. "How'd you get access to those files, Dane?"

"Not the right way," he told her.

Delancort gave a theatrical sigh. "Well, you have just made us all accessories to your crime by showing it to us, so why not proceed further?"

"Because Rubicon employees have never ever hacked into protected governmental servers at any time," Kara said flatly, as if she were reading the words from a page. Delancort shot her an acid look and she shrugged. "What? I sounded convincing that time."

Marc continued, "Before I left Croatia, I used the IAEA's access to get a line on a reference I came across." It had been his last act before Schrader closed down his system access for good, spoofing the Europol network to get him into the files that Jurgen Goss had been unable to penetrate. In a few days, a week at best, the intrusion would be flagged and most likely traced back to Marc's user ident, but he was hoping that by then it wouldn't make a lot of difference.

"*Exile,*" said Delancort, reading the tags on the top of the scanned pages. "Another of those very muscular-sounding martial code names. What does it attest to?"

What Marc found on the NATO server had only served to cement his belief in the danger that was at hand. "It's the classification for a weapons project the Russians developed during the Cold War."

Lucy gave a low murmur. "Oh, I heard of that. Baby thermonuclear packages, designed as covert munitions-in-place. The US Army had their own version, size of a trash can."

Marc took a breath. "I reached out to Rubicon because I believe, despite Strategic Arms Limitation Treaties to the contrary, that one of these devices is not only still active and viable, but that it got away from the Russians and into the hands of a non-state actor."

"I know you said you have something of great import to share with us," said a voice from behind him, and Marc turned to see Ekko Solomon enter the room. His expression was grave. "But this . . . Marc, are you certain of what you are saying?"

His throat became dry, and all the doubts that had been swirling around him now filled Marc's thoughts in a riot of noise. "The last time someone told me I was wrong about something, I threw my whole life away to prove I was right." He silenced the turmoil in his mind and straightened. "I wasn't wrong then. I am not wrong now."

Solomon held his gaze, and he felt as if the other man was looking right into his soul. "Very well." At length, he gave Marc a pat on the shoulder and took the chair next to Delancort. "I will hear you out."

Lucy wanted to interrupt the Brit at almost every juncture, and it became a physical effort just to say nothing and let Marc's explanation wash over her. Halting at first, he quickly got into a pace as he unfolded a story that made her eyes widen. At her side, she saw Kara running searches and checks on each name that came out of Dane's mouth, starting with low-life Serbian mobsters and their crooked cop pal through to the people he had been working with at the NSNS's field investigation office in Split.

On the surface, Dane's story about a dissolute Russian general cashing in his last chip for enough walking-away money had the ring of truth, but then adding in the presence of some of the most brazen conmen on the planet threatened to knock the legs out from under his narrative. She noted that but said nothing. Delancort, on the other hand, went for the throat and did his best to blow holes in Marc's story at every possible turn.

Kara used another wall-screen to pull up a nuke-map profile of an Exile device's projected yield, and to hammer the point home she centered it on the site of the building they were sitting in. The colored concentric circles expanding outward painted a grim picture. "If it goes off here, that's at least fifteen thousand people dead instantly. Pretty much everything north of Port de Fontvieille is gone. Monaco ceases to exist."

Lucy couldn't stop herself from glancing out of the window at the city beyond, warm in the morning sunshine, and picturing it in ruins.

Kara's eyes narrowed as she continued. "Put the same thing in a more densely populated city . . . Mumbai, Paris, Tokyo . . . You could expect that casualty count to double or triple. And that's just the people who would die quickly."

"*Maudit,*" Delancort said quietly, suddenly sobered by the possibility of such devastation.

"The general . . ." Solomon drew them all back to the moment at hand. "His involvement in this lends considerable weight to the intelligence Mr. Dane has brought us. How much do we know about him?"

Marc talked about the man's connection to the Kurjak syndicate, but it was Kara who once more mined something valuable from the sea of data that was constantly being sifted by Rubicon's analysts and expert systems. "We're continually monitoring our friends in the Combine," she explained. "For obvious reasons, because they've tried to kill most of the people in this room at least once."

Lucy sneered, in spite of herself. The Combine was a collective of international power-brokers who worked in the shadows of global conflict, acting as the quartermasters for the violent, the angry and the vengeful on the world stage. If there was a bush war, a terrorist attack, a criminal conflict taking place, they were likely to have a stake in it. The way she understood it, they were the scions of a clandestine network that had been profiting from violence since the days of the First World War—and by manipulating, encouraging and more recently, *initiating* terrorist atrocities, they kept the world's engine of fear running at a high tempo.

Marc paled and Lucy felt a pang of sympathy for him. Of all of them, Dane had lost the most to the Combine's schemes. "You're telling me *they* are part of this too?" he asked.

"A unique weapon of mass destruction coming onto the black market?" Solomon said grimly. "It would be a miracle if they were ignorant of such a thing."

Kara continued. "Our sources in Moscow believe it was Combine assets that helped orchestrate Oleg Fedorin's fall from grace. It's a good fit, because the man who is set to replace him in the Russian high command is a friend of Pytor Glovkonin, whom we are well aware is a highly placed partner in the Combine."

Marc's eyes narrowed. He and the oligarch Glovkonin had crossed paths more than once, and Lucy could imagine what was going through the Brit's mind at that moment. "But if they disgraced Fedorin as a means of getting their hands on that device, then it backfired," he snapped. "Fedorin is gone and so is the weapon."

"True," said Kara. "He dropped out of sight in Moscow a week ago. Hasn't been seen since . . ."

"Not exactly." Marc tapped a few keys and brought up long-lens photos of an older man with Slavic features. "I took these shots myself. Here he is in Split, from a couple of days ago. And I believe the men with him are the ones he sold the bomb to."

"So we locate these Kurjaks," said Delancort, and he glanced at Solomon. "Sir, if you are willing to authorize the asset transfer, we might be able to actually buy the device from them and turn it over to the NSNS before the Serbs sell it on to—"

"Too late for that." Marc shut Delancort down before he could go on. "One of them is dead, and the other is on a lead held by the man who *does* have the device. His name is Ramaas. He did his best to run me over when I tried to stop him from getting away with it. I got a look at his face, later I got a name . . ." He brought another image up on the wall screen and Lucy saw a grainy photo of a brawny, darkskinned man with scars and dreadlocks. "This was him in the late nineties, the most recent shot I could track down. He's changed his haircut since then but not his behavior. I got this image from the mug book of the Anti-Piracy Operations Center in the Seychelles."

"Checking . . ." said Kara, as she ran the same data. "The international coalition database for Operation Ocean Shield has a file on him. I have it. *Abur Ramaas*. Listed as a known active participant and organizer in a large number of maritime piracy incidents in the Gulf of Aden. Suspected ties to several Somali bandit clans and the Al Shabaab extremist group." As she read on, her usual flippant tone became muted. "There are pages and pages of warrants here. He's done a lot of bad things."

"And now we suspect he has a nuclear weapon in his possession?" Delancort peered at Marc. "Mr. Dane, I think I can speak for everyone here when I say you were rather conservative when you described this situation as merely *dangerous*."

Solomon's hands threaded together. "We are going to act on this," he said, after a moment. "Henri, direct our people to gathering more data based on Mr. Dane's information."

"Sir . . ." Lucy heard the challenge in Delancort's voice before it had finished forming. "If there is an actual device, if it is even in an operable state, should we not consider bringing the matter to the attention of a larger power? Our contacts at the UN or the American State Department?"

"The UN don't see it as a viable threat," Marc broke in. "Trust me, that ship has sailed. And the American government have never believed the Russians could perfect a compact nuke, because *they* couldn't. Without proof in hand, you're going to have a hard time convincing anyone of anything." He paused. "Just like I'm having a hard time now convincing *you*."

The room fell silent, and then it was down to Solomon to have the last word. Lucy studied his impassive, sculpted face. Ultimately, whatever happened next would be his choice alone. Rubicon was his company, backed by his fortune and his will.

"I believe in small acts that create large effects," Solomon began. "I believe that nations cannot always be relied upon to do the right thing at the right moment. This group was created to step into that breach. We do that today. If there is a threat to the world and it is in my power to do something about it, *I will*."

Solomon's words brought the briefing to an end, and Kara was the first out of the room, eager as ever to start mining data for whatever would come next. Lucy stood, Delancort rising with her, but Solomon was still seated, and he gestured to Marc.

"Sir?" said Delancort, a frown crossing his face.

"Henri, Lucy. Give us the room, please," said Solomon.

When they were alone, Marc closed the laptop and took a long breath. A weight lifted from him; he had a sudden sense that he was no longer shouting into the wind, desperate to find someone to believe him. "Thank you," he said at length.

"I owe you," Solomon told him. "After the incident in America . . . Without your assistance, the Combine and their partners in the Al Sayf terror cell would have done appalling things and I could not have stopped it. You helped me gain a victory in a long war that has few opportunities for such things."

Marc accepted that with a nod. It felt good to be doing something right. Belatedly, he realized that he hadn't experienced that sensation for a long time.

"But there is a question I must ask," continued the other man. "What do you want, Mr. Dane? Did you come here to give me this information and then . . . walk away? Go back to the NSNS, or something else?"

Marc frowned. "I'll be honest with you. I hadn't really thought that far ahead."

"Then let me put it another way. Does your responsibility toward this matter end now? I ask you that without judgment. Or do you wish to join us if we pursue the matter to a conclusion?"

"I . . ." Marc felt his color rise. "I've given you what I have. Beyond that . . ." He shook his head, and Gesa Schrader's words echoed in his mind. "I am not a field agent, Mr. Solomon. I learned that the hard way a year ago, when I barely came away from it with my life."

"I'm not sure I agree," came the reply. "You are resourceful. Dedicated. Driven."

"I was *lucky*," Marc countered sharply, and the healed bullet wound in his gut tightened in recollection. "And only just enough."

Solomon's gaze hardened. "You sell yourself short. And I think you know it. I think . . . Even if you do not wish to admit it . . . You *want* to be part of this." He leaned forward. "You want to be challenged."

Marc couldn't find an answer to that. Solomon pushed back his chair and stood up, pausing to straighten his sleeves.

"What you do next is your choice," he said, "but I would ask you to remain here for a while. Work with Kara. This office functions as a local crisis center for SCD operations and your insight would be valuable." Solomon walked away. "And while you are here," he added, "you may find you will change your mind."

— TEN —

Guhaad was no stranger to heat, but it was the strange texture of the air in the Emirates city that made him uncomfortable. Some quality of it felt wrong on his skin, and he could not rest there. His first night in Dubai had been a sleepless one, keeping a low profile inside a barracks-like building that had once housed transient workers but was now due for demolition amid the city's endless cycle of new construction. In the end, he had stayed up chewing a little khat and listening to the sound of the metropolis during the darkest hours, hearing the constant rush of traffic on the highways into the pre-dawn light.

Ramaas told him a man would be waiting for them when they arrived, and he was right, as usual. The Pakistani driver was pleased to see Guhaad, Macanay and Bidar go, speeding away in his truck the instant he was dismissed. The contact gave them food and water and as they rested, Little Jonas spoke to them from Mogadishu through the digital phone. Jonas's face, grainy and ill-defined on the screen, moved like that of a cartoon character, in fits and starts as he gave Guhaad all the information he needed.

Now it was late afternoon, and they were rolling along the line of Al Marsa Street in a silver G-Class Mercedes jeep. The route they were patrolling followed the length of the Dubai Marina to the west, but Guhaad's gaze kept drifting to the forest of skyscrapers on the other side, extending away over the Jumeirah Lakes district. To him they looked like strange alien machines made of glass and stone, things from some other world frozen in time as they advanced toward the ocean. He had only been in the city for a day, but already he was developing a directionless antipathy for it. It didn't seem real, somehow.

He wondered whether, if he walked to the foot of one of the towers and struck it with his fist, his hand would punch through it. Would it be thin and hollow, full of nothing but dust and dead air? Guhaad shook off the image. Lack of sleep was making his mind drift.

In the back seat, Macanay was scanning the area through a pair of bulky Pentax binoculars. Next to him were pages of printed photos, most of them downloaded from social media accounts, of an olive-skinned young man in various posed shots. Here he was in a bath full of crushed ice with two barely dressed supermodels; here tugging on the lead of an illegally bought pet tiger cub; leaning idly on the fuselage of a private jet; or taking a draw from a hookah in the shape of a golden AK-47. There were also a half-dozen pictures of a crimson Maserati Ghibli, including blow-ups of the car's number plate. Macanay's silenced Beretta pistol sat on top of the pages to stop them slipping off the seat, and another identical gun was in the door compartment at Guhaad's side, where he could reach it easily.

Guhaad had looked at the pictures earlier in the day, dwelling on the images that included sultry women in provocative clothing. He felt conflicted by what he saw, equally aroused and dismayed. He didn't understand why, and that made him irritable.

From what Little Jonas had been able to determine by digitally stalking the target, the man in the pictures had spent most of last night in a club out at the Meydan Racecourse before finally retiring to a private party in a penthouse apartment on the upper floors of the exclusive Silverene Tower. All of this he and his fellow rich kids had been more than happy to broadcast over their photo and messaging feeds. Guhaad expected that finding the target would present at least some challenge to him, but the man was more interested in screaming his boasts to anyone who would listen than maintaining a low profile.

Macanay jerked forward. "There it is," he said urgently, pointing with his free hand. "Quick! Bidar, get over there!"

Guhaad looked in the direction Macanay was indicating and caught sight of the fire-red Maserati emerging from a side street. Bidar said nothing, guiding the jeep swiftly across the lanes until it drew in behind the target's vehicle. Ahead of them, a tram snaked across the two-lane highway, bringing everything to a halt to let it pass.

Traffic on the wide road was sparse at this time of the day. Just past the point of high sun, most of Dubai's citizens were inside the air-conditioned buildings, the richer of them still sleeping off the excesses of the previous night. The punishing daytime heat meant that the city only truly came alive once the sun fell below the horizon. Guhaad would have preferred to undertake this mission after dark, but here that would have meant more people on the street to see it happen, and more chance something could go wrong.

"No police," said Bidar. "We should do it now."

"Not yet," Guhaad insisted, reaching for his gun. "But get ready."

The Maserati revved and shot away as the traffic lights flicked to green, and Bidar worked hard to keep the Mercedes close by without making it too obvious. As they passed the vast, overwatered swathe of golf-club greens to their right, the cars went beneath the curves of an elevated motorway junction, and Bidar stamped on the gas. There were no traffic cameras on this stretch of road to capture what they would do next.

The Mercedes pulled level with the Maserati, the jeep's front and back windows dropping in unison. Hidden in the shadows of the car's interior, Guhaad and Macanay put the muzzles of their guns on the sills of the windows and fired single bullets into the red car's nearside tires.

The Maserati suffered a catastrophic two-wheel blowout and threw itself about its own axis, spinning into a low barrier that it mounted and slid across. The car knocked down a speed limit sign and juddered to a halt on the median strip.

Bidar slammed on the brakes, and Guhaad was out of the Mercedes in an instant, with Macanay a step behind him. He sprinted to the other car and wrenched open the rear passenger door. A dark-haired woman—a girl, really—in a rumpled black evening dress fell out. She was shaking and crying, shocked by the sudden crash. Another, similar in looks and attire, was draped over her shouting out curses.

The sound of the women's distress triggered something ugly in Guhaad and he grabbed a fistful of dark hair, savagely yanking the girl the rest of the way out of the vehicle. He waved the gun at her and then at the second woman. "Bitches leave," he spat. "We know your faces. Speak of this and we will find you."

Both of them saw Guhaad's face, his pistol, and then Macanay at his shoulder with another weapon. They did not need to be told again, and they fled back down the road, their bare feet slapping on the hot asphalt.

Guhaad leaned into the Maserati, finding the target pressed up against the far side of the back seat. He looked dazed, or perhaps just hungover. The young man blinked at him and then he focused on the gun.

In the driver's seat, slumped against the deflating balloon of an airbag, another man who appeared to be some sort of servant was trying to extricate himself from his seat belt. *Bodyguard,* Guhaad guessed, given the driver's brawny form and his age.

He fired twice at close range through the back of the driver's seat, through-and-through shots that blasted jets of wet crimson across the white airbag and the steering wheel. Then he turned the gun on the target. "Kawal Daan," he said. "Get out of the car or I kill you."

The young man froze. The face that Guhaad had seen in all those photos, oozing arrogance and unearned privilege, was now that of a terrified child. Macanay got the other door open and dragged him out, hauling him toward the waiting Mercedes.

Guhaad pulled a cylindrical grenade from inside his shirt, tugged out the ring-pin and let the explosive drop onto the Maserati's back seat. Kicking the door shut, he ran back to the other car and climbed in as the white phosphorus charge exploded with a flash, setting the Maserati's interior alight.

Bidar jammed the Mercedes into gear and they lurched away from the broken crash barrier, rapidly picking up speed. Guhaad turned back to face the young man, who sat trembling next to Macanay. The other man's gun was pressed into his stomach.

Their captive's first words were "I have a lot of money," as if that would be his passport to freedom. He began to talk quickly, repeating himself over and over. "You don't want to kill me. I can make you rich."

"Can you?" Guhaad cocked his head. "What if I do not want riches, Kawal?"

The young man blinked as Guhaad casually mentioned his name again. He didn't appear able to grasp the idea that money might not be important to someone. "Wh-why else would you kidnap me?"

Guhaad smiled and gestured at Macanay to put away his weapon. In the distance, far down the road, he saw a flicker of light as the Maserati turned into a fireball. "This was for show," he told him, digging in a pocket for a ball of khat before slipping it into his mouth. "It is a lesson for you. To teach you that we are serious." He grinned, and weakly, so did the young man. "We are going to do business."

"What?"

Guhaad rolled the khat around his mouth, savoring the sensation of it. "We know who you really are, *Kawal Sood*." He aimed a finger at the young man. "You are going to tell me all about your grandfather."

Kawal's expression changed instantly, from slack fear to a sullen, juvenile sneer, and he seemed momentarily to forget his circumstances. "Him? I hate that old fuck!"

Marc looked up from the laptop's screen as someone tapped on the glass wall behind him. A door slid open and Lucy entered, putting down a cup of coffee in front of him. She crossed the conference room to the far window and looked out toward Monte Carlo, taking a sip of her own drink.

"Thanks," said Marc. "You've changed." Gone was the beachside outfit she'd been wearing earlier, replaced by rugged jeans and a cotton shirt.

"Work clothes," she explained. "Of a sort."

"Doesn't look like there's any Kevlar in there," he added.

Lucy shot him a narrow glare. "I'm not planning on getting shot at until tomorrow, at the earliest." She jutted her chin in the direction of his computer. "So you got something else?"

He sighed and shook his head. "I don't know. I'm just . . . Well, Kara gave me access to some of Rubicon's intelligence database. I was looking through it to see if anything connected with the Kurjaks but I came up empty . . ." Marc paused. "I read through all the tech-specs I could find on the Exile device, and now I'm trying to focus on Ramaas."

"The pirate." She eyed the picture of the man on the screen. "Johnny Depp, he ain't."

"I'm doing the usual analyst trick," Marc went on. "Put myself in his shoes. Where is he going to go? What's the move he was most likely to make to get out of Croatia?"

"Not a plane," noted Lucy. "He's not stupid enough to try and walk a radiological device through an airport, even a small one."

"Right. And the rail and road border crossings all have static radiation detectors, thanks to the IAEA. Unless Ramaas has a lead-lined coffin to put the case inside, they'd pick up something. Neven Kurjak is with him. He would know that."

"So it has to be a sea route," she said.

"He's a sailor," Marc added, with a nod. "He's well away from his stamping grounds back home in Somalia, so what's he going to do? Go for what he's familiar with. *Ships*." He angled the laptop's screen so she could see a list of names.

"MV *Pride of Trieste*. MV *Madonna and Child*. FV *Demolidor*. MS *Valerio Luna*. MV *Falcon Azure* . . ." Lucy read out the first few, but there were dozens more. "What am I looking at here?"

"Every registered vessel that's departed the area of interest within the past seventy-two hours," he explained. "There's a lot of traffic in the Adriatic Sea. Liners and ferries we can probably rule out, but yachts and merchant ships . . . We're talking about hundreds of sailings. Ramaas could be on any one of them." His neck was stiff with tension and he gave it a slow turn. "If anything, there's too much information. Solomon's company has access to a lot of data, for a private corporation."

"He's got plenty of contacts out there," Lucy countered, sidestepping the implication of illegality in Marc's statement. "I guess you could say that a lot of people owe him favors."

Marc nodded. "I'm one of them."

"Huh." Lucy leaned back against the glass and folded her arms.

"Funny thing is, Solomon would say the opposite is true. But then he's unusual that way."

"That is true," Marc agreed. "Not a lot of men make a mint and then decide overnight to become a defender of justice. Other than Bruce Wayne, I mean."

Lucy shook her head. "Didn't happen overnight. You're seeing a man who has gone a long way down that road." Then she fell silent, and Marc got the sense that she had said more than she meant to. He wanted to press her to go on, but past experience told him that would make her shut down completely.

Marc's gaze drifted back to the computer, and the endless digital stacks of intelligence files laid out before him. "I have to tell you . . . I never reckoned I'd be here again. Working with Rubicon."

"Is that what you're doing?" Lucy's question was deceptively light. "Truth to tell, I knew you'd be back, Dane. I was wondering what took you so long."

Something in her tone made him tense. Marc didn't like the idea that he was so predictable. "This isn't what I wanted," he began, reaching for the right words, before finally realizing he didn't have them. "Ah, *hell*. I thought I knew what I wanted. Not so sure now."

"Everything won't go back to how it was before." Lucy's voice softened. "Before London, before Dunkirk? Back to life in the van, watching stuff on a screen while somebody else went in harm's way?" She shook her head. "Not gonna happen. You already had one foot in the shadows before you got pushed all the way in. Take it from someone who knows, you can't cross back without it leaving a mark on you."

He wanted to argue with her, but nothing came to him. She was right, and he knew it.

Lucy jerked her thumb at the window, taking in the world outside. "No one out there gets that."

Slowly, what he had been grasping for started to pull into focus—the vague, ill-defined unease that dragged on him, that had been there for months, snapped into hard clarity. "I thought we had done something to make a difference, yeah? Stopping a terrorist attack, finding a traitor. I thought that meant something. But the people who were behind it, they sailed on." He saw the face of Pytor Glovkonin in his mind's eye. "Untouched."

"We did more damage than you think," Lucy countered. "The Combine lost a lot of ground when we messed up their little duet with Al Sayf. Turns out that shares in G-Kor took a nosedive after what happened in Washington."

G-Kor was the energy conglomerate owned by Glovkonin, and a key part of the Combine's clandestine support structure—not that anyone could *prove* it, of course. Lucy explained that the oligarch's company had been shorting stocks based on a crisis model that presupposed a devastating terrorist strike on the United States. When Marc, Lucy and the Rubicon team had stopped Al Sayf from making that happen, millions of dollars had been lost from G-Kor's coffers.

"They really don't like it when you hit them in the wallet," she concluded.

"But what about Glovkonin? He's done the vanishing act." Marc's former MI6 colleague John Farrier told him that the Russian's London home had suddenly become empty, his expensive cars and private jet abruptly disappearing along with their owner. "He got away. And so did Omar Khadir."

Khadir was Al Sayf's hatchet man, the other part of the unholy alliance between the power-brokers and the terrorists. While Lucy had helped agents from the US Secret Service to capture Jadeed Amarah, Khadir's second-in-command, the terror cell's leader had followed Glovkonin into the darkness. Lucy nodded grimly. "After DC I tracked Khadir to an apartment in Belgium, but when I got there he was gone. Left me a little something, though." She rolled up a baggy sleeve and showed him the faint trace of a shrapnel scar on the inside of her forearm. "What we hear is, Al Sayf are regrouping. They'll show their faces again, sooner or later. Preferably later."

"I know we saved lives," Marc replied. "But it doesn't feel like it was a win, Lucy. Just . . . holding back the tide for a while."

Lucy nodded again. "That's because *it is*. We're not one-and-done, this is a long game." She tapped the table. "You rolled up in here with plentiful evidence of that. There's always going to be another asshole with a bomb and a reason to use it. But what you need to remember is what's on the other side of that." Lucy smiled slightly. "You got a sister, don't you?'"

Marc gave a rueful nod. "She's not talking to me. I have a way to go before I can come back from what happened between us. I put her at risk."

"But she's alive, and her family are whole, right?" Lucy insisted. "That's because of *you*." Something suddenly occurred to her, and she pulled out her smartphone. "And so is this. Check it out."

She showed him a photograph of a tawny-skinned teenage boy with large brown eyes and an untidy mop of black hair. He was among a group of other teens of similar age and ethnicity, clowning around in front of what looked like an American farmhouse.

"Is that . . . Halil?" The last time Marc had seen the youth, he had been moments away from death in a highway diner, fated to die as the unwilling weapon in a brutal suicide attack. Marc and Lucy had saved Halil's life with only seconds to spare.

"The very same. I got Kara to keep a line on him. The State Department has Halil in a counseling program, with the rest of the kids Khadir used as his proxy soldiers. They're doing okay." She held up the phone. "See? This is what you need to remember. Not who got away. Who got to live, because of what you did."

He was trying to form a reply when an alert chime sounded from the laptop, and a new text window unfolded atop the others on the screen. His eyes widened as he read it.

"Trouble?" said Lucy, tensing at his sudden reaction.

He leaped out of his chair, pulling the laptop with him. "I need to talk to Kara, right now!"

They didn't really have him under guard so much as they were watching him as if he were a poorly trained animal. Neven pulled the scratchy material of the boiler suit tighter around him and wandered away across the deck of the tramp freighter until he found a covered area where he could stand out of the driving rain. Another man was there, one of the Greek ship's crew, and after a few moments of sign language Neven was able to beg a cigarette from him. They smoked in sullen silence for a while, and Neven took a long time over it. He was using it as an excuse to get outside, and the moment the crewman finished up and threw the butt of his cigarette over the side, he had the privacy he wanted.

As soon as he was absolutely sure he was alone and unobserved, Neven dug in the pockets of the greasy overall and found the compact, bling-gold satellite phone he had stuffed in there. Ramaas hadn't searched him and the warlord had no idea he was carrying it, but up until now there had been no chance for Neven to use it where he could get a signal.

He powered it up, his heart hammering in his chest, and felt his hope rise as a couple of reception bars blinked into life. Neven had spent the past few hours thinking about who he would call. There were a lot of possibilities, but in the end it was less about finding someone he could trust and more about finding someone whose loyalty he could *buy*. That quickly narrowed the options down to one.

Next to the name in the sat phone's memory were four different strings of digits. The first—the burner that Neven himself had supplied—returned a disconnected message. He swallowed hard and moved on to the next one, glancing furtively around. Eventually, Ramaas would notice that Neven was gone and come looking. He had no idea how long he had to do this, and he could only hope that at least one of his contact numbers was still valid.

Lucy followed Marc back across the atrium to the sunken conference area, where Kara Wei was working at her own computer. He started talking a mile a minute, and Lucy could only follow a little of the jargon-laced geek speak the Brit was spouting. Something about a phone intercept; he mentioned the name "Horvat" and she remembered his earlier comments about the guy being a cop on the take from the Serb smugglers.

Solomon came striding down the suspended staircase, the pace and tone of the conversation catching his attention. "Is there a problem?"

"More like an opportunity," said Marc, as Kara moved to an inset panel on a table and started reconfiguring the screens in the nearby windows. "Long story short, I put a digital tap on a burner phone belonging to Franko Horvat, one that was given to him by the Kurjaks. That phone's dead now, probably destroyed, but along the way I did get the details of the one-and-only caller in the memory."

"It has to be Neven, the surviving Kurjak brother," offered Kara, as she worked.

Marc nodded briskly. "That number just tried to ring Franko Horvat's desk at the Split police central precinct." He paused. "I've got a guy there watching it for me."

"If Neven is attempting to contact someone in Split, I reckon we can capture the call at the local cell nexus," Kara added.

"Get into the SS7 routing protocols," said Marc. "Then we'll be able to listen in, maybe even get a triangulation on Neven's location."

Kara paused and looked to Solomon. "With your permission, of course. Because to do that is, uh, not exactly allowed."

Solomon didn't hesitate. "Go to work."

"What makes you think Neven is going to keep trying to reach Horvat?" said Lucy.

"He will." Marc shot her a glance. "I saw the look on his face when Ramaas was hauling him away. Believe me when I tell you, he doesn't want to be anywhere near that guy."

The last number rang and rang, the chirping tone in Neven's ear cycling endlessly around. A tight knot of fear constricted his heart and he let out a low sob of desperation. If this didn't work, his one final lifeline would be severed and Neven Kurjak would truly be at the mercy of Ramaas. There would be no other choice but to surrender to the warlord's demands and hope that he would keep his promise not to take Neven's life when he had what he needed—

"Who the hell is this?"

When the line finally connected, Neven was briefly dumbstruck. He gasped and clutched the sat phone to his face, crouching low to the deck and out of the wind. "Franko! It's me. Don't hang up, for God's sake, please don't do that!"

After a long pause, the corrupt cop's voice sounded again. "*Still alive, are you? Like a cockroach.*"

Neven barely registered the insult. "I need help."

"*Fuck off and die. I have my own problems right now, thanks to you and your brother!*"

He went straight to the only card he had remaining. "I'll pay you. There's money no one knows about, safe from the police. Half a million euros."

"*Bullshit. I'm hanging up now. Have a nice death, you little prick.*"

"No! *No!*" Neven screamed into the phone. "God damn you, Horvat! All right, shit, I'll double that!" He gulped in breaths of wet, briny air and fought to compose himself. "I know you need it!"

That must have struck a chord, because Horvat didn't terminate the call. He could hear the rattle of a train in the background, the familiar sound of the suburban railway. Horvat was on a station platform somewhere in Split, and Neven experienced a powerful jolt of homesickness.

"*You've got thirty seconds,*" said the cop, after a moment. "*Talk.*"

"The African, that psychopath Ramaas, killed my brother!" The words gushed out of Neven's mouth. "The deal we made with the Russian, he came in and screwed everything up, took over. He believes he's on a mission from God! He wants me to take him to meet the Baker and I had to say yes—"

"*Why do I care?*" Horvat interrupted. "*Even I know that the Baker has been dead for years. Your new friend won't be happy when he finds out you're lying to him.*" He snorted. "*You've dug your own grave.*"

"Please, no," said Neven, and his hands started to shake. He could sense the conversation slipping away from him. "Just listen to me—"

"*No, you listen,*" snarled Horvat. "*My nice little operation has fallen apart because of you, and now I've got everyone in the city looking for me! You don't have any million euros, you don't have anything!*"

The line went dead. Neven cried out and shouted wordlessly into the phone, clutching it as if it were a talisman.

In the next second, a powerful hand closed on his shoulder and he was spun around. Ramaas stood there, the Greek crewman who had given Neven the cigarette behind him.

"What is this?" Ramaas plucked the sat phone from his hands and glared at it. He held it up, examining it from different angles. "Who did you speak to?" He grabbed Neven by the throat and hauled him off his feet. "Who was it?"

Neven told him everything in a torrent of confession, begging for his life. After a moment, Ramaas let him drop and walked away to the guard rail along the edge of the tramp freighter's deck.

"This disappoints me," he told Neven. "Now I will have to take certain steps." Ramaas raised the sat phone high and tossed the device away, into the black waves racing past the hull.

Neven dragged himself up from the damp deck, fully expecting to follow the phone into the drowning depths, but Ramaas waved him off. "This man will take you below, search you and lock you up," he told him. "I need to use the radio."

"Loss of signal," announced Kara, as the digital wavelength monitor on her laptop slowly flattened into a steady line. "Looks like that's all we're going to get."

Marc studied the mirrored display on the window screen behind them. Clever vocal parsing software listened in on the conversation between Neven Kurjak and Franko Horvat, deconstructing their words in real time and assembling a machine-coded translation from Croatian into English. Text scrolled up the window as the computer's simple artificial intelligence finished its job.

"Any locations?" Malte had joined them when the call intercept had begun, standing to one side and listening intently.

"Receiver is inside the Split metropolitan area," Kara reported. "Got him narrowed down to the nearest cell tower, but that's as good as it gets."

Marc handed her a scrap of paper with Luka Pavic's email address on it. "Do me a favor, send that as a priority message to this guy? Give him a digital recording of the call as well."

"Who is this?" she asked.

"Local cop," Marc explained. "He's a good guy. It could help him put that creep Horvat permanently behind bars."

Kara glanced at Solomon and he gave her a nod before she did as Marc asked.

"What about Neven?" Lucy studied the panel of text. "Can we lock down where he was calling from?"

Marc pointed out a string of data. "The call came in from a sat phone." The prefix showed it had been routed by a low-earth orbit satellite to a local provider on the ground and from there to Horvat. Backtracking through the information, it was a matter of isolating what satellite had accepted the signal and cross-referencing that with commercial orbital data.

Within a few minutes, they were looking at a zone of transmission centered over the Adriatic. "You were right," said Lucy. "He's on a ship at sea."

"But which one?" Marc folded his arms, thinking back to the long list of vessels. "We've got to find a way to narrow it down."

"Let's say we do." Lucy ran a careful eye over the map. "If we can pinpoint the ship, what's our next move?"

"We go in," said Malte. "Neutralize the device before it makes landfall."

"There's only one problem with that . . ." Marc used his own laptop to lay additional panels of data over the projected map, each one folding over the next in a stack of layers. The first showed plots of all the commercial shipping traffic heading south toward the Med in illuminated yellow trails, and then across that he added real-time weather data. The ugly swirl of a large low-pressure system imposed itself on the image, a radar return of heavy storm clouds moving north from the Strait of Otranto between the Italian and Albanian coastlines. "Boat or helicopter, you won't be able to get close. Unless you've got another way in, that's going to scrub any attempt for an at-sea intervention, right there."

Solomon gave a reluctant nod. "Regrettably, the Swedes have yet to complete work on the A26 submersible Rubicon purchased last year . . ." He ran a hand over his chin. "But the point is moot. Unless we know the exact vessel to target, we can only watch and wait."

Lucy stared at the translation of the telephone conversation. "Is this a misreading of a word here? From the context I think it's a name, but it looks wrong."

"Baker?" Marc looked at the same text. "Wait, no. Not *a* Baker, it's *the* Baker."

"Ramaas is in the market for a nice cannoli?" Kara raised an eyebrow.

"The name is an alias," Marc explained. "I saw it in the files on the Kurjaks. It's the nickname for some bomb-maker that worked with the Serbs back in the bad old days." He searched his computer's memory for the relevant data. "Here we go. From what the NSNS could determine, this guy helped the Kurjaks build the fake nukes they got rich off in the nineties. Red Mercury detonators and all that bollocks."

"So more bomb-*faker* than bomb-*maker?*" said Lucy,

"Nope." Marc shook his head as he ported the file across to the Rubicon mainframe for Kara to add to their data trawl. "NSNS could never hang a name on the Baker, but he was supposed to be the real deal. Word was, he'd been in the game for decades, came up in the days of Black September."

"Old-school terrorist," offered Kara. "That helps, Dane. I'll start a program on this guy. Maybe reach out to our assets in Mossad. They're always good with this stuff."

Marc glanced back in Solomon's direction, and noted that not once had the man given an order to anyone in the room. Everybody in the Rubicon team slotted straight into a role the moment that a problem presented itself, and Marc saw that he had done exactly the same thing. It felt oddly *correct*. There was an energy in the room that until now he hadn't realized was missing from his life.

Back in the NSNS field office, every day and every task had felt like an uphill struggle. But here and now, even if they didn't have a plan to deal with Ramaas right this second, there was motion toward one.

A sense of purpose, Marc thought.

The heavy padlock securing the tool room clattered and the metal door swung open. Neven looked up from the crate he was sitting on and blinked at Ramaas. He felt sickly and drained. The waves around them had grown as the tramp freighter forged on into the building storm, and even here below deck Neven had not been able to keep his food down. The bucket he had been given to use as a toilet stank of his stale vomit.

Ramaas gave Neven a sideways look with that dark, predator's eye of his and then beckoned him to his feet. "Come," he said. "Time for you to go."

Each time Neven saw the warlord, he was convinced it would be the last, and this was no different. He hauled himself up from the crate, disconnected from his body by a grinding, constant fear that had no end to it.

The deck lurched as he stepped out into the corridor. Neven heard noises coming from the starboard side of the ship—the clanking of metal on metal, the rattle of chains and men's voices.

"You believe you are about to die," Ramaas said from behind him. "I have told you. That is not my intention. Even if you did cause problems for me."

"Nothing I said or did will matter," Neven managed bleakly. "I was a fool to think I could get Horvat to help me."

"No one cares about you. No one trusts you," said the other man. "This is what you reap from a life of lies and tricks. But there is still a chance that remains."

They were moving toward the front of the ship's "castle," where the bridge and crew cabins were clustered. Neven heard urgent footsteps thudding on the deck above them and someone calling out a warning in a language he didn't understand. He risked a glance over his shoulder and saw that Ramaas was holding his dead brother's Python revolver in his fist.

"Redeem yourself, Neven Kurjak," said the warlord. "Do one righteous deed for me and for *Waaq*. For God."

"I've told you all I know," Neven muttered. "What more can I do?"

"All in good time." Ramaas had barely said the words when the chatter of automatic gunfire rang out and Neven heard the screams of a dying man.

He flinched, stumbling against the wall in fright, but Ramaas was on him, pulling him back to his feet. More shots sounded above them and then from ahead, past the door that led to the weather deck. The yellow flash of muzzle flare was visible through the rain-slicked windows. "What is going on?"

"The consequence of your actions," Ramaas told him, and shoved him outside.

Neven was startled as he saw that the vast shadow over the port side of the boat was not cast by a storm cloud, but was actually a wall of black steel. A container ship many times the size of the tramp freighter was cruising alongside them, and a web of cables had been strung from the other craft to the deck before him.

He saw lights on the bigger ship, and men moving on board with the spindly shapes of assault rifles in their hands. Others—all of them gangly and dark-skinned—were moving around the freighter's deck. Neven watched one of them walk to a pair of motionless bodies lying near where the smokers had congregated, and put a single shot into their heads.

Behind him, glass broke and a shotgun sounded. Then someone shouted something and Ramaas replied in the same language.

"The crew . . ." Neven cast around. All the Greeks were dead. "Why did you do this?"

"You made it necessary," Ramaas told him, pushing him in the small of the back toward the web of ropes and cables. "The call you made may be tracked to this vessel. The moment you did that, it meant this ship and its crew were compromised." He shook his head. "I could not trust them to be silent if others came to find us. You forced me to advance my plans."

One of the dark-skinned men came over and made Neven put on a life jacket and a winch rig. Ramaas left him behind, and in short order Neven was being hauled off the deck of the tramp ship like a barrel of cargo, the churning black waves passing beneath his dangling feet as he rose toward the hull of the massive container ship. He screwed his eyes shut and waited for the nightmare to end.

— ELEVEN —

One moment there was warm air on his face and the next it was cool evening breeze. Marc had no proper sense of the transition between the two moments. He had gone out onto the high balcony of the Rubicon office and found a place under a veranda to take a break, and then suddenly Kara was kicking his leg and he was awake again.

"I fell asleep?" He blinked and rubbed his cheeks. "Damn."

"Lucy said to let you. Said you looked like you needed it." Kara was holding a digital tablet in both hands and she sat down across from him. She perched on the edge of one of the square wicker chairs that were part of the balcony's modernist design ethic, as if she was afraid to settle more comfortably. Kara Wei was small and sparse of frame, and looked as if she might blow away in a strong wind.

"I told her to give you more coffee," she went on, "but nobody liked that idea."

"Sleep is for the weak," he said, managing a wry smile. "You need me for something?" Marc self-consciously reached for his backpack to make sure it was still by his side, still secure. He knew he was supposed to trust these people, but it was tough to let go of hard-learned instinct.

Kara pretended not to notice and flipped the tablet around like it was a flash card, the display reorienting itself to him. "I found the guy making the cannoli. Say hello to Jalsa Sood. Indian ex-pat. Political activist. Revolutionary. Freelance bomb-builder."

"The Baker." Marc looked at the picture displayed on the screen. It was old and grainy, the colors bled by time, and it showed a man with shoulder-length black hair and a piercing look in his brown eyes. The rumpled shirt and jacket he wore had the *Miami Vice* look that had been popular in the eighties. "I'm guessing this isn't a recent shot."

"He's been very good about keeping his face out of the public eye," Kara explained. "This is a smart one," she said, with a hint of admiration in her voice. "I mean, most terrorists don't make it out of their thirties, bomb-makers less so. It's not exactly a low-lethality occupation."

"Ramaas wants Neven Kurjak to help him find this guy." Marc returned to the questions that had been bothering him ever since they had intercepted the call to Horvat. "What for? I can't think of a single answer that isn't deeply troubling."

"True that," said Kara. "Sood trained as a physicist and engineer, top of his class. Got into politics when he was in his teens. Like you said before, he was into violent activism all through the seventies. First with the Tamils, then he turned freelancer. The guy was your straight-up genius recluse, with a real taste for exotic weapons tech."

"How did you find him?" Marc sat forward in his chair, taking the tablet from her and skimming through the files she had recovered. "The NSNS never got a sniff."

Kara brushed a length of her dyed hair back from her face and flashed a tight smile. "Not exactly so. They were looking in the wrong place, mistaking the work of other less talented 'bakers' for his and confusing the take. I can't blame them, though. On account of the fact the Jalsa Sood was killed in 2011."

Marc's head jerked up. "That doesn't track. Ramaas wants to meet a dead man?"

Kara cocked her head, playing with her hair again. "Well, when I said *was killed,* I should add *allegedly.*" She took the tablet back from him and flicked through a few pages, looking for something. "The intel I dug up is from Mossad. They say that Sood was assassinated by one of his clients after he botched a job for them. Word was, he'd lost his edge and become a liability."

"But you reckon that was a cover-up?"

She showed him a picture of a burned-out vehicle. "Car bomb in Libya. The kind of thing that someone like Sood could build out of pixie sticks and drain cleaner in an afternoon. The body was too badly burned to identify and there's evidence that a lot of Sood's money disappeared right after."

Marc took a breath as the data snapped into place. "He wanted to retire. Drop out of the game for good." He considered what else he had seen in the file. "Except . . . Geniuses get bored easily, yeah? He must have kept in with the Serbs, dabbling a little now and then to keep his skills sharp. I bet if you dig some more, you'll find a link between Sood and the Kurjaks. Money laundering, most likely—I reckon that's how they knew each other first."

Kara's head bobbed. "Agreed. And, of course, if we could find out where this dead-not-dead guy hides out, we would know where Neven is taking Ramaas."

The brief rush of discovery faded against the cold challenge of the woman's tone. "You don't know where he retired to?"

"Oh, there's a nice long list of maybes, based on possible sightings and intel the Israelis had on Sood's past financials. Greece. Morocco. The UAE. Canada. Myanmar. We can't know for sure without a lot more legwork to chase down dead ends."

"*Shit*." Marc sat back in the chair and looked away, out across the darkening bay and the clusters of yachts bobbing on the water. "We don't have time for that."

The expression on Kara's face changed, worry etched across her brow. "The Kurjaks knew where Sood went to ground. And there is a good chance that at least one other person would have that information too."

"Who?" Marc glanced back toward the office.

"I think that the people who 'killed' Jalsa Sood also know where he is."

Marc could see that as likely. If Sood's faked death was ever revealed to the world, the reputation of his so-called assassins would be compromised. Having his real location in hand would make sure the bomb-maker kept out of sight, for fear that he would be killed for real if he ever broke cover.

"What does Solomon say about this?"

"I haven't told anyone else yet," Kara admitted.

An unpleasant sense of foreboding gathered in his thoughts. If Kara had kept all this from the rest of the Rubicon team, it could only be for the worst of reasons. She was trusting Marc with it because he was still technically an outsider. "I don't want to ask the next question," he said, and then did it anyway. "Who claimed responsibility for Jalsa Sood's death?"

"*Al Sayf*," Kara said gently, and the air on the balcony turned hollow. "Who, of course, need no introduction."

Marc's hands reflexively contracted into fists and he fought down a surge of sense-memory before it could rise. The extremist terror cell was the tool by which the power-brokers of the Combine had spread fear across Europe and the United States, leading brutal attacks in Barcelona and Dunkirk, and attempts to do the same in the American capital. *Al Sayf* meant *the sword*, and by the edge of their weapons Marc had lost a life that he would never be able to return to. A sudden, directionless surge of energy tightened in his legs and he wanted to get up from the chair, walk it off, *damage something* . . .

He took a long breath, feeling the chill in his blood. "Did Mossad give you a name for the assassin?"

Kara nodded again, but another voice spoke as she opened her mouth to reply. "It's Amarah, isn't it? *Jadeed Amarah*. That's why you didn't want to say anything." Lucy stepped out of the shadows around the door leading back into the office. She had approached them both in complete silence.

Lucy's face was a cold, impassive mask. She was the one who had ultimately brought Amarah down, stopping Omar Khadir's ruthless lieutenant before he could take any more lives.

"How much of that did you hear?" said Kara.

"Enough," Lucy replied. "As soon as you said it was Al Sayf, I knew what would come next." She glanced at Marc. "You know Amarah's rep. He was designated executioner for the cell. He would have pushed the button that blew up that car and whatever poor dumbass was doubling for Jalsa Sood."

"We know where Amarah is," said Kara, after a moment. "He was rendered to a CIA black site in Poland last year, after the whole Washington thing."

Marc frowned. "Given what happened there, I doubt very much that the Central Intelligence Agency would be willing to work with us on this." He glanced up at Lucy, trying to read her and failing. "Hey, look—"

"Okay, then." She cut him off with a terse gesture. "Let's go talk to the son-of-a-bitch."

"Putting aside the not-inconsiderable issue of how we get close to the man to start with . . ." Kara shook her head. "He knows your face, Lucy. He'll remember."

"He doesn't know me." Marc said the words, and it was as though someone else had spoken for him. "I'll do it."

After the third day, Oleg Fedorin decided he was safe enough to chance spending some time on the balcony of the penthouse. He wore dark glasses and a panama hat, and stayed low around the whitewashed walls, unable to shake off the fear that one of the other nearby buildings might contain a surveillance team from the GRU. Vladimir tried to gently convince him that they were out of danger, but Oleg couldn't let go of his paranoia. The Russian military intelligence agency had eyes everywhere, even here in Brazil, thousands of miles from Moscow.

Eventually, the tension between them erupted into an argument and harsh words were exchanged. Things came out then, things that had been festering beneath the surface since the day they fled—or longer.

Because Vladimir was so much younger than him, wasn't he? And now that they were in a place where their secrets could become freedoms, instead of embracing that opportunity, Oleg's worst character traits had emerged. He could be cold, Vladimir often said. *Callous.* And always suspicious.

That had been a day ago. A mirthless smile twisted Oleg's lips as he looked out of the window, his gaze following the line of the Rua Santa Clara down to the Copacabana beach, visible as a slice of yellow sand between the white apartment blocks and green palm trees. In every sense, Rio de Janeiro was a world away from the restrictive, conservative life he had lived in Russia, where he had been forced to conceal his sexuality and his true self from everyone around him.

Always suspicious? *Of course he was!* Back there, no other reality existed. In the corridors of power, even the slightest hint that he had a secret to be exploited would have been seized upon to destroy him. For decades, Oleg Fedorin had denied who he really was, and still in the end his enemies had learned the truth. All those years of hiding had become meaningless overnight.

Oleg was afraid. He was rich now and he had escaped, but he was still afraid that his enemies would come for him, and that no amount of money would be enough of a shield. But more so he was afraid that he had driven Vladimir away with the choices he made.

Cold and callous. *True,* he considered, *but sometimes we must be.* That was the price of their escape. A trade in horrors, to sell the Serbians such a terrible weapon in order to secure a new life. *But what did Vladimir see in me when I made that deal? A frightened old fool ready to bargain away the future of thousands for his own hide?*

The door opened and Oleg jerked around, scrambling toward the Makarov pistol he had hidden beneath a magazine on the kitchen table. Then he heard Vladimir call out to him and the fear of death briefly went away.

Vladimir came in, bearing gifts of Xingu beer and Brazilian cigarettes. It was like him to do that, to bring a peace offering after a disagreement. But his expression was downcast even as he came to Oleg and they embraced. Something was amiss.

"Don't be angry with me," Vladimir began.

Oleg blinked. The statement seemed odd. After all, he had been the one to say the most hurtful things. He was the one who should have been apologizing. But then his gratitude at his lover's return turned to ashes. "What did you do?" he said, his chest tightening.

"I'm sorry." Vladimir stepped back and folded his arms. "I couldn't go on like this. After we left Moscow, I kept convincing myself you wouldn't do it, but you did, *you did . . .*"

"I had to!" Oleg reached for him, but Vladimir drew away.

"The guilt is eating me alive, Oleg. That you gave murderers and criminals *a nuclear bomb* in exchange for our lives? I can't accept that!" He shook his head. "What happens when it goes off and people die? How could we ever forgive ourselves?"

"I did it for you! I did it to protect *us,* don't you see?"

"I do." At last Vladimir took his hands. "And I've done the same thing. For us."

Oleg shook him off. "No . . ."

"I reached out to someone we can trust, a friend in the diplomatic corps in Kaliningrad. I told her we would give her information . . ."

"*No!*" Oleg shouted at him. "You stupid, stupid fool! Why would you do that?"

Vladimir's face flushed red. "Because I don't want to live with this! And what does it matter, anyway? The Serbians paid you! Why do you care if they are arrested and the bomb is recovered? We win both ways!" He gave a brittle smile. "We are still free and we make sure no one gets hurt. Don't you want that?"

"Fool," Oleg repeated, striding back to the kitchen. "Do you know what you have done? You have served me up to my enemies!" He grabbed the Makarov and pointed it toward the door. "Get your bag! We are leaving here now—"

The window across the room cracked and there was a sound like the low, fast buzz of a hornet. Oleg's hand was suddenly alight with pain as blood flowed from a new wound, and the pistol spun out of his grip. He cast about, finding the bullet hole in the glass, and across the way on another rooftop he saw the brief glitter of sunlight off a targeting scope.

The apartment's front door rattled open and three Hispanic men entered, all of them dressed in inconspicuous street clothes and baggy shirts to conceal the bulges of firearms. They silently deferred to a fourth man who came in last. Like them, he had the manner of a soldier rather than a spy, and Oleg knew immediately that whoever they were, they were not GRU agents. These were mercenaries, contractors.

The fourth man was Asian, Japanese at a guess. Short-haired and round in the face, he was of below-average height, but his build was spare and dense. In one hand he had a silenced Glock semi-automatic, which he used to point with. "You should bandage that, General Fedorin," he said, in passable Russian. "We will wait."

With trembling hands, Vladimir helped him use the towel to staunch the bleeding. One of the other men recovered the Makarov and then set off to search the apartment. Oleg heard him call the Japanese "Saito," but the name was unfamiliar.

"We don't have it here." He pushed Vladimir away and reached inside himself, dragging up the old persona he had worn as a soldier and a leader, and setting it back into place. He sat down on a chair. "If you're looking for the weapon, you're wasting your time."

"I know you do not have it." Saito's head bobbed. "And that is causing some problems for my employers. What did you do with the unit?"

"If I tell you that, you'll kill us both."

Saito glanced at Vladimir, ignoring the statement. "Guilt seldom expresses itself in convenient fashion. Nor does fear, for that matter. You were not expected to vanish quite so quickly, or completely."

Oleg's hand tightened around the makeshift dressing. "Who do you work for? Not Russia. Not the Americans. Someone else."

"Someone you can do business with," Saito offered. "If you are willing."

He had it then, the immediate understanding of exactly who he was dealing with. "You are Combine." Oleg couldn't help but scowl. He was more than familiar with the group, and did not make any secret of his antipathy toward them. "That makes sense. So Glovkonin sent you, yes?" When Saito didn't respond, he went on. "I should have known. I assumed G-Kor's failures would sink him, but he's scheming, isn't he? He and all his elitist cohorts, treating the world like it is their chessboard."

"You should know that you almost escaped us," Saito noted. "An unforeseen incident in Italy drew away much of our focus and in that time you slipped the net. You might have remained undiscovered if not for your companion's laudable concern for your emotional well-being."

Oleg glanced at Vladimir, but he couldn't find any blame for him. "This man, and the people who employ him . . . They're here because I didn't sell the bomb to *them*." He looked back at Saito. "That's the truth, isn't it? The Combine want the weapon. I wonder, were my troubles set into motion for exactly that reason?"

"The Combine's interest is in managing global stability." Saito's tone chilled. "By selling the device to a rogue actor, you have jeopardized a delicate balance."

"If I sold you the device, we would be dead by now!" Oleg retorted. "Your masters don't want it to make the world safer! They want it so they can use it how they see fit . . ." He paused. "Was that Glovkonin's plan? Blackmail the Kremlin, sell the weapon back to Russia at an inflated price? Or something worse?"

"Why do you care?" Saito cocked his head, his attention drifting toward Vladimir, who hovered near the door to the balcony. "You did not think twice about what would happen after it left your hands." He put away the pistol and produced an entirely different weapon.

The long, slender dagger was made of stainless steel. It resembled a kind of blade known as a misericorde, used in medieval times to deliver a killing blow to an unhorsed knight through the gaps in his plate armor.

Saito advanced on Vladimir. "You see him as a father figure, in a way." For the first time, the Combine operative spoke directly to the other man. "Is it because you were abandoned by your own father as a boy?" The blade glittered in the sunshine. "He can't protect you. But you can protect *him*. I know you want to."

"Vlad, say nothing!" Oleg tried to rise from his chair, but one of the other men pushed him back down.

Saito looked back at Oleg, and nodded in Vladimir's direction. "He is handsome." The dagger rose. "Unless one of you speaks, that will only be the first of what I take from him."

The name of the restaurant was Eternity, couched in all the overstatement and absence of irony that littered Dubai's playground for the idle rich. It took up the top two floors of a sculpted, 150-meter tower on the edge of the marina, emerging out of the building in a bloom made from green glass and matte copper. Petals of steel and stone formed platforms for a spectacular bar, a viewing gallery and the venue's private helipad. Baffles of white silk crackled quietly with the wind off the desert, and aside from the soft tones of a piano there was little other noise to distract the diner from his food.

He had the place to himself for the next hour or so. He liked being up here, cradled among the silk and the bare wood of the decking floor. In his more fanciful moments, he imagined Eternity as if it were a magical sailing ship that floated in the clouds, far above the crude concerns of the earth.

A good percentage of the restaurant and the building it capped belonged to him. One of many of his investments in the UAE, it didn't turn much of a profit but he enjoyed the freedom part-ownership gave him. Right now, the entire staff was focused completely on his needs, and in the passing of his years he had become accustomed to—and to consider that he had earned—such treatment.

He ate the cauliflower vinaigrette before him and savored each mouthful, occasionally giving his dining companion a sideways glance. The man in the seat across from him wasn't eating, and he looked uncomfortable out of his uniform. By day he was a high-ranking police officer, but here and now he was just a messenger.

"It happened very quickly," said the policeman. "We are doing all we can to expedite the investigation, but—"

"Spare me the excuses." He took a drink from a glass of ice-cold mineral water. "The women who were in the car, and the driver. Where are you with them?"

"The driver is missing. I believe the women have fled the city. A search is ongoing."

That created a frown. "The body. Is it *his*?"

"I would hope not."

He put down his knife and fork. "That is not what I asked you!"

The policeman blinked at his retort. "We don't think so. I'm awaiting confirmation from the coroner's office, but the burn damage to the . . . to the victim was very severe."

A mix of worry and annoyance colored his expression. He was angry and afraid in equal measure, thinking of the boy.

At once, he wanted to have him to hand so he could punish him for bringing this to pass, but also to shield him from greater danger. Promises had been made, after all, and there were debts that could not be repaid. The boy's father was long gone, and that meant certain responsibilities could not be ignored.

He turned back to his food, dismissing the policeman with a flick of his hand. "Leave me. I don't want to hear from you again until you have some answers."

The policeman was grateful for permission to depart, and gave a curt bow before walking quickly away.

He glowered at his food for several minutes, hands tense around the cutlery. The boy needed his father. *We both do. Things would have been so different if fate had taken another path . . .*

Raised voices reached his ears and he looked up. Men were crossing the open court of the restaurant, ignoring the demands of the staff to leave. One of them he knew—pale and drawn, nervous with every step he took—and seeing the new arrival set him immediately on alert. The other one was a stranger—towering and dark as thunder—with a predator's swagger.

Ramaas strode across the empty restaurant with the Serbian trailing at his heels like a wary servant, and he paid little attention to Bidar and Macanay as they formed a threatening barrier to discourage the staff from following.

"This city is a strange one," he said addressing the man in the white, collarless jacket who was the establishment's sole diner. "I have never seen anything like it in the real world."

The man was old enough to be his father, with a heavily lined, sun-bleached-leather face and hair run to white in a queue that snaked down his back. His gaze raked over Ramaas and he gave an arch sniff. "That is your first mistake, sir. This is Dubai. This is *not* the real world."

"I have been here less than a day, and yet I believe you." He approached the old man's table, which was set slightly up above the rest on one of the giant glass petals that formed the floor. "Many things here are a fiction, yes?"

"Perhaps you did not see the sign outside," the old man went on. "This place is closed for a private dinner."

"Very private," Ramaas noted, making a show of looking around. "I think there are many rich men in this city . . . But to have this place to yourself—that takes more than just money." He glanced at Neven. "This is the man, is it not? He looks different from your description." Before the Serb could answer, Ramaas did it for him. "There are doctors who can do much to make you hide the face you were born with, I hear."

"You have made a mistake," said the old man, pushing his plate aside. "You have confused me with someone else. My name is Vishal Daan, and this has always been my face." His tone hardened. "I think you should leave before someone calls the police."

"You are not afraid of me," Ramaas noted, amused by the idea. "Either because you are a fool or because you have known much fear in your time, and you master it." He gave Neven a nudge. "Let me hear you say it, Kurjak."

The Serb was already sweating through the suit he was wearing. "That man is Jalsa Sood."

"I don't know who that is." The old man shook his head. "Leave now. You are trying my patience." He glared at Neven and held the Serbian's gaze for a moment too long, enough that any iota of doubt Ramaas still had went away.

"You are the man they call the Baker." Ramaas stepped up onto the raised platform and helped himself to a drink. "I have come a long way looking for you, Sood. Do not worry, I am here for your skills and not your life." He indicated the Serb. "Do not blame Neven for betraying you. I left him with no other choice."

The old man glanced away as the wind picked up, bringing the faint rattle of a passing helicopter to their ears. He grimaced at Ramaas. "My name is Vishal Daan," he repeated. "I don't know him, and I don't know you. So go away and take your thugs with you!" He jerked his chin at Macanay and Bidar.

Ramaas smiled. "You should reconsider."

The sound of rotors was growing louder, and the shark-like form of a silver Augusta Grand helicopter emerged out of the evening sky, turning to present its side to the rooftop as it slipped past. The passenger compartment doors were open, and sitting inside where he could clearly be seen, Guhaad held a pistol at the head of a young Indian man in an expensive jacket.

The old man's face fell, and he failed utterly to conceal his shock. "Kawal—?"

"Your grandson is an overprivileged idiot," Ramaas told him flatly. "He believes wealth makes him safe. But you and I were not born into it like he was. We know better."

Suddenly the old man was on his feet, and he struck Neven violently around the head. "You cowardly, worthless wretch! What have you brought here?" He hit him again, and the Serb recoiled. "What have you told them?"

"Enough that you have my great respect," said Ramaas, interposing himself between the two men. "I am sorry we had to meet this way." He nodded toward the helicopter, and it orbited away, turning to line up for a landing on the helipad. "But you would never have spoken to me otherwise. And I do need your skills."

All attempts at denial vanished. "I am retired," Sood told him. "I have been so for many years."

"Your grandson will be killed if you refuse me again," said Ramaas. His patience for these games was waning. "Neven told me of the obligation you have to Kawal. And to his father . . . Your late son."

Sood's face clouded. "You have no right."

"I have what I take," Ramaas corrected. "And tonight, that is you."

Neven was the last to climb inside the helicopter, his clammy hands slippery on the seat belt as he fixed it in place across his lap. Ramaas dropped into the seat across from him and gave him a thoughtful look.

He couldn't meet the African's gaze. Neven's mind was spinning, grasping at possibilities. He had no contacts in this country, no safe places where he could run to. His avenues of escape were closed, and to his horror, the criminal knew that the only option now left to him was to throw himself on the mercy of the law. But who could he hope to surrender to? The Russians? The Americans? Did they even *have* an embassy in this dust-drowned country?

At his side, Jalsa Sood reached for his grandson, clutching at his arm. "Boy, how could you let this happen?" He was angry, almost shouting it, but an instant later the old man was shaking his head, near to tears. "It doesn't matter! I am sorry. I promised your father I would take care of you, I should have taught you better . . ."

There was a bump as the helicopter's engines increased power and Kawal had to shout to be heard over the sound of the rotors through the open hatch. "I don't need you!" He shook off Jalsa's grip as if his grandfather's touch was repulsive, and the gun that had been aimed in Kawal's direction dropped. "You stupid old man!" The words were venomous and brimming with adolescent resentment.

Neven saw the moment in Jalsa's eyes when he understood that the boy had never been a hostage at all. The old man's cheeks darkened and the anger came back. "You are part of this? Do you understand what you have done?"

"Shut up!" Kawal shot back, as the helicopter rose into the air again. "These men are going to make us rich!"

"We are *already* rich, you grasping little prick!" Jalsa slapped his grandson hard enough to cut his lip, but then Ramaas's soldier waved the gun in the direction of his kneecap and the old man drew back.

When Neven looked away, he saw that Ramaas was toying with a folding knife. His face came close to the Serbian's, and Neven felt hot breath on his cheek as Ramaas spoke. "You did what I asked," he said. "You brought me the boy, and through him, you brought me this Baker."

"You promised you would let me live," Neven shouted.

"That was a lie." The knife blurred in the dimness of the helicopter cabin and Neven felt it slice across his waist. "I am a brigand, Kurjak. What use do I have for promises?"

A shallow cut opened up the shirt he wore, pain burning on Neven's belly, but it was barely deep enough to make him bleed. He was briefly confused, as the death blow he had been expecting for days never came. Then he realized that Ramaas had cleanly severed the strap on the seat belt across his lap.

With one hand, Ramaas grabbed a fistful of Neven's jacket and pitched him out of the helicopter's open hatch, into the night air.

*   *   *

The black Peugeot 308 rocked gently against the chains that secured it to the deck of the shipping container in which they rode, and Marc found that sitting in the back seat of the car to work on his laptop was having a soporific effect. He shook it off and drained a bottle of water, pressing the heels of his hands to his eyes.

Inside the car, inside the cargo unit, the only light came from the sullen illumination of chemical glow sticks and a portable lamp rig sitting on the Peugeot's bonnet. He glanced at the Cabot diver's watch on his wrist. It was late afternoon, but it could have been the middle of the night for all he knew. Without any windows through which to watch the world go by, his sense of time passing had been knocked off kilter.

Hours earlier, after entering into neighboring Lithuania on board a Rubicon-owned cargo plane, the team had crossed into Poland under snap cover passports to rendezvous with the truck beyond the border. Now Malte had them racing like a rocket on the highway from Grajewo to Olsztynek, through a sheeting downpour of gray that seemed determined to follow them all day long.

Aside from the driver, the team on the ground was comprised of Marc, Lucy and Kara. There hadn't been time to source any local assistance from the closest Rubicon office in Prague, and the operation had the same kind of on-the-fly feel to it that Marc had become unpleasantly familiar with during his time as a fugitive from MI6. Everything was balancing on a knife-edge, all of it one misstep away from falling apart. He couldn't deny that some part of him was actually enjoying the thrill of being in the field once again, but that was swamped by more realistic concerns about getting through the next twenty-four hours alive and with the objective achieved.

Kara was dozing in a hammock strung from the walls of the cargo container, her slack face lit by the tablet screen she cradled in her hands. It was the first time he'd seen her sitting still. Usually, the petite Chinese American woman was constantly in motion, typing at a keyboard or moving from foot to foot with unspent energy.

As for Lucy, she cracked open the Peugeot's passenger-side front door and snaked in through the tiny gap. "Hey," she said, and nodded at the laptop. "You still worrying over that map? We scoped out the mission on the plane from France. Don't over-analyze. It's a good plan."

"Is it?" Marc looked down at the aerial captures of the target location. The area known as "Strefa G" was a compound within a compound, a highly secured sector of a hardened building on the grounds of a military base that—on paper, at least—belonged to the Polish national intelligence agency. "However you want to slice this, we're winging it."

"Having second thoughts? That's only natural."

"Nah." He shook his head, then paused. "Okay, *yeah*. But it's not that. This is all . . ." Marc sighed. "Too much like old times. And I don't like where that's taking me." He had spent most of his career in the British security services in the back of various nondescript vehicles similar to this one, glued to monitor screens while strike team operatives were kicking in doors elsewhere. This was dredging up bad memories again, all the things he wanted to put behind him. He met Lucy's gaze. "Sorry. I keep picking at it, don't I? I should just suck it up."

"Old habits die hard," she said, not unkindly. "I get where you're at. But this time, things are turned around. I'll be in here, you'll be out there." Lucy grinned at him. "You know what your problem is? You keep thinking you're still a back-seater." Then she turned serious again. "That could get you killed."

"Good pep talk, cheers," he allowed, his eyes drifting back to the map display. "Now all I have to concentrate on is how to infiltrate a CIA black site and convince a terrorist to rat out one of his mates."

"And do it before anyone in Langley hears about it," added Lucy. "So, y'know. *No pressure.*"

── TWELVE ──

The footprint of the Daan estate was large enough that it could have swallowed up the home of Welldone Amadayo three times over, and as Ramaas walked along the rose-colored marble floors, he found himself recalibrating his scale for what could be considered *excess*. The bomb builder's mansion was more of a palace, with dozens of opulent rooms and annexes that appeared to Ramaas to perform no real function. On the voyage from Europe he had wondered how rich a man who trafficked in death could become, and this residence told the story. Most of his kinsmen would aspire for something like this, but he found it cold.

The place had little life to it, resembling more a museum to one man's money than somewhere one could call home. Guhaad and the others saw it as a playground, helping themselves to food and drink from the well-stocked kitchen or playing with the dozen sports cars the old man had collected in his cavernous garage. Eventually, Ramaas had been forced to discipline his soldiers and remind them of the seriousness of their mission.

The security detail employed by Vishal Daan—or, more correctly, by Jalsa Sood—had already been dealt with before Ramaas's arrival at the rooftop restaurant the day before, leaving only a handful of residential staff and the old man's trophy wife. The warlord had quickly grown tired of the woman's histrionics and locked her in her rooms, but for their part the dozen or so staff went about their duties pretending that the African men with guns were not there. The grandson, Kawal, had helped that along by telling them that they would be safe, and so would their families, as long as no one raised the alarm.

Kawal reminded Ramaas of the youths he used to recruit to ride the pirate skiffs, gathered up from the beaches of Puntland. Shallow of spirit and lacking any kind of moral compass or empathy for their fellow humans, interested only in money and unable to look past their own immediate desires. Sood's grandson liked to think he was some kind of fantasy version of a criminal in the mold of an American rap star, all flash and no substance. He had already convinced himself he was a partner with the Somalians rather than their dupe. Ramaas was willing to let him continue to believe that, until the fiction stopped being useful. Kawal's connections in Dubai were smoothing the path, and he was determined to do all he could to spite his grandfather. Ramaas saw no reason not to take advantage of that.

Jalsa Sood's workshop was in a space on the lower level of the main house, joined to the big garage by a set of retracting doors. The area was dominated by the skeleton of a forty-year-old Maserati Bora, suspended on cables above the dismantled parts of its chassis. This was Sood's church, his retreat, where the genius who had once made clever devices of murder turned his hand to restoring the vintage supercar.

That work had been put aside in favor of the job Ramaas had given the old man. Crates of component parts, shipped in overnight from Saudi Arabia and Qatar, littered the floor. A group of identical steel-shelled suitcases were stacked in a low pile, and as Ramaas approached Sood's workbench, he ran his hand over their smooth metal surfaces.

Macanay straightened as Ramaas walked past him, chewing steadily on the mouthful of khat that was keeping him alert. He gave the warlord a wary nod and patted the Uzi submachine gun hanging from a strap over his shoulder, as if to say that *all was well*.

Sood turned, putting down a soldering iron, and glared at him. Tired and guarded, out of his rich man's clothes and in an ordinary robe, he looked his age. There was a collapsible bed in one corner of the workshop and Ramaas wondered idly if Sood had slept there last night while the warlord had taken the man's rooms for his own. He had toppled the king from the throne in his own palace, made Sood his servant. That amused Ramaas greatly.

"My wife—" Sood began.

"Safe," Ramaas said, before he could finish his sentence. "For as long as she keeps her silence."

"I will tell her."

Ramaas shook his head. "She has already learned that lesson." He jutted his chin toward the workbench. "The only concern for you now is to make me what I want."

The bench was littered with color photographs and complex blueprints, all of them showing every component and element of the Russian nuclear device in exacting detail. At the center of it all, one of the steel cases sat open beneath a powerful lamp, and inside it there was a cluster of metallic components and hardware that were identical to those shown in the pictures.

"How many of these do you want?" Sood said wearily.

"I'll tell you when it is enough." Ramaas glanced around. "They need to be perfect."

Sood scowled. "Without any radioisotopes to forge a reading, it won't be enough. This will be nothing more than a giant paperweight."

"I have that in hand," said Ramaas. A container of medical-grade iodine-125 bound for a radiology ward in Malaysia had already been hijacked for exactly that purpose. Ramaas pushed the old man out of the way and examined his handiwork.

"Where is . . . the original?" Sood licked his dry lips.

"I keep it close," Ramaas deflected. "And secure." He studied the old man. "Do you need people to assist you with the work?"

"No!" Sood snapped. "You force me to do this, fine, I will. But let me do it as I see fit!"

Ramaas shook his head and beckoned Macanay. Anticipating violence, the other man smirked and came over, slipping the Uzi off his shoulder. "I want to make sure you are not deliberately stalling." He nodded to Macanay and started walking. "Bring him."

They left the workshop through a set of glass double doors at the back, and emerged on the wide sun deck that surrounded the mansion's great oval swimming pool. Wooden panels on elevated frames, bleached white by the desert sun, cast grids of shade over the water.

Five black shapes lay on the bottom of the pool, the bodies of men in dark suits weighted down with chains from the workshop. The filtering system was still laboring to rid the water of the pink cast from the wounds of the corpses. Sood's security detail put up a good fight, but Guhaad killed them all in a matter of moments, doubtless eager to remind the warlord of his expertise in that area.

Sood grimaced at the sight and looked away. "You have already made your point," he muttered.

"I don't think so." A middle-aged Filipino woman—a household maid—was being walked out toward them by Bidar. She blanched as she saw the bodies in the water and fought back the urge to cry. "I think you are going to stall. It is the kind of man you are, Jalsa Sood. You will feel the need to be defiant in some way. I want to show you why that is a foolish idea." Ramaas nodded toward Bidar, and he shoved the maid in the small of the back.

She cried out and stumbled to the edge of the pool, blinking in the harsh sunlight. Bidar did not hesitate, and shot her in the back of the head with a silenced pistol. A jet of red burst from her mouth, and she spun and tumbled into the deep end.

Sood shouted out a curse and took a step toward the maid, but Macanay pulled him back. "Why did you—?"

"This will happen every day," said Ramaas, his tone hardening. "Someone will be brought here and executed. The faster you work, the fewer people will die."

"I said I would do it!" Sood shouted. "I give you my word! But it will take me several days, even at the fastest pace!"

Ramaas nodded. "And so several people will die. One for each day you work. As long as you work to my satisfaction, I will let you pick who dies. If not . . ." He let his gaze drift up toward the windows of the trophy wife's bedroom.

Sood jerked out of Macanay's grip and shook his fist at Ramaas. "You are an animal!" he roared.

"It upsets you that I kill innocent people?" The warlord walked to him, his dark and damaged eye glistening. "*You?* How many lives have your bombs claimed, old man? The false ones as well as the real? *You* judge *me?*"

"Why should I do any more for you?" Sood said, his flash of anger fading. "Life is cheap to you. When I give you what you want, I will die and so will Kawal!"

"You are too useful to murder," Ramaas replied, as if he were considering the possibility. "The boy, not so much. Think on that." He walked away. "And work faster," he added, throwing the comment over his shoulder. "Or don't. It is your choice."

Malte brought the Peugeot off the main highway past the village of Stare Kiejkuty and onto a narrower two-lane road that sliced through the frost-covered Polish countryside. To their right, a double fence of chain link topped by razor wire followed the line of the road for miles. A few meters past the fences, a wall of thin, towering evergreens screened the facility beyond from passing observers.

Marc looked up as a faded yellow-orange sign flashed past, bearing warnings in four different languages that the far side of the barrier was a military base where trespassers would be shot. He adjusted the thick-rimmed spectacles balancing on his nose and turned back to his laptop. "Okay, Kara, we're coming up to the entrance now. Light the blue touchpaper and stand well back."

"*Copy that, I think,*" said the voice in his inner ear. Kara's words were coming to him through a contact pad on the end of the arms of the fake eyeglasses. Hair-fine circuits threaded through the frames of the spectacles formed a distributed short-range radio transceiver that gently vibrated signals through his skull. Marc was essentially his own antenna, and the bone-induction communicator meant no one could overhear the incoming signal. He could respond with subvocalized replies, but it had the unpleasant side effect of making his jaw ache.

He opened and closed his mouth a few times to shake it off. "Here we go," he said aloud. "Commit to the hack . . . *now.*" Marc tapped the *enter* key on his laptop, and the computer sent a wireless ping back to a satellite transmitter in the truck, which was parked outside a highway service station half a kilometer away. In turn, that ping shot a packet of spoofed data up into space, where it would begin a few milliseconds of bouncing around the world until it homed in on an isolated server farm in Jakarta.

Marc heard the throaty snarl of a motorcycle engine and from the driver's seat, Malte spoke a terse warning. "Company."

He looked up again. Inside the fence line, a pair of ZiD scrambler bikes in olive drab were paralleling the car, each one ridden by an armed man in black tactical gear with forest-green flashes. On their shoulders each had a white-on-black patch in the shape of a vulture, and the word ALEPH. Marc did his best to appear indifferent to them, but he knew that the patrol riders were already radioing back to the front gate up ahead, warning them that an unknown vehicle was approaching.

Like Rubicon's Special Conditions Division, Aleph was a private military contractor, but that was where the similarity ended. Far larger than the SCD, and with a reputation for thoroughness, they operated forces in dozens of developing countries and worked with national interests as protective details in places where the real military didn't want to get involved. The base at Stare Kiejkuty was one such location.

First built for the SS during the Second World War before it fell into the hands of the Red Army, the base eventually became the property of Poland's intelligence agency in the 1970s and quietly served as a training center. But after the 9/11 attacks on New York City and the advent of the War on Terror, that changed. Hard facts were difficult to come by, but it was known that teams from the CIA had been resident at the facility, apparently using it as a covert prison for unlawfully rendered terror suspects. Public attention finally hit Stare Kiejkuty in the mid-2000s and the black site was shut down.

Or so the world believed. Far from letting it fall into disuse, the CIA had simply chosen to put distance between themselves and the Polish facility. Reopened sometime after 2012, the site was now privately managed by the Aleph PMC. Who paid Aleph and what the current function of the base was were questions a lot harder to find answers to.

Marc checked the progress bar on the laptop as it hit 100 percent and held his breath. The Aleph Corporation's core server in Indonesia worked on an architecture he was familiar with from his time at MI6, one with an existing zero-day exploit in its software that was going to get them inside. The data packet that was now infiltrating the distant server would temporarily add two identities to the base's lists of security-cleared visitors.

"*Clock is running,*" said Kara, seeing the same data stream he did. "*Estimate ninety minutes to burn. Don't stop to smell the roses.*"

"Copy that." Marc's throat was dry and his reply came out husky.

The car slowed and Malte turned off the main road and into the approach at the unmarked main gate. Another two guards in Aleph uniform were waiting for them, and one peeled off to approach the car while his colleague held a G36 assault rifle up and at the ready.

Closing the laptop, Marc rolled down the window and offered two high-quality fake IDs to the guard. "Agents Cahill and Durant," he said, affecting a passable American accent. "We've got priority clearance to interview an asset here."

The guard was wearing a digitally enabled headset and he scanned the passes with its built-in camera without replying. From the corner of his eye, Marc saw Malte's hand drop to the gearshift, ready to slam the Peugeot into reverse if they needed to make a fast exit—but then the guard was nodding, handing back the IDs. The gate opened and the car rolled forward into the treeline. The two ZiD bikes fell into flanking positions as Malte drove up a long, snaking road toward the base proper.

"*You sound Canadian,*" said Lucy, joining the conversation for the first time.

"Bite me, eh?" Marc replied, examining the pass cards. His own face looked back at him, with his beard now neatly trimmed and a pair of thick-framed hipster glasses across his nose.

The IDs were good enough to pass muster on a cursory check, but he didn't want to push their authenticity, no matter how many assurances Delancort had made.

To create brand-new identities would have taken time they didn't have and opened up more opportunities for something to go amiss. Appropriating the names of existing CIA agents was a smarter play, but it came with a different set of risks. In less than two hours, Aleph's central computer would send its regular scheduled update to the CIA's central database and register that two new arrivals had entered Stare

Kiejkuty's Strefa G compound—and then both systems would realize that agents "Cahill and Durant" could not be in two places at
once.

Another guard waved the car into a parking zone next to more ZiD
patrol bikes and the blocky shape of a Bearcat APC. Nearby, Aleph
contractors walked the perimeter with dogs, constantly on watch—
but they were looking outward, not inward. It was the one weakness
in the facility's set-up that Marc had been able to determine—Strefa
G had originally been built to keep people from getting *in,* not *out,*
and everything that had been retrofitted to it to make the place a
prison was built on that flawed foundation.

Getting behind the fence had been straightforward enough. Now
the hard part was beginning.

Lucy must have known what Marc was thinking. *"Simple in-and-
out,"* she said over the comms. *"Remember, we don't need to make good
on anything here, so promise that asshole whatever he wants as long as you
get the intel."*

Malte glanced over his shoulder and raised an eyebrow. "Your show,"
he said.

Marc nodded and blew out a breath. "Not a problem," he lied.

Although Jadeed Amarah had no clock, no way to reckon the passing
of the days apart from mandated times for sleeping and eating, he had
a grasp of the regularity of his interrogations. At first they had been
daily occurrences, soon after they had flown him through the night
to this cold and unknown place. Then the interval slipped to months
and finally to nothing.

He bore the scars that his refusal to speak had earned him, carried
them as if they were his badge of honor. The Americans and their
lackeys had done much in their attempts to break him, but he had held
true.

This was the lie he told himself. The fact was, he *had* talked. But
nothing Jadeed had revealed was of any consequence to his brothers
and mentors among Al Sayf. He offered up a few morsels of informa-

tion, but they were falsehoods one and all—part of the group's training was to give each of their warriors a cluster of lies to tell any interrogators, blind leads and fake facts that would waste the enemy's time and energy.

The other things he had told them, the real things, he salted in among the lies. The truth he told about the men who had betrayed his brethren, this cadre of Western elitists who called themselves "the Combine." He had no qualms about doing so. He owed them nothing.

It had been the Combine who promised Al Sayf their greatest victory, who had provided them with the tools to set the streets of America running red with blood. It had been the Combine who ultimately failed them, *betrayed them*. His hate for them was boundless. Those men were still free while Jadeed rotted here.

After the CIA had taken him, he resigned himself to becoming a martyr, at first believing that he could be a potent symbol in his incarceration. Perhaps, a figurehead that others might rally around and in whose name the war might be fought. But that hope of bitter triumph had faded against the harsh light of cold reality.

He was suffering the worst fate a revolutionary could experience. He had been erased from the world, his deeds unwritten and ignored. Amarah was a forgotten man, rotting here, valueless even to his enemies and . . . *Dare he think it?* Forsaken by his commanders?

So when the guards came for him, it was a shock. Hidden behind their masks, the figures in black marched him to an interview room where two white men were waiting, both of them dressed in suits. One, with glasses and a beard, sat in front of a laptop computer and looked as if he would rather have been anywhere else. The other was expressionless, moving to stand behind Jadeed as he sat down. The second man's presence was supposed to unsettle him, but Jadeed had played this game before. He rested his hands on his lap, the metal cuffs uncomfortable about his wrists.

As the masked guards left the room, Jadeed looked around. At length, his gaze settled on the bearded man and he cocked his head, drawing up some defiance. "What is it that your worthless nation wants of me today, American?"

The man glanced at his wristwatch. "Actually, I'm here to ask you what *you* want."

Marc kept his hands flat on the table between them, partly to avoid any hint of nervousness, and partly to stop them from tightening into fists. Across from him, a man who had led a group of teenagers-turned-weapons into a crowd of thousands of innocents sat indolently glaring, a sneer playing on his lips.

Marc had seen firsthand the horrors that Amarah and his cohorts in Al Sayf were capable of, and his blood chilled to imagine how much more damage they could have done, had he and Ekko Solomon's team failed to stop them a year earlier. It galled him to think that this terrorist could still be alive after everything his cadre had been responsible for, but the CIA had made good on their promise to bury Amarah in a deep, dark hole and make the world forget he had never existed.

As much as the Combine, Al Sayf shared the blame for taking the lives of people close to him, and for a moment Marc entertained the fantasy of launching himself across the table to wrap his hands around the terrorist's throat and choke the life from him.

Something of that intention must have flickered in his eyes, because the prisoner blinked and drew back, pulling his orange jumpsuit straight. "You have taken much from me," Amarah said, after a moment. "It will take forever to repay it all."

"Let's start small. How about a better cell?" Marc concentrated on letting a change wash over him. On the way to Poland, he had rehearsed this conversation a dozen times before realizing that he was approaching it wrongly. A lifetime ago, it had been Marc Dane sitting on the wrong side of an interrogation as men from his own agency had pushed him to admit guilt for a crime he had not committed. Now he reached back to that memory and took on the same tone, the same arrogant manners that had been used against him. "Maybe we can get you a nice plant."

Jadeed frowned and spread his fingers. "I want my *misbaha*. They were taken from me and I want them back."

"*Prayer beads.*" Kara's voice was quiet in his ear. "*Like a rosary . . .*"

"That can be arranged." Marc saw the opening and pressed on. "And more besides, if you're willing to assist us with something."

"I've already told you every story I know about the Combine," Amarah snapped.

"Tell me a different story," Marc insisted. "One about how you killed a man called Jalsa Sood in Libya."

Amarah was momentarily wrong-footed and he gave a shrug to cover it. "I have removed many impediments in the course of the work."

"Except you didn't that time. You didn't murder Sood with a car bomb, like you said you did." Marc opened his laptop to show Amarah the digital photos of the bombing's aftermath. "A bunch of ordinary people walking to market—you killed them in the blast zone. And some unlucky stiff who was probably paid to drive Sood's car. But not the man himself. You let the Baker fake his own death." When he said the nickname, Amarah's failure to hide his reaction to it told Marc he was dead on.

"You insult me," said the terrorist. "When the sword falls, all who meet its edge are taken."

"It would make you look weak in the eyes of your extremist cousins, wouldn't it? If it were known your group took money to fake a death instead of actually doing the deed. You were supposed to kill him, but he bought you off." Marc glared at the other man, his temper rising. "Tell me, who made the deal with Sood? Was it you, wanting to earn a little more cash on the side? Or was it your noble commander, Omar Khadir? Did you use the money to fund the bombing you supervised in Barcelona?"

"Dane." Lucy's voice resonated in his skull, a clear warning in her tone. *"Stay on point."*

Amarah's confusion slowly shifted, becoming annoyance and suspicion. "There is no way that the Central Intelligence Agency would suspect that Jalsa Sood is anything other than a corpse. We were thorough." And then a slow smile emerged on the prisoner's face. "So you are not CIA. I should have guessed that the moment I saw you." He leaned toward Marc and behind him, Malte unfolded his arms, ready for violence if it came. "Yes. I know who you are."

* * *

"Oh, shit." Kara unconsciously backed away from the monitor registering the audio pickup from Dane's glasses. "He's caught us? How
did that—?"

Lucy shot her a hard look and put her finger to her lips. "Wait." At
that moment, she wanted very much to have eyes in that interrogation room as well as ears, but they were taking a risk as it was sending an unauthorized radio signal out of the Strefa G compound. A
video stream would have meant more bandwidth, and more chance
that it could be detected or jammed outright.

She could hear Dane breathing steadily. "Get ready to abort," Lucy
told him. Suddenly the air in the back of the truck was close and
stifling.

"*You reckon so?*" Lucy couldn't be sure if Marc was answering her
or responding to Amarah.

"*Did your masters send you to kill me?*" demanded the terrorist. "*To
silence me? How will you explain that away? A suicide?*"

All at once, a critical moment of understanding flashed through
Lucy's mind. Kara was right, Amarah wasn't bluffing, and he *had* seen
through the false flag they were flying—but, more importantly, he
was making a serious mistake in the process. "He thinks you're with
the Combine."

Over the audio link, Lucy heard something like a wry snort. "*That's
what you think?*" Marc dropped his false accent and continued. "*I'm
sorry to tell you, you're not that important to us. But what you know about
Jalsa Sood is. So talk. If you want to live.*"

"Oh, shit," Kara repeated. "Well, I guess we're off-book now."

Amarah turned around and glared at Malte. "Nothing would give me
more pleasure than to watch you leave here with empty hands."

Marc watched his bravado falter a little, even as he spoke. *A year in
solitary confinement would do that to you,* he thought.

"What do you want with Sood?" continued the terrorist.

He considered the fate he wanted for Amarah and his cohorts. "We'll do what you failed to." Marc found it surprisingly easy to slip behind the mask of a Combine operative. It was a simple matter of remembering to subtract any humanity from every word he spoke. "Tell me where he is."

"Your masters like to make deals," Amarah said accusingly. "That is all the world is to them, like a game to be played." He shook his head. "We will make a deal, then. I will deliver Jalsa Sood to you. I know where he is. But it must be done in person. I know his new face. I will take you to him, in exchange for my freedom."

"You're a prisoner in a black-site holding facility surrounded by armed guards, dogs and fences . . . and you want us to bust you out? *Right now?*"

Amarah nodded briskly. "You asked me what I wanted. I am telling you."

Over the other man's shoulder, Malte was glaring at Marc and shaking his head.

"*Pull the plug,*" said Lucy. "*We're not set up for anything more than stealth infil and exfil, and the clock is down to less than an hour now. A brig break is a no-can-do.*"

"All right," said Marc, ignoring Lucy's warning. "We'll have to improvise."

"*Are you out of your damned—?*"

He took off the glasses and put them down on the table, pinching the bridge of his nose. If they walked out of here with nothing, then any chance to track down Ramaas and his bomb was gone. Marc snapped his fingers at Malte. "Give me your phone."

The driver warily complied. "What are you doing?" he said quietly.

"Like I said." Marc worked the laptop's keyboard. "Improvising."

"He's not responding," said Kara.

"Obviously," Lucy shot back. "*Damn.* He's going to wreck the whole operation."

"Actually, I think he's trying to salvage it . . ."

Lucy glared at the other woman. "Don't take his side." She switched channels on the headset she was wearing, keying into a different encrypted frequency. "Static calling Sky, ears on?"

"*Sky, responding.*" Ari Silber's voice sounded as if it was reaching them down a tunnel of distortion. "*Go ahead, Static. I'm guessing there's a problem?*"

Lucy didn't bother to tell Silber he was right. "We need to move up the timetable. How soon can you be on loiter?"

"*Twenty minutes and change, if I don't spare the horses. Is that what we're doing? Because if I commit, there's no do-over.*"

"I am well aware," Lucy replied, her lips thinning. "Start your approach now, but be ready for an abort. In case this blows up in our goddamn faces."

"*Understood, Static. Sky out.*"

She looked up and found Kara watching her. "So what do we do now? I mean, the plan was to ditch the truck and—"

Lucy cut her off. "It's out of our hands now."

Dane pressed the Rubicon-issue smartphone back into Malte's hand and he looked down at it. Framed by featureless black anodized metal, the handset's screen now displayed a simple GPS direction finder and a scrolling text block that read FOLLOW ME. Dane had connected a short USB cable to a port on the bottom of the device, and dangled it freely like a stubby tail.

Malte eyed it, and moved the phone around experimentally. The dart-shaped GPS indicator moved with him, keeping its target bearing.

Dane shot a look at Amarah, then typed something into his keyboard. There was a pinging sound and the scrolling text changed to DO WHAT I TELL YOU. Malte scowled. He disliked the Englishman's attitude and he certainly wasn't happy about putting his life in Dane's hands, but no other option was open to them, apart from admitting defeat and exfiltrating before their false identities expired.

Dane banged on the door of the interrogation room and the Aleph guard outside opened it. "My colleague needs to make a call," he said.

At length, Malte gave a nod and left the room, walking out into the corridor. The dart shifted, pointing him back toward the main entrance to the Strefa G compound. GO OUTSIDE, it instructed. He sighed and started moving.

Marc glanced at Amarah once more, and then went back to his computer. The prisoner lounged back in his chair, glaring at him. "What are you doing?" he demanded.

"You want out. I'm making that happen. Sit there, shut up and let me concentrate." Inside a partitioned ghost sector of the laptop's hard drive, Marc had hidden a dozen files showing internal schematics of the Stare Kiejkuty facility. They dated back to the mid-eighties, part of a packet of data stolen from the Russian military by anti-government hacktivists who had been more than happy to sell them for a princely sum of bitcoin to any anonymous buyer.

Marc's fixation with operational prep bordered on the obsessive, and it was part of the reason he had been so good at his job with MI6's OpTeam program. His changed circumstances forced him to lose some of that single-mindedness, but at times it still came through—and now he was glad that he had gone the extra mile in studying every possible aspect of the facility.

The Strefa G compound was close to the base's administration block, a few hundred meters away across an open parade ground that doubled as a helipad. Having paired his computer to Malte's smartphone through an encrypted wireless link, he could now map a series of digital waypoints directly to the other man's device. A video window in the corner of his screen showed blurry images from the phone's internal camera, the picture bouncing as Malte held it tightly in his hand as he walked.

Marc became aware of Amarah staring fixedly at him. "What?"

The terrorist leaned closer. "The Combine failed us in America. If it happens again, I'll kill you."

"Don't throw your weight around just yet, mate." The tension Marc was feeling expressed itself in a flash of annoyance. "You don't even know what bloody country you're in. Without us, you're stuck here." He turned back to the keyboard and issued the next set of instructions.

The arrow pointed Malte toward a low two-story building with the word *Administracja* written across the entrance. He kept his pace quick and steady, projecting the impression of someone who knew exactly what he was doing, even if that was far from the truth. Malte wasn't comfortable being treated like an avatar in some game, walked around by the invisible hand of a player sitting out of harm's way behind a keyboard.

Inside the building's entrance, an Aleph guard was standing sentry in front of double doors that led deeper inside. The arrow directed him to proceed through them and into the corridor beyond. Malte found the false identity pass and handed it to the guard, just as the phone gave off a low ping.

PASS WON'T WORK THERE, said the text box.

"Perkele," Malte cursed under his breath. The guard was already reaching for a collapsible baton on his belt and saying something negative.

The phone pinged again. PUNCH GUY, it suggested helpfully. TAKE HIS.

Malte let reflex take over and he threw a lightning-fast palm strike into the guard's solar plexus with enough force to make him choke and drop the baton. With his other hand, the driver grabbed a handful of the contractor's hair and pushed him down to meet his upcoming knee. The guard's nose broke with a wet crunch and he staggered back, dazed. Malte stepped in, slipping his hands and arms around the man's throat. He squeezed him into a sleeper hold and counted off the seconds until the guard went slack.

Malte dropped the unconscious man out of sight behind the reception desk, and snatched the guard's pass from its lanyard, moving quickly through the doors.

A corridor extended away from him, lined with offices and storage rooms. Malte glanced at the phone and the message changed again.

A334.

At first he wondered if Dane had mistyped, but then Malte noticed that each door had a four-character code stencilled on it. He started forward, scanning left and right.

Behind him, a side door opened without warning and another guard in Aleph's black-and-green uniform appeared, catching sight of Malte. He called out, closing the distance between them in two quick steps.

The guard got a hand on to Malte's shoulder, but even as it tightened, the driver was dropping and pivoting. Malte swung his arm down and put an axe-blow strike into the middle of the guard's forearm. Bone broke cleanly and tore a yell of pain from the man. He tried to disengage, but Malte grabbed the side of his head and slammed it into the wall, once, twice.

The driver finished him off with a hard cross that dropped the guard to the floor, his body slumping down against door A334. Malte kicked it open and dragged the injured man inside before anyone else could appear.

The room was noisy with the humming of air conditioners and the constant clicking of electronics. A quartet of computer servers stood before him, red and yellow LEDs blinking in complex but meaningless patterns along their flanks.

He held up the smartphone to his face as it chimed again. CONNECT PHONE + CABLE TO A SERVER, it told him. THEN EXFIL.

Malte weighed the device in his hand, considering what he was letting himself in for if he obeyed. Finally, he pushed aside his doubts and put the phone atop the nearest computer stack. There was a socket close by and he fitted the USB connector into it, uncertain what was supposed to happen next. The phone's screen instantly blinked black and a torrent of programming text scrolled across it.

The lights on the front of the server turned crimson, and Malte heard the ringing of distant alarms.

* * *

Contact.

Marc allowed himself a grin. It was starting to look as though this might actually *work*. In a few seconds, Malte's smartphone bridged the distance between Marc's computer and the air-gapped systems of the base's main servers. He fired off a bombardment of pre-programmed intrusion macros that landed like the digital equivalent of heat-seeking missiles, blowing open a hole in the mainframe's security firewalls that he could exploit. It was a crude, blunt-trauma hack that would make a mess of things, and Marc had already set up a timed self-destruct subroutine to make the phone short-circuit its own battery and catch alight. But before that happened, he gatecrashed the base's emergency functions and threw the virtual switches on every fire-warning subsystem in Strefa G. From the outside, the black site would have been a tough nut to crack for any covert-ops strike team—but from within, the protection was thinner and there were enough exploits open for Marc to cause chaos.

He paused to button his jacket and turn up the collar. Amarah gave him a quizzical look. Marc tapped the enter key and his reasons immediately became clear, as fire alarms started shrieking and the overhead sprinkler system gushed into life.

Amarah recoiled in shock at the sudden indoor downpour. Marc was on his feet, snapping the ruggedised laptop closed as the guard burst in. Outside, water was sluicing down the walls and the alarms were deafening.

The guard had a pistol in his hand and a hard cast to his expression that told Marc he would shoot first and ask questions later.

He jabbed his finger at Amarah and shouted at the guard. "What the hell is going on? Get him back to his cell!" The guard came forward and grabbed a handful of the prisoner's jumpsuit, hauling him up out of the chair. He took his eyes off Marc long enough for him to move around the table and plant a savage kick in the back of the man's right knee.

The guard crumpled and fell to the concrete floor, losing the gun as he went down. The weapon spun away across the water pooling beneath the table and Marc stooped to go after it.

Amarah rocketed out of his chair, seizing the chance to inflict violence having spent so many months unable to do so. His hands still cuffed together, he punched the Aleph guard in the face and then dove on him, using the frame of his handcuffs to press into the man's neck and choke the life from him. The guard fought back, but Amarah's pent-up hate was overwhelming him. Color faded from the guard's face.

Marc came back with the guard's HK45 pistol and aimed it at Amarah. "Get off him!" He shouted to be heard over the sound of the alarms. "We don't have time for this!"

Amarah slammed the guard's head against the wet floor with a splash and got back to his feet. "If you don't have the stomach to kill him, let me do it."

"Get out." Marc grabbed Amarah and shoved him into the corridor. He aimed the gun in the direction of the semi-conscious man and fired twice. "Happy now? Go on, move!" He forced him away and into the sheeting drizzle before the terrorist could see that both rounds had gone into the wall.

Keeping the other man in front of him, Marc marched Amarah swiftly along the hallway, holding the gun high against the prisoner's shoulder. They passed access doors to more cells where the handful of other detainees in the black site were already being held in lockdown, and soon emerged in an open junction where three corridors met at a heavy metal security gate. The door was already locked, and four more Aleph troopers were gathering there. Soaked through, they sported M4 carbines and hawkish glares.

"How do you plan to get by them?" Amarah hissed out of the side of his mouth.

"Shut it," Marc retorted, then called out to the guards. "I got this one, but something's going down in the cells." He shoved Amarah again, this time toward a branching corridor. "I'm gonna secure this prisoner," he added.

"This passage doesn't lead *out*," Amarah snarled.

"I know." Marc marched him through another set of doors and they emerged out of the sprinkler downpour and into the bitter cold of the exercise yard. "Keep moving."

Amarah ignored the order and halted, gesturing at a double stand of tall electrified fencing that walled in the yard on three sides. "Do you want me to dig, Britisher?" He spat the words at him, starting to shiver. "Or am I to be shot trying to escape?"

Marc considered the weight of the pistol in his hand, and for a moment he wanted to make that happen. It would be easy to do. Two shots, center mass. Watch Amarah go down to the dirt and bleed out. He deserved no better.

But that would solve nothing, help nobody. *So help me, I'll put you right back in here when we're done with you,* he vowed.

Marc shook off the moment. "Did you forget we have a bloke on the other side of that fence?" He heard the low, heavy growl of a turbo diesel engine and turned to see a black slab of metal bounce up the grass verge beyond and collide with the compound's barrier.

The big Bearcat APC smashed through both fences in a shower of sparks, the sheets of chain link rolling back like curtains, and it slewed into a fishtail turn. The driver-side door cracked open and Malte leaned out. He nodded toward the rear, his expression no different from the one he'd worn when picking up Marc at the Monaco heliport.

"Ride's here," said Marc, but Amarah needed no encouragement to scramble up into the back of the high-sided personnel carrier. As Marc followed the other man on board, the first shots whined off the armored hull. "Floor it!" he shouted.

Malte slammed the Bearcat into gear and the APC lurched forward, skidding across the frosty ground and back toward the distant treeline.

── THIRTEEN ──

The Bearcat lurched into a jackknife skid to avoid a rank of tire-shredding spikes and Malte accelerated into the wooden prefab guardhouse, losing only a little momentum as the APC smashed it down and rode on through the main gate in a shower of sparks.

Marc felt himself leave the floor of the crew compartment and bounce off the wall as the vehicle listed on its shock absorbers. The APC's heavy off-road tires screeched, leaving black commas of rubber on the highway as Malte turned the vehicle westward and they shot away.

Amarah was crouching low between two folding chairs attached to the bulkhead, cursing as he rocked back and forth. "Is he trying to kill us?" He shouted to be heard over the roar of the engine.

"Sit down and shut up." Marc grabbed a handhold to steady himself and squinted through one of the armored-glass windows in the back of the Bearcat, still clutching the HK45 pistol he had taken on the way out of Strefa G. They were already accelerating away from the grounds of the black site, but the Aleph guards were not going to let them go easily. He saw movement behind them, the spindly shapes of riders on motorcycles in pursuit.

The Bearcat swayed alarmingly again and there was a blare of horns as Malte threaded across the wrong lane, barely missing a tanker truck coming the other way. A wall of metal flashed past with a droning roar and then it was gone.

"*This* is your plan?" snarled Amarah.

Marc ignored him, hesitating as a squad of four ZiD bikes closed in on them. They were coming around in a line, rapidly eroding the APC's lead. For a moment, he thought about firing at the riders. There were small armored doors in the flanks and the rear of the Bearcat, like arrow slits on an ancient castle, through which he could aim the HK's muzzle. But he quickly discarded the idea; Marc's scores on the firing range were good, but it would be a waste of ammunition trying to draw a bead on one fast-moving vehicle from the back of another. He needed a smarter solution.

As he cast around the interior of the Bearcat, looking for something he could use, the leading Aleph rider showed no compunction in using his own weapon. Marc recoiled as a burst of bullets sparked off the back of the APC in yellow flashes. Guiding his ZiD with one hand, the lead rider had a compact submachine gun on a wrist lanyard in the other, and fired it toward the Bearcat's shielded wheel wells in hopes of blowing out the rear tires.

The attacker was close enough for Marc to recognize the distinctive shape of the firearm; a Swiss-made Brügger & Thomet MP9 machine pistol. Marc had an innate tech-nerd talent for absorbing and retaining hardware specs that proved invaluable in his analyst duties, but that was usually less helpful when being shot at. It was a kind of stress-level coping mechanism. Immediately a scorecard unfolded on the twitch-level of his thoughts—the gun had a thirty-shot magazine of 9mm ammo and it was capable of discharging over nine hundred rounds per minute. While that wouldn't be enough to chew through the Bearcat's reinforced bodywork, the vehicle's tires would be shredded if the bikers could land a few hits.

The pursuit took them through the middle of a small town in a blaze of noise and speed as desperate onlookers fled out of their path, but within moments they were back on the highway again. Malte put the APC into a swerving weave back and forth across the two lanes of the highway, but the other riders were coming up fast and all it would take was for one of them to draw a bead.

"We have to thin them out," Marc said aloud, and he grabbed at one of the folding chairs attached to the wall. Heavy plastic butterfly clamps held the chair in place, and he stuffed the HK pistol onto his waistband so he could undo them two at a time.

"What do you plan on doing?" demanded Amarah. "Lighten the ship so we float away?"

Marc jerked his head at the van's twin rear doors. "Open them."

"Are you mad—?"

"For crying out loud, stop running your bloody mouth and *just do it*!" The chair came away in Marc's hands and then he repeated the action with a second one.

"You'll kill us all, Britisher," said the terrorist, but he did as he was told. Crouching to keep himself out of the line of fire, Amarah turned the latch on the left-hand door and gave it a sharp kick as the Bearcat took a wide corner.

The door flew open, swinging back to crash against the side of the APC, and for a split second the leading ZiD rider had to pivot into the bend to make the same turn. Marc threw the folded chair out the back of the APC in a spinning-toss motion, aiming it right into the biker's path.

The chair flipped up in the slipstream and cracked the rider across the face with enough force to unseat him. At such high speed, motorcycle and rider were instantly parted, the uncontrolled bike rocketed away into a roadside ditch and the Aleph mercenary slammed into the icy asphalt.

The other bikes slowed momentarily, but none of them stopped to check on the status of their comrade. Bullets spanked off the open door and a hot round ricocheted inside the Bearcat, drawing an angry howl from Amarah.

Marc grabbed the other chair and tried his trick a second time, but his throw was off and the metal seat bounded across the road. One of the two trailing bikes juddered over it, almost skidding into a crash, but the rider was good and he recovered. Marc reluctantly drew the HK and blind-fired a couple of shots at the chasers, before retreating back into cover around the door frame.

He shouted toward Malte. "This isn't working, man. We need to lose these creeps!" Low hedges dusted with snow flashed past on either side of the road, and beyond them were gray, fallow fields and dense stands of trees. In his mind's eye, Marc recalled the local map he had pored over prior to the mission and something occurred to him.

He dashed to the front of the crew compartment, to the grille that opened into the driver's area. "Take a short cut!" Marc yelled, jabbing his finger at the fields. "Get us off the road!"

Malte saw the logic in it and gave a nod. "Hang on," said the Finn, and he spun the APC's steering wheel ninety degrees, putting them into a hard turn that was just on the right side of an uncontrolled spin.

Something heavy and metallic crunched against the rear quarter of the Bearcat, and Marc saw that one of the ZiD riders had been coming up on the outside, only to be slammed aside when the APC pivoted.

Malte aimed the heavy 4x4 at the hedge and the vehicle burst through it onto the frost-hardened earth of the field on the other side. The ground was rough and uneven, enough that the Bearcat's speed bounced it high on its wheels. As the vehicle briefly caught air, Amarah lost his balance, falling back toward the open doors.

Marc dove at him and barely caught the terrorist before he could be bounced right out of the APC, seizing fistfuls of his orange prison jumpsuit. Pain lanced through Marc's muscles as he overextended to haul Amarah back into the APC's rear cabin, and the man flailed, smacking him away once he was safe. "Get off me!"

"Next time I'll let you faceplant in the dirt, eh?" Marc belatedly noted that he had lost the HK45 in the heat of the moment, but for all the good it would have done he didn't miss it.

The last two bikes were still coming, kicking up divots of loose dirt and snow as they snarled across the field. They harried the APC like dogs trying to bring down a bigger beast, parallelling the vehicle and spraying gunfire along the armored flanks. Malte said something that Marc guessed was a Finnish swear word, judging by the venom behind it, and then the driver put the APC into another wide turn that brought them around in a rough circle. The ZiD riders were expecting a chase, and Malte's abrupt about-face caught both of them looking the wrong way.

The driver aimed the APC at the closest bike and pushed the pedal to the firewall. The Aleph merc made the mistake of skidding to a halt and he grasped his machine pistol in both hands, wasting the last of his ammo in an attempt to puncture the bulletproof windscreen.

Malte's forward visibility was cut sharply by the spiderweb fractures over the toughened plastic, but he still had enough to bear down on the shooter. At the last second, the mercenary gunned the throttle and tried to race away, but he was too slow to avoid the Bearcat's front left quarter as it slammed into his rear tire. The bike broke in two and the rider was thrown from his saddle in a tangle of limbs.

Marc saw movement back toward the highway. The merc he had used his improvised weapon on was still in the game. The man had lost his helmet in the crash, and Marc could make out his blood-streaked face as he came surging toward them.

Malte didn't wait around to play more bullfight games with the riders, and he put the APC back on course. They crashed through another hedge before speeding over a strip of fallow land and past a low, white-walled farmhouse, a blink of shocked faces at the windows as they zoomed by. The next field became a woodland and trees closed in around them, but still the chasers kept with the APC.

Marc glanced at his watch. If their timing was off, this would fall to pieces quickly. He knew that Aleph had to be scrambling other ground units to the area at this very second, and most likely they were calling in air-support backup as well. If they had help from the Polish military, Marc and Malte would most likely find themselves in cells next to Amarah's back in Strefa G before the day was out.

Up ahead, the woods abruptly terminated in a high, rusting fence but by now Malte had become adept at using the Bearcat's blunt, angular prow to make an entrance wherever he wanted it.

They crashed through and the APC churned up mud over a stretch of grass before hitting a broad expanse of tarmac. As wide as two country roads side by side, the runway extended from the fence line and into the middle distance. The landing threshold marks and designation numbers were bright against the tarmac, and to the west Marc could see the black shadow of an airport terminal building framed against the treeline.

Like the base at Stare Kiejkuty, the landing field that was now Olsztyn-Mazury Regional Airport had been built for the Second World War and decades later tainted by its use in unlawful renditions.

Now the airstrip was open for commercial, civilian business and those darker days had been airbrushed out of its history. *We're about to give them a reminder,* Marc thought grimly.

A twin-engine propliner was nosing off the runway onto the taxi apron as the Bearcat sped past, picking up speed toward the far end of the tarmac. With nothing but level ground between them and no obstacles in their path, the remaining pair of ZiD motorcycles opened their throttles and ate up the gap between them and the fleeing APC. Malte had the Bearcat going flat out, but the bikes were still gaining on them.

Marc looked at his watch once again, and wished that he was still hearing Lucy's voice through the concealed comm in his glasses; but she and Kara had to be long gone by now. Following the protocol they had planned for back in Monaco, the two women would have left the area the moment Marc had thrown away the script and called for ex-filtration.

He looked up into the sky, seeing only dull clouds. *Ari is super-punctual,* Kara had told him. *Like, he's genetically predisposed to being on time, every time.*

"Hope so—" Marc began.

"There!" Malte stabbed a finger at the treeline, and belatedly Marc saw that Ari Silber had chosen the low approach rather than the high one. A *very* low approach, in fact.

The blue-and-white fuselage of a T-tailed private jet hopped the top of the trees with barely a meter between its extended undercarriage and the leafy canopy. Less than ten meters off the deck, the aircraft moved like a fighter plane on a strafing run, screaming down toward them in a blur of metal. Malte saw it coming and stamped on the brakes, slowing the Bearcat into a juddering halt. The ZiD bikes shot by, coming around to race back toward them as the jet thundered over the heads of their riders. In that moment, the pilot flared the aircraft, briefly bringing up the nose to aim the jet's engine exhausts down at the tarmac. A searing plume of thrust blasted the bikes away like discarded toys and the APC shook as the tail end of the hot, fuel-stink gust washed over it.

Marc couldn't help but crack a grin as he watched the jet perform the kind of wing-over such aircraft weren't supposed to be capable of. "Actually, I was wrong before," he said aloud. "*Now* our ride is here."

Malte slammed the APC into gear and raced the rest of the way to the far end of the runway, while Marc and a stunned Amarah stood at the back doors to watch the jet come back around and execute a point-perfect touchdown.

The aircraft—a HondaJet HA-430 sporting a fake tail number and broadcasting no IFF transponder code—taxied easily up to the APC and turned, engines still idling. A hatch just behind the cockpit dropped open and Ari Silber stuck out his head. "We should be going," he said, and tapped the headset draped around his neck. "I'm listening to a lot of angry people." He grinned, his face flushed with the adrenaline of a combat landing.

Amarah took a step toward the plane and then halted, as if he had thought better of the action. "Where are you taking me?" he demanded.

"You're asking that *now*?" Marc resisted the urge to smack the guy and reminded himself of the part he was playing. "By all means, start walking if that's what you'd prefer. Then perhaps the Combine can break you out of another prison at some later date."

"I don't trust you," Amarah said coldly. "We are not allies!"

"Believe me, the feeling is more than mutual. But we both have something to trade, and we can't do it here." Marc turned toward the jet. "So make up your mind. Khadir worked with us and we were not allies either. Just people with common goals."

Mentioning Omar Khadir's name was enough to shock Amarah into motion and he gave a grim nod. "Very well." He pushed past Marc and climbed aboard the aircraft.

Alone on the tarmac for a moment, Marc allowed his mask to drop and blew out an exhausted breath. He looked away and saw Malte staring at him from the driving seat of APC, expressionless. The Finn beckoned, and then scrambled aboard the jet after Amarah.

Twenty minutes of heart-pounding, low-level, nap-of-the-earth flying later, they were racing over the Gulf of Gdansk beneath the radar-detection threshold, bearing west out of Polish airspace toward Scandinavia.

* * *

Bidar escorted the bomb-maker's grandson onto the sun deck, but to Ramaas's eyes the youth was acting as though he was there as his servant and not his jailer. Bidar ran a hand over his hairless scalp and glared at Kawal Sood's back in a way that showed he wanted to bury a knife in it.

Ramaas looked up from the maps and charts scattered over the low table in front of him, then back toward the mansion's swimming pool. "What do you want?"

Kawal gave a guarded smile. "I was wondering if I could get my phone back? I know security is a big deal and all, but I have my people I gotta stay in touch with . . ."

"No." Ramaas sighed inwardly. "It is important no one knows we are here. Guhaad made that clear to you."

"Well, yeah." Without being asked, Kawal took a seat across from the warlord. "But he doesn't get it, does he? How business is done?" Grinning, the youth leaned in, as if he was bringing Ramaas into a confidence. "It's not all about guns and shit."

Ramaas turned slowly to face Kawal. The younger man didn't seem to be aware of the true dynamics of the relationship between them, talking as if he was an equal, a comrade-in-arms. Kawal's manner was copied wholesale from the bluster and swagger of the American rappers whose music the youth so admired.

"Your grandfather's work is progressing well," said Ramaas, watching the immediate emotional shift on the younger man's face as he mentioned Jalsa. "But then he has been well motivated." Ramaas gestured toward the pool. The most recent addition to the bodies drifting in the tainted water was a gardener who Guhaad had selected from the staff a few hours earlier and shot dead. Apart from that daily crack of a single gunshot, the entire estate remained virtually silent.

Kawal didn't appear concerned by the bloated, floating corpses, his gaze turned inward to his own anger. "You gonna put that old bastard in there when you're done?" He hissed the question through gritted teeth. "I'd do it myself, if . . ." Kawal drifted into silence before he accidentally admitted to his own weakness.

"You have such hatred for your grandfather," said Ramaas. "And yet he is doing everything for you."

"*Fuck him!*" Kawal snarled furiously, the outburst coming from nowhere. "He's the one who drove my mother away when I was just a little kid!" Abruptly, it all poured out of him. "And my father? He's dead because of him!"

"Indeed?" Ramaas prompted. He already knew this story—Neven Kurjak had explained it to him on the ship from Croatia, held it up as the way through which they could get to Jalsa Sood—but he wanted to hear the youth say it.

"Fucking terrorist asshole," Kawal went on, his eyes shining. "My dad blew himself up working on one of that old bastard's bombs. And he never said he was sorry about it!" The youth looked away, rubbing at his face, and when he spoke again there was a note of deep sorrow in his words. "There was nothing left to bury."

"A tragedy," offered Ramaas. Neven explained how the death of Jalsa's son had been the catalyst for the bomb-maker's retirement from the game. He cashed out soon after, maintaining few contacts and very rarely taking on blind commissions from the Kurjaks—but the choice came too late for Kawal. Sood's grandson hated his grandfather with a directionless, white-hot fury.

Kawal stood up suddenly, abruptly enough for Bidar to drop his hand to his gun. The youth didn't notice. "I don't care no more. Once he's gone, all this belongs to me." He took in the mansion with a sweep of his hand. "Then I get the money and *I* am in charge!"

Ramaas eyed him. "There are more important things than money."

"Oh, right?" Kawal turned on him, gesturing aggressively. "Ain't you a pirate? What's that if not for the money, man?"

"I have a cause." Ice formed on the words and suddenly Ramaas was bored with the youth and his conceits. "What I am doing is for my God and my nation."

"Yeah, sure," Kawal sneered. "But you get paid along the way, no?" He shot a look toward Bidar. "Gotta have some paper."

Kawal's thoughtless accusation made a nerve in Ramaas's jaw twitch and he briefly considered ending the fool's misunderstanding about their association. Instead, he pushed the annoyance away and dismissed him with a wave of his hand. "Talk to Guhaad," he ordered. "You have contacts in the city? I want them to keep an eye open for people snooping around. Foreigners from Europol, understand?"

"Cops?" Kawal snorted. "They won't mess with—"

Ramaas cut him off with a nod to Bidar, who pulled Kawal away. "And don't speak to me again unless I demand it."

Kawal reacted, about to throw back a retort, but then he met the warlord's dead-eyed gaze and his bluster faded. Ramaas returned to his charts. The youth's voice had grated on him, and he needed the quiet to think and to prepare.

The cold breeze off the Öresund strait kept Marc from spending too long on the balcony of the apartment block in Ribersborg. It was overcast now, but he reckoned that if it cleared he would be able to see across the water to Denmark. In the other direction, the city of Malmö extended away northward. It was the first time he'd been in Sweden, and up until now the view from the balcony was the most he'd seen of the country, aside from the glimpses of the residential district below.

The escape flight from Poland seemed to take forever, each minute ticking past like an hour, but Silber had got them out of the country without issue, ghosting the HondaJet in to a Swedish provincial airstrip under a false flight plan. From there it had been a two-hour journey in the back of a windowless van, with Malte up front as usual and Marc forced to share the back of the vehicle with Jadeed Amarah. Fortunately, the terrorist didn't want to talk any more than Marc did, and the sullen silence carried them through to the safe house with barely a word uttered the whole way.

Ribersborg was quiet at this time of the day, and that suited the team just fine. Busy streets would have meant people to notice the arrival of the harried group of strangers who dismounted from the unmarked black van, and more chance of someone getting suspicious. The district reminded Marc a little of the South London housing estate where he had grown up, although the scrupulously clean streets and lack of any graffiti made it seem somehow artificial.

He wandered back into the apartment. Malte glanced up from the open-plan kitchen where he was busily cooking himself thick stew from a tin. Marc smelled gravy and his mouth watered. Another forgotten reaction resurfaced in him; he was always ravenous after air travel. Malte intuited this and nodded toward a cupboard stocked with more tins. Marc examined them in order, and bypassed the canned herring in favor of meatballs.

Marc wasn't sure if he was imagining it, but he could have sworn Malte's attitude toward him had thawed. *Maybe I earned a little respect from him, running the break-out on the fly,* he wondered. *Or not.*

Amarah entered from the bathroom, having helped himself to fresh clothes from the safe house's wardrobe. He had his orange prison jumpsuit rolled into a wad, and with a sneer he threw it onto the kitchen table. "Burn that," he said.

"Don't want to keep it as a souvenir?" Marc asked mildly.

The other man ignored him and pushed past, glaring at the available food. "Unless you want me to starve, get me something halal."

"We'll order in," Marc promised, shooting Malte a look. Because of his drastic change to the mission plan, that was one of the small details about this end of the operation that had not been prepared for, but right now the dietary requirements of a terrorist killer were not top of his priorities. "In the meantime, why don't you make good on your promise? We got you out. Now tell us where we can find the Baker."

Amarah took a seat and shrugged. "It's not that simple. I could tell you where he is, but that would do you no good. He changed his name, he changed his face. You wouldn't know where to start looking for him."

Marc sat down opposite the terrorist, once more drawing on his own experiences of being on the wrong side of a grilling. "My organization . . . The Combine has a lot of resources."

"So I have been informed," Amarah retorted. "But I tell you now— without knowing exactly, precisely where to find Sood—he will hear you coming and vanish before you can reach him." He made a vague, fluttering gesture with his hand. "And he will not surface again."

Over Amarah's shoulder, Marc saw Malte's expression harden and he knew the Finn was thinking about the application of a more *kinetic* method to make the terrorist forthcoming. But Amarah had spent months in a CIA-sponsored black site, weathering interrogation after interrogation and never leaking the information they wanted from him. The brute-force approach wasn't going to cut any ice.

"So where do we go from here?" Marc asked the question and watched Amarah mull it over. But before the other man could answer, there were four slow knocks at the front door across the room.

Malte put down his stew and opened the breadbin to reveal a pair of silenced Glock 17 semi-automatics hidden inside. He tossed one to Marc, who caught it easily; by reflex he checked to find that the slide lock was off and a round was in the chamber. Amarah retreated toward the door to the balcony, eyes searching the room for a weapon of his own.

A key turned in the lock and the front door opened carefully to reveal a weary-looking Kara Wei. She had a large grocery bag propped up in the crook of her arm and the door keys in the other hand. "Hey," she offered. "Sorry we didn't call first. My phone battery died."

Malte's combat-ready pose fell and Marc let the muzzle of his own gun drop away, relieved that things hadn't gone in a more dangerous direction.

There was someone else with Kara, a woman in a dark gray sweatshirt and a black hijab scarf that covered all of her head except the oval of her face. She had heavy spectacles like the ones Marc had worn during the Strefa G infiltration, and as she entered, the woman gave a brief, wan smile. Her whole body language was meek and self-effacing.

"You guys remember Lula," said Kara. "Right?"

Marc blinked as "Lula" met his gaze and he looked right into the eyes of Lucy Keyes. She looked like a totally different person, her face fatter and paler, her manner completely altered—but there was no mistaking the brief glint of cold amusement in her gaze.

"Yeah," he managed. "You . . . got here okay then? No problems?"

"Some," Kara said pointedly, handing the bag to Lucy, who dutifully carried it to the kitchen and started to unpack the food. "A few unexpected changes to the program. But we had to adapt."

"Right," Marc repeated. He glanced at Amarah, whose gaze had caught the packages of halal meats and bread that Lucy was removing from the bag. Marc's hand tensed around the grip of the Glock, waiting for the moment it would all go horribly wrong.

But Amarah's gaze raked over "Lula" and slid right off again. He went to the food and helped himself, giving no indication of realizing that the woman in the hijab was the same one who had kicked his arse up and down Independence Avenue a year earlier. *Then again, it is a pretty good disguise,* thought Marc.

They cooked food and ate, and the day passed into evening. While "Lula" took care of the housekeeping and Malte set up a watch station near the windows, Kara brought out a laptop and suite of recording gear as Marc sat down with Amarah to finish the conversation they had started earlier.

"You were about to tell me where to find Jalsa Sood," he said.

"What guarantee do I have you won't kill me the moment I tell you?"

Marc smirked, channeling the attitudes of every snide dickhead he had ever met. "Do you really think you're that important, Jadeed?" He deliberately used the terrorist's first name to belittle him. "Your only value right now is what I want from you. The Combine showed we were willing to work to your ends . . ." He nodded at the walls. "We wouldn't be here if that wasn't true. You're free of the Americans, free to do whatever the hell you want. So make good on the deal. *Where is Sood?*"

"Dubai," said Amarah, after a moment. "Living a high life, so I have been told. I suppose when one gets old and weak, soft beds and easy days have their appeal."

"How do we get to him?"

Amarah smiled. "Oh, for that, you're going to need me. And it will cost extra."

"Figures," muttered Kara, without looking up from her screen.

"I will need to make the introduction. Personally, face to face. Jalsa won't refuse to meet with the man who killed him, after all."

"I imagine not," Marc allowed, thinking it through. "Okay. We can arrange transport into the Emirates . . ."

Amarah raised his hand. "No. If this is going to be done, it will be done under my direction. You'll follow my lead . . . So I am certain I will not be double-crossed at the end of things."

Kara looked up at him. "And why exactly should we trust you?"

He gave her an irritated look. "Because I am Al Sayf, and we have paths around Dubai you are unaware of. A group of Westerners, blundering in like clumsy animals? You'll be spotted immediately. I have a way in, under the radar." He sat back, the annoyance giving way to arrogance. "Your oligarchs and rich old men can pay the way. For once, the Combine can work for me."

Marc pushed a pen and writing pad across the table toward him. "Tell us what you need."

There was a nondescript company staff car waiting for Saito when he disembarked on the tarmac at Paris Charles de Gaulle, and he peeled off from the line of passengers walking to the terminal building without breaking his stride. He climbed inside and the driver paused to hand him a sealed bag before they drove away, threading around the edge of the apron toward the less trafficked end of the airport.

Inside the packet, Saito found the usual assortment of clean cover documents, which he exchanged with the ones he had used to depart Brazil without alerting local security. A Turing secure smartphone was in there as well, and he frowned at it, wondering if his own personal communications had been compromised.

The phone activated of its own accord and asked him for a scan of his thumbprint and a facial-recognition image. When the device was satisfied, it connected him through a web of dark net servers to a familiar, rough-edged voice. *"Report. What happened in Rio?"*

It was typical of the Russian to open a conversation without preamble. Saito believed that it was because he felt his wealth put him above petty concerns like civility. The operative never expressed such opinions, however. He knew his place. Saito was the servant, and the Combine was his master.

"I have the information we require," Saito began. "We were able to locate Fedorin without issue. His traveling companion made an error of judgment, and my team was in place to exploit it to the fullest."

"What is Fedorin's status?"

"He won't cause any further problems." Saito glanced out of the window of the staff car as it descended into an underpass. Daylight briefly vanished as they sped along below the active runways, returning as they emerged on the far side across from the hangars designated for private corporate aircraft. "I used my discretion in the matter."

"Did you?" The tone of the reply told Saito that his explanation wasn't as satisfactory as the Russian would have liked, but then he didn't answer directly to this one man. Saito worked for the *ideal* of the Combine, not for the individuals within it. *"What about the device?"*

"It was not present," he explained. "But we assumed that would be so. Fedorin traded the device for his escape before he fled Europe. I am on my way to Croatia now. The general provided information on the identities of the men he dealt with."

"I want this situation contained," said the Russian, a rare flash of annoyance in his words. *"Quickly."*

"I am working as expediently as possible," Saito replied. "Additional information would be of great use in this next phase."

"I'll arrange it," said the other man. *"Who are these men?"*

The car rolled to a halt in the shadow of one of the hangars. A maintenance crew were already opening the doors, preparing the Gulfstream jet inside for immediate departure. "I need everything we have on a group of Serbian gunrunners known as the Kurjaks."

"Done," said the Russian. *"And to be clear, Saito. Whatever your 'discretion' may direct you to do, be sure to leave nothing behind."*

"As you wish." Saito bobbed his head in an instinctive bowing motion as the Turing phone's screen darkened. As he pocketed the new cover documents, his hand brushed over the secret, shielded pocket in his jacket where he kept the misericorde. The Russian's words served to remind him that he too was a tool of sorts. Like the weapon, something with only function, without conscience.

After he had given the Combine agent what was needed to prepare for the journey to the Emirates, Amarah told them that he needed his privacy for prayers and he retreated to the rooms they had given him. But when the door was closed and he was alone, he did not go through the motions of the *Salat Al-maghrib*. He sat and stared into space. Amarah had not followed the prayers for a long time, and with each day he did not, the distance between him and the beliefs he had grown up with grew wider.

Glimpsing the woman in the hijab among the Combine group had unsettled him. Once upon a time, seeing such a thing would have sent him into a rage, to think that she might be tainting herself to work with such infidels. But now it only served to remind him of the choices he had made. He avoided her, partly through force of habit, but more from an unwillingness to accept what she represented.

Captivity had given him time to ruminate on his past choices and the truths that he had devoted his life to. His original beliefs had been the spur that brought him into the orbit of Al Sayf in his younger years, enticed by the firebrand oratory of jihadi imams and stories of brothers who were fighting for honor and eternal glory. But what had really made Jadeed Amarah take that final step was his *hate*. Looking back now, he saw that the fuel for his revolutionary fire came from his hard life and a loathing for the Westerners. New clarity showed him that as much as he had cloaked it in rhetoric, the reality was that Amarah wanted to hurt those who had more than he did—the ones he saw as undeserving of their wealth, privilege and power.

During the time the CIA had interrogated him, the Americans had brought every weapon in their arsenal to bear on breaking Amarah. None had been more troubling to him than the interrogator who was also a Muslim scholar, a studious and pious man who explained to Jadeed over and over again how the acts he had committed were against Islam, against the words of the Prophet.

He lost something in those days, trapped in the ghost prison with the endless sermons from this man. A vital piece of himself withered and died—but it was not the one the Americans had hoped for. They wanted him to feel guilty, but that only showed how little they understood him.

Amarah's isolation did not stifle his hate. It *fed* it.

As he began to doubt, to rage silently in his cell at anything and everything, he asked himself questions that before he could never have voiced.

Did Al Sayf abandon him? Did Omar Khadir, the commander to whom he had dedicated his life, leave him to the mercy of their enemies? Was anything he believed in truly worth the effort?

That day, he had not prayed. And with each day that followed, it became easier not to. Amarah lived deep inside his own mind, and after the Americans had finally left him alone, that disconnection had grown.

What am I now? he wondered. *What do I have?* The answer was clear to him. It had become his new devotion, his creed redefined. *I have my hate.*

He nodded to himself, all thought of Gods and glory fading away. He would use these fools to take him from this place and back toward the lands of his youth. There were men there who could make use of skills like his, a soldier who had such raw enmity to power him forward. And once he was there, he would forge his own path—but not before murdering these Combine fools the instant the opportunity presented itself.

Marc stared out of the apartment window, his mind drifting. In the corner of his eye a dark shape moved and he turned as Lucy settled quietly into the seat across the table from him, cupping a mug of tea in her hands.

He watched her face change from the plain, open neutrality of the "Lula" identity and back to the woman he knew. Lucy took off the thick-rimmed glasses and pulled wads of padding from inside her cheeks. Her blank-eyed, docile look went away and she was suddenly stony and pugnacious.

She threw a glance in the direction of the door that Amarah had gone through, and then turned all her attention on Marc. "What the hell were you thinking?" Lucy spoke quietly, but with no less force than usual.

"I didn't have a lot of choice at the time," he told her, keeping his voice to the same level. "But it worked, didn't it?"

Lucy's jaw hardened. "I know we play things pretty fast and loose at Rubicon, but perhaps you didn't pick up on the fact that *I am in charge of this operation*." She leaned closer. "You countermanded me. I told you to scrub the mission and you went off comms and just made up some shit on the fly!"

"I did," he admitted. "It's par for the course for me. I'm getting pretty good at it."

"*Lucky,*" she corrected. "That's what you were. But that has a tendency to run out right when you need it, Dane." Lucy shook her head. "You should have backed off. We could have figured out another way to go at Amarah, or looked for a different lead on the Baker."

"How long would that have taken?" Marc shook his head. "You know as well as I do that it would eat up time we don't have!"

"It's a moot point now, anyhow. But I think you need reminding of something. This shit we do?" Lucy gestured around. "It's a team sport. So don't go cowboy on me again without making sure we're all on board first."

Marc heard the echo of Schrader's admonishments in her words and his jaw set. He didn't want to admit that she was right.

Lucy scowled. "You've committed us to this. We're working without a net, and now Aleph and the Central Intelligence Agency are both pouring on the gas to track us down. Good job. I guess you must have missed being a wanted fugitive, because you sure as hell are one now. And so are the rest of us."

"I made the right call," he insisted. "We've got Amarah in our pocket. Once he leads us to Sood, we can send that nasty little bastard right back where we found him."

Lucy let out a sigh. "You understand how dangerous this is? We can't afford a single mistake. If Amarah suspects we're not actually working for the Combine, there's no telling what he'll do."

"We can make this work," Marc assured her. "And speaking of which, aren't you taking a huge risk even being in the same building as him? What if he recognizes you?"

"Please." She gave a cold smile. "He looked right at me and didn't know it." Lucy indicated the hijab and her plain clothes. "Sexist throwback assholes like Jadeed Amarah only really look at women when they want something from them. In this outfit, I'm practically invisible to him."

"Still," Marc continued. "You need to be careful."

"Oh, you're just now getting that?" Lucy jabbed a finger at him. "Should have considered it when you went rogue on us back in Poland!"

He bristled at her tone. "The way I hear it, you're no better. Isn't that exactly what you did last year, back in London?" Lucy had ignored orders during a surveillance operation, and it had been a sore point between her and Solomon.

"You'd be dead if I hadn't," she said flatly. "Starting to regret it now."

"Jeez, you two . . ." Kara approached them, toting her laptop. "Get a room or something." She sat down between them and put the computer on the table. "While Amarah's out of earshot, I figured you both ought to see this. New intel feed from Delancort." The laptop screen showed a map of the Adriatic, with a set of latitude and longitude coordinates highlighted in crimson. "An Italian Guardia Costiera boat posted a report about the *Salina,* a Greek tramp freighter, one of the ships we were tracking out of Split. It missed a couple of scheduled call-ins and a day later it was spotted way off course, adrift and not answering radio hails."

She flicked to a series of blurry photos of the vessel. Marc saw that the ship's decks were awash and even from a distance there were signs of damage on board.

"Broken windows," noted Lucy. "Maybe bullet holes there?"

"Someone tried to scuttle the ship, but they didn't do it right." Marc thought aloud. "Five'll get you ten that the crew either abandoned ship—"

"Or they were iced." Lucy tapped the screen. "Bullet holes," she repeated.

"The coastguard will board the *Salina* when the weather calms down," added Kara. "Rubicon can probably get to it once it's been towed into dock."

"If that was the ship Ramaas used, he's long gone and so is the device," said Marc. He nodded toward the other door. "We've gotta work the lead we have."

"And quick," said Kara. "Delancort says encrypted traffic between Aleph's HQ in Berlin and their European assets has jumped. We're gonna need to move tonight before they close the net on us."

Lucy gave a weary nod. "Copy that. So, we'll follow Amarah's lead into the UAE, see where it takes us."

"He's going to try to stab us in the back," said Marc, after a moment.

"Of course he is," she replied.

— FOURTEEN —

Stepping outside, one moment Marc was being slow-chilled by the relentless air conditioning inside the airport terminal building, and the next he was engulfed in an arid inferno that hit him like a wall.

He stumbled and blinked into the midday glare, finding his sunglasses and rearranging the thin shemagh scarf around his throat to keep the sun off his neck. The heat was murderous and he had to resist the automatic reaction to retreat into the shade.

Amarah snorted and pushed past him, throwing the Englishman a withering look. "Follow me," he demanded, setting off across the roadway toward a parking area far from the lines of idling limousines and polished taxis that served the well-heeled visitors.

Marc trailed after him, careful to stay back a little, wary of everything around him and trying to take it all in at once. He glanced over his shoulder as Lucy fell in a few steps behind. She had changed into darker, shapeless robes beneath a black headscarf, her only break with the diffident "Lula" cover identity being those expensive sunglasses he'd seen her wearing back in Monaco.

"Welcome to Dubai," she said, quietly enough so her voice didn't carry. "Hot enough for ya?"

"Yeah," he offered, pulling a bottle of water from his bag and taking a swig. "In more ways than one."

Like it or not, Amarah was calling the shots now that they were in the Emirates, and even though Rubicon had an office in downtown Dubai, reaching out to them would be an act of last resort. Marc and Lucy were effectively on their own from here. Kara and Malte had split off from the group after they left Sweden, deliberately leaving a false trail for Aleph's hunters to follow, and that meant Marc and Lucy were now operating as a cell with Amarah as their direct responsibility. Putting their trust in a known terrorist wasn't an easy call, and Marc's thoughts kept wandering back to the additional $3-million fee Amarah had demanded for his promised "introduction" to Jalsa Sood. Solomon would never let him keep it, of course, but the issue right now was making sure that their erstwhile guide didn't figure out they were going to renege on the deal.

"That's gotta be his buddy," said Lucy.

Up ahead, Marc saw Amarah embrace a pudgy Arab with all the gusto of long-lost brothers. Straight away they were laughing and joking, and it was strange to see the man crack a happy smile. *Like a normal, ordinary guy,* he thought. For a moment, he could almost forget that Amarah had willfully suborned and killed innocents for his cadre's bloody and barbaric ends.

The Arab stood in front of a line of sun-bleached white busses and a crowd of wary-looking men of South Asian extraction, all of them migrant workers who had arrived in Dubai on the guarantee of lucrative employment contracts. He paused now and then to briskly direct a gang of thuggish-looking underlings up and down the lines of the new arrivals. The Arab's men barked at them with all the delicacy of drill sergeants, kicking at their bags of meager possessions or shoving them around. As Marc approached, he saw one of the thugs wander up to the Arab, holding a wad of green Bangladeshi and Pakistani passports forcibly confiscated from the workers. One of the men tried to step out of line, hands out as he reached to take back his papers, but he was met with a hard slap that sent him reeling.

Marc had heard the stories about luckless workers being promised fat paydays in the endless cycle of Dubai's construction industry, but the reality was more like what he was seeing now—a racket that was barely more than people trafficking and indentured servitude, in a nation where progress came from the steady stream of oil money and the blind eye that was turned to employee abuses.

The Arab thumbed through the passports and handed them off to someone else. He gave Marc a severe look, his smile ebbing briefly, but then it returned in a leer as he caught sight of Lucy. She looked away, her expression turning blank again. "What have you brought with you, Jadeed?" he asked.

"Tourists, Mahmud. Just some tourists." Amarah gestured toward Lucy. "Don't touch. This is my cousin's wife."

"And him?" The Arab waved at Marc, then closed the fingers of his right hand into a point and tapped them with the index finger of his other hand. "He looks like he's going to die of sunstroke!"

Despite the sweat pouring off him, Marc stepped closer to Mahmud and showed him a nasty smile, nodding down at the other man's hands. "I know what that means, mate." The Arab's gesture was a grave insult; *five fingers* meant *five fathers,* as in dubious parentage, and he clearly assumed it would slip past a Westerner's notice. Marc rolled the water bottle in his hand, squaring up to him. "Where I come from, a man who says that kinda thing gets glassed, yeah?" It would have been a simple matter to play dumb, but that could have caused problems down the road. *Better to go through the macho alpha-dog bullshit now rather than later,* he thought.

Mahmud blinked, seeing the flash of real anger in Marc's eyes, and then in the next second he blew out a raucous laugh, defusing the tension. "Ah, he's a sharp one! Forgive me, I meant nothing by it!" He waved toward the nearest bus. "Come, come! We should go!"

The vehicle was already loaded with sullen, silent men who didn't meet the gaze of any of them as they boarded. Marc scanned their faces, seeing only fatigue and fear there. Lucy took a seat on her own and kept her head down, while Marc dropped into a place across from the driver. As the bus pulled away, he saw the rest of the migrants trooping aboard the other vehicles and glanced at Mahmud. "So you handle these people, do you?"

The Arab grinned. "This city is opportunity, it says so on every billboard. New constructions each month, sprouting up like weeds! Someone has to build them . . ." He glanced back at the workers. "And here they are!"

Marc gave a sage nod, and looked at Amarah. "Your pal, he must be an important bloke. Generous too, I bet."

Mahmud sensed the hidden accusation in his words. "I pay my men well enough. They have a place to live and food to eat, you'll see." He leaned over. "You English and all the rest, you should be glad Dubai is here! This is a bulwark of freedom and democracy! Without it we'd be drowning in Islamists . . ." He choked off and showed Amarah a sheepish grin. "Well, you know. The bad kind."

"What do you care?" Amarah glared at Marc. "The Combine has its hands in half the corporations that own this city. So what if it is built on the back of slave labor?"

"They're not slaves," Mahmud interrupted hotly. "They get their wages . . . Eventually, after they've worked out their contracts, in a couple of years."

Marc looked back at the desperate faces of the migrants. None of them gave any sign of understanding the conversation going on about them, all of them looking mournfully at the glittering metropolis that flashed past the windows of the bus. "Is that when you give them back their passports? If they live that long?"

"We have to keep them in line somehow," Mahmud explained. "After all, these Indians . . . They're undisciplined."

The convoy of busses drove out across the city and through a series of massive building sites. The bare concrete spines of unfinished luxury hotels, condominium towers and office complexes grew up out of giant plastic-clad marquees, in gray pillars of sheetrock and rust-red fingers of naked steel rebar. Each was swarmed by figures in hard hats and dusty blue overalls, working to forge the next tier of the desert's miracle beneath the high sun's killer heat.

Finally, beyond the unfinished construction zones, the cityscape closed in to become tight streets, bordered by identical blockhouses where the workers were billeted after nightfall. The bus juddered to a halt and they disembarked.

The dirty, ramshackle worker-town was a million miles away from the airstream dreamland of the city proper. Marc had seen the same kind of class-clash disparity in places like Los Angeles or even back in his native London, but here the difference was so stark it was hard to believe these extremes of rich and poor could coexist in such close proximity.

He cast around, keeping one eye on Lucy and the other on Amarah. The buildings resembled military barracks or prison blocks, over-packed with humans and the mingled odors of cooked meat, sewage and diesel fuel. From the upper balconies of the nearest quarters, workers moving out for later shifts dithered to look over the new intake and several of them turned their attentions toward Lucy. As the only woman for miles around, even in her dark robes she suddenly had a lot of eyes on her.

Mahmud walked away to pass out orders to his men, and Marc orbited closer to Amarah, still keeping watch on Lucy in his peripheral vision. He knew full well she could take care of herself if circumstances demanded it, but to do so would be out of character for "Lula" and risked blowing her cover.

"Hey." He turned to Amarah. "You told me Jalsa Sood is with the rich set. This doesn't look like the better part of town. Why are we here?"

"This is how we get to Sood, unseen. The Baker and his family have many connections in the city. He will be told if strangers are seeking him out." Amarah pointed at a line of workers boarding the bus they had just left. "Coming through here makes us like them. *Invisible*." He sneered. "Mahmud and his friends shipped these fools around in cattle trucks, until the Emiratis started to complain that they didn't like looking at them. Now the white buses go everywhere and no one pays any attention to them."

"I get it. Good cover." Marc mulled that over. With no security to speak of and management who were open to financial compensation to look the other way, staying with the city's workforce was the ideal method for anyone who wanted to move around Dubai without being noticed. "But what if someone runs their mouth to the authorities?"

"They won't." Amarah glared at the workers with harsh antipathy. "These men are gutless and broken. They take beatings like whipped dogs." He nodded in the direction of the city proper. "If they wanted a better life, they could take it by force. There's an army of them here, but they're too weak-willed to shed blood." He shook his head. "They get what they deserve. They came here because they wanted wealth and now the wealthy have made them slaves."

Marc's eyes narrowed. "You're a real man of the people, aren't you?"

Amarah shrugged. "The weak die first. Why waste time on them?"

Marc was going to say something more, but then he became aware of Lucy approaching. She held out her smartphone to him like an offering. He took it and walked away with her trailing dutifully at his heels.

"Don't antagonize him," Lucy said softly. "He needs to believe he's in charge."

"Right now, he is," Marc replied, glancing at the phone as the device's encryption software opened a line. Making sure they couldn't be overheard, he put the phone on speaker and held it up. "We're here," he said.

"Indeed you are." Henri Delancort's voice issued out of the device. *"Tracking is active. I know we said that this operation would proceed under a reduced communications protocol, but information has come to light that Mr. Solomon felt had to be passed on immediately. There is good news and bad news."*

"I really hate it when you say things like that," Lucy muttered. "Cheer me up. Good news first."

"Aleph are looking in the wrong places for you. Signal traffic analysis indicates that the CIA have allowed them to take the weight of the hunt for Amarah, and thanks to Malte and Kara, that search is currently centered on Southern Spain."

"Bad news?" Marc didn't want to ask the question.

"The body of a middle-aged white male was pulled out of the Dubai Marina yesterday evening. Cause of death was blunt-force trauma consistent with a fall from a great height. It's not an uncommon end for people in that city, apparently. Too much wine and too many penthouses with balconies. But identification of this particular gentleman raised a red flag with Europol."

"Don't tell me." Marc felt his gut twist, and he said the name as the thought crystalized in his mind. "Neven Kurjak."

"It would appear so. Which means that he had reached the end of his usefulness in this matter."

"Shit." Lucy shook her head. "Neven was the weak link, he was our exploit. Without him in play, our options are narrowing."

She was right, but Marc was already thinking beyond that. "If Kurjak was here . . . and he was ditched . . . that means there's a good chance Ramaas or his posse are in Dubai as well."

"*How do you want to proceed?*" Delancort asked, after a moment.

Marc and Lucy exchanged glances. "Stick to the plan," she said. "We use Amarah to take us to Sood, and try to intercept him before Ramaas does."

"*And if that isn't feasible?*"

When Marc replied, his answer earned him a grim nod from Lucy. "Then the guns are going to come out."

Off the dingy entrance hall of the nearest blockhouse was a narrow room that stank of sweat and spoiled food, with every available meter of space filled by decade-old personal computers, dirty monitors and grubby keyboards. Half the stools in the makeshift Internet café were already being used, but Mahmud's arrival took care of that in short order. He didn't even need to give an order; the workers saw him and stopped what they were doing, filing out onto the street where they struck up wary conversations and smoked.

"What is to be done with the foreigners?" Mahmud licked his lips. "I can find a use for the woman . . ."

Amarah shook his head. "Do nothing for now. I need them alive to pay me." He eyed the computers. "What is all this? You actually expect me to believe that any of these machines are *secure*?" He glared at the nearest monitor, seeing a screen cluttered with random icons and pop-up windows generated by whatever accreted malware lurked inside.

"This is the best I have to offer," Mahmud replied, passing him a small zip-case. Inside was a voice-over-Internet phone handset, a Caracal semi-automatic pistol and a spare ammunition magazine. "Forgive me, brother, but—"

"It will have to do." Amarah waved him away, concealing the gun in the folds of his robe. "Wait outside."

Mahmud blinked, unhappy at being ordered around inside his own kingdom, but then he relented, pulling closed a thin folding door across the entrance to the room.

Amarah chose another computer and plugged the handset into a dirt-clogged USB socket. The two devices synchronized and a link across the World Wide Web immediately allowed him to make a point-to-point call without the need to route it through the UAE's telephone network.

He typed in an alphanumeric code based on chapters from the Medinan surahs of the Qur'an, a mnemonic he had committed to memory when he was first recruited into Omar Khadir's action cell. To anyone else, the numbers would have been meaningless, but to an operative of Al Sayf, they were a beacon, a way to reach out to the brethren.

A data window on the screen of the PC told him the connection had been made, and Amarah heard a click from the headset. He raised it to his mouth, but now the moment was upon him, he wasn't sure what to say. "I am here," he began. "Jadeed Amarah, by His grace and favor, peace be upon Him. I have escaped from the Americans and I am ready to return to the war . . . I . . ." He trailed off, losing momentum. *Was someone listening at this moment? Or was he shouting into the wind, his words being recorded by some distant machine for recovery by a man who would never come?* "I did not abandon my oath," he said, suddenly angry. "Did you abandon me?"

The line clicked again and an indicator on the data window blinked from green to red. He had been disconnected.

Amarah tossed the handset across the room with an angry snarl, the sudden rush of fury coming from out of nowhere. He wasn't sure what he had expected to hear on the other end of the line—Khadir's sonorous voice, his commander welcoming him back into the fold?—but it wasn't *silence*. He felt alone and hollow inside as he struggled to process the churn of his emotions. Slowly, his directionless anger began to solidify into something else. *Determination*.

If he was on his own . . . then so be it. He would not seek out new orders and wait to be told what to do. Jadeed Amarah would take things into his own hands.

The folding door opened with a rattle and he looked up to see the Britisher standing there, his face drawn and suspicious. "What are you up to in here? You'd better not be trying to give us the slip. Not if you want your bloody payday."

Amarah got up, straightening as he did so. "No. We have an agreement. I will honor it, as long as your masters do the same."

The other man folded his arms. "All right, then. So now it's your game. How do we get to Sood? And just so you know, there's a clock on this now."

He smiled thinly, his mind already racing with the possibilities of how he could turn this situation to his greater advantage. "It is simple. We will walk in through his front door."

"I told you what would happen if you wasted time," Ramaas's words boomed through the echoing space of the workshop.

The bomb-maker flinched at the sound of his voice and dropped the soldering iron he was holding. Sood turned to him, trying to recover his composure as Ramaas approached, with Guhaad at his side. "I am doing no such thing!" insisted the old man, and his face fell in sorrow. "What more do you want from me? I am not as young as I was, and your thugs barely let me sleep . . ."

He ignored Sood's complaints and his gaze raked over the results of the old man's work. "We've been here too long," said Ramaas, almost to himself. "We need to finish and move on." He glanced at Guhaad, his face darkening. "Too long away from home. People will start to question my absence."

Guhaad read the words like a command, and he pulled his gun, aiming it at Sood, letting the barrel drop toward the old man's knees. "Does he need his legs to do his labor?"

Sood's lined face stiffened in defiance. "I am not afraid of you!"

Ramaas moved to the open case on the workbench, running his hand over its metallic innards. "This is fine work. Even I cannot tell the difference." He glanced over at the vials of radioactive chemicals that had been brought to them by the idiot Kawal's so-called "contacts." Sood's grandson had proven useful for that, if little else. With the fluid inserted into the dummy weapons, anyone running a check of the inner components with a radiation detector would get an alarmingly plausible reading back from the case. *Enough to cloud the waters,* Ramaas told himself.

He was considering ending the agreement with the bomb-maker when the grandson dashed into the garage. "Yo, we got a problem."

Kawal panted and waved his hand, the thick gold bracelets around his wrist jangling together.

"Explain yourself," demanded Ramaas.

"Someone is here. For *him*." Kawal pointed at his grandfather. "Wants to see the old prick. Says he won't leave until he does." He described a gaunt Saudi who had come to the mansion's gate out of nowhere and demanded entry. He had two companions with him, an African woman in a hijab and a white man, probably a European.

"And you knew nothing of this?" Ramaas eyed the younger man. "You told me you knew this city, and all the comings and goings! I do not like surprises."

"I will dispose of them," offered Guhaad. He was getting bored with tormenting the hostage staff and becoming increasingly quick to offer violent solutions to every circumstance.

Ramaas was considering letting his war dog do just that when Kawal took a breath and started talking again, staring at his grandfather. "This guy, you know what he says to me? He says, *Tell the Baker the man who murdered him is here.* What the fuck does that mean, huh?"

All the color drained from Jalsa Sood's face. "No," he whispered. "Oh, no."

Ramaas knew what it meant. Aboard the cargo ship that had brought them to Dubai, he made Neven Kurjak tell him absolutely everything that was known about Sood, up to and including the stories of the bomb-maker's faked death. But until now, the details of exactly how that had happened were a mystery. "This is the assassin?" He loomed over the old man, daring him to lie about it. "Who is he? Why is he here? Did you summon him?"

"No, I swear it!" Sood shook his head frantically. "He . . . His name is Jadeed Amarah. The last I heard of him, he was arrested by the Americans . . . He was part of a plot to attack their president in Washington!"

Ramaas rubbed a hand over his chin. He had seen the news reports. "The Americans said it was Al Sayf." The warlord recalled the Al Shabaab militants in Puntland cursing the names of their distant brethren for failing in a glorious mission. Ramaas thought otherwise; from what he knew of Al Sayf, they were to be respected for their daring in striking at the heart of such a powerful enemy. "This man Amarah is one of them?"

Sood gave a nod. "We . . . had an agreement."

"Why is he here?" Ramaas repeated. "I will see if you lie to me."

"I told you, I don't know!" Sood retorted. "I worked with Amarah's cell in the past. I helped them with some designs a few years ago, and that's all! If he is here, he wants something from me."

Ramaas glanced at Guhaad, weighing the options. He had no desire to make a new enemy, not now when he had so many other things to take care of. Killing this unexpected visitor would be the expedient option, but it could have consequences that would jeopardize the warlord's plans. Drawing the attention of Al Sayf had too much potential to interfere with God's wishes. At length, he gave Guhaad a shake of the head and looked back at Sood. "You will go and talk to this man. You will make him go away."

"I will," Sood promised, and he almost bowed as he rushed off.

"Make yourself useful." Ramaas turned on Kawal. "Watch him."

"Hey, man, I got this." Kawal's face split in an eager grin, and he strode after the old man.

Guhaad made a negative noise, deep in his throat. "The old fool is lying. He must have sent a message out, called for help from this man Amarah!"

"Perhaps," allowed Ramaas, and with that he made a choice. He slammed shut the lid on the open suitcase. "It is time to leave. Tell Bidar and Macanay to find vehicles. We have what we need to move forward with our mission."

A feral smile split Guhaad's face, like a knife emerging from a sheath. "We can't leave any witnesses."

Ramaas nodded again. "Do it quietly."

The receiving room in the mansion was bigger than the apartment that Lucy Keyes had grown up in, and it was furnished as though there had been a closing-down sale on shiny pink marble and gold paint.

Swamped in the shapeless black folds of an ankle-length abaya dress, Lucy walked with small steps the requisite number of paces behind the men as they entered. Amarah found himself a couch to sit on, and Marc hesitated, glancing back at her even though she didn't meet his eyes. She kept her hands folded and her head bowed, and he got the message. Lucy couldn't break character with her "Lula" cover, not now they were right on top of the target. The Brit walked around the room, looking up at the high ceiling.

Lucy scoped out the space from the corner of her eye, watchful without being obvious about it. The hexagonal room had shadowed depths that were too dark to peer into, with arched openings that led away down shady corridors and windows barred by ornate wooden shutters. The way they had come in led to a covered path and back to the main gate, another door directly opposite to the mansion's interior. A couple of security cameras inside plastic domes over the lintels covered all angles of the chamber. She could smell orange blossom, and while the room was cooler than the blazing heat outside, there was still a heaviness in the air. The breath of a dry desert wind made the wooden blinds mutter and creak. Lucy tasted it on her lips, like dust.

Amarah was watching her. He'd been doing that more and more since they arrived in Dubai. Every time his attention wasn't on something else, his gaze drifted back in her direction. She adjusted the thick glasses balanced on her nose and deliberately let her face go slack, breathing through her open mouth and maintaining a vacant look.

If Amarah made the connection between "Lula" and the woman who had helped the US Secret Service bring him down, this operation would be blown. Lucy ran through the options in her mind. All of them ended in her putting Jadeed Amarah down for good. If it came to it, that wasn't something she would have a problem with.

Two men entered from the other door, both of them of Indian extraction. She recognized Jalsa Sood immediately from the photos of him as a younger man. Despite the weathering of his face and his silver-white hair, it was undoubtedly him. He seemed off balance to her, but then that was to be expected. Being confronted out of the blue by the man who had helped convince the world you were dead would do that for anyone.

Sood's companion had a variation on the face Lucy had seen in the surveillance photos of the bomb-maker from the 1980s, and that told her that he was family. But beyond that he was nothing like the old man. Jalsa was dressed conservatively in an expensive but understated thawb, while the younger man was wearing an over-styled designer tracksuit and enough gold to sink him.

Sood greeted Amarah in halting Arabic, then switched to English as he took in Marc and Lucy. "This is . . . very unexpected," he began, forcing a smile as he bowed to them. "Welcome to my home. I am Vishal Daan, you have already met my grandson, Kawal."

"Hey." Kawal barely glanced at Marc, but he gave Lucy the kind of lingering appraisal that made her immediately want to take a shower. She simulated a demure smile that only encouraged him.

For his part, Amarah was looking over the old man in a similarly predatory manner, but for different reasons. After their greeting, he dropped back onto the couch and gave a languid nod. "Let's dispense with the lies. They both know who you really are, Jalsa."

"Ah." His face fell, but then Sood recovered and he sat down on another couch. He picked up a brass bell from a low table and shook it, sending a trilling ring echoing away from them. "The maid will bring us tea," he explained.

"Hospitable as always," Amarah replied, then he looked up at Marc. "Here he is. *The Baker.* Alive and well, as promised."

The younger man turned from eyeing Lucy to glare at Amarah. "Yo, did you bring some shit to our door, man?" He tensed, squaring off for violence. She had seen the exact same body language a thousand times on the New York street corners where she had spent her teens. "What the fuck do you want here, huh?"

"Kawal!" Sood shouted him into silence, his cheeks darkening. "Forgive my grandson, he is ungracious . . ." The old man took a breath and his next words hardened. "But he makes a fair point. Who are these people?"

"You're famous, Jalsa. They wanted to meet you."

Sood stiffened, and his eyes darted around the room. He was afraid, that was clear, but Lucy got the sense that there was something else to it. She glanced at Marc and a silent communication passed between them. *He's hiding something.*

"Sir, the organization I work for would like to employ you as a consultant." Marc opened with the approach that Rubicon's behavioral-modeling team had said would be the best option. "This would be on a purely technical level, of course. You would be well compensated."

"No. *No.*" Sood gave a weak shake of the head and looked away, briefly showing his age in a flash of vulnerability. "Where is that maid? I need something to drink . . ."

He seemed frail and tired. For a moment, Lucy could almost imagine that she *wasn't* looking at a man who had built hundreds of bombs that had claimed thousands of innocent lives. *Almost.*

Kawal glared at Marc. "How much money you talkin' about? Would have to be a lot, or else you can get the fuck out."

"No!" Sood got to his feet. "I am not interested! I want you to leave!"

Amarah gave a shrug and stood up. "Well. I told you I'd bring you to him. I never said he would like it." He sniffed the air. "You will still pay me."

"Pay *you,* bitch?" Kawal was getting up a head of stream now, and he stalked across the room toward the terrorist. "Man, get lost before you get hurt! You know who we are with now?"

Sood spoke over his grandson. "You are silent for so long, Jadeed, and then you come to me, to my home, in the middle of the day? You bring strangers to my door?"

Amarah bristled at his tone. "It was necessary."

"For you? But not for Al Sayf." Sood shook his head again. "You are not here with their blessing! You are trading my safety for gold from these foreigners!"

Marc held up a hand. "Please, there's no need for this. We can come to an arrangement—"

But Sood wasn't listening, and Lucy saw the same rising anger in him that Kawal showed. He jabbed a finger at Amarah. "Al Sayf do not exist anymore! The Americans are rooting them out and killing them for what you did in Washington!"

"That is a lie!" Amarah spat back. "They are . . . regrouping." Suddenly, the terrorist appeared uncertain of his own reply. "Khadir will return . . ."

"As he did for you?" Sood retorted. "You were left to rot in a cell! What does that tell you?"

"It tells me that I am owed," growled Amarah, and he looked toward Marc. "This man is a mercenary in the employ of the Combine. You know who they are, Jalsa. They are far richer than you!" He sneered. "I have a deal with them. I have made good on it."

"You have been lied to, my friend." The new voice came from behind Lucy, and she spun, tensing up as part of the shadows detached itself from the gloomy corner of the room and came into the light that spilled through the wooden slats.

The dark and thickset man smiled like a killer, flexing his hands as he strolled toward the group. *Abur Ramaas,* thought Lucy, as his black and damaged eye swept the room. *That can't be anyone else.*

The color drained from Marc's face and Ramaas saw it, chuckling to himself. "I like listening to your conversation," he said. "So little truth there. But this least of all." He aimed a finger at Marc like it was a gun. "This is not a Combine man. He is *police.*" Ramaas sounded out the word, long and low, then met the Brit's gaze. "You followed me from Croatia. How did you do that, policeman?"

"You're hard to miss," said Marc, after a moment.

"What?" Amarah's face creased in a terrible instant of naked fury, and he spat out a string of curses. "What did you say?" Then he wasn't looking at Marc or Ramaas anymore. He was glaring at Lucy. A slow wave of recognition came over him at long last, becoming anger and loathing. He rushed at her, and before she could react, he grabbed at her hijab and her fake glasses, tearing them away. "*You?!*" he spat at her, dragging a pistol from the folds of his robes and aiming it in her direction. "Worthless American whore!"

"Surprise, motherfucker." She dropped the act with a shrug, her defiance rushing back in to fill the void and washing away the timid "Lula" in a blink. "And here was me thinking you were too damn stupid to notice." She spat out the pads that filled her cheeks and showed him a sneer.

"What the—?" Amarah's gun draw kicked off a cascade of swearing from Kawal and he pulled a weapon of his own from his belt, a shiny gold-plated Sig Sauer that looked more like a toy than a real fire-arm. He swung the weapon back and forth, unsure whom he should be aiming at. "Back off!" Kawal's eyes widened in fear.

Amarah took a step aside. He knew if he fired, no matter what his target was, Kawal would light him up.

"Now it is interesting," said Ramaas, amused by the turn of events.

"Tell the boy to drop his weapon," said Amarah.

"This asshole brought the cops!" Kawal shouted. "We gotta smoke them!" He gritted his teeth and snarled. "I'll fucking kill you!"

Ramaas's mood shifted like the wind over water, suddenly becoming thunderous. "Then *do* it!" He pointed at Sood. "You want to be a brigand? Show me you possess the will. The old man is useless now. End him, if you have an ounce of strength."

"What?" Kawal's hand flexed around the grip of his pistol, and Lucy kept very, very still. The younger man was totally out of his depth, and his bravado had given him nowhere to go but down.

"Shoot him!" barked Ramaas. "But you won't! Because you are as useless as he is!"

Kawal exploded in a torrent of swearing, suddenly swinging the Sig toward Ramaas. "*Fuck you!* You don't tell me what to do, you son-of-a-bitch! I don't answer to you—I can do whatever the goddamn hell I want! You are in my house now, this is Kawal Sood's house and I don't ever—"

Amarah fired a single round that went straight through Kawal's chest and splattered blood and lung tissue over the marble walls and gold pillars. The younger man staggered backward and Amarah hit him again with another, this time putting the kill-shot through the side of his face.

Kawal fell back over one of the couches and collapsed into a twitching heap. The bomb-maker cried out and rushed to him, clawing at his grandson's body in shock and horror.

"He would not be silent," said Amarah, through gritted teeth.

"He was tiresome," agreed Ramaas, his mood shifting again. "But you and I, we have no quarrel."

"I want to kill the whore and the Britisher," continued Amarah, the raw need for his revenge like acid. "I have no interest in your business."

"Indeed." Ramaas gave Lucy a rueful smile. "That would put me in your debt. A problem solved." He took a step back, studying Amarah. "And it would make you free, I think."

Lucy's lip curled. "Aw, look at you two. Like kindred scumbags." Her mind raced; if she could get Amarah to *react* instead of *think*, she might get an edge she could use. "Hey, if you wanna blow each other, go right ahead, don't be shy. We won't judge."

Ramaas drew a knife and tossed it onto the blood-spattered table. "Use that on her. A bullet would be too swift." He turned toward the door. "As much as it might be entertaining to remain here, I have other priorities to attend to . . ."

"You'll both be dead before you get out of the compound." Marc's words were cold and controlled. "There's a strike team embedded outside right now. They heard those gunshots. Anyone comes out who isn't me or her gets a .300 round through the eye." Lucy had to admit he sounded fairly convincing.

"I will take that bet," said Ramaas, his smile widening. "I have killed everyone else in this house. Three more bodies matter nothing to me—"

"*Kutha sala!*" Sood screamed the words at Amarah with a force and venom that Lucy would not have believed the old man capable of. He came up from the ground in a blind rush, his white cotton robes soaked with his grandson's blood and Kawal's golden gun in his trembling fist. Sood mashed the pistol's trigger and fired wildly, spitting rounds in an uncontrolled arc.

Lucy glimpsed Marc throwing himself out of the line of fire and she did the same, her combat instincts kicking in as she dived across another of the low couches. She landed badly, her breath blowing out in a gust.

Everything else unfolded in flashes, actions stacking atop one another with such speed that it made her head swim. Ramaas reacted as though he had been kicked in the chest and he staggered backward as a random bullet hit him in the right bicep, carving out a ragged chunk of blood and muscle.

Amarah fired into the old man as Jalsa came lurching across the room, hitting him in the stomach. Jalsa crumpled like paper and crashed to the tiles. Dark blood filled his hands as he tried to cup the edges of his ragged wound.

In the same moment, Lucy saw Marc dragging an oil lamp up from the table, pulling it into a swing which he directed toward Ramaas's head—but even injured, the pirate warlord was able to get up a hand and deflect the improvised weapon away. He smashed the lamp and bellowed in pain as he punched Marc with his wounded arm without thinking. The hammer-blow connected and she saw Marc reel back and go down.

"Enough!" snarled Ramaas, and he glared at Amarah. "Do what you wish here. Just make sure they are all dead!" He lurched away, clamping his free hand over the new wound to staunch it as he vanished into one of the corridors, unwilling to ignore his own mission in favor of the two interlopers.

Lucy dragged herself upright as Amarah spun toward her, holding the wicked knife the warlord had left behind. "Your turn now," he said.

—— FIFTEEN ——

bet you dreamed about this, right?" Lucy let a mocking lilt enter her voice. "Night after night, in that six-by-nine where the CIA put you?" She licked her lips provocatively. "Is it going how you thought it would?"

Amarah scowled, infuriated by her tone. "I will silence you."

She knew his type down to the last detail, the kind who believed women were for beating or for using, who wrapped up their ignorance and cruelty with words like "values" and "honor" to conceal the fact that they were just bastards. Color, creed or religion didn't factor into it. Some men just *hated.*

And that meant she could push his buttons. Lucy eyed the jagged-edged blade he twirled in his right hand. "You want to stick it in me, big man? Reckon you can keep it up?"

He lost his cool and dove at her with a sudden flurry of slashing attacks that cut through the air in flashes of bright steel. Lucy retreated, dodging from side to side, staying just beyond his reach. She watched his motion, looking for patterns and strike points.

If Amarah was smart, he would have taken his reprisal the quick way and shot her dead where she stood. But here was someone who considered himself *righteous* and *wronged,* who had probably spent every day of his incarceration coming up with ways to get payback on the skinny black girl from Queens who had put him in that cell. He wanted to cut on her and take it slow.

Amarah snarled and changed tack, shifting his grip to go for a downward stabbing motion. Lucy didn't let him get there. She stepped to him, coming inside her attacker's reach to shorten the distance and hit him hard with a punch to the chest. She followed it up with a cross-hand move that was meant to disarm him, but Amarah had enough of his wits about him to deflect that approach and he reeled back.

Lucy cursed inwardly. They hadn't been able to take any weapons with them when they left Sweden, and she felt naked without a gun. If their roles had been reversed, Amarah would have had two bullets in him by now, but this was going to have to go the long way round.

The terrorist went back at her, going for the stab again, and Lucy brought up her hands to block his strike—but it was a feint. Amarah deftly flipped the combat knife around his palm and hit her hard with the heavy pommel, cracking her across the cheekbone. Flares of pain lit up inside her head and she lost her pace.

She was too close to the wall, in danger of losing room to maneuver. As the thought occurred to her, it was already too late to react. Amarah grabbed at the thick folds of her abaya and shoved Lucy back. He slammed her bodily into a shade across one of the open windows, and she felt the wooden slats splinter apart across her shoulders under the force of the sudden impact.

Her legs caught on the ledge of the window and she lost her balance before she could grab for a handhold.

Lucy tumbled backward out of the window, grasping for Amarah, pulling him with her as she fell into the blazing yellow sunshine outside.

Briefly blinded by the sudden change in illumination from the darkened reception room, they fell a story and landed hard atop the wide, square-framed veranda that shaded part of Jalsa Sood's swimming pool from the midday heat. The wooden frame cracked alarmingly under their weight.

Amarah was atop Lucy, holding her down as he pressed the knife toward her throat. She pushed back with both hands. All she could see was the black shadow of his head framed by the sun, and the dazzling mirror-bright line of the blade. The knife's razor tip puckered the skin of her neck where it touched.

* * *

Everything was blurry and made out of pain. At least, that was how it felt inside of Marc's skull as he blinked back to awareness and rolled over onto the cool marble tiles. It took agonizing moments for him to drag himself away from the edge of semi-consciousness. He tasted copper in his mouth and he could already feel the side of his face starting to stiffen with the beginning of bruises.

There was a liquid, wheezing noise that rose and fell around him, and Marc's hand clutched at his chest, afraid that the freight-train punch from Ramaas had broken something in his lungs. Then he figured out that the sound wasn't coming from him and he righted himself, turning toward the noise.

Fighting through dizziness, Marc's eyes labored into focus. Hard sunlight flooded the reception room through a window behind him, shattered bits of wood lying all around it. He cast about, Lucy was gone and the room—now bereft of all shadows in the unfiltered daylight—was a mess of broken furniture and spilled blood.

The wheezing was the sound of a man's life ending. Kawal Sood was dead, slumped in an untidy heap, his head and torso a mass of red, and his grandfather was trying to hold on to him, as if he feared at any moment someone would tear the two of them apart.

Jalsa Sood's white robes turned crimson as the mortal wound in his belly blossomed. The old man was crying and struggling to force in every breath of air he took.

Marc moved to him. Kawal's bloodstained Sig Sauer lay forgotten on the tiled floor between them.

"My boy," wept Jalsa, cradling Kawal's ruined head. "My boy is dead. I killed him. I killed them both."

Crouching there, ending a little more with each exhale, the bomb-maker was stripped of all the lies about who he was and what he had done. Marc saw a grandfather and a father buried under regrets, destroyed by the life he had made for himself. He felt the smallest flicker of sorrow for Sood, before a voice in the back of his mind reminded him of a certain truth. *He has more blood on his hands than just this. Sood is reaping the harvest of a lifetime of violence.*

Marc picked up the gun, weighing it in his hand. "What did you do for him, Jalsa? What did you do for Ramaas?"

Sood looked up, but his eyes were fogged with pain. His hand dropped from Kawal's bloody cheek and it fell to his lap. "I knew I would die. *Time*. But Kawal. Not him."

Marc leaned in, pushing away every human reaction that tried to come to the fore. "Where is the device?"

The old man's hand snapped up and grabbed him by the collar, blood smearing Marc's shirt as Jalsa pulled him close. Pink froth gathered at the edges of Sood's mouth as he spoke, his words drowned and fluid. "Right." He had to push it out in gulps of air. "Cylinder. Nine . . . Nine rods."

"I don't know what that means . . ." Marc began.

But Sood was already gone.

A bead of crimson grew where the knife rested on Lucy's throat, and Amarah grunted in frustration as he tried to press the weapon into her. Their hands locked around the hilt of the blade and each other; both of them struggled with all their might to resist or to kill. Locked in an obscene embrace, seconds seemed to extend into hours. The need for revenge and the desire to survive were perfectly matched, but the stalemate could not last.

Amarah gave a wordless snarl and renewed his inexorable pressure with a flex of his shoulder blades, making the muscles in Lucy's forearms buzz with the exertion. Then without warning, the wooden struts holding up the thick sailcloth of the veranda splintered and finally broke in half. The entire front section of the platform gave out and came apart, dropping the two of them into the deep end of the swimming pool below.

Lucy twisted out of Amarah's grip as they hit the water and went under, arms flailing as she desperately tried to put some distance between them. Lucy rolled as she sank, kicking off her shoes, and her feet slapped the bottom of the pool as she pushed away again. The water was clouded and over-chlorinated, and it was hard for her to swim through it as the black abaya clung to the contours of her body. The material dragged on her, and she pushed at debris from the collapsed veranda, groping toward the surface overhead.

A dark shape blocked her way and she reflexively shoved at it. The last of the breath in Lucy's chest erupted out of her mouth in a shock of bubbles as the shape resolved into the drifting corpse of an Arab man in a tuxedo. Blank eyes glared back at her from a face made pallid by days in the water.

There were others in there with them. Numerous bodies drifted in the ornate pool. Sickened, Lucy thrashed her way past the dead man and broke the surface, spitting tainted water from her mouth. She spun, trying to get her bearings, but everywhere she looked there were floating corpses.

I have killed everyone else in this house. Ramaas's words came back to her. *Three more bodies matter nothing to me.* He had not lied. The pool and the sun-drenched patio around it had been turned into a mass grave.

Amarah exploded out of the water behind her, still clutching the shiny steel knife in one hand, and she saw sunlight flash off the blade. Lucy lurched forward, splashing through the shallows toward a mosaiced staircase leading out of the water, and she had one hand on a chrome banister when a savage pull dragged her backward.

The terrorist was still waist-deep in the pool, and he had a length of her clothing in his hand, curling the material around his wrist. Amarah yanked on it with all the strength he could muster, and Lucy clung to the banister, crying out in anger. He tried to stab her with the knife, but the blade whistled through empty air, centimeters from her exposed back.

Her bare feet skidded on the bottom of the pool. If she slipped, Amarah would reel her in and plant the knife in her heart. Lucy struggled, fighting to slough off the robe and get free. A horrible possibility flashed through her mind: *Is Lula going to be the death of me?*

And then someone shouted her name and she twisted, glimpsing a figure atop the remains of the ruined veranda.

Marc had Kawal's golden gun in his fist and he fired off two shots, one after another. The first went wide and fizzed into the water, but the second was true and hit Amarah in the right shoulder. He screamed and toppled into the pool with a heavy smack, losing the knife and his grip on Lucy's clothing.

Suddenly free of him, she dragged herself the last few meters out of the water and across the patio. The sickening taste of the tainted water clogged her throat and nostrils, and she wanted to retch.

Marc scrambled down off the half-destroyed veranda and ran to her, shielding his eyes in the sunlight. "Are you okay? I mean, I saw him with the knife, I thought—"

"Gimme that," Lucy broke in, as she snatched the gold-plated pistol from his hand and turned back toward the pool.

One arm hanging uselessly at his side, Amarah was wading out toward the edge of the water, grasping for the ledge. Lucy didn't hesitate. She put a pinpoint shot through the man's heart, killing him instantly. Amarah's body toppled backward and sank into a spreading cloud of crimson.

"Damn," said Marc. "Uh, okay."

"I wasn't going to let him give a speech." Lucy bit and tore at the shapeless black abaya until she finally shrugged out of the waterlogged dress-robe, revealing the soaked trousers and T-shirt beneath. "You didn't really think we were gonna send him back to the CIA when we were done, did you?"

"Yeah," he admitted. "Kind of."

"This way is cheaper than airfare." She turned away, glaring into the distance. "And you can't tell me you didn't believe he had it coming."

Marc gave a grim nod. "No argument there." Like Lucy, he had been a front-row witness to the murderous ambitions of Jadeed Amarah and his cohorts.

Lucy sighed. "Thanks for the assist." She stopped herself from suggesting that next time Dane should go for a kill-shot, reminding herself that it didn't come as easily for him. She pushed that thought away and ejected the Sig's magazine. "Only four rounds left. *Shit*. Where's Ramaas?"

The rattle of a submachine gun cut through the air, followed quickly by the revving of a powerful engine. "There's your answer." Marc pointed in the direction of the ground-floor garage. "Come on!"

*   *   *

The throaty rumble of a supercharged V8 echoed through Sood's workshop as they made their way through it, staying in cover behind support pillars and shelves laden with vehicle spares. Marc saw a workbench that had been abandoned in haste, with tools scattered on the floor and a stool lying on its side. Whatever the Baker had been cooking up for Ramaas was in the process of being cleared out, and if he got away from them now, their one and only shot at stopping the pirate warlord would be gone.

He looked around for something to use as a weapon and settled on a bright red crowbar lying atop a tool chest, brandishing it like a short-sword. At the far end of the workshop were two half-open doors that led into the garage proper. Marc could only see a slice of the space beyond, glimpsing the sleek shapes of vehicles hidden under black antistatic dust covers. He ducked back as he saw a bald man toting an Uzi walk past, keys jangling in his hand.

"Is he in there?" Lucy whispered the question and held up the gold Sig pistol, her finger resting on the trigger guard.

Marc heard the sound of a trunk lid closing and the engine revved again. Voices in a language he didn't recognize carried from inside the garage, echoing off the walls, and he nodded.

"They're leaving," said Lucy. "We gotta go!" She took a breath and then kicked open the door. Marc shouldered the door on his side and followed her through.

"Nobody move!" shouted Lucy, leading with the pistol.

Idling at the mouth of the garage was a silver supercar that resembled an art deco bullet, a low and long-nosed two-door coupé sporting a large Mercedes-Benz trefoil and axe-blade scissor doors. Ramaas was already in the driver's seat of the SLR McLaren, and part of Marc admired the choice he'd made in picking which of Sood's car collection to steal. Another of his men was half-out of the passenger door, clutching a short-frame shotgun, and he froze, a grin on his lips.

Two more of the warlord's gun-thugs were helping themselves to a second car—this one a BMW Z4 roadster in candy-apple crimson— and Marc saw the bald guy with the Uzi whip around, heedless of Lucy's warning. The submachine gun chattered again and the spray of shots punched holes through the workshop doors and sent the two of them diving for cover.

The SLR's snarling roar sounded and the car shot away and out onto the asphalt, even as the scissor door was still descending. More shots came from the men in the Z4 as they hit the gas and followed Ramaas's lead into the daylight and away.

Lucy sprinted to the garage door and raised the Sig into a two-handed aiming stance, but at the last second she held her fire, and watched the back of the Z4 disappear behind the over-elaborate stone fountain in the mansion's courtyard. "We need to get after them!"

"Way ahead of you," said Marc, grabbing a handful of the dust sheath over the nearest car. There were a half-dozen other vehicles up on racks or parked in the corners of the garage, but they didn't have the time to window shop or compare marques. He dragged the cover off a metallic blue Audi S5 and slid into the driver's seat, fishing his grimy sunglasses from a pocket. Lucy grabbed the keys from a rack on the wall and tossed them into his lap as she vaulted into the passenger seat.

"Go!" she snapped, and he put the car into gear, launching it out of the garage in a wheel-spin skirl of noise. The Audi responded easily, and Marc threaded around the fountain and powered down the distance toward the front entrance. The gates were hanging open as they bounced onto the road, and Lucy jabbed a finger toward a retreating blur up ahead. "There's the Beemer . . ."

"I see it," said Marc, narrowing his focus to the road as he applied pressure to the accelerator.

"Get up there." Lucy dropped the window and the hot wind whipped through the S5's interior. "I need to be closer. We are going to fuck up his shit."

Marc pushed the Audi up through the gear changes and slipped across the three-lane highway. Low concrete walls flashed by as they turned onto First Al Khail Street and continued to accelerate, speeding past signs for an expensive residential district called the Lakes. The name appeared odd to Marc's eyes, conjuring up visions of pastoral English countryside rather than a transplanted greensward on the edge of the desert. Less secluded than Sood's isolated estate, the houses were

still in the top tier of private villas in the city, and the high walls surrounding the buildings echoed with the roar of engines as the cars shot
past.

Ahead, he glimpsed the red BMW weaving between a pair of white
people carriers and scanned the road beyond it, trying to spot the
silver supercar.

"Those losers in the other car are not the priority," said Lucy, following the same train of thought. "We gotta get on that Merc's tail
and stick to it."

"Easy ask," Marc replied. "Not so much in the execution, though.
That SLR's got six hundred-odd horses under the hood. If we get to
a straightaway, he's gone."

"Then pour it on," she retorted.

"Copy that." He passed one of the people carriers on the inside and
there was a brief flash of bright crimson as the BMW blinked past and
fell behind, disappearing into the Audi's slipstream. The driver hadn't
seen them coming and he reacted way too slow to run any interference for Ramaas.

As the road curved to the right, Marc leaned into the turn and continued to put his foot down. The BMW would be racing to catch up
to them, which only gave Marc and Lucy a small window of opportunity to get in range of the SLR before they would have trouble
coming at them from in front and behind.

The road passed the sculpted lawns of a golf course on the right,
and to the left dozens of marble towers rose out of the near horizon,
catching the rays of the morning sun. The light blinked off something
else: a low-slung silver arrowhead just ahead, two lanes over and
moving swiftly into the feeder lane of a motorway interchange.

Marc yanked the steering wheel and the Audi screeched across the
road, cutting over the paths of other drivers who hit their horns in a
blaring chorus of disapproval. He ignored them and slipped into a
trailing position a few vehicle lengths behind the SLR. The other car
was losing speed as it approached the complex cloverleaf junction, but
Marc didn't follow suit, betting on the Audi's traction control to keep
them from losing it on the turn.

They followed an overpass across the sixteen lanes of the Sheikh

Zayed highway that bifurcated downtown Dubai, and the road branched just as Ramaas woke up to the fact that he had a tailgater. The SLR descended the exit ramp and started to gain speed.

"Get me close!" Lucy shouted again, propping up the gold pistol on the door frame. But Marc was already committing himself to a different approach. "Hold on!" he called, and aimed the Audi's prow right at the rear quarter of the supercar.

The two vehicles met in a heavy crunch of fracturing plastic, with enough force to dent the panels on the SLR's side frame. Shards of tail lights scattered like shrapnel. The silver car skidded and recovered, before lurching across the Audi's path and into another feeder lane that would take it onto the wide highway they had just crossed.

Marc stamped on the accelerator and rear-ended the SLR again, this time shunting the supercar into another skid that didn't allow Ramaas to make a clean recovery. The car snaked across into another lane and sideswiped a green SUV, sending the 4x4 off on its own uncontrolled slide. As the SLR slewed back, Lucy fired off a shot that blew out the passenger-side window in a shower of glass.

Marc hunched forward in his seat, as if that would give him a fraction more speed, and went for it again. Part of the Audi's front bumper and a section of the grille were already dislocated from the frame and trailing against the asphalt as he slammed the cars together for the third time. The busted grille splintered and tumbled away, but the impact took part of the SLR's rear bumper with it, and popped the lock on the supercar's boot hatch.

As the car passed in front of them, the hatch yawned open and revealed the contents of the trunk. "*Oh, shit,*" cried Lucy. "Are they—?"

"Yeah." Inside, lined up in a row, were five identical steel-shell suitcases. Each was a perfect duplicate of the Exile unit that Marc had last seen in the hands of Neven Kurjak.

"Which one?" The inevitable question was forming on Lucy's lips, but she never got to voice it. The SLR's swerve sent one wheel over the rumble strip on the edge of the highway before Ramaas managed to regain control of it, but not before the shuddering and rolling of the car's motion bounced one of the cases clear out of the trunk and into the path of the oncoming traffic.

Marc swore and stamped on the brakes, desperately veering to avoid the steel case as it landed flat-side down and spun wildly across the asphalt, like a stone skipping over a lake.

Lucy's head snapped around to follow the path of the spinning case, unable to take her eyes off it. She felt a sudden fist of panic in her gut as the case ricocheted off a guide rail and directly into the path of a cargo truck speeding up along the outside lane.

She wanted to close her eyes, momentarily terrified that a world's-end whiteout flash would be the next thing she would see, but then the truck rode right over the case and flattened it, scattering smashed pieces across the roadway.

"So not that one," managed Marc, answering her unfinished question. "Bloody hell . . ."

"Remind me to get some clean underwear after this," she shot back. Ahead of them, the silver roadster was drifting across the lanes again, in the direction of the elevated metro line that parallelled the road. The highway was a canyon boxed in by an orchard of shining towers, all blue glass and pale sand-colored stone, and it extended off toward the horizon in a ribbon of black. If Marc was right—and he usually had a handle on the numbers—the fancy Merc would soon leave them eating dust.

She weighed the pistol on her hand. *Three rounds left.* She would have to make every one count. "Get us alongside!"

Marc nodded and changed gear, aiming them into the supercar's slipstream. Lucy kept expecting Ramaas's vehicle to light the afterburners and blaze away, but he didn't. Then she saw why.

The thug they had glimpsed in Sood's garage, the man with the shotgun, emerged from the broken passenger-side window. He clung to the car's hardtop, reaching backward, and Lucy realized that he was trying to slam shut the yawning trunk hatch.

As their car came closer, the hatch went down and locked, and the baby-faced thug looked back toward Lucy. His hand dropped to grab at his belt and she knew he was going for a gun.

For the second time that day, the action came to her without hesitation, powered by a cold kind of combat logic that was born out of hard training and harder experience. Lucy leaned out of the window and into the hurricane of air blasting down the road. *Two moving vehicles, close range, dry air, a 9mm bullet.* All the variables threaded through her mind in a fraction of a second, as easy to her as breathing. The Sig bucked in her hand, the sound of the discharge swallowed by the wind. The thug grew a rosette of red on his chest and sagged against the side of the car. One arm flopped away and his hand ground against the speeding road surface.

Lucy turned her head to suck in a breath of air and as she turned back, the shadow in the silver car's driving seat was in motion, pushing at the body of the gun-thug. The injured man was still trying to claw back inside when Ramaas forced him the rest of the way out and let the slipstream rip him away.

"Bollocks!" Marc mashed the brakes again and the car lurched aside, narrowly avoiding the thug's body as it wheeled past them and into the path of the traffic behind.

Ramaas used the moment to pour on the coals. The Merc roadster began to pull away from them as they passed the marina and the towers around them started to thin out. Lucy shot a glance at the Audi's speedometer. The needle was already at ninety and still climbing, but the Merc kept adding distance.

"We're never gonna catch him in this thing," muttered the Brit.

"I'm open to any suggestions," she began.

Suddenly, Marc's head snapped around as he saw something in the Audi's wing mirror. Lucy looked in the same direction and saw the red BMW convertible coming up fast on the outside, headlights on full beam and blazing. The bald guy with the Uzi was in the passenger seat, and he was taking his time with his aim as the Z4 matched pace.

"Marc . . ." Lucy warned. He didn't seem to hear her. "Marc?" She shouted at him. *"Dane!"*

He pumped the brakes as the thug with the Uzi fired off a burst, and the positions between the two cars reversed. The bullets missed the passenger compartment, but Lucy saw the blue metal of the Audi's hood grow a bunch of silver impact craters as the rounds hit the front of the car.

Marc worked the steering left-right, left-right in an experimental motion. "I think he might've hit something important," he called out over the roar of the wind. "Feels mushy . . ."

Ahead, they were catching up with a group of slow-moving trucks spread out over the middle lanes. Marc found a way to thread the needle between two of them as the BMW tried to drop back and parallel them again. The bald guy fired off another burst, but they were already behind the truck and the rounds went harmlessly into the back of the wagon.

"I can't get a bead on that asshole while he's on the wrong side of us," Lucy complained.

Marc's eyes were fixed on the horizon. "We're losing Ramaas," he grated. "We don't have time to screw around!"

"Faster, faster!" Bidar shouted eagerly at Guhaad as he ejected a spent magazine from the submachine gun and rammed a fresh one into its place. "Faster would be better!"

Guhaad scowled. When this was over, he was going to punish Bidar and remind him which of them was in charge. He took in the road around them, alert for the blue car to re-emerge from behind one of the slower-moving trucks. They were passing out of the city now, the landscape around them flattening as the expensive, lavish towers gave way to construction sites and cranes. Signs in English and Arabic suspended over the highway told him they were going in the right direction; the Jebel Ali Free Zone industrial area was a few miles ahead, and within its boundaries there was a sprawl of unmarked roads and unmapped buildings. Once they were inside, they were as good as ghosts.

He chanced a look over his shoulder, searching for the signs of the police, but saw nothing. If the Dubai cops had been alerted to the chase, they were still rushing to reach it.

"Come on, come on!" shouted Bidar, brandishing the Uzi. "Where is the white rat?"

Out of nowhere, the digital satellite phone stuffed into Guhaad's pocket buzzed angrily and he pressed it to his ear. "Yes, boss?"

"*Where are you?*" demanded Ramaas.

"Chasing the policeman. The one who came after you."

"*Don't take too much time with him,*" came the reply. "*Deal with it quickly. They know we are here, we can't wait for you. They must not follow us!*" The line cut and Guhaad's scowl deepened.

"There! I see it!" Bidar pointed and bellowed out the words. Guhaad remembered him doing the same, long ago in the gunwale of a skiff as they sighted an overladen freighter in the Gulf of Aden.

This is no different, Guhaad told himself. *We killed the foreigners there. We'll kill them here . . .*

As they passed through the pack of cargo trucks, Guhaad looked ahead and saw another, larger vehicle snaking along the highway. He reached across and yanked on Bidar's belt. "Hold your fire. I have an idea."

The desert gusts whipped around the Audi's interior, dragging sand in with them and stealing away all the moisture in Marc's mouth. He blinked behind his aviator sunglasses and squared his shoulders, wishing that the Audi had a nitro button he could mash to gain a burst of much-needed velocity.

"There he is!" said Lucy. She aimed the pistol in the direction of the BMW as the red car suddenly vaulted forward and cut left across the lanes. Marc accelerated again to match him, but the convertible had already vanished behind the rear of a dust-caked eighteen-wheeler carrying a load of wide-gauge water pipes. He glimpsed flashes of red as the BMW passed up the length of the truck on the far side, moving to overtake it.

"Where's he going?" said Lucy.

Marc shook his head, dropping back. "No idea. I'm gonna go around, try to get behind him . . ."

To the right, he saw a clump of buildings settled in the middle of the sands—a giant shopping mall clustered at the foot of a hotel complex in the shape of a giant's gateway—and for a second he thought that the BMW was going to head for the off-ramp. But then Marc saw the bald man stand up in the footwell as the car passed the truck's cab, and aim the submachine gun at the big rig's driver.

A pennant of flame spat from the Uzi's muzzle and a full-auto discharge shredded the windscreen of the truck and the luckless man driving it. At high speed and instantly out of control, the rig swerved wildly and the oscillation translated down the length of the trailer, rocking it hard enough to pull the rear wheels away from the asphalt.

Marc saw it coming and stomped the Audi's brake pedal into the floor.

The truck cab swung as the BMW sped on and away. The rig jackknifed and the transfer of momentum was so brutal that it flipped the entire vehicle onto its side and back down across four lanes of the highway. The cables holding the water pipes snapped and the truck shed its load directly into the path of the Audi and the traffic behind.

Lucy reflexively grabbed the "oh-shit" handle over the door as Marc wrenched the steering wheel from side to side, desperately trying to find a path through the bouncing, rolling pipes that came tumbling toward them. The Audi pitched hard on its shocks, but in a fraction of a second they ran out of room. The yawning end of a pipe section struck the back end of the car with enough force to break something in the drive train and the Audi lurched into an unrecoverable skid. They hit the safety barrier on the right side of the highway with a flat crunch of rending metal, and the airbags deployed to smother the impact.

Marc lolled back in his seat, choking on dust, and tore the airbag away from his face. Across the road, cars were swerving into one another and juddering to a halt as they came upon the obstacles strewn over the highway.

His shoulder and his neck ached as though he had been kicked by a horse. Lucy squirmed across the ruined interior toward him and coughed. "Get out."

"Yeah." Marc kicked open the driver-side door and they got clear of the broken Audi. Oil was already pooling beneath it, and white vapor coiled from the bonnet. "Lost our wheels," he said thickly.

"Maybe not . . ." said Lucy.

A few meters away, a glassy footbridge crossed over the road, connecting to the shopping mall and a metro station that resembled the cocoon of a huge moth coated in bronze. It was incongruous out here, with little else around, but the complex was simply waiting for the dead desert around it to sprout more homes, more towers, and more money.

An athletic young man in the tan uniform of the Dubai police force came sprinting over to them, his face a mask of worry. "Are you all right?" Marc gave him a weary nod and he shot a look at the disorder of the pile-up forming on the road before him. "Oh, no. I have to call this in." The young cop started back toward the footbridge.

In the shadow of it were a cluster of vehicles. A handful of the ubiquitous bone-white SUVs that swarmed the city's backroads were grouped next to a svelte, airstream shape that shimmered in the heat. People who had been gathering around it were now gawping at the road accident.

But the car . . . The car was low and swift even standing still, and Marc blinked at it in amazement. "Bloody hell, is that a . . . ?"

"For cryin' out loud." Lucy glared back at him as she brushed dust off her face and chest. "Close your mouth. It's just a goddamn machine."

The *goddamn machine* was a Bugatti Veyron in a green-and-white livery, and it looked as if it was designed to go into orbit and back rather than hug the blacktop. Marc had heard that Dubai's police department had a stock of expensive supercars in their patrol fleet, but he'd only ever half-believed it.

"Hey!" His thoughts caught up with him and he reached out to grab the cop's shoulder. Like his car, the young man was well sculpted and perfectly manicured. "There was a silver SLR McLaren, you must have seen it burning rubber up here a moment ago . . . And a red BMW drop-top . . ."

The police officer nodded. "I was reporting it. There have been calls about a shooting near the marina . . ." He looked back at the mess on the highway. "But this . . . We have to get help here!"

"No doubt," said Lucy. "Except there's a terrorist suspect in that silver roadster. We need you to get after him."

"A terrorist?"

Marc nodded. "We're undercover officers with Europol," he lied, reaching for the first thing to come to mind. "Been tracking him from Eastern Europe."

"And every second we stand here talking, he's getting further away." Lucy nodded at the Veyron. "My friend here is looking at that thing like he wants to marry it, so I'm guessing that means it is fast. You see where I'm going?"

The cop held up his hand and his manner became stiff. "These cars are not used for high-speed pursuits," he replied, in a rote manner that told Marc he had given this reply more than a few times. "They are for display only. For public-relations engagements." He took a breath. "If you are who you say you are, present your identification and I will—"

"You'll call it in?" Lucy snapped, and Marc saw her temper fray. "*Nah*. Hand over the keys."

The cop snorted. "I will do no such thing—" He fell silent as the gold Sig Sauer came out of nowhere and pressed itself against his chest. The bystanders watching the scene saw the weapon and broke away in a panicked rush.

Marc shrugged. "You'd better do what she says, mate."

"There are no keys," insisted the police officer. "The cars operate on a radio-frequency ID chip system. Only we can drive them."

The young man shifted, trying to conceal something, and Marc grabbed at his arm, pulling it up. He wore a black plastic bracelet around his wrist, like a fitness monitor. "A chip like the one in there?"

"No," he insisted, struggling against Marc's grip.

When Lucy spoke again, her voice was ice cold. "Is that car worth your life?"

"It . . . it's worth eight million dirham!" he blurted.

Lucy pulled back the hammer on the pistol. "Is *that* how much your life is worth?"

The blood drained from the young cop's face, and he reluctantly removed the wristband, slapping it into Marc's palm. "Do you know what you are doing? We have very strict laws in this nation. Do you understand what your punishment will be?"

"We'll take our chances." Lucy shoved him back with the gun. "Get his weapon, too."

Marc snatched the Caracal pistol from the man's holster. "If it makes you feel any better, we're on the level about the terrorist."

"The only criminals I see are you two," the policeman shot back.

"I'll try to bring it back in one piece," said Marc, and he ran to the car, with Lucy on his heels. He pulled open the supercar's door and failed to suppress a faint smile.

Lucy sent him an acid glare over the roof of the Veyron. "Stop enjoying this," she said sternly.

"Belt up," he replied as he climbed in and thumbed the ignition button. "And *hang on.*"

— SIXTEEN —

This is a cop car?" Lucy sank into the passenger seat of the Veyron and took in the dark leather all over the interior. "My best shoes don't look this fine." She shook her head, frowning at the excess. "I swear, this city is like Billionaire Disneyland . . ."

"And then some. Here we go." Marc tapped the RFID bracelet against the locking module behind the steering wheel and the car slipped away from the hard shoulder as if it was made of liquid mercury. He applied steady pressure to the gas pedal and the Veyron responded with a rolling engine note as the revs grew.

She had to admit, it was pretty damn smooth, and even with the traffic flashing past alongside them it felt as though they were hardly moving. In other circumstances she might have appreciated the ride for what it was, but right now all that mattered was that this thing was *quick*, that it could catch up to Ramaas before he decided to get off the freeway and vanish.

"There's gonna be a lo-jack in here somewhere . . ." She bent forward, feeling under the dashboard and around her feet. Her hand found a black box beneath her seat, out of place against the upholstery. "Wait, I got it. Never mind." Lucy used the butt of Kawal's gun to crack it open and rip out the GPS tracker inside.

Marc located the control that triggered the Veyron's lights and sirens. "What do you reckon? Blues and twos?"

"They'll see us coming," she replied.

"That's pretty much a given anyway in this motor," he countered, and flipped the switch. Gripping the steering wheel firmly, Marc slowly increased the power.

An angry voice spluttered from the radio built into the dashboard, and Lucy silenced it with the twist of a dial. "If the local five-oh weren't on to us before, they sure as hell will be now, Dane. Tell me you can handle this thing."

"I've driven one before."

"Really?"

"Well, not so much driven. More like, *stood next to*. But I got it. It's cool." They hurtled between a pair of water trucks that seemed to be standing still, and Lucy's gaze caught the needle on the analog speedometer as it effortlessly topped a hundred miles per hour and continued to climb.

She glanced behind her, through the slit-sized back window at the road retreating behind them. She couldn't be certain, but in the distance, up in the sky, Lucy thought she could see a helicopter. "Gimme the gun you took," she ordered.

"Jacket pocket," Marc instructed, unwilling to take his hands off the wheel at such speeds, even for a second.

Lucy pulled the Caracal semi-automatic and checked it over. As with the car, the cop's gun was immaculately cared for. *But like his wheels, never used in anger,* she noted.

"Target," said Marc. "Red Z4, center lane, coming up fast."

She grinned, holding the Caracal in one hand and the gold-plated Sig Sauer in the other. "Shall we give him a ticket?"

Marc had to ease off the gas to make sure they didn't overshoot. "Do it quick. We still have to find that SLR before the next junction."

"It's cool," she repeated, but the words were lost in the sudden roar of wind that whipped into the car as she pressed the switch that dropped the power window.

"The police . . . ?" Guhaad saw the strobing flicker of warning lights as the supercar emerged from the slower traffic falling away behind them.

"Not the police," Bidar shouted, slurring the words a little and bearing his stained teeth as he squirmed in his seat. "It's *them*!" He had been chewing on the last of his khat supply since they left the bomb-maker's mansion and it was making him bold. He rattled the Uzi in his hand. "I have to kill them twice, brother!"

Guhaad's eyes flicked around. They were on a clear stretch of highway, with nothing but eight lanes of open asphalt between the two vehicles. He tensed. This time, they could not afford to fail. He held the wheel firmly. "Do not miss!" he yelled, pitching his voice to be heard over the engine.

Bidar laughed wildly as he dragged himself up onto the passenger seat, clutching the submachine gun to his chest. "Come on!" he yelled into the wind.

The green-and-white racer came upon them, moving like a fish through water, and Guhaad glimpsed a dark woman's face inside the vehicle, eyeing him coldly. She had a gold pistol in her hand. "Now, Bidar! Now!"

With a shout, Bidar bobbed up from the passenger seat and leaned across the back of the BMW, one hand clutching the back of the driver's seat to steady himself, the other holding the Uzi extended toward the police car. He was laughing.

Guhaad's eyes snapped back to the road, but from the corner of his vision he saw the double muzzle flash from the gold gun, flaring brightly in the half-second before Bidar pulled the trigger. Then in the next instant Guhaad's face was spattered with hot blood jetting from wounds in Bidar's chest.

Bidar's laughter became a scream and he lurched forward, collapsing over the driver. His gun-hand tightened in an involuntary muscle spasm, his arm dropping to point the Uzi downward. The weapon discharged with a droning rattle, spitting brass shell casings into the slipstream, and discharged the remaining ammo in its magazine through the back of the BMW, blowing holes in the chassis and tires.

Guhaad felt the car rebel against him. It shuddered and gave off an accusatory howl, before pulling sharply into an uncontrollable turn toward the hard shoulder. He couldn't see properly, not with Bidar's blood all over him and the dying man collapsed across his arms. He tried to apply the brakes but the pedal thudded uselessly against the floor. He was still trying to arrest the turn when the BMW careened off the road and slammed into a gravel-choked ditch.

* * *

"You got him?" said Marc, risking a glance away from the road as they accelerated again.

Lucy twisted in her seat, discarding the gaudy gold pistol in the footwell, now that it was spent and its slide locked back. "Maybe," she admitted. "He skidded off the highway."

"Can't go back and check." He stabbed a finger at the sat-nav GPS screen built into the Veyron's dashboard. "Exit is coming up." The digital screen showed another cloverleaf junction approaching fast, roads branching off the motorway and into an area known as the Extension, a sprawling industrial estate that formed part of the economic Free Zone around the port of Jebel Ali.

Her head jerked up and he knew that her keen sniper's eye had spotted their quarry. "Is that him? I see something silver, at one o'clock."

As Lucy said the words, sunlight flashed off a bright metallic object at a distance and Marc drew the Veyron across the lanes to bring it closer. The car was moving into position to take the exit ramp. He hesitated. "Anywhere else in the world, I'd say yeah, for sure . . . But this is Dubai. Every trust-fund kid with an Amex Black card probably has a Merc SLR in their garage."

"So get me close!"

Up until now, Marc had been afraid to really push the Veyron, but they were running out of road. He flicked the gearshift and put his foot down. The supercar's quad-turbocharged engine responded instantly to his demands and poured velocity into the road, automatically deploying the rear air spoiler. G-force pushed the two of them back into the cockpit seats and the Veyron swallowed up the distance in a swooping surge of power. Marc had to brake a heartbeat later to avoid overshooting the silver SLR, even though both cars were topping a hundred and fifty as the curve of the off-ramp loomed before them.

Lucy was at the window, the Caracal pistol in a two-handed grip, the desert wind shrieking now, tearing at each exhale from Marc's mouth. "It's him!" she shouted, and fired a shot into the other car that hit but did nothing to slow it.

Marc couldn't stop himself from flicking a look to the side, and he regretted it. He got an impression of a shape inside the SLR—long and angular, aimed out across at them—before his mind caught up to what he was seeing.

"*Gun*—!" cried Lucy, as the pump-action shotgun Ramaas was pointing at them discharged.

Marc jerked the Veyron's wheel as she yelled, and felt the impact rather than saw it, hearing the grind and clatter of heavy-gauge pellets screeching off the roof, the door, and the hot ricochets rattling around inside the vehicle.

Lucy recoiled back against him, letting out a bark of pain.

"Are you hit?" he shouted.

"Get after him," she shot back, one hand clamped to her face. "Go, go!" Blood was already running over her fingers, but Lucy voice was filled with anger instead of pain. "Goddamn that son-of-a-bitch!"

The SLR's remaining undamaged tail light flared red and the car swung its long nose toward the exit ramp, accelerating as it went. Marc gave the Veyron's steering wheel a savage twist and the tires screeched as the streamlined prow veered after the other vehicle.

The cars crowded in on each other as they both took the exit way too fast, leaving streaks of rubber on the road as their traction control systems briefly warred with mass and gravity to keep them from spinning out.

Eight open lanes narrowed abruptly to two, and it was as if the blacktop had folded in on itself. Suddenly, room to maneuver was sparse and made more dangerous by an increase in other traffic. None of that bothered Ramaas, however, who immediately floored it as they pulled off the wide highway and onto the local road. Marc gunned the Veyron's engine and paced him, coming up fast to nudge the SLR's rear bumper. He glanced at the speedo; they were bouncing around the hundred mark, and the less-maintained surface of local road was translating up through the shock absorbers in a steady, teeth-rattling vibration.

Ramaas veered sharply into the oncoming lane to drift around a dusty sedan and back again. Marc followed suit, in time to see a truck coming the other way fill the Veyron's windscreen. His mind told him to hit the brakes, but he let instinct overrule it and accelerated through a blare of horns, barely threading the needle as the truck thundered past.

Lucy made a growling noise and drew her hand down her face. A couple of red streaks crossed her brow and vanished into the dark line of her close-cropped hair. "That stings," she hissed, and extended her hand out of the window to plant two shots in the SLR's rear.

"Don't shoot at the trunk," Marc snapped. "Remember, *bombs*."

"I was aiming for the tires, but no joy. He must have run-flats . . ."

The traffic was thinning out, but the road was growing less even by the second and it became an effort to keep the Veyron steady at high speed. The chase kicked thick clouds of dust into the air, and Marc kept dropping off the pedal. The speedometer needle fell by margins in quick jerks.

"Keep on him!" Lucy demanded. "The road curves up ahead . . ."

"We can try to run him off, copy that," Marc finished the thought for her. As they approached the turn, he glimpsed a long, flat build-ing rising from the sands in the middle distance. The nondescript warehouse had to be Ramaas's ultimate destination.

The SLR picked up speed again as Ramaas attempted to put more distance between them, but Marc wasn't about to let that happen. He felt the all-wheel drive bite as he shifted gears and the streamers of desert sand whipped up around the car as it gained a fresh burst of speed.

Then something at the apex of the turn shifted. Marc had assumed it was an outcrop of rock, but it was a man in a brown dishdasha robe, concealed behind a tarp that blended him into the landscape.

Now revealed, in his hands was the distinctive drainpipe shape of a Russian-made anti-tank rocket launcher, familiar to anyone who had ever watched front-line war reports from the world's brush-fire hotspots. He pointed it at the archway-shaped grille in the Veyron's hood and fired.

Marc saw the flash of backblast and wrenched the wheel over as hard as he could, but it wasn't enough to get clear of the rocket. The shooter's lack of good aim sent the warhead into the road surface di-rectly in front of the car, but the high-explosive charge inside was enough to blow a meter-wide crater in the cracked asphalt and flip the Veyron into the air.

The ground revolved around them as if they were inside a jet doing a barrel roll. The car's multipoint harnesses kept Marc and Lucy pressed tight to the seats as gravity pulled them this way and that. The Veyron described a single aerial spin before it hit the highway again, and then more across the asphalt and the sand as it began to destroy itself. Wheel cowlings, sections of the bonnet, the lights bar and the rear spoiler were all ripped from the frame until the car finally came to a shuddering stop, back on its wheels.

Marc felt dizzy and sick, raising his hands to claw away the airbags that had blown out to cushion him from the crash impact. It had been bad enough losing the Audi back down the motorway, but this was a hundred times worse. His head and shoulders ached where he had been whipped around by the G-force, his joints singing with stress. For a moment, he couldn't bring himself to move—but then the odor of burned plastic and spilled gasoline reached his nostrils and it was like an electric jolt to his system.

"Lucy?" He grabbed for her. "We have to . . . have to get out." The doors were jammed into the car's framework and wouldn't open, but the shattered windscreen was hanging loosely out across the broken prow of the Veyron. He hit the quick-release buckle on the seat harness and lurched forward. *"Lucy!"*

The man in the brown robes was walking calmly toward the car from the road, picking his way through the trail of broken Bugatti pieces and sizzling debris. He tossed the spent launcher tube away, drawing a revolver. Marc saw him look up into the air and then break into a jog, coming closer.

Lucy's head lolled forward, and then snapped back as she came to from a daze. Sleepily, she barely gave the man in the dishdasha a sideways look before she raised the Caracal pistol and shot him through the windscreen. "Asshole," she muttered.

They helped each other out of the wrecked Veyron and slid down into the sand. Marc looked back at the ruined supercar and felt a pang of guilt. Not because he'd stolen the vehicle, but because he had been party to the destruction of something beautiful.

"How much is eight million dirham, anyhow?" Lucy asked, surveying the wreck.

"Two million," he replied. "We just wrote off two million dollars' worth of car."

Lucy patted him on the face. "Don't cry. They can sue us." She went to the man in the robes, who was still alive, and stooped to get his revolver. "You." Lucy prodded the injured man in the chest. "Where is Ramaas?"

He pointed toward the warehouse, gasping through shallow breaths.

"How many men does he have?" Marc asked the question, but the injured shooter looked at him blankly.

"That's all we're getting from him," Lucy concluded, and for a moment Marc believed she was going to finish off the man in cold blood. Lucy caught his look and waggled the pistol in her hand. "Just conserving ammo," she explained, tossing the revolver to Marc. He caught it and checked the chambers.

They trudged the rest of the distance toward the warehouse, following in the lines of the SLR's route. The car's tire tracks ended at one of three wide roller doors at a loading dock, but there were no other entrances along the sunward side of the building.

"How do you want to do this?" said Marc. "He could be doing anything in there—"

As he spoke, there was a grinding rattle as a chain drive came to life, and the roller doors began to rise, thin lines of shadow appearing at their bases to grow larger with every moment.

"Cover!" Lucy shouted, and they sprinted into the shadow of an empty guardhouse facing the roadway.

The warehouse's interior was dark, but Marc saw a glitter of silver through one of the doors. The SLR was in there, parked askew with the scissor doors folded up like extended wings and the trunk hatch yawning open. The boot was empty.

He held his breath, waiting for someone in the cover of the darkness to start shooting. Instead of gunfire, he heard the high-pitched, nasal snarl of revving motorcycle engines. "What the hell?"

The stuttering revs became a scream of acceleration and from out of the shadows, streaming around the stalled Mercedes, came four identical KTM dirt bikes. Each one was ridden by a figure with their face obscured behind a white crash helmet, and all of them had the same kind of brown dishdasha as the man with the rocket launcher. But what made Marc's heart freeze in his chest was the silver steel case strapped across the handlebars of each of the bikes.

Lucy hesitated, seeing the same thing, before she committed to opening fire, trying to take out at least one of the riders as they sped past. If she hit them, they didn't let it slow them down. The bikes roared out across the asphalt at full throttle and the pack broke apart, each heading off in a different direction across the sands.

Marc burst from cover in time to see one of them slow as they passed the injured man left behind by the wrecked Veyron. The rider drew a gun and killed the other shooter with a bullet to the head before powering away again.

"Smart bastard," Lucy growled, watching them go. "There's no way we can track all of them!"

Marc swore, glaring around as the motorcycles disappeared into the heat haze off the desert. The Exile weapon and the doppelgangers Jalsa Sood had constructed had slipped through their hands. "Ramaas must've had this planned from the start. He's turned it into a bloody shell game—"

A shriek of torn air cut through his words and a wall of concussion hit them both, throwing Marc and Lucy into the dust as the warehouse behind them exploded into a ball of orange flames and black smoke.

The hot stink of combusted petrol washed over them and they both choked. Bits of tin roofing fluttered down out of the skies, scattering all around. Marc was momentarily deafened, and he pulled on Lucy's arm, trying to drag her away. "We have to get out of here," he managed.

But a sudden wind was whipping up and when she turned back to him Lucy was pointing toward the highway. A squad of green-and-white police 4x4s were bounding over the road toward them, and above, a helicopter had settled into a menacing hover.

Lucy raised her hands and let her gun drop into the sand at her feet. Marc saw a man in a tan-colored uniform aiming a rifle at them from the helicopter's crew bay, and he did the same, feeling all the fatigue held back by his adrenaline come over him in a rush.

After a female doctor had dressed the cuts on her head, a woman in a perfectly pressed green hijab and police uniform came to take Lucy's statement, but as she barely said anything past her name and a demand for a phone call, the conversation was somewhat one-sided. The identification Lucy had on her, under the "Lula" cover, was good enough for a cursory check but it didn't hold up to an in-depth examination. Instead of giving the locals more information, she decided to play the waiting game. She hoped a solution would present itself *before* the Dubai cops ran out of patience.

They put Lucy in a clean, modern cell and she passed the hours sleeping and waiting for the police to interrogate her again. A day went by. When they didn't come, she became concerned. Somebody was going to be punished for all the mayhem that had been unleashed in the city, and if it wasn't her . . .

She frowned. While Marc Dane had served in the British military and been trained by the security services, he didn't have the black-ops preparation like Lucy Keyes did. He hadn't gone through the rigors of SERE the way she had at Fort Bragg, back when Lucy was still wearing army green for Delta Force. The Survival Evasion Resistance Escape program had taught her how to be ready for anything up to and including "enhanced interrogation techniques," but as far as she knew, Marc had never had to face that kind of thing. And here they were in a city that was pretty much a law unto itself.

Lucy pushed away the troubling possibility. *The Brit's tougher than you're giving him credit for. He'll be okay.*

But when she saw Marc for the first time since they'd been arrested, she knew that her fears had been on the money. Two burly police officers marched her out of the cell and down a series of brightly lit corridors until they emerged in a parking garage where an armored prisoner-transport van was waiting.

They shoved her inside, and there he was, handcuffed to a rail along the middle of the compartment. He had bruises on his face and a split lip that hadn't been there after the car crash. "Hey," offered Marc, his voice scratchy.

There was already a stocky policeman sitting in there with him, and a second man climbed in after Lucy, securing the cuffs around her wrists to the same restraint rail. The other cop sat down with his back to the door and started toying with his iPhone as the van started up and pulled away.

"You made some friends?" Lucy glared at the cop, who ignored her.

Marc shrugged. "You know how it goes. *I fell down the stairs.*"

"Fuck these guys," she said, with real heat. Her curse drew the attention of the man with the phone and he gave her a severe look. "Yeah," she told him, "I'm talking about you, needle-dick."

"That's not going to help," said Marc. Rays of sunlight came through the slit windows in the top of the van as they turned and picked up speed. He leaned over and she did the same, so they could talk quietly to one another. "I ran the same Europol line I gave before, told them Ramaas was a terrorist and we were chasing him down." He gave a weak grin. "They didn't buy it. I reckon someone up top in the Dubai police knows who Jalsa Sood really was. I reckon they're going to try and fit us up for the murders at his place. Gloss over Jalsa's terrorist past and make it look like it was a high-end car theft gone wrong, or something . . ."

"Yeah . . ." Lucy considered that. It wouldn't do for it to become public knowledge that the city had been home to a notorious bomb-maker for the past decade. "And meanwhile, Ramaas has gone dark."

Marc glanced around. "The way I figure it? They've already got an inkling who we really are . . . They must have checked us out on the international crimes database. I mean, Europol and me are not exactly on the best of terms after I split from Split and then there's your reputation with the US government . . ."

She gave him a hard look that prevented Marc from adding any more to that sentence. "So. Extradition."

"Don't hold your breath," he corrected. "I'm willing to bet they'll keep us around for a while. Foreigners behaving badly always plays well with the locals, right? They'll take us to the central nick in Al Awir . . . And that'll be the last we ever see of each other."

"If we're lucky." Lucy thought it odd that the pair of them had been put in the same van with two male cops, considering the UAE's laws about fraternisation between genders. She considered another possibility—that they were being driven to some isolated spot out in the desert where they would be quietly disappeared. The look in Dane's eyes told her he was thinking along similar lines.

Lucy watched him intently for a moment. "What?" he said.

"I know you got an idea, Dane. I mean, you're good at this stuff, right? *On the fly?*"

He scowled. "Most of my ideas involve me being in a better position than chained up in the back of a paddy wagon."

"Hey, you already broke out of *one* prison this week. How hard is it going to be to do it again?"

"We got no weapons, no tech, no backup," said Marc. "Don't think I don't appreciate your renewed confidence in me, but I can't spin straw into gold."

"We get to Al Awir, or wherever, and that's game over," she told him. Lucy felt her anger kindling. "I had a gutful of the convict life once already. Not doing it again, not here." She glared at the cop with the iPhone. "I'm already sick of this place and everyone in it." She remembered the glittering spires of the rich districts and the crushing inequality they had seen in the concrete dorms of the worker-town. Prison would be little better.

The police officer met her gaze. "You both be quiet," he said firmly.

"Or what?" Marc snarled. "You going to slap me around a little more? Of course, there's only two of you this time. Don't like those odds, do you?"

For the first time, Lucy noticed that the other cop in the back of the van had a swollen eye hidden underneath the sunglasses he was wearing, and he shifted uncomfortably at Marc's words. *Tougher than you're giving him credit for,* she thought again.

Very deliberately, Marc met Lucy's gaze and then shot a sideways look at the cop who had spoken. Marc's eyes flicked to the man and then down to his phone. He cocked his head. The gesture said, *Get me?*

She did. Lucy looked at Marc, at the police officer with the black eye and then gave an imperceptible nod.

So that was how they were going to do it, the brute-force approach. Crude, but neither of them could afford to be choosy right now. She smiled thinly. That was fine with her. A bit of rage-work would do a lot to even out her foul mood.

Lucy was subtly adjusting herself when the van came to a sudden halt, braking with a lurch that rocked the prisoners in their seats. The cop's iPhone gave off a soft ping and he made a disgusted face.

Lucy hesitated, thinking about how she might take him down. With the cuffs, there was only so far she could move.

The last thing she expected was for the transport's back doors to swing open. Lucy smelled seawater and rust, and she heard the calling of gulls. Without a word, the two cops got up and climbed out of the vehicle, but not before one of them tossed the keys for the cuffs on the floor between Marc and Lucy's feet. Puzzled, they both watched the police officers disappear out of sight through the open doors.

She shot Marc a wary look. "How did you do that?"

"Do what?"

"Was it the phone, or something? You send him a message?"

"With what?" Marc clutched at the keys and opened his cuffs. "Happy thoughts?" He did the same for Lucy and she shook off the steel bracelets, massaging her wrists.

She stood up and took a step toward the door, but Marc's hand shot out to grab her arm. "Wait a second. What if this is a set-up? Could be they're letting us go so they can shoot us while we're trying to escape."

Lucy mulled that over. "Possible," she admitted, "but I am damned if I'm going back to jail again. I'll take my chances."

Warily, they scrambled down out of the back of the van and onto a concrete dock. Marc scanned their surroundings. "We're on the coast."

Off to one side there was the vast construct of the Palm, an artificial island growing out of the Dubai waterfront, and in the other direction there were the numerous slips and moorings of a massive yacht club.

The two cops returned and climbed back into the rear of the prisoner transport, closing the doors behind them. The van's engine had been idling all the while, and now it rumbled again as it drove away, leaving Lucy and Marc alone—and quite free—beneath the harsh sun of the day.

"I honestly have no idea how or why that happened," said Marc, after a moment.

"It did not come cheaply," said a voice from behind them. Henri Delancort leaned out from beneath a sunshade over a motor launch tethered to the dock. As they approached, Malte Riis climbed out of the boat, his pale face impassive beneath a straw hat. He gave Lucy a brief nod and walked on past her, in the direction of the city.

"Where's he going?" said Marc.

"Malte has the admirable task of containing any blowback from your little escapade in the desert," said Delancort, and he beckoned them impatiently. "Well, come on. *Vite, vite.* Before the locals have a change of heart."

Lucy climbed into the launch and Marc followed suit. "Rubicon sent us a boat?" added the Brit.

"This isn't Mr. Solomon's boat." Delancort shook his head and pointed to a mooring out past the artificial island, where a sleek giga-yacht in silver and sky blue lay at anchor. "*That* is Mr. Solomon's boat," he corrected.

The rain was hammering down so hard on the plastic cowling around the payphone that Horvat had to jam the blocky pink handset into his ear, so he could hear the voice on the other end of the line. "*Listen to me, Franko. As your lawyer, I have to tell you that this is the only card you have left to play. You've got to come in and surrender yourself to the police. They have the city sealed up tight!*"

"Piss off," he spat back. "Turn myself in? Those bastards all hate me!"

"*I don't disagree,*" came the weary reply. "*But if you come in, we can play it by the book. Cut a deal.*" There was a pause. "*I've heard some things. It's not just the cops who are looking for you. You've made a lot of enemies over the years, you know that. I'm told people are asking questions. Not locals.*"

Horvat grimaced through the rain at the frontage of the bank across the street, finding the ornate clock above the door. He watched the sweep of the minute hand, knowing exactly how long it would take to run a trace on the location he was calling from.

"*I can probably get you a reduced sentence,*" the lawyer went on, "*but you'll need to come clean about everything.*"

"I am not going to prison!" Horvat snapped. "I won't last a day! Too many people in there I put away want a piece of me."

"*Just talk to—*"

A jolt of paranoia ran through him. "You're trying to keep me on the line, aren't you? Are they there with you right now?"

"*No, Franko, no—*"

He shook his head. "I'll make my own deal. You're fired!" Horvat slammed the phone down. He turned up his collar before jogging out across the rainy street and into the bank's main entrance.

He gave the duty manager a false name and got rid of her as soon as the woman gave him access to the safety deposit vault in the basement, where his box was waiting. There was hardly anyone around at this time of the morning, and Horvat dragged the metal container into a private booth off the vault. He dropped it onto a table and blew out a breath.

His comfortable life as a corrupt cop was now in tatters, and that meant Horvat could trust no one and take nothing for granted. He could only go back to what he knew would work—blackmail.

Inside the box was a stash of money, an untraceable gun as well as more fake IDs and blank credit cards—a "parachute" package that he had gathered up over the years for just such a turn of events. But the real riches were a shopping bag filled with stolen files, compromising photographs and old tape cassettes that contained enough dirt to ruin the lives of a lot of high-profile people. Horvat upended the box onto the table and began to transfer the contents to a sling bag he had brought with him.

The annex's privacy curtain slid back and Horvat whirled angrily around, furious at this disturbance, his hand snatching at the pistol.

A round-faced Asian man in a black jacket and trousers stood there, holding a silenced gun of his own. "Good morning, Detective

Inspector Horvat," he began, his words careful and firm. "Step away from the table."

Horvat released his grip on the pistol and did as he was told. "Who the fuck sent you?"

"My name is Saito," he replied. "I was not sent to find you specifically, per se. But we have crossed paths because you are a node in my investigation."

"A what?" Horvat bristled at the man's lecturing tone. "I am a police officer. You can't threaten me!"

"Technically, you are not," said Saito. "There is a warrant for your arrest." He glanced at the blackmail files. "You stole the security monitor hard drive from the Queen's High casino. Where is it?"

"How do you know—?"

"Where?" repeated Saito, taking a step closer. His gun never wavered.

Carefully, Horvat reached into his bag and removed the book-sized computer component, and put it on top of the pile. "Listen to me. There's a lot of stuff here. It's worth hundreds of thousands of euros, millions maybe. How about I walk away and you get to keep it all, eh?"

Saito gave a brief shake of the head. "I have a counter-offer," he said. "As I stated, I am not specifically interested in you. But you are the only person I have been able to locate who can tell me about the man that Neven and Bojan Kurjak were dealing with, before the former vanished and the latter was killed."

"The African?" Horvat's brow furrowed. This line of questioning was not what he had been expecting. "You're talking about that pirate with the dead eye . . ."

"Tell me everything you know about him and you can walk out of this building." Saito let the gun muzzle drop away as a gesture of good faith.

Horvat chewed on it for a moment. He had nothing to lose. Bojan might be dead, but the Serbs and their new friend were ultimately responsible for all of his woes, and if he could do something to ruin their lives, the venal and spiteful part of Horvat's nature demanded that he do so.

He dredged up every minor detail he could recall about the pirate and the Kurjaks, everything he'd ever overheard or seen in recent days or before. Saito recorded him speaking on a slim digital device the size of a pen, prompting him for clarifications now and then, but mostly staying silent.

"Ramaas," he said, when Horvat was done. "The man's name is Ramaas?"

Horvat nodded. "So I can go now?"

Saito approached the table and separated the pile atop it into two. He pushed one half—the money, the gun and the IDs—toward Horvat, and the other—the blackmail files and the hard drive—he patted with his hand. "I will keep these. My employer might find them useful."

Horvat wasted no time shoving his spoils into the sling bag and getting out of there. Huffing and puffing, he took the stairs up from the basement as fast as he could and dashed across the bank's wide hall toward the main doors, desperate to get away.

It was only as he got to the doors that his brain caught up to the fact that the bank was empty. Horvat's head whipped around and his heart sank as he saw a rank of blue-and-white patrol cars parked outside and officers in the black tactical gear of the Special Police unit aiming assault rifles at him through the driving rain.

He hesitated on the threshold. Had the man who called himself Saito set him up, or had he been too long on the phone to avoid a trace?

Then Horvat saw Saito emerge from the stairs to the basement. He had turned the dark jacket he was wearing inside out, and now Horvat could see the word POLICIJA written across the back. As he walked up, Saito was unscrewing the silencer from the muzzle of his gun. He aimed the pistol at the glass frontage of the building and pulled the trigger, blind-firing in the direction of the patrol cars outside. The black-clad tactical team reacted in kind.

"No!" Horvat screamed, pushing open the door and raising his hands. "Don't, it wasn't—"

But they were already returning fire, and Franko Horvat went down in a hail of bullets.

SEVENTEEN

The yacht was called the *Themis*, and the Greek Titaness of mythology she was named after greeted them in the atrium beyond the sun deck where they boarded. An abstract meter-high statue made of copper showed a woman holding a sword, point down, in one hand and a set of balanced scales in the other. The sun glittered off the sculpture's androgynous face as she stared out at nothing.

"Lady Justice," said Lucy, and gestured at the piece of art. "Isn't she supposed to have a blindfold on, or something?"

Delancort shook his head. "That's a detail that artists added in the fifteenth century. Justice should never be blind. At least, that's what Mr. Solomon has told me."

"Is he here?" Marc glanced at the French Canadian.

"Still in Monaco." Delancort walked past him. "He's been very busy. More so, after the mess you made for us in Dubai." He sighed. Solomon's aide had listened carefully as Marc and Lucy had filled him in on what happened in the Emirates as they sailed across from the dock, taking in everything with stoic nods of the head. "Despite what you may believe, my job is not solely to clean up after you."

"We didn't have a lot of choice," said Marc. "We got here too late. Ramaas was already in play."

"And now he is, as the Americans say, *in the wind*. And you found yourself arrested. Your divergence from the script in Poland was bad enough, but this goes well beyond that."

Somewhere off toward the front of the boat, a bell trilled twice and Marc heard the rumble of diesel motors beneath his feet. *Themis* was weighing anchor and preparing to set sail.

"We could have got out of it," Lucy insisted. Marc decided not to disagree with her. "We were working on a thing."

Marc halted, glancing around the brushed steel and azure glass of the yacht's modernist interior. The vessel had the same design aesthetic that he had seen before, on Solomon's private jet. It was all clean, smooth lines, every surface and accessory resembling a perfectly machined part for some colossal, elegant engine. The boat had to be a hundred and sixty meters long at least, and Marc wondered again about the enigmatic billionaire's resources. "How did you get them to release us without charge?" He looked out of a panoramic window, beyond which the towers of Dubai were beginning to diminish.

"When you missed your scheduled check-in, we employed digital assets to track your whereabouts." Delancort raised an eyebrow. "I wasn't surprised when Kara back-traced warrant searches based off your fingerprints to the Dubai police force. From there, it was simply a matter of applying the correct leverage."

Lucy's expression stiffened. "You paid them off? Are you telling me that Solomon cut those assholes a check so we could walk?" Her voice rose as she spoke. "Have you been over there, Delancort? Have you seen what it's like outside the malls and the nightclubs? The last thing the people running that city need is more money—"

"Calm down." Delancort shook his head. "Remember who we are talking about. Do you believe for one moment that Ekko Solomon has any illusions about the human rights abuses taking place out of sight here? You know him, Lucy. You know he would not be a party to enriching those responsible for such things."

"So explain what you meant by 'leverage,'" she demanded.

Delancort gave a familiar Gallic shrug. "We did have to agree to replace the Bugatti you destroyed with one from Mr. Solomon's personal collection. But as to the matter of your incarceration, well . . ." He paused, framing his words. "Rubicon owns controlling stock in a large investment bank that several Dubai interests are in partnership with."

"You mean, *owe money to,*" corrected Marc. "I've heard the stories about investors overspending to keep that city from falling back into the desert."

"Quite," allowed Delancort. "The suggestion was made that certain loans would immediately be foreclosed unless an accommodation could be met. And so it was."

The explanation wasn't enough for Lucy, however, and she scowled. "Serve them right if that place drowns in the sand," she muttered. "I need to go clean up."

"You both do," Delancort said curtly. "I will get to work on the information you gave me. In the meantime, there are cabins set up on the guest deck."

A shower and a change of clothes made Marc feel almost human again.

He helped himself to the contents of a medical kit that the *Themis*'s crew had thoughtfully provided, patching up the various bruises and cuts that a couple of days on the wrong side of Dubai had left him with.

By the time he exited the cabin, it was late in the day and the sun was dipping toward the horizon as the yacht hugged the Emirati coastline, heading northeast into the Strait of Hormuz. The boat's powerful engines were making good headway, the blade-like silhouette of the *Themis* cutting quickly through the littoral waters.

Finding his way back to the main deck, Marc mentally unfolded a map of the region. It was another of his more useful skills, one that had made him invaluable as an Officer Observer back in his days with the Royal Navy's Fleet Air Arm, the knack of being able to hold a chart in his head as though he had it in his hands. Allied with a superlative sense of direction, it meant he rarely got lost.

If he guessed right, the *Themis* would enter the Gulf of Oman by nightfall and then they'd be free to set a course for . . . *where?* He doubted very much that Solomon would want them to come and pick him up in Monte Carlo. The Horn of Africa, and the pirate Ramaas's home territory, was a lot closer.

Marc paused to watch the ocean, letting his mind drift with the waves for a moment, listening to the steady rush of the water along the hull. He hadn't had a single moment to stop and process what was going on around him since that day in the gym, when Luka Pavic had brought him the information from his cousin. It was hard to grasp that it had been less than a week since that happened. It felt like months. The confrontation in the burning building, tracking Ramaas to the casino and then getting shut down by Schrader . . . All that had been the precursor to the course he was on now, working with Rubicon's Special Conditions Division and grasping his way toward stopping a ruthless killer from doing something terrible.

I've been here before, he told himself. *Last time we got through more by luck than judgment. This time . . . ?* Marc sighed, and from out of nowhere came a sudden, acute pang of loneliness. For a second, he had a total and true sense of just how far away he was from his old life. Unbidden, the emotion turned bitter and he frowned as a question he had kept silent for over a year now pushed its way forward. "What the hell are you doing with your life, man?"

"Say what?" He turned as he heard Lucy approaching. "Who are you talking to?"

"Myself. I know—first sign of madness, my mum always used to say."

Lucy gave him an odd look. "She still around?"

"No."

"But your sister is, right?"

"Yeah," he said, at length. "We don't talk much, though."

"Make the effort." Lucy had a look in her eyes he hadn't seen before, one that Marc couldn't place. Then it was gone and she was all business again. "But not right this second. C'mon. Solomon wants us downstairs."

"I thought he wasn't on the boat."

"Trust me, he can be in two places at once if he wants."

Lucy led Marc below, through sections of the yacht that were used as a reception room and a library, before bringing him into a large compartment that took up most of the width of the hull.

Marc's first thought was of the Hub White facility at MI6's headquarters in Vauxhall Cross, a compact, carefully engineered crisis center banked with video display screens and data consoles. The light level in the room was low, illuminated by the screens and a soft blue glow that came from several door-sized panes of glass that extended from floor to ceiling. Like the smart windows in Rubicon's Monaco office, the panes here were filled with waterfalls of information moving in a constant flow of new intelligence.

Kara Wei stood up from a keyboard and gave them both of them a jaunty wave. "Hey. Glad you're not dead."

"Us too," said Lucy.

"Got something you might want to look at." She offered Marc a set of chunky, over-engineered digital glasses with a laser projector built into the frame. He eyed them warily. "Put these on," Kara told Marc, making the motion for him. "Can't see it without them."

He slipped the glasses over his nose and recoiled. Floating in front of him was a blurry, pixelated image of a distorted metal box. He blinked. "What is this? It's out of focus."

"Use your hand." Kara grabbed his wrist and moved it so his fingers were up in front of his face. The image of the box immediately reacted as though he had touched it. "Synthetic haptic response, see?"

"Oh, right." Marc reached out and put his fingers where the box would be if it were really there. He pinched a corner of it and found he could move it around. The virtual-reality device responded smoothly to his gestures. "So, what? There's a motion tracker in the specs following my hand movements?"

"Yeah, you got it. We built that image out of high-definition object data that was uploaded to the UAE national police server. Recognize anything?"

"You look like you're swatting flies," said Lucy. "Or signing something."

"It's the suitcase." Marc kept his head steady, and slowly turned the distorted lump of steel around in mid-air. "The one that fell out the back of the Merc when we were chasing it."

"The fake bomb?"

"Yeah, lucky for us." He studied the ruined interior of the simulated device. "It's a mess. I suppose the local coppers must have recovered it from the roadway."

"They have any idea what it was supposed to be?" continued Lucy.

"It would appear not," said Kara. "Probably a good thing."

Marc tried to visualize what the fake would have looked like when it was intact, and he felt a chill run up his spine as he recalled what he had seen in Neven Kurjak's case back in Croatia. The ruined replica of the Exile device was convincing, even half-smashed. He pulled it closer to him, trying to examine the cylindrical sections that made up the core of the unit, but the image began to lose definition.

Right cylinder, nine rods. Those had been Jalsa Sood's dying words to him, but without an intact example of his work, Marc could only guess at what the old bomb-maker had been trying to tell him. Unable to gain any more from the image, he handed the VR glasses back to Kara.

Delancort entered, working at a digital pad. "Mr. Solomon will be conferencing with us in a few minutes—we're just waiting for an optimal satellite position for the link," he explained, and his usual unflappable mask faltered. "Something is up," he admitted. "The usual levels of signal encryption have been doubled."

Marc and Lucy exchanged glances. "So while we've got time to kill, some questions," she began. "Do we know what the Dubai police are doing about the kills at Sood's place? I mean, there's a dozen bodies there, including an escaped Al Sayf terrorist. Once they figure out what they have, it's going to be a big deal."

"They're nothing if not good at being discreet," said Delancort. "Malte has been monitoring them. The public line is that the estate belonging to one Mr. Vishal Daan has been closed off because of . . ." He glanced at his pad to find the relevant data. "A *gas leak*."

"The locals are going to want to make this all go away," said Kara. "I would not like to be them when the CIA find out they're sitting on Jadeed Amarah's corpse."

"Is that likely to happen?" said Lucy.

Kara gave an airy shrug. "Oh, someone may have dropped an email containing that very information on a secure server at Langley. Just saying."

Marc nodded at the screens. "So what about the two jokers in the red BMW we ran off the road, and the guy Ramaas ditched? Got any intel on them?"

Delancort found another file, and with a swipe of his hand he migrated it to one of the glass panels. Marc saw still images of the crimson Z4 abandoned in a roadside ditch. "Malte managed to intercept this for us. The body of an African male of unknown identity was found in the vehicle, dead from multiple gunshot wounds." He glanced at Lucy, then away again. "Police on site reported that there was evidence of another person in the car, but no one else was found in the area."

"So the driver bolted," said Lucy. "Which means he's either lying low, or more likely he connected up with Ramaas after his boss pulled the dirt-bike trick." She looked toward Kara. "You got any leads on that?"

"There's like thousands of motorcycles in Dubai alone, not counting unregistered ones." Kara gave a slow shake of the head. "Give me full access to all of their traffic cameras and a week to sift the data and I might be able to find the bikes. Emphasis on *might*."

"No time for that. We need to go back to core principles," said Marc firmly. Intelligence analysis and pattern matching was something else he was good at, and he called on those talents right now, grabbing another digital tablet. He began to leaf through the intelligence data they had on the warlord. "Forget everything else. Ramaas is at the middle of all this, he has been from the start. We've got to put all our energy into tracking him down."

"We need to find out where he sleeps," agreed Lucy. "We get to him, we get to the weapon."

"What makes you so sure?" said Delancort.

"Gut instinct," she replied. "A guy like that, he hasn't got a lot of trust to spread around."

"It's time," said Delancort, and he stepped aside to face one of the smart-glass panels.

The data displayed here became a haze of photons that flickered and re-formed into an image of Ekko Solomon, seated behind his desk at the Monaco office. It was late afternoon there and the sun was still high in the sky behind him. The glass panel suddenly became a doorway, and Marc imagined it was a portal through which the other man could step through.

"Mr. Dane, Lucy. You are both uninjured?"

"More or less," said Marc. "Thanks for the get-out-of-jail-free card."

"*It is only money,*" said Solomon, and from the corner of his eye Marc saw Delancort actually wince at the words. "*And after what has happened in the past hour, it would seem that an investment in intelligence about Abur Ramaas is about to become a far more valuable commodity.*"

Lucy made a face. "I don't follow."

"*While you were being extracted from Dubai, events have proceeded apace,*" Solomon said grimly.

Marc's throat became dry as his mind raced with the worst of possibilities. "Tell me he didn't . . . set off the device?"

"*Not yet.*" Solomon tapped a control panel inset on his desk. "*Observe. I am relaying you a video file that was passed on to Rubicon from a contact we have in the Chinese Ministry for State Security . . .*"

One of the wall screens blinked into life, and Marc was suddenly looking at Ramaas, as the man sat indolently in a large wicker chair against a stone wall. Waxy evening light filled the room, but there was little other detail to make it clear where and when it had been shot. Marc knew, however, and he glanced at Lucy, getting a nod from her. "That's Jalsa Sood's mansion," he said. "Which means this must have been recorded in the last few days."

Ramaas leaned back in the chair, beckoning whomever was holding the camera to bring it closer. "*Take a good look at me,*" said the pirate warlord, enunciating his words in steady, measured English. "*You men of power. See this face and know who and what it is that is coming to punish you.*" He pointed a finger at his dead, dark eye. "*I will show you something. You will see.*"

The video jumped in a hard edit to show metal decking, in some location that Marc did not recognize. The camera panned over a sheaf of military blueprints covered in Cyrillic text and found a steel case lying there. Thin, spindly fingers came in to open the steel lid and reveal the device inside.

Marc tensed in spite of himself, and he felt a strange pressure behind his eyes, like a tiny pre-echo of the nuclear weapon's contained destructive power.

"*There is a name for this thing,*" continued Ramaas, over the playback. "*Exile.*" He sounded out the word. "*But I call it what it is. This is a piece of the sun.*" The camera zoomed in on a metal plate riveted to the inside of the steel case, blurring before it sharpened again.

"What's he doing?" said Kara.

"He's showing us the device's registration tag," Marc explained. "So it can be checked out by the people in the know . . ."

"Proving his bona fides," added Lucy.

The view cut to Ramaas in his chair. He sat in it like a king upon a throne. "*My nation has been through much hardship, thanks to all of you. Our shoreline poisoned and our harvest from the sea stolen away, by you. Our cities ruined by your soldiers. And before that, our lands were taken by your colonials through force of arms. When we defended our-selves, when we did what we had to in order to survive, you called us brig-ands. Pirates and criminals.*" He gave a humorless smile. "*But we have learned from you in that time, oh, yes. You have taught us.*"

"I don't like where this is going," said Lucy quietly.

Ramaas stood up slowly and walked toward the camera. "*The lesson is, that a nation, a man, can go beyond being a criminal if his wrongdo-ing is large enough. And what crime is greater than war?*" He pointed out at his viewers. "*You fired the first shots. Now I have the power to de-clare a war on you, if I wish. Somalia will no longer be the whipping boy of the West. You will no longer ignore my nation. We have your weapons now. You will listen to us.*" His face filled the screen. "*You will respect us.*"

"He has just handed the world's superpowers a reason to bomb that country into the dust," noted Delancort. "The man is insane!"

"*Perhaps not,*" said Solomon. "*Keep watching.*"

There was another clumsy edit and the grain of the video changed. *A different camera,* thought Marc. There was no audio. The point of view panned around inside the back of an empty van as the vehicle rolled along a road, before dipping to show the same steel case at the camera operator's feet. The lid was open, the mechanism clearly visible. A gloved hand closed the lid as the van came to a halt and the view bounced around as the person holding it got out and started walking. The camera was aimed down at the ground, but it caught glimpses of other people's feet passing by and flashes of the steel case in the camera operator's hand. It was a bright day in whatever city the weapon had been taken to. The pavement turned into a white-striped crossing and then the ground underfoot changed from asphalt to a path through a park. Presently, the camera stopped moving and panned up. The steel case was resting against a metal fence, and just past it was a waterfront, with land visible across the distance. The view shifted until it found a blurry point on the horizon. The blur gradually resolved into the Statue of Liberty.

Marc heard Lucy swear under her breath. "That's Battery Park," she said stiffly. "Mom would take my brother and me there for picnics in the summer."

The show wasn't over. The image cut to a different stream of video. The set-up was the same; the interior of another van, the establishing shot of the Exile case and then motion as it was picked up and carried out onto the street. This time, the pavement was made up of diamond-shaped slabs and the ambient light was dull, from an overcast sky. Marc instinctively felt something familiar about the glimpses he was getting. Somewhere with older architecture, somewhere European?

This time, when the case was put down on the ground, the camera rose to show a wide open plaza of stone cobbles. In the distance was a set of minarets and distinctive onion domes clustered together. "St. Basil's Cathedral in Moscow," said Marc. "This was shot in Red Square."

Then, for the third and final time, the video flickered into a new view. It began with the camera operator pointing the lens down at a black rucksack similar to the kind that were owned by thousands of world travelers. Gloved hands opened the rucksack and removed the familiar steel case, opening it briefly to show off the inner workings before returning it to its place. Gray paving stones and dozens of pairs of feet flashed past as the person with the camera made their way through a dense crowd. Then finally they halted, showing the rucksack again and a silver corner of the case peeking out from inside. The camera was set on the ground and tilted upward until the view was filled by the tiers of a massive building with a swooping roof in the style of a feudal Chinese palace. Crowds of tourists milled around in front of the building, posing for snapshots.

"I know where that is, I've been there," said Kara. "That's the Gate of Divine Might. One of the entrances to the Forbidden City."

"New York, Moscow and Beijing," said Delancort. "I will say this for him, he is not one for aiming low."

"How did he get them there?" said Lucy.

"We've been off the grid for more than a day," noted Marc. "Long enough to sneak the cases in on a cargo plane or something . . . And we know our guy has the contacts to do it."

At length, the video playback returned to Ramaas once more, and he was nodding to himself. *"Which of those devices is the real weapon? If you test us, you will learn."* He let that sink in. *"If you attempt any action against us, if your militaries advance toward our nation, you will learn."* He waved the camera away, as if he had become bored with it. *"Now, go and think on your crimes, and consider what compensation you might provide for them."*

The recording ended and Marc released a breath he had been holding. "This guy, he's got some stones. Ramaas is using the bomb for a power play. He's declared Somalia a nuclear-armed rogue state."

"He doesn't have the authority to speak for the whole country," said Delancort.

"Who would have the courage to stand against him?" said Solomon. *"He already has a substantial power base . . . And by threatening the superpowers on their own terms, there are many who would consider him a heroic figure . . ."*

"Delancort is right. Ramaas must know that this makes him the most wanted man on the planet!" Lucy said hotly. "He's painted a target on his chest and invited America, Russia and China to step up and take a shot! What's going to stop any one of them sending in a black-ops team to blow the shit out of his little pirate empire?"

"That won't be the first option," noted Marc. "Right now, the CIA, the FSB and Chinese state security are tearing that video to bits in analysis, trying to track down whomever shot the footage and make sure they don't have a loose nuke in their backyard . . ."

"But there's only one device," said Kara. "Marc, you said you saw it in Croatia, when Ramaas got away."

"But there were five in the boot of the Merc we chased," he said. "One got run over. Three we saw in the video. That leaves one unaccounted for, and it could be anywhere." He frowned. "Like I said before . . . Ramaas is playing a shell game with us. We don't know which are dummies and which are not."

"*But now we know what he wanted with Jalsa Sood,*" said Solomon. "*A smokescreen.*"

"Sood told me something before he died." Marc relayed the bomb-maker's final, cryptic statement. "Maybe if we can get a better look at the devices on the video, that might give us a steer?"

Kara nodded. "Let me see if I can work up something with the digital imaging guys at the Palo Alto office." She dropped into a seat in front of a computer console. "It'll mean getting them out of bed, but they do like a challenge . . ."

"That's a start," said Marc, glancing at Lucy. "But Lucy was dead-on, what she said before. We've got to find this guy and figure out what his *real* game plan is."

Lucy gave Marc a nod of agreement.

"So we have to break it down. What does Ramaas want?"

"Money," offered Kara, without looking up from her console. "What did he say at the end of the video?"

"*Consider what compensation you might provide,*" repeated Delancort. "That certainly sounds like a man looking for a pay-off. One could read that as a tacit offer to cash in his nuclear device for recompense."

"It fits the pirate *modus operandi,*" said Marc, but Lucy could tell he wasn't convinced. Both of them had stood in the same room as Abur Ramaas and they shared a similar impression of him. "Take a hostage, demand a release fee. Except this time, the hostage is a city and not some unlucky freighter crew."

"But you don't buy that?" Lucy prompted.

"Nope." The Brit gave a firm shake of the head. "He's sending mixed messages, isn't he? Asking for money, that's a brigand move. But earlier on he's kicking off about the injustices done to him and his country. Ramaas is demanding *respect.*"

A chill prickled Lucy's skin as another possibility occurred to her. "There's a third option. He's doing this out of ideology. Because he believes in something. And zealots are always the hardest ones to predict."

"Kara will concentrate on supervising analysis of the video," said Solomon, shifting in his distant, sun-lit office. *"But I believe that if Rubicon is to be of use, we must commit to an act of intervention now, before Ramaas solidifies his position."* He looked out of the screen and directly at Marc and Lucy. *"Agreed?"*

They both gave a nod. "So, circling back to the question of the hour," said Marc, "where the hell is he?"

"Henri, show them the intercept data," ordered Solomon.

Delancort frowned, but he did as he was told. With more flicks of his wrist, Solomon's aide sent digital information windows to the display panels around them. Lucy recognized a "heat map" of Somalia, with areas along the coastline dotted with zones of glowing colors. The regions were clustered largely in the areas of major urban centers, hot reds and oranges in the cities fading to cooler blues and greens in the more sparsely populated areas.

"You may not be aware that the Horn of Africa has one of the highest usage-per-person rates for cellular telephones on the planet. Somalia alone has a dozen different telecommunication suppliers serving the population."

"That's because landlines are unreliable," said Lucy. "Collapsed infrastructure and graft in the government means phone lines don't get fixed. The people out there are adaptable . . . They use what they have to hand."

"Indeed," said Solomon. *"Rubicon has invested heavily in the region . . . Including fronting a major cell phone provider. This map shows the areas where Rubicon-manufactured SIM cards are in use."*

"That's a lot of coverage," noted Marc.

"That's deliberate," said Delancort, off a nod from Solomon. "For some time now, we have been discounting the cost of SIMs in this region, undercutting or buying out the competition, all to widen the spread of Rubicon's market share."

"You're listening in." Lucy felt that chill on her flesh return. "You're running all the phone conversations in your network through an Echelon server, sifting for keywords."

"Most recently for specific references to Abur Ramaas," said Delancort. "Nothing from the man himself or his close confidantes, but we've assembled some consistent locational intelligence in the last fifteen hours."

"*It is for a greater good,*" insisted Solomon, seeing the look on her face. "*America and the NATO powers have been doing the same for decades, for far less altruistic reasons.*"

Lucy's eyes narrowed and she hovered on the verge of expressing her disquiet about Solomon's revelation—but then a voice in the back of her head reminded Lucy that she had come into her employment with Rubicon with her eyes wide open. She had known from the start what tools Ekko Solomon had at his disposal, and how he wanted to use them. Lucy glanced at Marc and once again, she knew he was thinking the same thing.

They had hacked into a cellular network only a few days ago to capture a call from Neven Kurjak's smartphone, but he had been just one man, and a known criminal. This was an intrusion on a far greater scale, involving hundreds of thousands of innocent people. Was it right to do something like this?

For today . . . With these stakes . . . I'm going to say it is. She took a breath and buried her misgivings. *Tomorrow, though . . . That may be different.*

"Okay," Marc broke in, "if we're all going to pretend we're happy ignoring the egregious violation of civil rights that just happened, let's not waste the opportunity. What have you got?"

Delancort told them the cell phone traffic picked up spikes in conversations that included Ramaas's name and that of Welldone Amadayo, an influential local power-broker who was suspected of widespread corruption. By all accounts, Amadayo had been killed by the pirate warlord's men and in the ensuing vacuum, those among the rich elites in Mogadishu and nearby regions were running scared. The intelligence gleaned from thousands of local phone calls over the past few days showed that Amadayo's private estate was now home to a cadre of armed men whom no one dared to challenge.

"You reckon Ramaas has taken this Welldone guy's place for himself?" Lucy turned the idea over in her mind. "That's pretty thin."

"We know that Ramaas was there the day before he flew to Croatia to meet with the Serbians," said Solomon. *"We believe that he murdered Amadayo."*

"He likes the personal touch," muttered Marc, then looked up. "Think about it. He didn't need to go to Split in person, he didn't need to go to Dubai to find Sood. He did all that because he wants to look people in the eye."

"That sounds like someone who likes to send a message," offered Kara.

Lucy folded her arms. She wasn't convinced, but then again in the past she had pulled the trigger on operations with less intel than this. "Okay. So we infiltrate this dead guy's place and track Ramaas from there? That's the plan?"

"There's no time to spend on surveillance and prep," added Marc. "It would have to be a lightning-strike raid."

"Did you just volunteer?" Lucy raised an eyebrow.

That knocked him off his pace. "I, uh, well . . ." He swallowed hard, realizing what he was getting into. "I am the only one here who's seen the device up close. If it's there—"

She shook her head and spoke over him, turning to look toward Solomon. "Ramaas knows our faces now, and so do his men. If he's as dialed in as we think he is, he'll make us the moment we step off the plane, or the boat or whatever. And a land crossing over the border from Kenya or Ethiopia could take days." Lucy ran the scenario in her head. Ramaas had threatened nuclear detonation if military force was deployed toward Somalia, so that meant that flying in by helicopter wouldn't work either. If the American drone assets patrolling outside the border didn't interdict them first, odds were that the locals would shoot them down before they could reach the outskirts of Mogadishu where Amadayo's estate was located. "We need the quick and direct approach," Lucy went on, and nodded toward Marc. "Out of the sky like lightning, just as you said." A plan began to form.

"I have the sudden sense I am going to regret those words," said the Brit.

A smile pulled at her lips. "You know how to use a parachute, right?"

— EIGHTEEN —

Marc hunched forward in the canvas seat and tried to ignore the steady vibration coming up through his feet and into his bones. The skin of his face felt raw and uncomfortable beneath the breather mask clamped over his nose and mouth. It had been necessary to shave off all his scraggly facial hair in order for the mask to make a good seal, and now he was resisting the urge to scratch. Cool, pure oxygen had been cycling into his lungs for the last couple of hours and he was finally getting past the light-headedness as his body equalized itself to the air mixture.

He cradled a smartphone in his gloved hands, one of Rubicon's hi-spec custom models that packed a ton of cutting-edge tech into something small enough to slip into his pocket. The unmarked device was built out of scratchproof glass surrounded by a reflectionless carbon-fiber shell, and it replaced the one that he had lost in Dubai. The spyPhone, as Kara Wei liked to call it, advanced in capability each time he got a new version—and that happened a lot, as she took every opportunity to remind him. He had no idea what happened to the phones that got left behind in the field, but knowing the attention to detail shown by Rubicon's Special Conditions Division, he didn't doubt they had some kind of self-bricking mode that rendered them useless after the fact.

Marc busied himself configuring the new device's settings to the way he liked them, trying to find a moment of peace in the mundanity of the task. It didn't work.

He shifted uncomfortably in his matte black jumpsuit and tactical rig. It was fresh out of the package and scratchy, and along with the mask, helmet, gloves and webbing, he felt as if he was wearing a costume more than a set of working clothes. Everything occurring around him had an artificial feel, as though it was happening to someone else. He frowned and pulled himself back to the moment.

The phone's satellite communications link blinked a green icon in the corner of the screen and in a moment it had flash-loaded data from the handful of contact blinds Marc had set up for himself. One of the off-grid phantom servers he employed ghosted the office email account Marc had used while working at the NSNS in Split, and he was about to scrub the numerous threatening messages from Schrader and de Wit when he noticed one of them was from Luka Pavic.

He read on. Pavic spoke better English than he wrote, but the salient points in the email were clear enough. The day before, an anonymous source had called in to the precinct with information about the whereabouts of one Franko Horvat, and his plans to rob a bank in the city. Marc didn't think for one second that the corrupt cop would ever have done something so blatantly stupid, but the police in Split had no choice but to respond to the tip-off.

Horvat had come out of the bank shooting, so the officers on site had said. Pavic's tone, even through the email, seemed unconvinced. But no one was going to look too hard at the brutal death of a man who was uniformly detested by crooks and cops alike.

Still, Pavic noted that there were questions that had no answers trailing in the wake of the bank shooting. A large safety-deposit box that had apparently belonged to Horvat was found empty and the bank's video security system had suffered a strangely convenient malfunction in the hours surrounding his arrival. More than that, Pavic said there was a rumor going around the station house that the gun recovered from Horvat's side had not been fired.

Marc tried to dismantle this new piece of information and figure out what it meant. The list of people who wanted Horvat crossed off was long and varied, but the timing of his death was too expedient. It felt like a loose end being tied up. Marc's frown deepened and he filed away the information for later consideration. He had more immediate matters to concentrate on, and he slipped the phone into a Velcro-sealed pocket.

"*Hey.*" Lucy's voice came through the radio bead built into his helmet, and he looked up. She stood before him, swaying slightly with the motion of the deck underfoot, dressed in the same gear as him. Only her eyes were visible, and they had her usual deceptively sleepy aspect to them. "*Still dizzy?*"

"I'm good," he replied, the mike in his oxygen mask picking up his words. "This is all a bit new to me," Marc went on. He looked away, taking in the cabin around them. The unpressurized cargo bay of the big C-130 Hercules resembled the inside of a railway carriage, one that had been stripped to the bare metal and redecorated with sheets of thermal cloth and bright red netting. Two crewmen in the uniform of the Omani Royal Air Force shared the space with them, but they had been ordered to keep themselves to themselves. Since Marc and Lucy had buttoned up in their tactical gear somewhere over the Gulf of Aden, they hadn't shared a word with either of them.

"*It's a piece of cake,*" she told him. "*All you gotta do is follow me and fall out a door.*" Lucy reached down and tapped the digital auto-altimeter on his wrist. "*This'll do the rest for you.*"

Marc couldn't help but throw a look toward the far end of the bay, where the Herc's cargo ramp was sealed tight. "I jumped out of a plane a couple of times, in OpTeam training with the SIS. But that was during daylight. And not so high up as to give me frostbite."

Lucy indicated the ice crystals gathered around the edges of the circular window near his head. "*We've been climbing for a while now. When we get to thirty thousand feet, we'll be in the zone. Can't fly lower than angels two-six out here, on account of SAMs and the like . . .*"

"Right." Marc craned his neck around to look out into the ink-dark sky, hoping to catch sight of the sea far below him, but all he saw was the steady blink of the aircraft's running lights and the blur of the blades on the turboprop engines. He met her gaze. "Is this you getting back at me for what happened with the Veyron? Cause that was not my fault."

"*Hey, this was your idea.*"

"It bloody well wasn't," he insisted. "You really like this whole 'falling from great heights' thing, don't you?"

Her eyes showed her smile. "*This'll be more fun than that wire-drop we did in New Jersey, trust me.*" Lucy straightened and became serious.

"*All right, you wanna run through it this one last time, or have you got it?*" She patted a window pocket on the forearm of her jumpsuit, where a map was stowed.

Marc shook his head and patted his own. "No, I'm good." He drew another deep breath of cool, metallic-tasting air through his mask. "Sooner we go, sooner we're down, right?"

"*Glad you said that,*" she noted, as the crewman started moving toward them. "*Last gear check.*"

Marc got to his feet and did a slow pirouette, letting her tug on fasteners and tabs. The parachute on his back felt awkward, pulling him off balance from the smaller pack hanging from his chest that contained an oxygen bottle, reserve chute and mission gear. He did the same for her, making sure nothing was loose.

She put her hands on the straps over his shoulders. "*These feel tight?*" The straps crossed over his chest and down around his crotch, hugging the contours of his body.

"Very."

"*Then that's not tight enough.*" Lucy yanked on the tabs and Marc lost a breath as he was almost throttled by the embrace of the straps.

"Thanks," he grunted.

The Omani jumpmaster paused to shout something to Lucy and she gave a nod in return. "*Here we go!*"

Marc felt the crewman's gaze rake over him and wondered what the guy was thinking. According to the flight plan, the Hercules was on a scheduled cargo run from the RAFO's base at Thumwait to a Kenyan military airstrip outside Mombasa, and the aircraft could not deviate from that course. But orders from high up in the Omani Air Force's chain of command had swapped out the usual cargo in favor of a man and a woman in high-spec stealth gear, with no explanations as to why. From what Marc understood, Ekko Solomon regularly played golf with the RAFO's chief of staff and getting them the use of the C-130 was the cashing-in of an old marker.

"*This won't be like the jumps you've done before,*" said Lucy. "*This is HAHO, high-altitude, high-opening. The chute will pop a few seconds after we hit sky, so be ready for it.*"

The ready light flashed on the cabin wall and the cargo ramp dropped open. A wall of polar-cold air rumbled in through the gap and Marc felt it wash over him. As they marched toward the widening gap, out beneath the tail of the Hercules he could see only depthless midnight blue. "So you've done this a bunch of times when you were with Delta Force, right?"

"*Actually, this is my first.*"

"What? Really?" The standby light changed to green and the jumpmaster gave a thumbs-up.

"*Nah,*" she said, and there was the smile again. "*Later.*" Without hesitating, Lucy stepped up to the edge and fell out into the void.

Then Marc was where she had been standing and he looked down, seeing moonlight off the Indian Ocean far below. "Green for go," he said to himself.

Marc pitched forward and gravity took him.

The thunderous wind plucking at the sleeves of his jumpsuit and the drag on the pit of his stomach told Marc that he was falling, even if the deep night around him was strangely static. Out of the corner of an eye, he briefly caught sight of a black shadow on the sky, a blink of light as the Hercules vanished away on its course. Then the aircraft was lost to him and he turned, orienting himself toward the ground.

He barely had a moment to steady himself before a mule-kick impact slammed him in the chest and pulled at his shoulders. His head snapped back and there was a flash of pain as the parachute exploded out of his pack, unfolding perfectly into a wide arc of aerofoil. Lucy had warned him that some HAHO jumpers were hit so hard by the violent wind at altitude that they were knocked unconscious, hence the auto-deploy linked to his altimeter.

Marc's hands snatched at the dangling control lines and a surge of relief shot through him as he grabbed hold. He gave the chute's steering an experimental tug and it let him drift right, then left.

"*Good deployment,*" radioed Lucy. "*I'm below you, your seven o'clock.*"

"Roger that." He looked and found a vague shape. Dull green glow strips on her gear vest and boots showed Marc where to find her. "I got you." As the more experienced jumper out of the two of them,

Lucy was the lead and she was carrying slightly more gear than Marc, in order to even up their weight so they would descend together.

"Stay on my six and follow me down. We got distance to cover, so stay sharp. Maintain radio silence until we're on the dirt."

"Copy." He nodded, not that she would have been able to see him.

They described a slow corkscrew turn away from the ocean and the coastline of Somalia made itself apparent far below them. Marc flicked a look at the map and saw where the bright splash of light that was Mogadishu extended out to the southwest. From high above, the city resembled a spray of hot orange sparks frozen in time. Looking northward, the color faded away as the urban sprawl petered out and became scrubland. He picked out other smaller townships up along the coast, reaching into the lawless regions that Ramaas and his pirate clan had made their heartland.

Their landing target was out beyond the eastern end of the Somalian capital, in an area that Welldone Amadayo and his wealthy friends had bought up over the last few years. Satellite photos showed naked plots of ground ready for the new rich to move in and start building, with Amadayo's estate being one of the notably larger domains. Marc recalled seeing clusters of single-story brick-and-clapboard houses grouped around one edge of the walled estate, like fungus growing on a rock. The dead man's neighbors were the ordinary and the poor, and Marc wondered how they felt about living next to a rich man's fortress.

Lucy continued her wide downward turn and Marc made sure he kept on her, trying not to tense up too much on the control lines. Now he was starting to pick out detail from the city below, and the tranquil nature of the first part of the descent faded. Being able to see buildings and streets turned the ground from something abstract to something real, and he was suddenly very aware of how fast they were falling. He ran through what he remembered from jump training with the SIS, repeating it to himself in preparation.

Marc checked the map again. They were still kilometers away from the drop zone, and now Lucy was vectoring into the wind up the coast as they silently drifted over Mogadishu's wide dusty highways and the endless grids of its side streets. Identical clusters of houses went on forever, broken here and there by bald patches of earth or clumps of greenery.

He wasn't really sure what he'd been expecting to see from up here. Most Westerners only knew the country and its fractured capital from war movies and disaster-laden news footage, but the place was quiet—no running battles in the streets, no fires burning out of control. How much of that was real peace or a deceptive mirage he couldn't tell, not until he was down in the dirt.

His radio crackled. *"Here we go,"* said Lucy. *"DZ in sight."*

"Yeah, got it." Marc looked for and found the Amadayo estate, becoming clearer now as it rose out of a low hillside. He could see light spilling from the windows in the mansion house and what looked like a makeshift tent city out in front of the building.

They orbited over the walls of the estate toward waste ground beyond. Marc kept expecting the sudden report of gunfire from below, but no one looked up as they flashed by above, under the silent black canopies.

Then the ground was zooming up to meet him and Marc braced. He hit hard and stumbled across the uneven earth, skidding to a halt and panting from exertion. The night's ambient heat enveloped him and he was immediately slick with sweat inside the insulated jump-suit. He gathered up the billowing chute and had the helmet and oxygen gear off as Lucy came jogging up to him. He stowed the jump kit with hers in the hollow of a dead tree, and then set to work stripping off all the cold-weather layers that had kept him from getting frostbitten on the way down.

Lucy handed him a pack that contained a Heckler & Koch MP7 submachine gun, extra ammo magazines and a stubby suppressor. Marc had been issued with a Glock pistol in a thigh holster as well, but the real weapons in his personal arsenal were an Amrel mil-spec tablet computer and a few gadgets he had purloined from an equipment locker on board the *Themis*.

"You saw the tents?" Lucy was checking her gun, and didn't look up. "Looks like Ramaas decided to move in and redecorate."

"He's not going to be in there," said Marc. "He's too smart for that."

"True," she replied, "but I'll bet someone here does know where he's

at. We find that guy . . ." Lucy ratcheted the slide on the MP7 to un-
derline her point. "And I'll ask him real polite like."

Marc put his own SMG on a sling and gestured forward. "Ladies
first."

"So gallant." Extending the wire stock and foregrip, she pulled her
weapon close to her shoulder and set off, fast and low toward the wall
of the compound.

As they got closer, Marc smelled cooking meat wafting over from
a makeshift barbeque set up in the remains of the ornamental garden.
They halted in the shadows cast by the wall and he used a pocket monocular to scope out the front entrance down by the road. "Gates have
been pulled off the hinges and left where they fell," he noted. "I can
see a technical parked across the driveway, and a couple of lads with
AKs." The vehicle was a battered Toyota pickup truck with a heavy
.50 caliber machine gun in the bed, the blunt barrel aiming skyward
at nothing. Marc felt his gut tighten at the thought of what might have
happened if the weapon had been manned by someone alert during
their descent.

"Not the front door, then," said Lucy. They moved away until they
found a section of wall out of sight of the guards.

From his pack, Marc removed a snake-like cable ending in a micro-
camera and connected it to the tablet, before sliding it up and over the
wall. The tablet's screen gave them a fish-eye view of a scorched lawn,
and clumps of bushes.

As he reeled the camera back in, Lucy scrambled up and over, and
then Marc did the same, staying low and rolling longways across the
top of the wall to minimize his silhouette.

They were barely into cover when two men walked past, following
the path up to the big house. Something was clearly funny, because they
were both braying with laughter as they passed by the two intruders.
The men were wearing dirty green fatigues and they toted AKM assault rifles by the barrels, swinging them around carelessly as they
joked. Each had a jet-black shemagh around his neck.

When they were out of earshot, Marc leaned close to Lucy. "Those
guys don't look like bandits."

"More like militia," she agreed. "We need to get a closer look."

They crawled through flower beds now left untended and around fountains that had run dry. The green of Amadayo's gardens was already dying where it had been left to rot. Snatches of conversation reached them, and as they got closer to the mansion house, Marc could hear loud music playing from within. The sound was echoing off the walls and around the interior spaces stripped bare after the politician's murder.

Lucy took a guardian position close to a smashed window and Marc dug in the "bag of tricks" again, this time retrieving a toy-like device that resembled a large cotton reel made of black plastic. A titanium tube, it ended in two cast-urethane hemispheres that were ribbed like the wheels of a dune buggy. Little whip antennae protruded from one surface, and a small stabilizer hung down from the rear. Marc activated a remote-control program on the tablet and the wheels gave a spin as it came to life.

He held it up for Lucy to see, and her face appeared on the tablet, relayed through a wireless camera in the frame of the device. "You know why they call this a 'throwbot?'"

"Why?" She was humoring him.

He smirked and threw the device overarm through the broken window. The wheeled drone landed on the carpeted floor inside and automatically flicked itself over into the correct position.

Marc was now looking through the throwbot's eye, and with smooth motions over the tablet's touch-sensitive surface, he guided it silently from room to room, deeper into the mansion's interior.

"What are you seeing?" whispered Lucy.

"We absolutely do *not* have an invite to this party," he replied. The wheeled drone kept to the shadows, but Marc's view on the screen was clear enough to show dozens of men milling around in the largest hall of Amadayo's house. They were sitting or crouching, gathered in front of a bedsheet hanging from one wall that was being used as a makeshift screen. A video projector and a portable DVD player were rigged up nearby, and the loud music Marc had heard before was the soundtrack over herky-jerky propaganda videos of firefights and bomb detonations. The men watching the screen were dressed like the guards outside—the same style of fatigues, with webbing rigs that looked like

Chinese Communist issue and the ubiquitous shemaghs in black or red-and-white check. He worked the drone backward, retreating from the room and into the corridor, but not before the throwbot's camera caught sight of a familiar black flag covered in white Arabic script, pinned up over the entrance atrium. It was the *al-rāya,* the infamous jihadist banner.

"Confirmation," he said quietly. "These aren't Ramaas's pirates. These blokes are Al Shabaab."

"What the hell are *they* doing here?" hissed Lucy. "This isn't their turf . . ." She drifted off, and shot a look into the night sky.

"It is now," Marc corrected. "We know Ramaas has dealt with them before . . . Maybe he turned this place over to them as a way to get them on side? Along with the bandit clans, they're the largest armed force in the country after the army . . ." He realized that Lucy wasn't listening to him anymore. "Hey!"

"You hear that?" she said.

"What?" But as the word left his mouth, he caught a noise on the wind, over the steady thudding of the music from inside the mansion house. A deep, rattling drone that was growing louder with each passing second.

He turned in the direction of the sound in time to see an angular shape emerge out of the darkness and sweep low over the wall of the estate, the rumbling engine note changing as it pitched up and slowed suddenly. Marc saw a pair of large black rotor blades chopping at the air, suspended at the ends of wings that supported a muscular fuselage between them.

It was unmistakably a V-22 Osprey, the next-generation tiltrotor troop transport that was a hybrid of helicopter and turboprop airplane; but only the United States military flew the V-22, and the livery of the aircraft was all-black rather than the usual American battleship gray. *This isn't right,* Marc told himself, instinct kicking him back up to his feet.

The Osprey's wing-tip nacelles tilted to the vertical as the aircraft passed directly over their heads and a powerful downdraft blasted Marc and Lucy back against the stucco walls of the mansion house. Flashes of firelight from the guards at the gate reached toward the Osprey as they opened up with their assault rifles, but the aircraft was already pivoting into a pedal turn, a drop ramp at the rear falling open to deploy troops onto the roof of the building.

Lucy looked back at Marc and her mouth moved, but her words were swallowed up by the noise of the rotors. Sudden movement on the screen of the tablet dragged Marc's attention back to the device and he looked to see the face of one of the Al Shabaab fighters filling the view from the throwbot's camera. The man was agitated, shouting and waving his hands around.

"Shit!" Marc tapped in a three-keystroke code, setting off a small explosive charge inside the little drone, enough to destroy the throw-bot and likely take off the fingers of the fighter who had grabbed it. The tablet screen blinked the words SIGNAL LOST, and he was jamming the device back into his pack as Lucy reached out to grab his shoulder, leaning close to him.

"We need to get—" Lucy was shouting to be heard over the drone of the Osprey's engines, but she never got the chance to finish. Muzzle flashes blinked behind her and she was suddenly thrown forward against Marc, collapsing onto him.

Over her shoulder, he saw men in green fatigues running up the driveway toward them, firing from the hip.

Saito's ingrained sixth sense, the kind of instinct that only came from years of soldiering, was ringing a wrong note from the moment his boots touched the sun deck on the mansion's top floor. The hairs on the back of his neck prickled and an ill-defined tension blossomed in his chest. It felt *wrong*.

The deployment from the V-22 was clean and fast, as he expected from the team, and as they kicked open the doors and rushed inside, he shot a quick look at the VTOL aircraft as it turned in place and side-slipped away from the building. The hurricane force from the ro-tors battered at the ground and the loose grasses of the ruined lawns, kicking up a wall of dust that billowed out in a rolling wave. Make-shift tents around the rear of the main house were blown down as the Osprey dropped in to land on Welldone Amadayo's seldom-used tennis court, several hundred meters away. The rotor pitch thrummed at idle, and he knew the aircraft would be ready to exfiltrate them at a moment's notice.

Satisfied that their escape route was secure, Saito unlimbered the Vector CRB carbine strapped across his chest and thumbed the weapon's fire-select lever to burst mode. The three other operatives with him were already moving through the sun gallery and rooftop lounge in a staggered line, their movements quick and economical. His misgivings ebbed but did not entirely fade.

As they reached the open stairwell leading down into the building proper, two men in faded surplus camos came sprinting up to meet them, leading with the AKM rifles in their sweating hands.

Saito's point man and the second operative in the line gunned them down with chugs of fire across the face and neck. They had to shove the bodies back over the banister to get past, sending the corpses spinning back down to the ground floor.

The third operative was a man named Byrd, who carried a wide-mouthed pistol-design launcher capable of firing 40mm grenade shells. Saito beckoned him to the top to the stairs, and Byrd took the lead. He sent three rounds down the stairwell, each one with a shock-and-stun warhead. A thunderous roar echoed through the building, but as they descended to the second floor, the tempo of return fire coming back at the team was still fierce.

Sustained barrages from Kalashnikov rifles tore into the walls and ceiling, shredding what little of the mansion's interior decor was still intact. The enemy fire was wild and uncontrolled, but the sheer force of it was impeding any chance to progress. Byrd lurched forward to unleash another salvo of grenades, but the floorboards beneath his feet burst apart in ragged splinters as someone below directed their fire through the ceiling. He fell down in a bloody heap, and Saito reeled away, his mind snapping back to a conversation held hours earlier.

As the Combine team staged for the attack on the far side of the Kenyan border, Saito had underlined his misgivings about launching an infiltration into Mogadishu without current reconnaissance data . . . and he had been overruled. Hours of low-level flight along the coastline, skimming the crests of waves in the darkness, had given him more than enough time to know that he was right and his paymasters were mistaken.

But Saito was a servant, and he did not call the shots. They were here now, and their mission remained the same. *Locate and terminate the pirate warlord, find the weapon the Serbs gave him.* Everything else was irrelevant.

He erased the doubts in his mind and pulled the pins on fragmentation grenades still clipped to Byrd's body, and then tossed the smaller man over the ledge and into the melee below. Saito fell back as more explosions rumbled through the house.

"This is a hornet's nest," snapped the point man, a grim Spaniard named Ruiz. "We were told to expect minimal resistance!" He shot a look at Mayer, the other member of the team. "I'm not getting paid enough to die here!"

Saito ignored them both, listening to the shouts from below. The shooters on the ground floor were regrouping, and he could hear them calling to one another and shouting battle cries in the name of their holy war. These were not Ramaas's brigands, then. He gave a nod. *A clever maneuver.* The pirate had allowed his jihadist militant allies to occupy this estate and unknowingly become a trap for anyone tracking him back to this location.

"They're coming up," snapped Mayer. "I hear them, must be another stairwell."

"We kill our way through," Saito ordered, as a door further along the corridor slammed open and more armed men boiled out onto the landing. "Advance and fire!" He called out the command as he followed it himself, striding forward to meet the new attackers with his carbine spitting flame.

Lucy howled with pain and Marc reacted without thinking. He pulled her aside with one hand, his other gripping his MP7 as he swung it up toward the advancing shooters. He had no time to aim and be cautious about it; Marc squeezed the submachine gun's trigger and fired off a snarling discharge of rounds on full-auto, cutting down the first rifleman with hits across his torso and belly. The second shooter dove into cover behind a stone planter, spraying bullets from his AKM high into the walls and missing by a wide margin.

Lucy let out a bone-deep groan and her knees bent. Marc took her weight and they both dropped. His free hand touched her back and he dreaded the prospect of feeling blood seeping through her tactical vest—but instead his fingers touched hot, burned fibers around the ragged impact points.

She swore violently and pushed him away. "I'm okay." Lucy ground out the words through gritted teeth. "Plates in the body armor took the rounds. Fuck me, that burns . . ."

"Incoming!" Marc saw movement as more of the jihadis spilled out of the front of Amadayo's mansion. Lucy brought up her own SMG as Marc did the same and they both let off bursts of fire toward the new surge of attackers. "We can't stay here," he said. "We've got no good cover!"

"Yeah," Lucy nodded, shaking off the pain. "Hell, what did we step in? The mission just got blown wide open, we need to get gone!" She fired off another three-round salvo. "Open to suggestions, smart guy."

"What about that VTOL?" He jerked a thumb toward the roof. "Like it or not, someone else has just gatecrashed this thing."

"And good luck to them," Lucy retorted. "But unless you wanna stick around and find out who kills who, we need to extract and re-group!"

The original plan had been to get a location for Ramaas from someone in the Amadayo mansion and then appropriate some local transport to reach his location. Now that had tuned into *get away or get dead*.

"Garage!" Marc stabbed a finger in the direction of an outbuilding across the drive from the main house. "We need wheels, as long as you're happy letting me drive again."

"Drag me on a goddamn skateboard for all I care," she snapped back at him. "Go, go!" Lucy put down a wave of cover fire and Marc sprinted across the gap between the wall of the house and another raised flower bed.

He skidded behind shelter and then returned the favor, shooting at a cluster of riflemen behind the bullet-pocked fake marble columns of the entrance portico. He heard a scream and saw someone fall in a spurt of blood.

Marc didn't let his mind even start to process the grim facts of what he was doing. He drew on his training, concentrating on navigating through the moment-to-moment havoc of the firefight.

Enemies. Targets. Objectives. Survival. He reduced his actions to those terms and shut out everything else.

The slide locked open on his MP7 and he ducked back into cover to reload, exchanging the spent magazine for a full one. Lucy slapped him on the shoulder as she slid in behind him and nodded toward the outbuilding. She didn't need to remind Marc that there were easily fifty meters of open space between the flower bed and the garage. "I'm gonna pop smoke," she told him. "We'll both go on my word."

"Got it." Adrenaline was pumping through him now, and he rocked on the balls of his feet, anxious to get moving again.

Lucy pulled the pin on a smoke grenade and lobbed it out toward the house, drawing a fresh fusillade of fire from the shooters. As white vapor jetted from the metal cylinder, explosions sounded from inside the mansion and glass shattered.

"Looks like those dicks from the Osprey are getting into it," she offered.

"Why would the US risk sending a team here, after that video from New York?" said Marc, taking a deep breath. The smoke was thickening into a bank of white fog.

"I don't think they did," Lucy replied, then she slapped him on the arm. "Now!"

The two of them sprinted out from behind the flower bed and Marc followed Lucy's lead by firing suppressive bursts toward the front of the building. Heavy 7.62mm rounds hummed through the air around them and cracked at the flagstones by their feet, but the shooters were firing blindly. Crossing the distance to the garage seemed to take forever, as the smoke turned everything into a whiteout—and then suddenly the heavy wooden doors rose out of the haze. Marc shouldered one of them open, shoving Lucy through before pulling it closed behind him.

Inside, the garage was pitch dark. The still air within was hot and stale with the smell of engine oil. Lucy's tactical flashlight snapped on and a broad beam illuminated the interior of the outbuilding, washing this way and that across the floor and the racks of tools against the walls. "Oh, hell no," she muttered.

The garage was empty.

The jihadists kept coming, drawing fire from Saito's team down the corridor and the stairwell, splitting their focus as new fighters mantled the bodies of their dead brethren and attempted to box in the Combine mercenaries.

If we remain here, we die. Saito made the calculation and knew that no other outcome was possible. Byrd was already gone, and Mayer had taken a glancing hit to the leg that was bleeding badly. The numbers of the Al Shabaab fighters were overwhelmingly in the enemy's favor, even with the skill and experience of the Combine team on Saito's side. *It will be a retreat, then,* he decided, and gave the order. Laying down the last of their grenades, Mayer and Ruiz moved back up to the top floor and Saito served as rearguard, gunning down the men who tried to come after them.

Reaching the sun deck, he stepped aside as his men tipped over lounge chairs and a massive glass-fronted refrigerator to block the path of anyone trying to follow. Saito pressed a hand to the throat mike around his neck. "Aerial? Mission abort. I say again, mission abort. Extract us from the roof . . ."

He looked in the direction of the Osprey and his heart sank. A squad of men in fatigues were trying to approach the aircraft. They were moving and firing in poor order but as with those inside the mansion, there were more than enough of them to pose a serious threat. At the rear of the tiltrotor's fuselage, he could see a crumpled figure in black sprawled on the cargo ramp, apparently dead. Saito looked to the cockpit and glimpsed movement inside.

"Copy that!" The pilot's voice was tight and urgent. *"They're closing in, I'll try to—"*

Yellow light flashed out under the wing and Saito winced as a cry came over the radio bead in his ear. When he called out to the pilot again, the man did not reply and the Osprey remained where it was, rotors a blur as it sat unmoving on the tennis court.

"We have lost the aircrew," he announced dispassionately. "We have to get away from this building . . . Follow me!" Saito slipped his carbine over his shoulder and used a chair to boost him to the apex of the mansion's angled roof.

Gripping the red tiles, he hauled himself up and then bent down to assist Mayer, who endured the pain from his wound with quiet gasps. The material of the other man's trouser leg was now dark and wet with blood. Ruiz came up last, swinging himself onto the roof in a single motion.

Their boots clattered on the tiles as they ran along the length of the mansion, careful to distribute their weight as they moved. The steady drone of the Osprey's idling engines was like an endless peal of thunder, but beneath the noise Saito could hear the excited shouts of the jihadist soldiers and the crackle of more gunfire. White smoke billowed up from the courtyard outside the house, and he hunched forward to minimize his visible outline. It was dark up here, and anyone down on the ground might not see them at first glance—but all it would take was one observant man with a rifle and they would be picked off to plummet to their deaths.

Ahead, the east wing of Amadayo's mansion came to an abrupt end, but a high wall extended away toward the outbuildings and the edge of the estate beyond those. Saito jabbed a finger in the direction of the wall and dropped down onto it in a cat-fall.

He saw movement below him as a gunman came around the corner of the mansion, but then there was a buzz of suppressed fire from Ruiz's Vector and the man dropped. Mayer and the Spaniard followed him down.

They were almost at the roof of the lower outbuilding when a fresh salvo of gunfire erupted all around them. Mayer reflexively put his weight on his wounded leg and it folded under him.

Saito had one foot on the low roof as Mayer toppled straight into the terracotta tiles and smashed right through them. He disappeared into the gloom below, but the damage was already done. The tiles came apart in a clattering rush and the roof unzipped as it caved in on its supports.

Silently cursing their luck, Saito went down and Ruiz came with him, mercifully out of the firing line but into the black, oil-stinking darkness. He hit a concrete floor hard and rolled over, ignoring the pain, grabbing for his carbine.

Thread-thin red targeting lasers stabbed out from their guns, meeting a pair of green beams that aimed back toward the Combine team. A dot of emerald light wavered on Saito's sternum and finally a white man with sandy hair and a smoke-dirty face came out of the shadows. He had an MP7 aimed and ready, and at his side was a black woman wearing the same tactical gear.

"And who might you be?" the gunman asked, his British accent laced with tension.

NINETEEN

Hello, gatecrashers," said Lucy, her tone dangerous and mocking all at once.

One second there had been gunfire cracking off outside the garage, and the next the sky caved in and brought with it these men with their guns and their injuries and their hard-eyed glares. It didn't take a genius to figure out that this was the team from the Osprey, but they bore no resemblance to any American military unit that Marc was familiar with.

"PMC?" he prompted. Their loadout and equipment were more high-end than the hardware used by the Aleph mercenaries Marc had traded fire with in Poland. "Who sent you?"

The slender Asian man with a Vector carbine over his shoulder shot a look at the other two new arrivals, and Marc knew that he was the one in charge. "I could ask you the same question."

A spray of automatic fire cut through the air overhead, across the thrumming rumble of idling aircraft engines. Lucy reacted, panning up her SMG toward the hole in the roof, hunting for more threats. "This is really not a good time for small talk," she snapped.

One of the other mercs moved to the double doors and peeked through a crack in the frame. "She's right. Movement out there. They're bringing that technical around, probably going to use the fifty to hose us all in here. We have to go." He glanced around, finding the single rear door leading out toward the gardens. "That way."

"Be our guest," offered Lucy. "Can't be more than two dozen of those assholes dug in out there."

The Asian man's eyes never left Marc's. "I imagine we came to this place looking for the same person. Bad timing that we were all ensnared in the trap he left us." He held up his hands. "But we could work together."

The merc by the door crouched by his injured comrade and helped him up, shaking his head angrily. "Unless one of these two has a tank in their pocket, how is that going to help us?" He jutted his chin in the direction of the door. "We go for the VTOL, we'll be cut down, same as the crew."

Marc caught the man's meaning and seized on it. "You lost your aircrew?" The Asian man gave an irritated nod, and off that Marc let his MP7 drop. "I can fly that thing."

"You can?" Lucy raised an eyebrow.

"I've read the manual," he muttered.

"Damn it, Saito," snapped the other mercenary. "Say yes, and then we can all get out of this shithole!"

After a moment, the Asian man nodded. "But there is the small matter of getting to the aircraft."

Marc held out his hand to Lucy. "How many grenades you got left?"

"Couple of frags . . ."

"Perfect." He glanced around. "I need wire, or cord or something . . ."

The injured man clutched at something on his belt. "Will this do?" He handed Marc a clutch of plastic zip-ties with his bloody fingers.

"Good enough." Marc dropped his pack on the concrete floor and fished out a second throwbot drone.

The fighters grouped in the rear gardens were looking in every direction at once, convinced that the arrival of the black helicopter-plane was the opening shot in the great war their demagogue leaders had long promised. Afraid to venture out of cover across the clear ground between the ornamental planters and the tennis court, for fear that more troops might come charging out of the aircraft, some of them warily kept their rifles trained on it. Others pointed their weapons at the sky, ready to shoot at the next invader. The Osprey did not move, its rotors still spinning in humming blurs, the whole aircraft crouching low to the ground like some giant, angry insect.

The fighters imagined hordes of helicopter gunships out there in the black night, locust-swarm masses rolling in over the shore to drop squads of horribly beweaponed Western soldiers. Some of them fired into the dark, convinced they saw enemies in every jumping shadow.

Others—the older men who had fought in real battles rather than the days of turning guns on panicked civilian apostates—kept themselves in better order, watching the outbuildings where the enemy infidels had to be hiding.

The door at the rear of the garage opened briefly, enough to show a narrow sliver of darkness within, and then it slammed shut once more. All guns turned toward it as motion caught the eye of the fighters, and for a moment the idling Osprey was forgotten.

Something small and fast came bouncing over the flagstone path that wound its way through the gardens of the Amadayo mansion. No larger than a beer can on its side, the device rolled toward the men in cover and dragged behind it a makeshift train of plastic strips and green, fist-sized spheres. A glassy eye in the middle of the little machine got a glimpse of a black-hooded rifleman staring blankly at it, and the robot accelerated toward him.

The rifleman shouted in alarm as his mind caught up to what he was seeing. He brought his AKM to his shoulder and opened fire, trying to shoot the drone before it could get close, but he was too late. Hauling a cluster of M67 fragmentation grenades with it, the throwbot sped into the middle of the group of fighters and self-destructed. Chain-fire detonations of the grenades turned the blast into a sustained rumble, and even as the sound was fading, five figures burst from inside the garage. Throwing smoke canisters to cover their exit, they sprinted through the chaos toward the Osprey.

Marc charged into a wall of wind as he rushed for the grounded VTOL, and again the aircraft's massive rotors swallowed up all other sounds around them. He threw a look over his shoulder and saw Lucy firing from the hip as she came up behind him.

Back past the gap between the mansion house and the outbuildings, someone was trying to maneuver the Toyota technical so that the heavy machine gun in the flatbed could be aimed in their direction. As he looked, the muzzle of the big MG grew a flickering crucifix of fire, and tracer rounds marched up the lawn toward them.

He followed Lucy and the man called Saito to the rear of the Osprey, ducking under the H-shaped tail to scramble up the cargo ramp and on board. Saito went back to haul in the body of a dead man lying on the grass, and as Lucy put down cover fire, the other two mercenaries from the garage climbed in.

The Osprey's interior was loud and vibrating with the endless rumble of the props. It had the same stripped-to-the-bare metal look as the Hercules that brought them from Oman, every surface covered with pipework and cable conduits. As he dashed forward to the cockpit, Marc felt more than he heard the low thuds of stray .50 caliber bullets punching through the aluminum fuselage and out the other side.

A horror was waiting for him up there. Slumped forward over the central control console was another of Saito's team. The pilot's face had been destroyed by a high-velocity round that had hit him in the cheek, and there was a mess of blood, brain matter and bone fragments across the inside of the canopy. He fought down an instinctive urge to retch and dragged the dead body away from the controls, dumping it back on the floor of the crew cabin.

Marc dropped into the pilot's chair and let experience and muscle memory take him through the next few moments. He secured his seat belt, put his feet on the pedals, and then allowed his hands to fall naturally to the joystick and throttle. His eyes scanned the digital screens in front of him and he automatically wiped one clean of the blood droplets that had spattered across it.

"Get us airborne!" Lucy was suddenly at his shoulder, shouting into his ear. "C'mon, do some of that pilot shit!"

He reflected that now was probably a bad time to tell her that he had exactly *zero* hours on this type of aircraft. Thanks to his naval training and his time with the SIS OpTeams, Marc *was* experienced with a half-dozen models of helicopter, and he did have enough fixed-wing hours to get most things off the ground and down again in one piece. The Osprey was half-helo, half-prop plane; *how hard could it be?*

But he had been expecting to find something that resembled a helicopter's control set, not the hybrid laid out in front of him. Marc gripped the joystick and felt the vibration from the rotors through his fingers, felt his gut tighten. Time slowed. It was all on him now. Ten seconds more and the Al Shabaab fighters would be swarming them.

He shook off the flash of fear. The Osprey's engine nacelles and rotors were aimed up at the sky, which meant right now it was acting like a helicopter. *That, I can fly.*

"Hang on to something." Marc pushed the thrust control lever forward, applying power to the rotors, and the Osprey leaped off the ground far quicker than he expected. The tail slewed around as Marc over-corrected, shredding the canopy of a stand of acacia trees as the VTOL slipped through the air, threatening to yaw away from stability and spin them back into the ground.

His gaze locked on the controls, Marc saw flashes of muzzle flare at the periphery of his vision as the Osprey's nose swept past the fighters shooting up at them. Marc's thumb found the wheel switch that controlled the angle of the aircraft's wing-tip engine pods and clicked it forward. The nacelles tilted past a sixty-degree angle and suddenly the Osprey was behaving like a fixed-wing airplane. The transition moment came as a shock. Acceleration pushed on him as the aircraft thundered above the heads of the gunmen, flashing over the roof of the mansion and across the grounds toward the high walls of the estate.

Marc chewed on his lip as he struggled to find the rhythm of the VTOL's flight, over-correcting again as the Osprey's center of gravity shifted. He aimed the aircraft away from the surrounding residential district filled with two-story houses, and followed the open road. His first instinct was to micro-manage the Osprey's fly-by-wire digital controls and he smothered the urge, letting the aircraft find its own level. *If I can just get the pace of this bird, I can do this . . .*

But this had been a liftoff from a hot LZ and the escape was by no means assured. Marc flinched as bright orange jags of tracer lanced past the nose and he shot a look out of the canopy to the dusty highway below. A trio of technicals, most likely reinforcements called in by the extremists, were racing along the road in the wake of the VTOL.

Each carried a heavy gun in the rear aimed directly at the Osprey, bracketing it with streaks of fire as they pursued.

Once more, Marc felt the hits as the aircraft took rounds in the belly. Red warning lights flashed on the screen in front of him, signaling damage to the hydraulic systems. He worked the nacelle controls again, trying bring the rotors to full horizontal flight mode, but the Osprey fought him. He tried to work the flaps, and found no joy there either. The VTOL dragged in the air, refusing to answer his commands. "We got a problem," he shouted over his shoulder. "I can't gain altitude!"

Lucy pushed away from the cockpit and scrambled back down the length of the Osprey's cargo compartment.

Saito's injured man was already down on the deck, leaning up against the fuselage. He was pale and sweaty, on the verge of passing out. She dismissed him and stepped over the body of the mercenary who had been hauled in before take-off. The two surviving, combat-capable men were crouched at the open cargo ramp in the rear, trying to pick off the drivers of the pickups with their carbines. They were having no luck; Lucy was an exemplary shot, and even she would have admitted that firing from a moving airborne platform at a moving ground target at these speeds was nothing but a waste of ammunition. For a moment she wished she had her custom sniper rig with her.

"What is he doing up there?" Saito's teammate was Hispanic, but that was all she could be sure of about him, other than the fact that he was pissed as all hell. "He said he could fly this thing!"

"Damage," she shouted back, ducking as a hot round whickered off the lowered ramp. "What else you got on this bird?"

Saito glanced back at gear bags secured to the walls of the compartment. "I don't think that—"

Lucy didn't wait for him to finish. She went to the first bag and tore it open. Inside was crash-survival gear for water or desert landings. She kicked that one away and moved on to the next. It had a lock on the zipper, and she sawed at it with her combat knife, slicing through the ballistic mesh of the bag instead. Saito was reaching out to stop her, but she was already in.

The knife cut through cloth and plastic and into wads of paper. The bag was filled with used currency, US $100 bills wrapped into individual bricks. "Hey, Benjamin," she said aloud, seeing President Franklin's face staring up at her. Lucy turned back to Saito. "Bribe money?"

"Emergency funds," he called back.

Lucy gave a nod. "I'd call this an emergency." She ripped the cash bag from the straps holding it to the wall and dragged it to the cargo ramp. Before Saito or the other mercenary could stop her, Lucy had slashed open the bottom of the bag and booted the contents of it into the Osprey's rotor wake.

A torrent of money burst into the air and began to fall across the path of the technicals, hundreds of thousands of dollars raining down on the road below. It was enough to stop the shooting, but for a moment Lucy was uncertain her plan would work. The fighters were opportunists, that was true, but were they so pious they would ignore a literal windfall in favor of their righteous anger?

Not so much, she reflected, as the three pickups skidded to a halt and the men on board spilled out onto the road. Trailing smoke, the Osprey extended the distance between them, its course beginning a curve that would take the aircraft around the northern edge of Mogadishu.

Saito gave a humorless grunt and stepped away from the ramp, kicking a loose c-note into the wind. "That was a very expensive exfiltration. In more ways than one." His gaze raked over the injured man and the two dead. "Ruiz, secure them." The other mercenary accepted the order with a nod and moved off.

Now that she could catch her breath, Lucy was measuring Saito, searching for tells that could give her a clue as to who he was and who had sent him into Somalia. "My guess is you work for someone who doesn't worry much about money." She gestured at the cabin. "Gear like this don't come cheap."

"American and British," Saito said in reply, pitching his voice up over the sound of the engines as he studied her in return. "But not military . . . At least, not for some time."

"Like knows like, right? That practically makes us cousins."

Saito smiled thinly. "I am not being paid to shoot at you."

"For now," Lucy added, as the Osprey's deck tilted alarmingly.

They grabbed at handholds on the walls of the cabin and she lurched to a window, afraid that she would see more ground fire snaking up toward them. The aircraft had gone into a circular path passing over what looked like a set of derelict municipal buildings, a hospital or a school.

"We're losing height," snapped Saito. "What is he doing?"

Lucy saw the engine nacelle at the end of the wing tilting back upward. "Landing . . ." The Osprey hopped over an angled fence and a line of half-collapsed bleachers, kicking up a tornado of yellow dust. Dane was putting them down in the middle of what looked like an abandoned soccer field, and they hit the ground with a heavy crunch that shook the fuselage.

She worked her way forward as the rotors wound down, and Lucy could smell the acrid odor of burned insulation and the stink of hot engine oil.

Marc raised his hands off the controls as she reached the cockpit; he was breathing hard. "I had no choice," he began, preempting the question. "We got a leak in the hydraulics back there. I was having problems with getting any height and if I keep us in the air, something's going to seize up. Then we'd go down if we wanted to or not . . ."

Saito was behind her. "We are still inside the city limits. We can't remain here."

Lucy glanced out through the canopy, then pulled the glare cover off the MTM tactical watch on her wrist and checked it. "We've got around five hours until sunrise, and then everyone is going to know where we're at. Locals would have heard the engines but we got decent cover here . . ." She thought it through. "What are our options?"

"If we don't fix the Osprey, then we are walking out," Marc said bluntly. "If the damage isn't too bad, we might be able to patch it . . ."

"Ruiz has experience with mechanical systems," said Saito, beckoning the other man over. "How long will it take?"

Marc climbed out of the pilot's chair. "I have no idea." He blew out a breath. "We should probably have a backup plan, just in case."

He gave Lucy a meaningful look and rubbed his earlobe; she got the inference. The drop into Somalia had been set up from the start to be as near to a zero-footprint operation as humanly possible, because the eyes of every major nation's intelligence agencies would be watching the country like hawks. Long-range communication with Rubicon was only to be initiated in the most extreme circumstances, so essentially Marc and Lucy had been on their own since the moment they jumped from the C-130.

But all that planning for a stealthy mission had gone out the window with the firefight at Amadayo's mansion and the chaos of their escape. *Making it up as we go,* Lucy thought grimly. *Again.*

She knew that Rubicon were listening. All it would take to reach them would be a string of code words spoken in the clear over any cellular phone in Mogadishu. The signal traffic analysis programs that Kara Wei had infiltrated into the region's cell network would pick them out like a whisper among the roar of a crowd. But to do that would be throwing in the towel. Ramaas and the Exile weapon would still be out there, and they would be no closer to stopping him. It gnawed on Lucy that they still didn't have a handle on whatever the hell the pirate warlord was planning.

"Okay." She folded her arms across her chest, putting that problem aside for the moment. An unpleasant awareness was pushing its way to the front of Lucy's mind as her gaze left Marc's face and turned back to Saito and Ruiz. "If we're going to work together, then we need to put all our cards on the table. You agree?"

Saito gave a wary nod. "Agreed."

The Brit had been on the money when he pegged these guys as contractors, but the vibe coming off them was leading Lucy toward one unpleasant conclusion about their origins. She decided to roll the dice and see what came up. "So why don't you start by telling me what made your bosses in the Combine send you down here?"

Saito's poker face wasn't quite good enough to hide his tell. "You are a perceptive woman," he replied, after a long moment.

At her side, Marc's reaction was exactly what she'd expected it to be. "Wait, *what?*" His hand snatched at the Glock pistol holstered on his thigh. "The bloody Combine? Lucy, when did you know that?"

"About a second ago," she told him. "It's the only explanation that makes any sense."

"It would appear you have an unresolved issue with my employers?" Saito said lightly. "I am dismayed."

Ruiz snorted. "Don't you get it, man? These two? They work for the African. Ekko Solomon."

"Ah." Saito's head bobbed in a sage nod. "Of course. A truth dawns. Yes, that explains much." He gave a grunt of amusement. "Fate is not without a sense of irony."

Marc came forward with the gun in his fist, but Lucy put a hand on his arm. "Easy now, cowboy. Let's not do anything we might regret."

"Like throwing in with these pricks?" spat Marc. "My friends are dead because of the Combine and their fucking games!"

Marc's anger rolled off Saito. "I know nothing of that. You and I have never met . . ." He trailed off, and looked at the Brit as if for the first time. "But you are familiar to me. Yes. I've seen you before." He leaned back, nodding to himself. "You were in Split. The Queen's High casino. You failed to stop Ramaas from making his escape with the device . . ."

"How do you know that?" Marc demanded.

"I viewed footage from the casino's security system."

"Those hard drives holding that video were stolen," said Marc. "By Franko Horvat." He paused, as if he was connecting the dots. "You were there. In the bank. You're the reason he's dead, I'll bet."

Saito cocked his head. "And now I am here."

Marc looked at Lucy. "That's how the Combine tracked the nuke. The Kurjaks to Horvat, Horvat to Ramaas, Ramaas to Amadayo."

"Except we were set up, eh?" interjected Ruiz. "The intel was a trap."

"My heart bleeds for you," growled Marc.

Saito eyed the gun in Marc's hand. "If you want to turn this into another firefight, it is your choice to make. I have a rudimentary grasp of this aircraft's controls but I would prefer you to pilot it for us rather than have to kill you."

Lucy's hand dropped to her own weapon, and she saw Ruiz do the same.

"Do you want to do Ramaas's work for him?" Saito said lightly. "You may find it hard to believe, but the Combine want the same thing you do. We are here to neutralize Abur Ramaas and the Exile nuclear device he has taken possession of."

"Why? So you can turn it over to your bosses?" Lucy eyed him.

"Think what you will," Saito replied. "The fact remains, the Combine is interested in maintaining global stability. A pirate warlord with a weapon of mass destruction in hand cannot be allowed to threaten that."

"The last people I knew who threatened the Combine's *stability,*" Marc began, his voice low and cold, "I had to watch die in a firestorm. I'd rather shoot you in the head and take my chances."

Saito's gaze shifted back to Lucy, unfazed by the threat. "Do you feel that way? I sense not. You are more the pragmatist than your English friend. You understand there is a tactical decision to be made here, yes?"

She hated herself a little for the nod she gave him in return. "Enemy of my enemy and that shit, yeah, I heard it all before. But sharing the same foxhole don't make us allies."

Saito glanced at Ruiz and gestured for him to put up his weapon. "Perhaps a show of good faith will help." He explained that Amadayo had been the Combine's primary asset in Somalia, but he was not the only one. A man named Kaahi, an officer of the Federal Government with responsibility over the national television station, was also in the employ of the group. "Kaahi's intelligence directed us to the mansion," Saito noted. "Clearly he was sending us into an ambush."

"He's Ramaas's man," said Ruiz. "On the take at both ends. Obviously decided it was time to burn his bridges with the Combine."

"So it's likely this Kaahi bloke will know where the target is." Marc reluctantly holstered his gun. "Ramaas has got to have his hands in the Federal Government somewhere. Otherwise, they'd have turned him over to the United Nations the moment that bomb-threat video went live."

"We find Kaahi and interrogate him," Saito said to Lucy, then looked to Marc. "Meanwhile, you will help Ruiz repair the Osprey."

"All that before sunrise?" Marc snorted.

"Exactly." Saito walked down the cabin and pulled a panel off the wall, revealing a storage compartment behind it. Inside, Lucy saw the wheels of a dirt bike and an electric engine in a skeletal frame. "So, let us not waste any more time, yes?"

Marc leaned close to her and spoke in a quiet tone. "How did we end up working with our enemies again?"

"Bad karma?" she suggested, gathering up her gear.

Solomon stood on the balcony, looking out over the lights of the city. Below, the night was young and Monte Carlo was open for business, the clubs and casino packed with people seeking a taste of elegance and adventure in their lives. He frowned, his hand reaching up to toy with the slender chain around his neck. The people down there were sailing across the surface of the world, insulated from the harsh realities of it by money, position or just indifference. He doubted that many of them understood that their reality was only one version of things, balanced atop a thousand other truths that were harder and more unpalatable.

And the hardest truth of all was one that Ekko Solomon had learned with a blood cost. *The world turns on secrets, and most of us are better off not knowing them.*

He ran a finger over an odd-shaped piece of metal on the end of the chain. To most, it would have appeared to be an abstract thing, a discolored steel talon; but a soldier would see it for what it really was, the trigger from a Kalashnikov assault rifle. The gun it came from had been destroyed long ago, but Solomon kept this part of it as a constant reminder to himself of where he had come from and what he had done to rise from there.

He heard Delancort's careful footsteps on the balcony's wooden decking. "Henri," he said, without turning around. "Any contact?"

"No, sir," said the French Canadian. "But that is as expected. Our people in Mombasa say the C-130 touched down on schedule. Lucy and the Englishman were not on board."

"You do not approve of Marc Dane's involvement." It wasn't a question.

Delancort sighed. "I admit he has a useful skill set and has proven to be resourceful . . . But I have to question his commitment, sir."

"He just dropped into one of the most lawless regions in Africa," Solomon replied. "To help us. Is that not commitment?"

"With all due respect, isn't it Rubicon that is once again helping *him*?" Delancort walked to the edge of the balcony. "He brought this situation to us. We were peripherally aware of both the Kurjaks' and Abur Ramaas's existence, but this business with the Exile device . . ." He trailed off. "Dane only came to you because no one in Europol would take him seriously."

"You think I am indulging him?" Solomon's eyes narrowed. "You saw the pirate's threats, Henri. This is not some phantom Dane is chasing. It is a credible threat to the world." He nodded to himself. "And if we can do something about it, we will. That is the principle Rubicon was founded upon."

"*No nation but justice,*" said Delancort, translating the Latin quote that sat beneath the Rubicon corporate logo on the office's wall. "You have set yourself a high bar, sir."

Solomon nodded again, his gaze briefly dropping to the moonlit waters of the bay. "Redemption is a long road." His hands tightened on the rail ringing the balcony. "I wish I could do more. It does not feel like it is enough."

"Ramaas won't succeed in trying to blackmail the three largest nation states on earth," Delancort said, with a sniff. "He's deluded if he thinks he can. The only variable is whether he dies before or after the weapon is detonated."

Solomon gave him a look. "Do not underestimate him. I grew up around men like Abur Ramaas. He is a jackal, and jackals are as intelligent as they are vicious." His gaze lost focus for a moment as he pictured the other man, imagining the warlord as if he were a shadowy mirror of himself. Solomon shook off the mental image.

"Believe me when I tell you, this game of his has not yet been fully revealed."

Delancort hovered on the cusp of a reply, but then the door to the balcony slid open and Kara Wei was standing there, pale and wide-eyed. "There you are! You need to come see this, sir. We got another flash traffic upload from our source in Beijing."

Solomon and Delancort exchanged glances. The woman Kara was referring to was an asset Rubicon had cultivated inside China's security services, a remnant left in place from other, past operations to defy acts of terror.

"Ramaas put up another video," Kara explained. "Everyone—and I mean *everyone*—is going to scramble once it gets around."

"He's made more threats?" said Delancort.

She shook her head. "It's more like he's sending out party invites."

The Zero MMX dirt bike had a quiet electric motor rather than a gasoline-powered one, so it sped them along the highways of Mogadishu like a ghost.

Lucy resented the fact that she had to play passenger to Saito's driver, but the Japanese mercenary was the one who knew where to find the target, and after threading through darkened alleys and dimly lit streets they emerged across from a six-story building in the Warta Nabada district. Saito hid the bike between a low wall and a parked panel van, and together they slipped into the courtyard of a shuttered apartment complex across the way. Both of them were shadows, their faces hidden behind dark shemaghs that covered head, neck and shoulders.

Lucy scanned the building through a monocular. A sign in English and Arabic script over the entrance said it was a television station belonging to the Federal Government, but she saw little sign of official presence there. No soldiers in Somalian Army uniforms, no policemen—but there were a handful of twitchy, stringy-looking youths armed with rifles gathered around a cargo truck and a weather-beaten Yukon SUV. Harried civilians were moving in and out of the building in twos and threes, carrying boxes or equipment cases that were going into the back of the truck.

She panned up, finding an orchard of antennae and satellite dishes on the roof. Some of the offices were illuminated, the yellow glow of their lights spilling out through the wire anti-frag meshes over the windows. Lucy passed the monocular to Saito and let him make his own survey. "Looks like they're pulling out," she offered. "How do you know this Kaahi character is even in there?"

"Because I'm looking at him right now." He pointed. "Third-floor window, second across."

Lucy could make out a thin man in a white shirt and red tie gesticulating angrily at a woman in a hijab. He was trying to direct her to do something, but she was reluctant to obey. Finally, he turned away and disappeared from sight.

Saito handed back the monocular. "He's leaving and taking anything useful with him," said the mercenary. "It makes sense. Kaahi knows that the Combine will become aware of his duplicity. He doesn't want to be here when that happens."

She jutted her chin toward the men at the entrance. "Those boys look like bandits to me. Ramaas's men, I reckon."

He nodded. "Kaahi still has value to Ramaas. The man is a government official, after all. He'll want to keep him alive." Saito paused, checking his gun before pulling his headscarf tight. "There is a side entrance. We go in that way, low profile. Isolate Kaahi and interrogate him." He gave her a look. "You will do as I tell you, yes?"

"For now," she replied, flicking the safety off her SMG. "Lead on, man."

Saito followed the low wall into a pool of gloom beneath a busted street light and then crossed the road when the attention of the gunmen was elsewhere. Lucy stuck to him like she was his shadow, letting the Combine operative take point as he eased open the side door and entered the building. But her finger never strayed too far from the trigger of her MP7, and she was ready to put a few rounds in Saito's center mass if he tried to dry-gulch her.

They found a service stairwell and started up it. Saito was well trained, that was clear from how he moved. Back in the day, Lucy had been on transnational exercises with Delta and their opposite numbers in the Tokushu Sakusen Gun, the Japanese Self Defense Force's counter-terrorist unit—but those men had always kept their faces hidden behind balaclavas and did not mix with the US Army operators off mission. Saito had the same hard-trained and precise economy of motion in his movements as the TSG guys, and Lucy couldn't help but wonder how the man had ended up in the employ of the Combine.

Was it something like her own circumstances, the last grab at a final option after all others had faded? Lucy was indebted to Ekko Solomon and the Rubicon Corporation for saving her life after her own commanders had thrown her to the wolves. Was Saito following a similar path? Was he damaged goods forced to leave behind his nation's service? Or had he joined the Combine out of a more basic, less principled impulse?

Marc had not exaggerated when he said that Saito's paymasters killed his friends, and it was equally true that the Combine had spent time and effort trying to do the same to everyone in Rubicon's Special Conditions Division at one time or another. It was hard not to take it personally.

More than once, the SCD had crossed swords with the shadowy cadre of power-brokers and arms dealers, and it never ended well. The Combine were old money, the top tier of a rich elite who wanted to stay there by manipulating a status quo of global brush-fire wars and terrorist horrors. Rubicon was everything they were not, a vigilante force that answered to no one.

No one but Ekko Solomon's conscience, she corrected herself. Lucy tried not to think too hard about that. She had vowed that as long as she could keep looking at herself in the mirror each morning, she would continue to be part of Solomon's crusade. *If that ever changes . . .* She pushed the thought away.

Saito paused as they reached the third floor and opened the door from the stairwell a crack. Voices wafted out from the corridor, a man and a woman arguing in the local dialect. "That's him," whispered Saito.

* * *

"But who are these men?" Esme asked the question, and Kaahi's anger grew at her impertinence for asking it. "Why are they here so late at night?"

"That is not your concern!" he snarled at her. The woman was supposed to be his assistant, but she talked to him as though she was his mother. "Just do what I tell you!"

Esme made a sour face. "You cannot blame me for asking. You must have heard the reports coming in from the east of the city—people are saying that there was a gun battle! They are saying the Al Shabaab militants camped out there were attacked by the American military again, and—"

"Just shut up!" he bellowed, silencing her with the interruption. "You don't know anything!" Kaahi pushed past her and strode toward his office. "Get back to work!" He threw the last comment over his shoulder and wrenched open the door.

Esme was more correct than she knew, but Kaahi wasn't about to tell her that. He was on his way out of this city, out of this country. In a few hours, the money Ramaas had promised him would be in his hands and he would be on the first jet to France, or Spain, or whatever country he wanted.

That belief evaporated as he entered his office and found two people waiting there, a man and a woman in military apparel. Neither of them had been in the room a few moments ago, before he left to give Esme her dressing-down.

He took a breath to call for help, but then the man pulled the scarf he was wearing away from his face and all the energy in Kaahi's body faded. The Japanese he had met in a street café earlier that day was standing there, no longer looking like some dissolute foreign tourist. Kaahi's mouth moved but no sound emerged.

"You were paid to provide a service," Saito told him gravely. "Imagine how disappointed I was to learn that you reneged on that agreement."

A dozen options flashed through Kaahi's mind. His eyes darted around the room, as he realized that his only escape route was back through the door. He weighed the lies he could tell in an attempt to deflect the blame. He even considered violence, but the guns carried by Saito and his companion ended that train of thought half-formed.

In the end, he decided to stall for time. "I . . . can explain," he began hopefully.

"Cut to the chase," snapped the woman, in a coarse American accent. "Where's Abur Ramaas, dickhead?"

Saito gave her a wan look and then nodded. "Indeed, yes. That is the most salient question."

Kaahi's hands knitted together and his eyes strayed to the clock on the wall. *If he could keep these foreigners talking* . . . His rescue was on the way. All he had to do was delay long enough for it to arrive. "You can't go after him. Not now. The odds are in his favor. He's changed everything."

"I disagree," Saito said, and he drew a long, needle-like knife from a vertical holster on his webbing vest. "You are making it necessary for me to compel you." The Japanese glanced at the American, as if he was uncertain how she would react. The woman showed no response to the open threat.

Something occurred to Kaahi. "You haven't seen it, have you?"

"Seen what?" demanded the American.

He took a step toward a portable DVD player on his desk, but she lifted the gun slung at her hip, aiming at his belly. Kaahi paused and raised his hands. "Press play," he told her. "Ramaas sent a new message to your president and all the rest of them. Watch it and you'll understand."

Lucy scowled, and then she tapped the button on the little device. The disc inside whirred into life and the screen flickered before resolving into an image of Ramaas. It was filmed in the same kind of floating, handheld camera style as the earlier "declaration" she had seen on the *Themis*, but the backdrop was different. The walls behind Ramaas's head were old, painted metal patched with rust. It had an industrial look to it, like a factory or something similar.

"*You men of power,*" he began, showing his teeth. "*You have had time to think on the lesson that I taught you.*" Ramaas leaned in, until his face filled the screen. "*Now you must pay for your sins against my people and my nation. You must pay in treasure or in blood. You choose.*" He chuckled, rubbing at the cheek beneath his damaged eye.

The camera followed him to a table, upon which was a commercial maritime chart showing the coastline of Somalia. Scattered atop it were photos and blueprints of the Exile device—but no sign of the steel case itself.

"*You will give me respect,*" Ramaas went on, "*because I will show you all that you are no better than me. A brigand.*" He patted the blueprints for the bomb. "*There will be an auction,*" he continued. "*In twenty-four hours' time. Here. You will pay me for the right to know where the weapon is hidden.*"

"You sneaky son-of-a-bitch," muttered Lucy. "So he is about the money after all."

Kaahi gave a nervous giggle. "He has out-played you!"

On the screen, Ramaas was still talking. "*Bidders must be present at the location of my choice. No more than two representatives from each interested party. And believe me . . . There will be* many *interested parties.*" He reached out and took the camera from the hands of the person using it and carried it to the map. The screen blurred as the autofocus shifted and the chart became sharp and clear. A thick finger tapped the paper where a red cross had been drawn in the ocean. "*Here,*" intoned Ramaas. "*And bring no warships or aircraft within one hundred miles.*" The disc clicked again and the playback halted.

"What's out there?" said Lucy.

"A commercial gas-drilling rig," Saito replied, thinking it over. "Abandoned in place following this country's misfortunes. A good location for such a gathering. He's planned this well."

She chewed her lip. "I don't like the implication there, about *interested parties.*" Lucy shot a look at Kaahi. "Let me guess, you're in this because he used your connections to upload the video, am I right?" Off his nod, she stepped around the desk until Kaahi was between her and Saito. "So who did you send it to? Washington, Beijing, Moscow . . . And where else?"

Saito answered for him. "Anyone who is interested in owning a nuclear device. I would imagine that list is lengthy."

Kaahi drew himself up, finding some shaky defiance. "How does it feel to be the victim this time?"

"He has not succeeded yet," said Saito, and his hand moved in a blur. The long, thin stiletto blade he held pierced Kaahi's neck above the collarbone and sank in deep.

Lucy reacted with a jerk of motion, but it was too late to stop it happening. Saito held the weapon in place for a beat as Kaahi gasped out his final breath. Then the blade whispered back and out and the man fell to the floor, crimson jetting from the entry wound.

"*Shit!*" Lucy took a step toward the dying man. "You didn't have to—"

"He told me what I needed to know," Saito went on, and he was moving again.

From the corner of her eye, she saw him come at her and she twisted, cursing her own reaction. It happened quickly, even as Lucy snatched at her gun.

Burning, screaming agony exploded across her back and her belly as Saito was on her, pushing the blade in through a tiny gap in the plates of her body armor. She screamed and tried to pivot, but the pain was incredible, lighting her nerves on fire.

Her knees turned to water and Lucy crashed to the floor, falling next to Kaahi as the light in the man's eyes faded. Gray fog crowded the edges of her vision, and dimly she was aware of Saito tearing her gun from her nerveless hands.

"You will not die from this." His voice seemed to come from a great distance, echoing down a tunnel. "Unless you remove the blade, and then you will bleed out in under an hour." He was pulling at her gear, stripping her equipment. She swatted at him, felt a blow connect, but it was all so far away.

The pain became a tidal wave, and then blackness washed up over her.

TWENTY

They both reeked of spilled hydraulic fluid and the fixes they had cobbled together inside the Osprey's fuselage looked like a mess, but finally Marc had been able to help Ruiz get the VTOL back to something approaching operable condition.

Marc climbed back into the pilot's seat on the right-hand side of the cockpit and prodded at the keyboard next to the multifunction digital screen before him. He paged through sub-menus and found the diagnostic display he needed. Green status tabs illuminated one by one, and he blew out a breath. "We're okay," he said aloud. "I think."

He sensed Ruiz behind him, seeing the man's reflection on the inside of the cockpit windows. "Piece of cake," said the mercenary, wiping grime off his hands, although his tone gave the lie to his response. "Just be ready to spin us up. The moment Saito gets back, we're out of here."

"We can make it across the Kenyan border in a couple of hours—" Marc began, but Ruiz spoke over him.

"Job's not done," insisted the other man. "Like it or not, you're in this with us now."

With the work of patching up the Osprey's damage to keep him occupied, Marc had been able to put aside his enmity at working with the Combine operatives, but now he had a moment to dwell on it, his manner darkened again. "I don't think so."

Ruiz dropped into the co-pilot's seat and glared at him. He pointed at the two body bags in the cargo compartment. "Byrd got himself killed in the house, and then we lost these on the way out. Mayer back there, he's wounded bad—"

"All the more reason to evac," Marc broke in.

Ruiz talked over him again. "And that asshole Ramaas is laughing at us. This don't end here, you get me?"

Marc chewed on that for a moment. "Don't try to tell me you're going after Ramaas because you want some payback. You want him because the Combine want him."

The mercenary snorted. "Yeah. You think anyone else has got the stones for the job?" He gave Marc a withering look. "You and the woman thought *you* were gonna stop him? Don't make me laugh." Ruiz shook his head. "That rich dick Solomon and all of his crew, you're just day-players getting in the way. Oughta stay back, let the better men do what's needed, you get me?"

"Better men?" Marc repeated, his ire rising. "The Combine is nothing but a bunch of bastards with more money than morals! You're either too stupid to get that or you don't give a shit!"

Ruiz sneered and got up. "Hey, you wanna die poor and righteous, be my guest. I want payback and I wanna get paid, so fuck everyone else." He walked away, muttering to himself.

A reply was forming on Marc's lips, but it faded as he saw movement outside. A fast shape came bouncing across the football pitch from out of the darkness, and by reflex he grabbed for the pistol holstered on his thigh. He'd left his MP7 back in the rear compartment while the work of repairs had gone on, and now he wished he hadn't.

Then Marc heard the low keening of an electric engine and knew it was Saito's dirt bike returning. But something was wrong; the bike only had a rider and no passenger. He scrambled out of the gunner hatch behind the cockpit and went after Ruiz, who was already at the rear of the aircraft.

As Marc ducked below the Osprey's wing, Saito was climbing off the bike, sharing a quiet word with Ruiz. The Hispanic merc's expression became cold and he turned on Marc, raising the Vector carbine hanging on his shoulder strap.

Marc's Glock pistol was already in his hand and he aimed it at Saito, ignoring the weapon that was coming to bear on him. "Where is she?" He spat out the question.

Saito made no attempt to go for his own gun. "There were some complications."

A rush of ice flooded through Marc's veins. "You killed her?!"

"No. She was alive when I departed," Saito replied. "Your friend is strong. She had a good wound. I believe that a woman of her resilience will be able to survive it. And if not . . ." He paused. "Well, that would be unfortunate."

"If she's dead, you'll be next." Marc spat out the words, meaning every one of them.

Saito shook his head. "Killing her has no value to me. Alive, she will be a distraction. Something for Ramaas's brigands to deal with while I position myself to take advantage of the situation." He glanced up to the night sky, as if gauging something unseen. "I could not have her close by, you must see that. She was too dangerous. An unpredictable element. But you, I do need. I require a pilot."

"*Fuck you.* I'm not helping you anymore." Marc's mind was a churn of conflicting emotions. If Lucy was out there somewhere, if she was hurt, he had to reach her. He owed her no less. "Tell me where she is!"

"The locals will have found her by now. But you should be more concerned about your own fate." Saito stepped around the bike, closing the distance between them. "And the matter of the Exile device."

Marc kept the Glock aimed directly at Saito's face. If he shot him, the Japanese mercenary would be killed instantly, but then Marc would perish a split second later as Ruiz opened fire in retaliation. Part of him wanted to do it, heedless of the consequences, and he had to stop himself from tightening his finger on the trigger.

"Ramaas released a second demand to the world," Saito went on. "He has called a gathering on an abandoned drilling rig off the coast. He is planning to sell the weapon to the highest bidder and I need to be there."

Marc never wavered, but inwardly he was racing to assimilate this new information. Saito had to be telling the truth, at least in some form. He needed Marc to fly them out of here, and as Ruiz had made clear, the Combine's mission was far from over.

"We are ready to depart?" Saito directed the question to Ruiz, who nodded. He looked back at Marc. "Then this is how we shall proceed. You will drop that gun and take us out to the rig. You will assist us in completing our recovery of the Exile device and when that is done, you are free to go."

"Else I end you here and we do it the long way round," said Ruiz. "Your call, *pendejo*."

"Why the hell would I agree to that?" Marc ground out the words. "You reckon I'd actually trust you?"

"Because you know that you have no better option." Saito cocked his head. "We know where Ramaas is. Your mission is the same as mine. *Find him*. Are you going to abandon it for the woman?" He paused again, considering something. "Do you think, if the roles were reversed, she would do the same for you? You know what is more important."

A hideous, chilling kind of acceptance rose up in Marc's thoughts, a realization that Saito was actually right. Weighed against the threat represented by Ramaas and his stolen Russian nuke, Lucy Keyes was just one life. There was an entire city's worth of potential victims out there right now, and if the warlord's schemes were not stopped, a horrific death in nuclear fire was waiting for them.

"If it will salve your conscience," Saito added, "blame me. Understand that I have given you no other choice in this."

"That's how you people work, isn't it?" Marc's reply was loaded with venom and bitterness. "That's the Combine's style. Find where people are vulnerable and *squeeze*."

"Yes," agreed the mercenary. "But ultimately, the decision is yours."

"Fuck you," Marc repeated, his anger crumbling into despair. The pistol in his hand wavered, and the muzzle dipped.

Ruiz saw his cue and spun his Vector carbine around, slamming the butt of the weapon into Marc's head, knocking him down to one knee. The mercenary wrenched the Glock from his hand and then came back to strip the sat phone and survival knife from Marc's gear vest.

Dazed, Marc spat out blood from a cut on the inside of his cheek and lurched back to his feet. He burned with humiliation, and as his hands contracted into fists, he wanted nothing more than to give in to his anger.

Saito saw it in his eyes and there was a flicker of concern on the mercenary's face, there and then gone. "I imagine you are considering doing something dramatic and foolish. I would advise against it."

Marc wanted to make a threat, to say something that would let him believe he wasn't giving in without a fight—but there was nothing to be done. Saito was holding all the cards, and he hated himself for having to admit it.

And more than that, Marc knew that the moment the Combine mercs were done with him, they would discard him with the same callous disregard they had shown Lucy. But while he was alive, he still had a chance to do something. *What that is, I have no bloody idea.*

At length, he took a breath. "So let's go, then. Sooner we're done, the sooner I never have to look at you again." Marc took a step toward the Osprey, then stopped, as another thought occurred to him. "You said you left her alive."

"I did," Saito replied.

Marc smiled coldly as he found the smallest of victories in the moment. "Trust me, mate . . . You're going to regret that."

The pickup screeched to a halt outside the television station and Guhaad jumped down from the flatbed, shoving aside a youth toting an AK-47 who stood in his way. The young gunman was barely a teenager, and he blinked at the bigger man in confusion as his jaw worked on the ball of khat in his mouth.

"Where is Kaahi?" Guhaad demanded. "He isn't answering his phone. And I don't like to be kept waiting!"

The youth with the gun blinked again, and then pointed in through the doors of the TV station, toward a fretful-looking woman who had been waylaid by more of his comrades.

Guhaad strode into the building and the men he brought with him followed, sensing his annoyance and mirroring it in their swagger. The youths intimidating the woman saw him coming and immediately they ceased their games. All of them knew who he was and where he stood in the hierarchy of Ramaas's organization.

His mood had been fierce since his return to Mogadishu. He still burned with anger at the humiliation of being sidelined during the race from the bomb-maker's home, and although the warlord had made nothing of it after they made their rendezvous to escape Dubai, Guhaad was convinced that others saw his actions as failures.

If anything, the lack of criticism from Ramaas made things *worse.* Guhaad knew that Zayd had not returned from his mission in Europe, and he knew that the warlord had given the other man a new and more important task to accomplish. Jealousy ate at him. Ramaas was planning something big, something dangerous, but he still deflected every question Guhaad put to him about it. He would not explain what was going to happen with the Russian bomb. The only conclusion Guhaad could draw was that Ramaas did not trust him with that information.

He fumed. He wanted Ramaas to understand he was just as capable as the cold-eyed sniper, but fate continued to conspire against him. Resentment simmered and his anger moved like water, searching for the path of least resistance. Guhaad loomed over the woman, directing it toward her. "Who are you?"

"My name is Esme . . ." She looked at the ground, fingers clutching nervously at the edges of her hijab. "I work here . . ."

"Where is Kaahi?"

"Upstairs." She pointed. "His office is on the third floor, but they won't let me go back up there."

"Get out of my way." Guhaad pushed her back toward the cluster of youths, instantly dismissing her. He took the stairs at a pace until he reached the upper floors. The place was in disarray, but he ignored the mess. He didn't care about what was happening here, only that Ramaas had told him to deal with Kaahi.

The resentment flared again. This was a job for someone less important, Guhaad told himself. Ramaas was mocking him with this little duty.

"Boss?" One of his men was at an open doorway, and his face was stiff with surprise. "I found him . . ."

Guhaad didn't need to enter the room to know that Kaahi was already dead. He could smell the fresh blood in the close, unventilated office. He could see the pool of dark crimson soaking into the thread-bare carpet around the man's fallen corpse.

"They cut on him," said the man at the door.

Guhaad's eyes narrowed and he tried to imagine what had happened in the office. Someone with a blade had come here and ended Kaahi silently. *Why?* If the attack was some attempt to strike at Ramaas by killing one of the government men in his pocket, then it was a poor one. There were many more where Kaahi came from.

He looked down and saw that his boot was resting on another patch of bloody carpet. Guhaad refocused and picked out more spatters of red. *A trail.* He backed away a step and now that he knew what to look for, he saw a path of wet marks leading out of the office and down the corridor. At the far end there was a door hanging half open, leading to a fire escape stairwell. There was a smudge of crimson on the handle.

He found the woman collapsed on a landing halfway between the second and first floors. She was wearing a black coverall like those Guhaad had seen on American special forces soldiers, and there was a red-soaked scarf tied around her belly as a makeshift bandage. The hilt of a narrow dagger was wrapped in the wet cloth.

Her face was the color of wet clay, filmed with sweat and drained by blood loss. Guhaad gave a grunt of surprise as he realized *he knew her.*

She tried to back away from him, but she was already pressed into a corner. He sized her up and waited for her to remember him too. After a moment, he saw the light come on in her eyes. "I didn't think I would see you again," he grinned. "But maybe Ramaas is right. Maybe God does have a plan for all of this."

The woman was tough, he could see that. She bit down on her pain and gave him a defiant look in return. "Sorry about . . . messing up your ride."

He nodded. The American and the white man, the English who had been with her in Dubai, they had been responsible for running him off the road. This one, she had killed Bidar and left Guhaad for dead in a roadside ditch. He wondered about what he was going to do with the woman to repay that indignity.

"You are a long way from New York City," he told her. "You came a long way to die."

She eyed him. "You don't know me."

Guhaad laughed at that. "My Uncle Yarisow, he drives the taxi in Manhattan. I hear that accent when I talk to him on the telephone."

The woman gave a pained chuckle. "Oh, yeah? Are you like him? Maybe you're. . . . you're for hire too?"

"What is she saying?" The rifleman standing behind Guhaad made a confused face.

"Go down to the next floor and wait there," he snapped, the order coming from him before he thought it through.

His jaw stiffened. He knew exactly what the American woman was suggesting, and his first instinct was to take out his blade and slit her throat then and there—or better still, walk away and let her bleed to death.

But he did neither. She had the right mixture of arrogance and desperation in her voice, a tone that Guhaad had heard many times before. How often had he stood on the deck of a captured cargo ship or a rich man's yacht, and listened to some overfed Westerner saying the same thing? *How much money to let me live?*

He enjoyed the feeling that gave him, the control and the strength of it. The thrill of power made his resentment and disgrace fade. The American worked for important men, *wealthy men*. That was certain. So what harm would there be in taking a taste of that? Guhaad found himself liking the idea. Ramaas could busy himself with the Russian bomb and Guhaad . . . He could deal with this. He was capable.

And if it became a problem, he could simply kill the woman and dump her in the ocean.

He folded his arms. "You have something to offer me?"

"Take me to . . . a doctor. Then the airport." She straightened up, wincing with pain as the knife in her gut shifted with the movement. "Half. Half a million dollars for a taxi ride."

He grinned, knowing that he had her life in his hands. "No. Double it."

"Asshole!" Her head lolled forward and she took a ragged, panting breath. "*Shit*. Shit, okay. A million. My people will pay that."

"If you are lying—"

"I'm dying," she shot back. "Yeah, yeah, I know the drill. So we doing this?"

He nodded, and shouted out to the gunmen to come back up.

They carried her out to the waiting truck, and Guhaad told the driver that things had changed. Kaahi was dead, just as Ramaas wanted, but now something else had come up. They were going to see the old man, the *dhakhtarka* who lived down on the waterfront.

As the pickup's motor turned over, Guhaad climbed into the flatbed and leered at the American woman in the dimness. "Don't die on the way," he told her. "I don't like to waste money."

But she wasn't listening to him. The woman was looking up into the night sky, as if she was trying to pick out something.

Guhaad heard a noise on the breeze. It sounded like a helicopter, but deeper and heavier, a rumble from powerful engines that faded off into the distance.

Despite the pain she was in, the American gave a weak smile. "Still alive," she said to herself.

"We will see," Guhaad replied, and banged on the back of the pickup's cab. The vehicle lurched forward and sped away.

The Calypso XV gas rig had been built by men who said it would be a monument to new ideals and greater prosperity for the nation of Somalia, but those sentiments had been lies from the start.

Like the multinational corporations that had sent their fleets of factory ships to drain the coastline of fish stocks and the criminals who sank barges full of toxic waste in the shallows, the Calypso was the product of minds who saw the lawless, poorly governed seas off the Horn of Africa and wanted to plunder them. With no national administration to waylay them and few with the will to enforce applicable laws, the men from the West buried a great concrete pylon in the ocean and started drilling for natural gas.

Calypso XV was all that remained of their ambition, almost a decade later. Abandoned in place after poor yields and a faraway financial crisis conspired to ruin its creators, the monopod rig protruded from the dark waves like a gray stone tree trunk. Its canopy was a blocky mess of industrial machinery. Rusted, decaying pipes festooned the structure. The multiple decks were derelict, and for a long time they had been left to fall apart and tumble into the sea.

For Abur Ramaas, it was one more sign that his path was the right one. God had allowed venal men to build this thing, and then punished them with its failure. There was a certain kind of justice to that, the warlord reflected. And in the spirit of balancing the scales still further, he had taken control of the Calypso rig as part of his schemes to unite the pirate clans of the surrounding regions.

As a boy, Ramaas had listened to the Christian missionaries who told him stories about the ancient history of Europe and the massive stone fortresses that dotted the landscape. Now the Westerners would have to come to his castle. Fitting that it sat atop the ocean, amid the seas he had known since he was a youth. From here, he would return Somalia to the strength it had always been denied. He would free his nation from the shackles of the West for all time, and make himself a king in the process.

We have never been pirates, he told himself. *We are not criminals. We deny the laws of those who say it is so.*

Ramaas looked out over the water from atop the gangway where he stood, and showed his teeth. Very soon, he would have everything he wanted.

"Boss?" He heard an awkward shuffle of feet and turned to see Little Jonas approaching him along the creaking deck. He was only a few years Ramaas's junior, but the man's small stature and odd gait made him appear strangely childlike, and so "Little" he became. "More boats out there." He waved in the direction of the sea and the black horizon with his bad right hand; it was crooked like a talon, although it didn't affect the man's skills with computers.

Jonas had a sharp mind and a wicked streak, both qualities that had ultimately brought him into Ramaas's orbit. Jonas's father and mother had fled to America in the 1990s and he had been raised there. An affinity for both crime and technology had soon brought him to the attention of the authorities, and Jonas ultimately found himself fleeing his adopted country for the nation of his birth—and it was there that his skills were found to be of use to his familial clan. Jonas was the one who set up the voice-over-Internet network Ramaas used to coordinate with his men, and Jonas was the one who had learned how to hack the shipping logs of the cargo vessels sailing through the Gulf of Aden, all the better to target the richer pickings and let the loads of lesser value pass unmolested.

With his help, Ramaas was turning the wheel of history, pulling Somalia back toward what it had been in years past—a place to be feared, where those who crossed its sea-lanes would have to pay a tribute or perish.

Ramaas smirked. Now that ideal seemed small. Now his name was being spoken in the castles of all the world's warlords, and he liked how that felt. "What boats?" he demanded. "American? Chinese?"

"Yes. Russian too. They are obeying you, boss. They are staying out past the line you gave them, and no jets have flown over us." Little Jonas said it with an air of confusion, as if he couldn't quite believe it was happening.

"Fools," said Ramaas. "Do they think *we* would obey *them* if our places were reversed?" He laughed at the idea.

Below, bobbing on the surface of the calm ocean, a docking platform rose and fell in the gentle swell. Moored to it were a cluster of smaller boats—a few military-style rigid inflatables, a handful of raider skiffs and two out-of-place motor yachts. This was the fleet that had brought the supplicants to Calypso XV, along with a couple of helicopters parked on the broad landing platforms atop the rig. Ramaas's "guests" had been given accommodation in the abandoned living quarters, and it amused him to imagine these men from their great nations being forced to spend a night inside the stinking, rusting hull of the old rig. After all the indignities his nation had suffered, it was another small victory.

"Will any of them kill each other before dawn?" Ramaas wondered aloud. The bidders were not just from the nations he had directly threatened; arms dealers, envoys from terrorist factions and what the Americans like to call "non-state actors" were in there too. "Rats," he said to the air. "A cage full of rats all wanting to tear out each other's throats . . . but too afraid to take the first bite."

"Another message came in over the radio," said Jonas. "Someone else wants to join our game."

"Did they pay the toll?" Ramaas took a deep breath of salty air. All interested parties had been required to lay down a quarter-million-dollar payment just to be allowed to approach the rig.

Little Jonas nodded. "The Combine are on their way now. They don't like to be left out of things."

Ramaas gripped the gantry's rusted guide rail and for a moment he didn't know if he should spit or roar with laughter. Finally he nodded and let a smile crack his face. "This is good," he muttered. "Let them come! It is right they should be here. I want them to see it."

There was an implied dismissal in Ramaas's words, but Jonas remained, absently kneading the wrist of his crooked hand. He shot the other man a questioning look and finally he said what was on his mind. "We are not challenging the crew of a ship or the fat, rich men in some office a thousand miles away, boss. These are soldiers."

Ramaas waved the words away. "White men sent ships to kill us before and they failed to wipe us out. They sent troops here when I was a child! But we are still here and they are gone!" His voice rose, drawing the attention of some of the other men nearby on the gantry. "I will make these ones vanish too." He bit out the next words, making every one of them a bullet. "And we will still be here."

At first Lucy supposed they were going to murder her anyway, as the pickup stopped at a decrepit mini-mall sandwiched between a pair of three-story apartment blocks.

The pain was making it hard for her to concentrate, but she shrugged off an offer of help from one of the gun-thugs and made a point of hobbling into the building herself. She couldn't afford to show weakness.

The back door opened into what had once been a tiny fish market, but the smell of dried blood was layered over the briny odor baked into the walls and the floor. She cast around, finding a steel table with a sluice grate in the middle of it and a workbench laden with surgical tools. It reminded her of a Mob doctor's den she'd once seen in New

Jersey, but back then it had been someone else with a wound on them and Lucy had been the shooting party.

Stark light was thrown from a fluorescent strip in the ceiling, and from out of the gloom around its edges came an older man with the kind of gangly, ropey build Lucy had come to associate with the locals. His face resembled a piece of ancient petrified wood, all cracks and pits, and it was framed by glasses with thick frames and a grubby kofia cap.

He frowned at her as if he were some distant relative coming across a wayward child. "Oh, daughter, what happened to you?" The old man's voice had a lilting accent Lucy couldn't immediately place. He took off his cap and stuffed it in a pocket, waving her over to the steel table as he moved to a butler sink to wash his hands. "Guhaad, is this your doing?" He glared at the man who had captured her in the TV station.

The gunman shook his head. "If I wanted her dead, why would I be bringing her to you, old fool?" He waved at the air, as if he was dismissing a nagging insect. "Make sure she doesn't die."

Half the money she had promised Guhaad was already filtering its way into a set of Wells Fargo and Bank of America accounts held by fake names up and down the Eastern Seaboard of the USA. Lucy had spoken to the cab-driver uncle in New York via cell phone as they rattled down the highway, not exactly at gunpoint but as near as damn it. It turned out that good old Uncle Yarisow had a sideline as a hawala broker, a less-than-legal conduit for money that Somalian immigrants used to send cash back home. Rather than trusting banks, brokers like Yarisow maintained an informal network of transactions based on bonds of clan loyalty and familial trust. Guhaad was cutting him in for a fat percentage of the agreed fee, which Lucy was drawing from an emergency Rubicon slush fund. Making the call and activating the money transfer would raise a red flag back in Monaco, but the exchange wouldn't be interrupted. *I hope,* she added silently.

She couldn't stop herself letting out a moan of pain as she climbed onto the table. The old man came over and unwrapped her makeshift bandages. Lucy smelled the pungent copper tang of her own blood and mint from his breath. He smiled at her, adjusting his glasses. "We have some work to do. Tell me your name."

"Lucy." She had to grind out the word. "What's yours, Pops?"

"Pops." He repeated the word with a grin. "I like that. Yes. *Pops.*" A fresh wave of agony rocked through her as the old man touched the hilt of Saito's knife where it was still lodged in her, and his expression became serious. "Daughter, this will be harsh for you. Strength now, yes?"

Lucy felt the blade start to move, and a firestorm burst across her nerve endings. She couldn't stop herself from releasing a scream—

—and time blurred around her like fog.

She shifted, gathering bits of consciousness back to her, and saw light glistening through the contents of an IV saline bag hanging from the fluorescent light fitting above.

Lucy's hand slid down to where she had been stabbed, fingers finding a deadened region of flesh there, bound beneath thick gauze bandages. She blinked to find focus and her gaze raked across the room, settling on a silver steel spike resting across a kidney basin. Saito's misericorde blade had been excised from her and cleaned.

"You can return it to whomever gave it to you," said the old man, as he came into view. He held up a hand to stop her from rising. "Not so fast, Lucy American. Go gently or the stitches will break."

"What happened . . . ?"

"You passed out from the pain. It was good. I kept you under while I worked, it seemed the best idea." He came close and she smelled mint again. "It has been a few hours."

"You speak good English," Lucy noted.

"*E parlo italiano,*" he added, with a wan smile, switching from one language to another. "*Russkiy slishkom malo.*"

"An educated man, huh?" She drew a shaky breath and slowly took stock of her body's condition, mapping it out.

"And your next question is, *Why is a clever old man living in a place that smells of stale fish?*" He chuckled. "I have been here since before you were born, child."

"Right. So where is . . ." She reached for the gunman's name. "Guhaad?"

"He hasn't gone far." That was as much a threat as it was a warning. The old man offered her his hand and she rose to a sitting position. "Move slowly. I used surgical staples to close you up, but they will open again if you decide to dance."

"I'll keep that in mind." Lucy took in the room and immediately saw it through a soldier's lens, looking for things that could be weapons if the need arose. Guhaad's men had taken her guns and her knife. Her eyes hesitated on Saito's dagger.

"For now," continued the old man. "*Tea*." He wandered off, disappearing through a set of dirty plastic flaps hanging across a doorway, and she heard him talking to someone else, the words too indistinct to be clear.

She slipped off the steel table, ignoring a faraway throb of dull pain from her gut. Lucy crept around the room as quietly as she could, trying to get a sense of who her new caretaker was. The old man clearly had some medical training—that was obvious in the professional manner with which she had been patched up—and by the look of him he had to be in his seventies if he was a day. One table was overflowing with piles of old books and vinyl records, and she frowned at it. What Lucy needed right now was something more modern: a cellular phone she could use like a rescue flare to contact Rubicon. Her own sat phone was gone, probably taken while she was unconscious. There was no way to know when Guhaad would get back, and she wasn't hopeful about her chances of dealing with the gunman and his pack of thugs in her current condition. She needed another option.

The old man came back into the room. "Tea will be ready in a—" He stopped and gave her a stern look. "What did I tell you?"

"I'm not dancing." She forced a smile, and tapped the books. "Quite a collection you got here."

He flashed his teeth, showing a gappy grin, and came over, fishing out a dusty hardback with a sun-bleached red cover. "Relics of times past," he explained, cracking open the book. The yellowed pages were dense with tiny lines of Cyrillic text. "Before the Civil War here, back when I was your age . . . I was a doctor with the Army. We were Socialists then, you understand? The Soviets were our allies . . ." A shadow passed over his face. "Well. We believed they were." He tossed the book back on the pile, as if he was suddenly annoyed with the idea of what it represented. Instead, he picked up one of the old records, and Lucy saw that the label said it was a recording of *La Bohème*. "At least the Italians left us with some culture, eh? They were in charge when I was a boy. " The shadow in his eyes returned again. "They cut up our lands like meat. And it has been the same way ever since."

He was giving her an opening, so she took it. "I thought things were different now. AMISOM is here, right? The African Union Mission helped put your own people back in charge."

"Did they?" said the old man. "What do we have now? A government of splinters? Backed by troops from Kenya, Uganda and other countries who care nothing about this one?" He shook his head. "They are content to let us eat ourselves as long as we do it quietly. It is a crime, daughter. A crime." He put down the record and wandered away.

"Is that why you work for Ramaas's men?" she asked.

He stopped, his back to her. "He is a beast, that one. But is that what we need? A wolf instead of sheep?" The old man turned back toward her. "Everyone is tired of following politicians who only talk and talk. Even *your* people feel that way." There was a pause. "You hope that the older you get, the more you would come to ease with the way the world is, yes?" He shook his head. "Not so. I am angrier with the men in power now than I have ever been." He gestured at the air. "Let him burn it, daughter. Let him burn them all. How else do we make them understand?"

The plastic flaps moved and a skinny young boy in a pale blue soccer shirt backed into the room, bearing a tray with cups and a pot of tea. He rasped out a breath with each step he took, his lungs laboring. Lucy caught the aroma of hot apples and her mouth watered.

When the kid turned around, she saw that his right leg was missing from the knee down, replaced with something made of leather and grubby pink plastic. With exaggerated slowness, he brought them the apple tea and poured out measures for both of them. Lucy took hers gratefully and gave him a wink.

"Look at him and then at me," said the old man, nodding at the boy. "A lifetime of years between us, and what we have in common is what the West took from us. My past . . . His future."

"He was . . . wounded?" Lucy found a chair and sat down, cradling the tea in her hands. She was still shaky from blood loss and fatigue.

"He was born that way," explained the old man. "Deformities from the contamination of the water table. Another gift from the Italians."

"I don't follow you." Lucy sipped the tea and watched the boy cross to the table where she had been patched up. He set to work cleaning up the mess that had been made in saving her life.

"Uranium. Lead and cadmium, mercury." The old man ticked them off on his bony fingers. "Poisonous remains from chemical factories and hospitals. Ships laden with it were deliberately drowned out in our seas and every time there is a tsunami on the other side of the world, it washes up on our shores. Slow venoms to go along with all the rest."

She said nothing, taking in his words. Lucy had heard stories about organized crime groups accepting bribes to spirit away toxic waste from corporations and governments that didn't look too hard at where the material was headed.

"So many gifts we have been given," he said bitterly. "Until our sons started attacking ships in the Gulf, no one knew we existed. Until America made a film of it."

Lucy put down the cup, listening to the seething fury in the old doctor's words. "If you think that's true, why did you save my life?"

"I don't blame you." He smiled again. "You are not rich. You do not toy with lives for profit. I see it. You're a soldier, yes? I was too, once. Like those poor fools on the ships . . . Just ordinary people made to serve the ones with no hearts." He paused. "And also I was told to. Guhaad tells me. He is Ramaas's right hand."

She licked her lips and leaned in, deliberately holding eye contact with the old man, trying to bring him into a confidence. "Ramaas is threatening to kill a lot of innocent people. People like me, old men like you and kids like him." Lucy nodded toward the boy. "Ramaas has put a gun to their heads."

"People in the West?" he asked. When she didn't reply, he went on. "It is hard for me to feel sorry for them. All my life, they have been coming here to use my country for whatever they wanted." He got up and left his tea untouched. "And now we have a chance to oppose this, you want us to do nothing?" He walked out of the room before she could frame an answer.

TWENTY-ONE

Marc eased the controls over and put the Osprey into a wide turn, circling the aircraft around the Calypso rig with the platform on the starboard side. Looking out of the canopy, he could see the wide landing pad lit by portable floodlights and the flicker of human shadows moving around on the lower levels.

Night had fallen, dark and moonless, so the flight out from the coast across the sea became a test of his piloting skills as he worked the controls and struggled to keep them on course to the pirate haven. The V-22 was a good aircraft, and more forgiving than its checkered reputation had led Marc to believe—but it wasn't meant for solo flight and handing all the tiltrotor's systems alone was hard work. He was sweating it, not allowing himself to think more than a few minutes past the operational bubble he was working in. The black ocean was constantly pulling at the old, steady terror that lurked far back in his memory.

In a perverse way, it was a small mercy. Full focus on keeping the Osprey in the sky stopped Marc from dwelling on his current situation and his fears for Lucy.

"Are you going to land this thing or keep circling until we run out of gas?" Ruiz called out from the cabin behind the cockpit.

"Sod off," Marc snarled, snapping back to the moment. On the way to the rig, he had briefly entertained the idea of putting the aircraft into a ballistic attitude by standing the Osprey on its tail, then opening the rear hatch to send anything not tied down into the ocean. Unfortunately, the V-22 wasn't designed to fly that way and attempting to would have put the aircraft in the drink. All he could do was play along for now and hope that an opportunity to extract himself from this mess would present itself.

He sharpened the turn and took a deep breath, aiming the nose at the helipad while putting the Osprey's wing-tip engine nacelles into helicopter mode. The big three-bladed prop-rotors hammered at the air as the aircraft slowed and dropped toward the deck. There were few crosswinds, a stroke of good fortune that Marc was only too happy about. As they came down, he heard the synthetic female voice of the Osprey's on-board computer giving out monotone warnings about the aircraft's sink rate, but it was too late to go around. He had already committed to the touchdown.

For one sickening second, Marc feared he had overcompensated and was about to send them off the edge of the helipad and into the sea, but then the oleos in the Osprey's undercarriage crunched as the aircraft's weight settled and they were down. Fighting off a tremor of adrenaline in his hands, Marc blew out a breath and robotically worked his way through the shutdown checklist. In another time or place, he would have relished the chance to fly the tiltrotor, but here and now the gravity of the larger situation overshadowed the challenge.

By the time the Osprey's systems were secured, Saito and Ruiz had already disembarked from the aircraft. Marc followed them out on the deck of the derelict rig. As he passed Mayer on the way out, he saw that the unconscious Combine mercenary was pale and his breathing was shallow.

"Your man needs serious medical attention," he told Saito.

"He knew the risks," replied the other mercenary.

A group of gunmen emerged from behind a gray EC135 helicopter parked on the far side of the landing pad, all of them toting Kalashnikovs, their eyes darting around the Osprey. They reminded Marc of a pack of wary hyenas. Some of them wore surplus military kit, but the majority were garishly outfitted in brightly colored uniform shirts from Premier League football teams.

At the lead, a lanky man in a Manchester United shirt that was two years out of date sized Marc up with a sneer, and said something to his comrades. The group split apart and Abur Ramaas was suddenly there, large as life and scowling like a storm cloud. Marc saw that his bicep was wrapped in a grubby, blood-stained bandage, his trophy from the melee escaping Jalsa Sood's mansion in Dubai.

"Did I not make myself clear to your masters?" said the warlord. "The Combine is not welcome in Somalia."

Saito let the man's words roll off him. "My employers were disappointed by your retirement of Amadayo and Brett. But what is done is done. This is a different matter."

"Always the businessmen," muttered Ramaas, scanning the group. "But the blood is just as red and the money is just as green as all the rest." His gaze settled on Marc and his eyes widened. "*You* are here, policeman?" He barked out a laugh. "You have not learned your lesson yet?"

"What can I say?" Marc masked his real feelings with a shrug. "Sometimes I don't take the hint."

Ramaas nodded. "You're stubborn." He clapped a large, thick-fingered hand on Marc's shoulder. "That will get you killed one day." He eyed Saito. "You are with these fools now?"

"Not by choice."

"Ah." Ramaas made a face at his men and they laughed. "If you are here, it is because *Waaq* wishes it. I won't question that." He drew back. "You will be present to see how the game ends." The warlord gave a dismissive wave and started to walk away.

"How long can you keep this up?" Marc said to his back. "You're not Somalia, man. How many people do you really speak for—your clan at best? You're a pirate with delusions of grandeur." He took a step after him, drawing a deep breath of air laced with salt spray and rust, ignoring the guns that were raised in his direction. "You're trying to run with the big dogs, but you have to know . . . They're never going to let you keep that bomb."

"*Keep it?*" Ramaas threw him a glance over his shoulder. "Is that what you think I want, policeman? To sit on it like the Americans or the Russians do, making threats forever?" He glared at Saito, his tone turning sour. "Such acts only have value to merchants and their servants." Then the warlord laughed again. "What good to a soldier is a weapon unfired?"

* * *

When Lucy was certain the old doctor was out of earshot, she caught the attention of the boy and gave him a warm smile. "Hello," she began. "Can you speak English?"

"A little." His head bobbed.

"What's your name?"

He grinned back at her. "Rio." He paused. "You are from America?"

"I am."

Rio considered that. "I've seen it in films. It's big."

She nodded. "That it is."

"People there seem very angry."

Lucy kept her smile in place. "Often true. But not everyone. Not me."

He jerked a thumb in the direction of the doorway. "I shouldn't talk to you. He will be upset."

"We don't have to tell Pops," she said, making a conspiracy of it. Lucy gave him another wink and he laughed. She pressed on. "Hey, Rio. Can you help me with something? I need a phone." She raised a hand to her head, making the universal "call me" gesture. "I bet you have one, right? Can I buy it from you?" Secreted inside a hidden pocket in her tactical jumpsuit was a fold of crisp $100 bills, and she pulled one out to offer it to him.

Rio half-reached for the money, then frowned. The bill was stained dark where Lucy's blood had soaked into the paper. "I should not take it." For a moment, avarice warred with the kid's wary nature—and then he suddenly brightened. "We can play for it!"

He fished in the pocket of his baggy cargo shorts and came back with a handful of playing cards. His plastic foot clicking on the floor as he moved, Rio put three of the cards down on the operating table and slipped them around.

Lucy knew this set-up. Seeing it played on block corners every day of her youth as she grew up in Queens, she knew that it was the classic example of the "short con," a way to sucker in marks with what looked like a fast and easy version of *Find the Lady*. It was all about using sleight of hand to misdirect, so you would be chasing a Queen card back and forth without knowing that it had never been where you thought it was in the first place.

Rio showed her the cards and then mixed them up, waiting for her to give him the nod. She decided to play along, and gestured with the hundred.

The cards moved, the boy's hands blurred, and Lucy pointed. *Wrong card*.

"Sorry!" He held out his hand for the money, pleased with himself.

She didn't give it to him. "You got this wrong, young blood. You're supposed to let me win one time. Then you up the bet. Take me for more." Lucy reached out and took the cards. "Let's do this another way. My turn."

Rio started to complain, but she was already working the deck. Lucy flashed an Ace of Spades in one hand, the Queen of Hearts and the Ace of Clubs in the other. It was an easy slip, if you knew how to do it. As the cards went down, she made it look as if she dropped the red face card first when it was actually the black Ace. With a flick of her wrist, the cards were swapped and now anyone watching would be tracking the wrong target from the start.

But the boy was sharp. He knew the trick, and he didn't fall for it. Rio found the Queen and flipped it over, his momentary dismay turning to a smug smirk of victory.

Lucy admitted defeat and handed over the bill. "You're good at this, kid. Who taught you this, was it Pops?"

The plastic flaps over the doorway crackled and Lucy cursed inwardly as Guhaad strode in, with the doctor trailing behind.

"His father taught him," said the old man.

Guhaad grimaced and pawed at the cards. "This is a stupid game."

He tossed the cards away and Rio gave a gasp of dismay. "That's because you never win it," said the boy, with as much defiance as he could manage.

The gunman's nostrils flared and he raised his hand as if he was going to strike Rio. The boy recoiled but the blow did not come. The old man nodded at the doorway and Rio dashed away—taking with him the c-note and any chance Lucy might have had to part the kid from his phone.

"You shouldn't threaten the boy," the old man told Guhaad. "Ramaas won't be pleased."

"He won't say anything," Guhaad snapped back. "Not if he knows what is best for him."

And suddenly, Lucy saw something she had been missing. The same curve of the jaw, the same pug nose. *Rio is Ramaas's kid.*

The old doctor met her gaze and he guessed the train of her thoughts. "Now you can better understand why Ramaas has such rancor in him. Rio's mother died during childbirth. There were not enough medicines, because of the sanctions." He sighed. "And then the boy himself . . . his leg . . . his lungs . . ."

"Stupid game," repeated Guhaad, picking up the Queen of Hearts and glaring at it. "The prize is never where it is supposed to be."

A shell game. The grim certainty crystalized in Lucy's mind with an abrupt, definite weight.

Events from the past few days shifted and locked together, one thing trailing into another. She remembered what Marc had told her about the confrontation in the Kurjaks' casino, then she drew up her own recall of the frantic chase down the highways of Dubai and the ambush that had been waiting for them in Welldone Amadayo's mansion house.

And she knew what she had to do.

"Is the woman fit enough to move?" Guhaad was asking the old man. "I want her gone!"

Before he could reply, Lucy was on her feet. "Change of plans, handsome," she told him. "I'm not going to the airport. Take me to Ramaas."

Guhaad let out a splutter of incredulous laughter. "Why should I do that?"

"Hey, you don't want him to know you're making bank on the side, I totally get it." She walked stiffly toward him, ignoring the pain in her gut. "But think how impressed Ramaas is gonna be when you bring him someone else who wants to bid on that bomb." Lucy tapped her chest. "I work for a rich man. But then you already know that."

Guhaad's hand dropped to the gun in his belt. "Maybe I shoot you instead. You are too much trouble."

Lucy shrugged. "Your call. But do that and you won't get the rest of the cash we agreed on. And old Uncle Yarisow will be real disappointed."

"What is she talking about?" said the old man, but Guhaad waved him to silence.

At length, the gunman's face shifted from annoyance to something darker. "All right. Come with me."

"You should have left when you had the chance, daughter," called the old man, as Lucy followed Guhaad out toward the street.

"No can do," she replied. "I gotta play the hand I've been dealt."

The contact was waiting for Zayd exactly where he said he would be, loitering beside a battered blue panel van parked at the mouth of a narrow alley. A few hundred meters away, sparse traffic on the main road rushed back and forth in a steady rising-falling whirr of noise. A police car howled past, casting spears of light briefly over the walls of the buildings rising over the backstreet as its siren sounded. There were few pedestrians out at this time of the night, and that was all to the better.

Zayd looked around, the sniper's sharp eyes instinctively analyzing the angles of attack. He considered where he would like to be for the best sight-lines and patterns of fire. One city was very much like another to him, all of them cluttered masses of hides, kill boxes and cover. In the end, he reduced them all down to abstract patterns through which he could weave a bullet and send another soul off toward death.

Without a word to the driver of his taxi, he got out and dragged his gear with him. One was a long, thin case made of ballistic black nylon that resembled the cover for a fishing rod, the other a heavy sports bag that hung off a long strap going over his shoulder.

The contact knew his face and nodded in greeting. He extended his hands in an offer of assistance, but Zayd pushed him away.

"No one touches these but me." His words were harsh and brittle.

He had been traveling for many hours to get here and his temper was frayed with fatigue.

"Whatever you say." The contact blinked and rubbed a hand over his dark features. The two men were of similar height and build, close enough in aspect that someone with an educated eye might have guessed there was some clan connection between them. Zayd saw it in the other man, but he gave little consideration to the fact beyond that. He wasn't here to spend time comparing the complex networks of who might know who and what person might be related to which other. The contact wasn't going to be a friend, just a means to an end.

"What is your name?"

"The name that the *gaal* gave me is Eddie," he began. "But I am—"

Zayd cut him off before he could say more. "That is good enough. Show me."

Eddie nodded, his head moving in short jerks. He led Zayd to a metal door in the wall of the alley, opening a massive industrial padlock. The door slid open and a draft of musty, machine-warmed air wafted out.

Looking in, Zayd saw that the door led into an antechamber lined with lockers and electrical switchboxes on the walls. On the far side was a barred gate that opened into the mouth of a tunnel threading down into darkness.

He followed Eddie inside and put down the bags. The contact offered him a plastic carrier bag. Inside it was a clip-on flashlight, a laminated map of the service tunnels below, a tea flask and some khat wrapped in newspaper.

Zayd handed the khat back to him and took off his jacket. "I don't need that."

"You could be down there a while."

"I will manage." Under his jacket, Zayd wore a shirt of identical color and cut to the one Eddie had on beneath his dark blue fleece. He held out his hand to the other man.

Eddie frowned, then exchanged the fleece for Zayd's jacket, pausing only to give him the security pass he wore on a lanyard around his neck and a cap bearing the logo of the local metro system. "No one will give you a second look wearing this," he explained. "The meeting place is marked on the map. The others will be waiting for you there."

Zayd put on the cap and the fleece. "What about the communications?" Once they were in the tunnels, the digital satellite phone he carried would be useless.

Eddie nodded again. "There will be radios you can use. I wrote a frequency on the map."

Zayd glanced at the diagram and saw the numbers. "Good. You will relay the message if . . ." He paused, reframing his words. "*When* Ramaas calls?"

"Yes." He glanced out through the half-open door toward the driver in the waiting taxi. "That man. Is he one of us?"

Zayd shook his head. "A Kenyan. He doesn't need to know. But Ramaas was very specific about *our* people. Get the word out to anyone in the clan and our allies. Tell them to leave the city." As he spoke, he unzipped the sports bag and removed a folder containing his kunai blades. "Be careful how you say it. Don't start a panic."

"What's that?" Eddie pointed at something else inside the bag, a dented silver case with ribbed flanks.

"Not your concern," Zayd told him, and pulled out a wad of cash which he handed over. "Just make sure you have a way out when the time comes." He secreted the blades about his person and turned on the flashlight before gathering up the bags again.

Eddie licked his lips. "What exactly are you going to do?"

"We are going to pay back those who wronged us," said Zayd, disappearing into the sloping tunnel.

The glow of pre-dawn was lightening the sky as they forged away from the coastline and out into the deeper waters of the Gulf of Aden.

Lucy kept one eye on the gunman who had been left behind in the machine room to guard her, and another on the grimy porthole in the hull. Now and then she caught a glimpse of a blurry shadow on the horizon—the derelict gas rig. She kept her distance from the gunman, who had a vacant, cow-eyed look about him and a tendency to mutter.

Guhaad's boat was a medium-sized pirate dhow called a jelbut, the kind of vessel that in years gone by would have been a trawler. These days it served as mothership to a flotilla of skiffs for sorties against prize ships traversing the sea lanes off the Somali shore. The wooden hull creaked and moaned in a steady rhythm, the waves slapping off the bow as its diesel engine drove it onward.

Along with Guhaad, Lucy had counted only four men on board. She guessed that he wanted to keep his side deal with her as secret as he could, the better to avoid cutting in others for shares of his payday in order to buy their silence. All of them were armed with AKMs, pistols or machetes, and without a gun of her own, Lucy felt positively underdressed.

She drank tepid water from a plastic bottle and used the action to hide a survey of the machine room. Tools and mechanical spares for the boat lay scattered around on a nearby workbench, and she mentally evaluated what would be the best choice for an improvised weapon.

The hatch slid open and Guhaad entered with another armed guard, holding a satellite phone in his hand. Lucy heard the faint burble of a voice on the other end over the grumble of the dhow's engine. "It is time," he demanded. "Give him the password for the money."

She shook her head and jerked her thumb at the rig in the distance. "We're not there yet."

"Yarisow has to do this now," Guhaad insisted. "You pay the rest of the money or I will feed you to the sharks!"

"My gut says not to trust you," she retorted.

"And yet . . ." Guhaad showed Lucy an ugly grin and he rested his free hand on the butt of a .45 semi-automatic stuffed in his waistband.

"Fine." She reached out and snatched the phone from him. "I know the script for this. Done it more than once." Lucy raised the handset to her ear. "You listening, mack? Write this down." From memory, she quoted a six-digit numerical sequence that would allow Guhaad's uncle back in New York to unlock the remainder of his fee and close their deal. As he read it back to her, in the background Lucy heard the sound of an FDNY fire truck racing past and the noise gave her a strange, sudden pang of homesickness. She grimaced and tossed the phone back to Guhaad.

Lucy turned away, putting her hands flat on the workbench. She started silently counting down from ten.

Guhaad said something she didn't catch and ended the call. He barked out an order to the other guard and the man left her alone with Guhaad and the mutterer. She heard shouting from the deck above and immediately, the boat lurched into a hard turn. Out of the port-hole, the derelict rig drifted from sight as the dhow turned away toward the open ocean.

Lucy had counted down to *three* before they made their move. *Predictable*. She turned on Guhaad, becoming angry. "What the hell?"

The pirate thug glanced at the other man and grinned. Without even looking at Lucy, he hit her with a vicious backhand slap that knocked her against the workbench. He couldn't have telegraphed it more, but she took the hit and let it stagger her.

Guhaad pulled the .45 from his belt. It was an old World War II-era Colt, the barrel a dark tunnel aiming at her face. "You should have trusted your gut," he told her, enjoying the taste of his double-cross.

She knew the script all right. He was going to beat her, assault her, and then with her throat cut Lucy would go over the side to feed the fishes. The only variable would be if Guhaad decided to let his men come in and get their fill before they finally ended her.

He waved the gun at her. "Take it off."

Lucy lowered her gaze to the floor and let the tears come. "Wh-what are you going to do?" Her voice became plaintive and wavering.

Guhaad liked that. It emboldened him. "Take it off!" he shouted, and with his free hand he grabbed at her collar and pulled. The material ripped, revealing part of her bare shoulder beneath. She staggered away, toward the wall.

Across the room, the mutterer was watching the drama play out, fingering the grip of his rifle. He shifted from foot to foot, and Lucy knew he was wondering about when he would get his turn.

For a moment, she became "Lula" again, drawing on the meek and timid mask. "Don't hurt me . . ."

They were the magic words. Guhaad put the gun down on the

workbench and started to unbuckle his belt. Almost as an afterthought, he shot the guard a hard look and yelled at him. "Wait outside. I don't want you staring at me, idiot!"

Muttering irritably, the other man accepted the order with a nod and slid through the door, latching it shut behind him.

Guhaad chuckled and turned back to Lucy, still working at his belt. He walked straight into her attack.

Lucy put the head of the short claw hammer she had secreted in her right hand directly into Guhaad's cheek, and she did it with enough force to shatter his malar bone. As he fell, she had to flip the hammer to dislodge it, and it took her another two hard strikes about his temple to put the thug down for good. He was just an obstacle now, something to be removed from the world.

Guhaad twitched as he started to die, making wet gasping sounds and moans that were more animal than human. Lucy smothered his face with an oily rag and started a performance of her own, faking little cries of pain every couple of seconds and punctuating them with occasional sobs.

"You actually fell for that," she whispered to the dying man. "I mean, you knew I was capable, right? And still you reckoned you could smack me around." Guhaad tried to grab at her, but his hand flapped at nothing. "You're gonna die as poor as ever . . . That cash I promised you will evaporate by nightfall."

He let out a low hiss, but she kept up the pressure. The bank code Lucy had provided to Yarisow was the digital equivalent of fairy gold. Rubicon's financial servers would retroactively nullify the money transfer within twelve hours, and along the way embedded tracer software would be able to map the route of blind accounts the crooked hawala broker used to launder pirate income. That data would anonymously appear in an email to a contact at the FBI shortly thereafter. Although he didn't know it right now, old Uncle Yarisow had less than a day before men in blue windbreakers would come around to kick in his front door.

When her would-be killer was still, Lucy left him where he had fallen and grabbed Guhaad's pistol, checking the magazine and making sure there was a bullet in the chamber. She searched him, finding some more ammo, the thug's sat phone and a familiar needle-like dagger. She pocketed Saito's weapon and scowled. The stitches in her gut pulled as she moved and Lucy winced. Her pain meds were wearing off.

She was slow, dehydrated and outmatched four to one. Guhaad had let his dick do the thinking for him and paid the price, but that play wouldn't work again. *I need to do this cold and quiet,* Lucy told herself.

Working quickly, she took the empty water bottle and stuffed it with a long tail of fine wire wool from a box on the workbench. Packing the bottle until it was full, she kept up her breathless gasps. A shadow at the bottom of the door told her that the mutterer was right outside, listening in to the show.

The mouth of the makeshift bottle-silencer fit loosely over the muzzle of the Colt. It wasn't an ideal match, but with the steady rumble of the dhow's engines it would be enough to smother the sound of a shot.

Lucy took a position by the door and gave out a final long, strangled moan. She started counting down from ten again.

At *four,* the hatch slid open and the mutterer peeked in. He stepped into the room and she put a bullet through the man's neck. The reek of burned plastic and hot metal curdled in the air as he dropped to his knees, clutching at the spurting wound. She sent a second shot into his right eye.

Lucy put the man's AKM over her shoulder and cat-footed out onto the mid-deck. The three other gunmen were at the back of the boat, clustered around the helm and smoking cigarettes. She crouched at the foot of the stairs and listened for a couple of minutes, keeping her breathing silent, mentally mapping the positions of the remaining thugs and waiting for the ideal moment.

One of the men came forward, his bare feet slapping on the deck as he approached the stairwell. Lucy shifted position, putting herself in the deepest part of the shadows.

When he was almost on top of her, Lucy gave a low whistle and she heard him react. A head appeared in the open hatch with the muzzle of a rifle alongside it.

Lucy grabbed the gun barrel and yanked it hard, hissing in pain as the motion made her stitches stiffen again. The rifleman overbalanced and fell down the stairwell, causing a burst of laughter from his pals on the weather deck. He landed in a heap on the lower level and she fired twice at point-blank range.

The improvised suppressor fell apart as the wire wool melted and fizzed. Lucy grimaced and tossed it away. She thought about going for the AKM but she could already hear the laughter turning into concern. Now there were footfalls as the last two men left the helm and came across the deck, calling out to their comrade.

She started counting down again, this time marking off the steps to the stairwell. On the mark of *three,* Lucy bobbed up out of the open hatch and twisted like a gun turret, pivoting from target to target. She took down one man with a shot in the thigh and the stomach, but the last member of Guhaad's crew only got a glancing hit across his shin.

He was getting back up as Lucy scrambled out of the hatch. She ran straight into him and shouldered the man against the guide rail. He clawed at her face and pulled the trigger of his assault rifle, but the AKM was pointing at the deck and it only succeeded in ripping splinters out of the wooden planking. Lucy gave him a savage head-butt and he cried out. She shoved the man back again, and this time his feet slipped on the deck. He tumbled over the rail and fell head-first into the sea. The dhow chugged on regardless, leaving him to flail and yell as he drifted off, falling further and further behind the boat.

Lucy got to the helm and turned the wheel until the bow was aiming roughly in the direction of the derelict rig, visible on the horizon as a black blob. The pain in her belly was a constant gnawing ache now, and when she peeled back her shirt, the bandage beneath was spotted with blood.

"Secure and regroup," she said aloud, giving herself the order. Lucy used a rope to lash the helm in place, and then left it unmanned as she made a quick pass through the dhow from stem to stern. With her injury it was hard work hauling the dead men up to the deck, stripping them and rolling them overboard, but she managed it. Lucy found more ammo, some water and a bottle of painkillers, all of which were welcome.

As the rig grew before her, she used the satellite phone that had belonged to Guhaad to make a coded call to a dead-drop message box monitored by Rubicon. Her situation report was clipped and to the point; the mission was incomplete, the situation unfavorable, the directive unchanged. *Find Ramaas and stop him.*

Sitting in the shade of the weather deck, Lucy used the contents of an expired first-aid kit to re-dress her wounds and then sat silently, watching the rig approach and figuring out a plan.

She tossed her jumpsuit over the side and cobbled together a new outfit from the least soiled clothes she could find—cargo trousers, threadbare Nike trainers, a baggy soccer shirt and her bloodstained tactical webbing. The rest of the first-aid kit bandages she used to wrap around her chest, and the oversized shirt did the rest to disguise her gender. Lucy rubbed dirt into her face and found a bandanna for her head. The AKM on her shoulder completed the disguise, and she studied herself.

Not my best look, she thought. *But it'll sell.*

She brought the dhow in at the far end of the floating dock beneath the derelict rig and cut the engines. No one challenged her; they knew this was Guhaad's boat, and Ramaas's right-hand thug could go wherever he wanted. A khat-chewing guard threw her a spaced, disinterested wave as she dropped down to put a rope over a mooring cleat, and Lucy returned it. He looked away, already forgetting about the new arrival.

She started up one of the rig's service ladders, rising carefully hand over hand toward the upper decks of the wind-blown platform.

Mayer had died quietly, succumbing to his injuries during the night. Marc watched Saito zip the corpse into a body bag alongside the other dead Combine mercenaries and saw nothing resembling emotion on the other man's face. If anything, Mayer's passing was a minor inconvenience to him, like a tool breaking. Ruiz ignored the whole process, camped out on the drop ramp at the rear of the Osprey's cargo bay with his gun across his lap and a constant scowl on his face. The two Combine operatives had elected to spend the night on board the parked tiltrotor, watching the clock as the hours ticked down toward the time for the auction, and that had prevented Marc from getting access to the cockpit and the V-22's radio.

Marc's thoughts were churning and he hadn't been able to catch any more than an hour or two of sleep. Unspent energy rolled around in him, and he tried to walk it off around the perimeter of the gas rig's giant landing pad.

Below his feet on the lower decks, Ramaas's brigand army was stirring. There was tension in the air, a strong sense of violence being held barely in check. After their arrival, Marc had glimpsed groups of other invitees from the warlord's list of the wealthy and the dangerous. He caught sight of two Americans whose hushed conversation died when he came close. They had the tight-lipped, vigilant look of covert operatives, and Marc briefly considered opening up to them, trying recruit them as allies—but he had no way to make the Americans trust him.

Marc found an isolated corner of the gantry around the helipad and propped himself up on the safety rail. A line of bright orange sunlight glistened at the horizon, turning the ocean into a sheet of beaten copper, and he leaned into the strong breeze off the water, as if it could give him the answer he was grasping for.

The rusted decking of the gantry creaked and Marc glanced in the direction of the sound. Under a shadowed section of the platform, a skinny figure emerged from the gloom and aimed an assault rifle in his direction. Marc backed away, raising his hands.

The gunman's face was hidden behind a red scarf, and he made the universal gesture for begging a cigarette. "Sorry, mate," Marc replied, shaking his head. "Don't smoke."

"Good," said the gunman. "It's a nasty habit, Dane." The scarf came down and a dark, familiar face was looking back at him.

Marc experienced a moment of brief mental dislocation. "Lucy?" He took a step toward her, then halted. His head darted around, looking to see if anyone was watching them. "Holy shit, how did you get out here? Are you okay? How . . ." He forced himself to stop and take a breath. "I'm glad you're alive." A sudden weight of guilt dropped on him. "I wanted to go back for you, but Saito—"

"It's all right." Lucy kept to the shadows, watching all the angles she could. "You had to make a hard call. If you'd come after me, I would have smacked you upside the head."

"Yeah, well . . ." He frowned. "I still feel like shit about it."

"Good." She shouldered her AKM rifle and pulled a pistol from a pocket. "Here, take this. Reckon you're gonna need it before the day is out."

Marc considered the gun, then handed it back to her. "As much as I agree with you, better not. If Saito sees it, I'm not going to be able to explain it away."

She shrugged. "Your call."

He met her gaze. "I was afraid . . . he'd killed you." A shadow of that bleak possibility washed over him.

"I'm built tough," she replied, but there was an edge in her voice. Lucy was in pain, and she moved stiffly. "Just running a little slow now, is all."

He listened intently as Lucy explained how she had got out to the rig and survived Saito's attack. In turn, Marc gave her his side of events.

"We need to figure out what to do next," Lucy concluded. "If we have to, could you get the Osprey out of here quickly?"

He nodded. "Two minutes from a cold start, maybe, yeah. But what does that get us? We still don't know where the Exile device is and Ramaas won't volunteer that information. He's holding all the cards here, Lucy."

She gave a humorless smile. "You're more right about that than you know. I think he's running a game, Marc. This is three-card monte, this is a scam. Except the stakes are a lot higher."

"Yeah." Everything she said had been echoed in Marc's mind over the past few hours. "The Mercedes back in Dubai . . . When we shunted it, there were five cases in the boot. We know one got smashed, the other three we saw in the video demand."

"So where's the last one? I've been wondering that myself."

Marc said what both of them were thinking. "Here? Everything I've seen of Ramaas makes me guess he'd have it close to him."

"I'd agree with that, if only he hadn't faked us out at every damn step of the way through this whole thing. But short of searching this place from top to bottom with a particle detector, there's no way we can be sure."

He looked out at the horizon. "You can bet that the Americans, the Russians and the Chinese are looking for any excuse to drop a rain of cruise missiles on this rig. If they believe the bomb is here, they'll send this place to the bottom."

"But none of them want to take the risk that the case is on their turf." She sucked in a breath through her teeth. "Man, he's one clever son-of-a-bitch. Ramaas has all of them chasing their tails while he sits back and laughs his ass off."

Marc nodded. "He's got every gun in the world pointed at him, but he doesn't give a toss about it."

Lucy's lip curled. "And all those ordinary people back in Somalia trying to drag themselves out of the chaos, everyone Ramaas pretends to be fighting for, they just want to get back to something like a regular life. There's no ending to this that works out good for them."

Marc gripped the rusted safety rail. "Then we have to change the game." His jaw stiffened as the frustration and anger he felt inside rose to the surface. "I've been behind the curve on this. Missing the chance, over and over." He shook his head. "Not this time, Lucy. We have to end this before it's too late. Once Ramaas strikes that match . . . Nothing we can do will put out the fire."

She gave a grim nod. "You better get back to Saito. He'll get suspicious if you're not around." Lucy pulled her disguise into place and moved toward the shadows.

"And what about you?" said Marc.

"I'll be around," she told him. "I'm gonna try something. Call in a favor."

"Be careful," he warned.

Lucy flashed him a last, daring smile as she walked away. "You and I both know, we left that behind *days* ago."

— TWENTY-TWO —

The signal for the gathering was the sound of a warning horn that echoed mournfully around the steel compartments of the decrepit drilling rig. Under the guns of dozens of pirate riflemen, Marc followed Saito and Ruiz down through the decks until they emerged inside a wide-open area that had once been one of the rig's main machine spaces.

The steel deck was warped and rusty with neglect. Stubs of metalwork that should have been taken away for salvage stuck up everywhere, the remains of frames and the stems of sawn-off bolts like the roots of rotten teeth. In the middle of the derelict atrium there was the end of a shaft that fell away down the center of the concrete pillar that supported the rig, and Marc watched a tanned man in a dark jacket walk to the edge and look down. He kicked a lose piece of scrap over the edge and Marc heard it clack and rattle down into the dark. Both of them listened for the sound of a splash, but it never came.

The man in the jacket noticed Marc's attention and shot him a warning look. He had ink-black tattoos on his cheeks, numerals and ornate crosses that signified a senior position in Los Noche, one of the largest and most ruthless South American drug cartels. Very deliberately, he spat into the abyss and then walked away.

Marc's gaze tracked upward. The open space had the shape of an arena, with the lower level served by several entrances and a ring of grid-work walkways raised above it. More gunmen milled around up there, and he saw a youth holding a video camera, scanning the room to capture all the action. At the top of the chamber, a rough tear in the ceiling showed a light well above, allowing fingers of pre-dawn glow to filter in through the stale, unmoving air.

"Remain where I can see you," Saito warned. "If you become a liability, your use to me is over."

"You can swim home, then," Marc shot back. Saito and Ruiz stood close to each other, their attitude mirroring that of all the others gathering in the chamber. Every one of the attendees was watching the rest with belligerent expressions on their faces. As well as the group from the cartel and the CIA operatives he had seen before, Marc picked out what had to be the Chinese contingent—two unsmiling Asian men in business suits—and a pair of grim-faced Saudis who might have been al-Qaeda. He counted at least eight interested parties, all of whom were dressed in the kind of neutral, overcut clothes that could easily hide firearms. Only one other group stood out, a pair of colonels in North Korean army uniforms who plainly didn't care who knew where they were from.

A hatch opened and one of the brigands came in, pushing a crate on a wheeled dolly. He gestured inside. "Guns. Radios. Phones. In here!" He pushed it toward the North Koreans and pointed angrily when they made no move to obey. "Do it!"

He had four men with AK-47s standing behind him, and they all took aim. After a long moment, the two colonels sourly unhitched their leather belts and removed their sidearms, placing the weapons holsters and all into the empty crate. The brigand waved a metal-detector wand in their direction, the kind airport security guards used to scan passengers, and he barked at the officers when it went off several times. They made a performance out of giving up their hardware, and when it was done the process was repeated over and over as the pirates systematically disarmed everyone in the room.

Men with rifles on the upper gantries wandered back and forth over their heads, talking in low tones and glaring down at the assembled group. Marc searched for signs of a red scarf, and for a moment he feared the worst; but then he saw an athletic figure on the far side of the compartment, standing close to a towering, short-haired woman and a blunt-faced man he guessed were the contingent from Moscow.

* * *

Lucy was careful to stay back from the rest of the gunmen and do nothing to engage them. *So far, so good.* If they weren't dizzy with all the khat they were chewing, then they were animated by the promises that were floating around the rumor mill. *Ramaas was going to make them all rich. Ramaas was going to kill all the foreigners. Ramaas was going to declare war on the rest of the world.*

She guessed that the truth was in there somewhere. But for now, she was passing unnoticed and her boyish frame wasn't drawing attention. How long that cover would last, she couldn't tell. When it crumbled, she had to be ready. Lucy needed a fallback.

And here it was, potentially. The bull-necked guy was unknown to her, but he had the look about him that made Lucy peg him as Spetznaz. The elite special forces of the GRU, his kind were notorious for being as hard as nails and utterly dedicated.

The woman, on the other hand . . . Built broad like a shot-putter, she had classically Slavic features and a severe blond buzz cut. Lucy knew her face well enough. The last time she had seen it, a set of crosshairs had been between the pair of them.

"Rada Simonova," Lucy said quietly, as the rest of the room's attention stayed on the men collecting the guns.

The GRU officer stiffened, picking her name out of the noise, and turned slowly to face her. Simonova's long-fingered hands bunched into fists. "Who are you?"

Lucy stepped closer. "Grozny, three years ago. Remember those Chechen separatists with their anthrax?"

"The Americans don't know about that," said the woman. "Which means there is only one person you could be." She cocked her head. "*Keyes.* Not dead, then?"

"Not for want of people trying."

"Ha." Simonova gave a half-smile. "I wonder how this rabble would feel if they knew someone like you was loose in here. That might earn me an advantage with the pirate king, wherever he is."

"Seriously?" Lucy glanced around, making sure no one was listening in on their conversation. "That's where you go first, Rada? Selling me out? Not very sisterly of you."

"There aren't a lot of us in our game," said the Russian. "Maybe I want less competition."

The black-ops community had always been a traditionally male-dominated arena, and Simonova was right when she said that female operators were in the minority. It was half of the reason why Lucy had recognized the Russian while she had been scouting around the derelict rig. When there were only a few like you, you tended to know the faces and names of your contemporaries.

"We were after the same thing in Grozny," Lucy went on, "and we're on the same side here. That's why I didn't shoot you then." Her hand slipped to the butt of the rifle hanging from her shoulder. "You're not gonna make me regret that, are you?"

Simonova looked away. "You must be truly desperate to come to me for help, Keyes." She continued before Lucy could reply. "Let me guess; your African patron sent you in here, but now you've got no way out. So you're grasping at the closest thing you have to an ally."

"I am the only one of us who is currently armed," Lucy reminded her. "How long do you think you and your boyfriend there would last if these hyenas start shooting?"

"That is a good point," allowed Simonova. "So tell me what you want."

"Backup, for when this all turns to shit. Which it will."

"You sound so certain."

Lucy nodded. "We've been tracking this joker Ramaas for days. He's not gonna follow the playbook, believe me."

"*We?*" Simonova looked around. "You have company, then?"

She ignored the question. "Just remember, your people have got the most to lose here."

"What makes you say that? My comrades in the FSB have turned Moscow inside out looking for the weapon. Nothing has been found. Perhaps it never even existed."

"Uh-huh? Moscow wouldn't have sent a pair of top-kick GRU operatives in here if they didn't believe the threat was real," Lucy retorted. She moved so she was standing directly behind the Russian woman. "We know about the Exile Program. And if that bomb detonates, an hour later every nuclear scientist on the planet will have a read on the isotopic signature from the blast. And that'll lead right back to your government. I know your president is pretty bullish, but is he really ready for that?"

Simonova said nothing. The isotopic signature of a nuclear device was the equivalent of a radiological fingerprint, and with the correct spectroscopy equipment any physicist worth their salt would be able to determine the precise origin of the nuclear material in the suitcase bomb, down to the site of the plant where it was enriched. "If you know where the weapon is, tell me," said the Russian. There had been a playful tone to her earlier words, but now it was gone.

"I got an inkling," Lucy admitted. "But I don't know for sure. You in or out?"

"In," replied Simonova. "For now."

Lucy wanted to know what she meant by that, but across the compartment, some of the gunmen started chattering loudly. There was a thud of bolts from a sealed hatchway, and the men raised their guns and began shouting. She mimicked their actions but said nothing.

The hatch swung open on creaking hinges and it was time for the main event.

It was an apt description, Marc thought, because Abur Ramaas entered the room like a champion prizefighter walking to the ring, surveying the faces of everyone around him with an imperious sneer. A rough-throated cheer rose up from the warlord's soldiers and Ramaas accepted it with a harsh bark of laughter. Following at his heels were more armed men, along with a gangly, smaller guy clutching a laptop to his chest. The computer immediately caught Marc's eye—it was a ruggedised military-specification model similar to the kind he used, for now left behind back on the Osprey.

Like knew like. Marc recognized another hacker when he saw one. The guy bounded over to a raised area of decking at the back of the compartment where a portable generator had been set up, and started connecting the laptop.

Marc shifted slightly, trying to get a better look, but Ramaas came forward and blocked his view. "Policeman," he said, sounding out the word. "This is going to be a great day. You will see."

"Is that right?"

"Oh, yes," Ramaas added mildly. He walked to the crate filled with confiscated guns and communications gear, waving away the man who had been pushing it around. "Let me start as I mean to go on," he continued, addressing the room.

With a sudden surge of movement, Ramaas strode to the crate and gave the dolly it was resting on a hard shove with his boot. It slid across the deck and the back wheels slipped over the edge of the open drill shaft. Captured by gravity, the whole thing shifted and fell into the black void in a clattering disarray. The crate, contents and all, disappeared down the shaft and was gone.

Laughter filled the room as Ramaas strode back to the raised platform where the pirate hacker was unfurling a collapsible satellite dish. The warlord clapped him warmly on the shoulder, and then sat down on a tool chest that had been positioned like the throne of a king upon a scrap-metal dais.

"And so here we are," Ramaas intoned. "How does this taste to you?" He looked across the room, deliberately making eye contact with anyone who would meet his gaze. "All of you, so used to being the ones with the guns. The ones who are in control. But not today. Not on this glorious, great day." He leaned back. "I am captain now."

His words sent another ripple of mocking laughter around the room, and everywhere Marc looked he could see the faces of men who were itching to draw blood on any of the foreigners corralled before them.

"Let's just get this over with," said one of the Americans. "We're here. So tell us how much you want."

Ramaas glanced at the hacker, who gave him a nod in return. The hacker flipped the laptop around and Marc got a quick glimpse of the screen. He recognized what looked like routing protocols for financial transfer operations. *They're setting up a link to some offshore bank account,* he guessed. "It's going to be an auction," Marc said quietly.

"A simple game." Ramaas stood up and produced three white envelopes from inside his leather vest. He toyed with them, slipping them back and forth between his fingers. "Our first sale of the day." He fanned out the white packets. "Three devices. Three locations. But only one authentic item. Each of these contains a paper . . . and on it, the name of a city." He grinned, his dark and damaged eye glittering wetly. "The three highest bidders win these." He waved at the computer. "Come and make your offers, if you wish. Or wait for the next item. The choice is yours."

Slowly, reluctantly at first, representatives from the different groups came forward and stood out of sight of the rest in order to type out their bid into the laptop. Every one of them was greeted with a fresh series of catcalls and hisses from the assembled crowd of brigands, who made each approach to the warlord's "throne" into a walk of shame.

"Listen to them," growled Ruiz, as Saito returned from his trip up to the keyboard. "A pack of barking dogs." He glared in the direction of Ramaas, who drank from a bottle of beer and sat languidly as he watched the representatives come and go like supplicants. "And look at him! He's loving every second of this charade. Making fools of everyone!"

"You're surprised?" said Marc. "Ramaas has got power over everybody in this room and he doesn't care who knows it. Right this second, he's holding the world hostage, so he's going to enjoy it for as long as it lasts."

Saito gave him a cold look. "He's a thug who had a stroke of good fortune, nothing less. And soon it is going to run out. The Combine understands men like him. They will let him swing his cock around and shout about how impressive he is. Ramaas will make so much noise, he'll never hear the shot that kills him."

Marc shook his head. "You underestimate him and you'll regret it. People will die, if you play him for a fool."

Saito gave that flat, humorless smile of his. "What I see is an opportunist who deludes himself into thinking he is something more. What is that phrase you British use? *He has ideas above his station.*" The mercenary nodded in the direction of the dais as the gunmen made sport of the man currently standing in front of the laptop, a morose European whose allegiance was unclear. "These people are illiterate, vicious thugs led by a man who is only a little better educated. We shouldn't have to sully ourselves by dealing with a nation of them."

"Ramaas isn't Somalia," Marc snapped. "Not everybody in that country is a pirate! But then the Combine never really thinks hard about the people, do they? Just see resources for exploitation. You're no different from your bosses in that respect."

The Japanese man cocked his head. "You buy into the narrative too easily. Poor fishermen exploited by developed nations become pirates to feed their starving people. Like your Robin Hood, yes?" He grunted in derision. "Look around. How many of these men do you think were peaceful tuna fishers once upon a time? They had a chance to go back to that lifestyle when the military started patrolling the Gulf. There haven't been factory ships in these waters for years. Too few wanted to go back to the old ways. They like the easy money and the taste of blood."

Ruiz showed a wolfish grin. "Now that, I can understand . . ."

"Do you know why Abur Ramaas has gained so much influence?" Saito continued. "Because he pulled together the clans in Eyl and everywhere else, all on the promise of gold. He delivered and they went to him willingly. Whatever fraction of his countrymen have to suffer because of what he wants . . . I do not imagine that is something which troubles his sleep."

The gunmen jeered the last of the representatives—one of the North Korean officers—as he walked stiffly away from the dais, and Ramaas rose to his feet, idly tossing his empty beer bottle into the shadows. "I wonder, who paid the most to earn themselves peace of mind?" He leaned in to converse with the hacker and whatever answer he got was enough to make him roar with laughter. "Oh, so very predictable."

The warlord strode out into the crowd and pushed his way toward the Chinese. He tossed an envelope at them and then walked away, forcing one of the representatives to scramble down and retrieve it from the deck. Next, he went to the Americans and slapped a second envelope into the hand of one of the CIA operatives, before finally giving the last to the woman from the Russian contingent with a mocking flourish. Ramaas's gunmen liked the performance and they cheered it on.

Marc glanced at Saito. "Hard luck," he began. "Looks like you got bid-sniped."

"You really do not understand what is going on," said the mercenary. "This is just the opening gambit. The real play begins now."

Marc scanned the faces of the Russians, the Americans and the Chinese, trying to get some sense of what it was they saw written on the pages of their expensive prizes, but all of them held flawless poker faces.

He waited to see which of them made a move to leave immediately, even an involuntary glance toward the exits from the machine room. If they had bought the data that told them it was *their* city that was under threat, the need to communicate that to home base would be paramount. But no one moved or spoke, and the shape of an unpleasant possibility began to gather at the edges of Marc's thoughts.

"Are you satisfied with your purchases?" Ramaas asked. "No returns or refunds, I am afraid." He grinned at his men. "Our friends there have made us very, very rich!" A roar of approval echoed around the compartment.

Saito waited until the jeering ebbed before he spoke up. "The location of the device is not the most valuable thing you have to sell. Let us stop wasting time with your games and cut to the heart of this."

For a moment, anger flared in Ramaas's eyes. He didn't like having someone else push the script. But then the ire faded and he was back to playing his role as bandit king once again. "You're right. We will talk about the real prize." He produced a fourth envelope, identical to the previous three, and used it to fan himself. "Here it is. The remote radio frequency for the device and the seven-letter code that gives direct access to the weapon's control protocols . . ." Ramaas held it up over his head. "With this in hand, the device can be disarmed . . . or detonated . . . at will." His face split in a wide, shark-like grin. "What am I bid?"

Lucy tried to steal a look at the paper in Simonova's hand, but the Russian had it hidden away before she could get close. She fought down the sudden impulse to snatch it from the other woman, the consequences be damned, just so she could have some idea of where the threat was located. Lucy's home town of New York was in the firing line as much as Beijing and Moscow, and even as she tried to convince herself that it was all part of Ramaas's greater shell game, she couldn't help but experience a surge of fear for the city of her birth.

She closed off that part of herself and drew on her training. Lucy let herself go dead and cold, holding her focus on the target. She imagined herself in a sniper's blind, silencing her breathing, letting in everything around her, analyzing every variable. *Read the landscape. Look for the anomalies.*

Simonova showed no emotion, her face gaunt and statue-still. Across the room, the CIA operatives and the Chinese agents from State Security were equally stoic. None of them were meeting the gaze of the others, none of them showed the reaction that a warning about their own city would have instilled. That meant that either all those operatives had nerves of steel or that something else was going on.

The next round of bidding began, and it became an ugly screaming match. The Saudis and the mysterious Europeans fought over one another, upping the money on offer into tens of millions of dollars in the first few moments. Lucy watched as the Combine's representative added in his bids every so often, but to her dismay the major powers did little to stop the cost rising and rising. She kept expecting the Americans or the Chinese to drop in a sudden, show-stopping bid that would freeze out the rest, but they let it climb. Finally, the auction turned into a two-way duel between the Combine and the North Koreans, each topping the next until the bidding tipped the scales into the $200 million range.

Lucy found Marc and they shared a look across the chamber. The same question was on both their lips. *What the hell is going on?*

"Enough!" shouted Ramaas, bringing his fist down into his palm with a smack that echoed like a shot. He gripped the last envelope in his hand. "I am getting dizzy!" He snorted and his words were buoyed by the ferocious amusement of his gunmen. "Come and claim your prize!"

Both the Japanese mercenary and a North Korean came forward, but Ramaas nodded to one of his bodyguards and the man shoved the Combine operative back.

"Not you," Ramaas told him, bearing his teeth. "Never you. The lesson has to be taught to your masters. We have not forgotten how they sent the toxic wrecks to our shores. They are owed nothing but poison." He threw the envelope to the North Korean as the army officer stepped away from the laptop, the final cash transfer signaling it was complete. "Here. You have earned this!"

The man clutched the paper to his chest and held it close, scowling at the rest of the representatives, and smug in his victory. But then Ramaas gave another nod to his bodyguards and a gunman blocked the North Korean's way with his assault rifle.

"What now?" said the army officer. "Our dealings are over. We are leaving."

"Not yet. Open it," ordered Ramaas. "Let everyone see." He was eager for it to happen.

A growing sense of unease clawed at Lucy's gut as the sullen officer tore open the envelope.

The man flushed bright red with fury as he read what was written there. "*What is the meaning of this?*" he bellowed, turning on Ramaas. "The Democratic People's Republic of Korea will not be insulted by the likes of you!" He advanced on the warlord. "You will give us what we paid for!"

The officer's words were drowned out by a torrent of mockery and hateful laughter from the gunmen in the gallery, their taunts reaching a climax that made the metal walls vibrate.

"How dare you!" shouted the officer, and it was then that Lucy saw what was written on the paper. The seven-letter code was *FUCKYOU*. "We will rain fire and death down on your worthless nation!" the North Korean went on, screaming in rage. "You have made an enemy for a thousand years!"

"And you were idiot enough to give your money to me!" Ramaas shot back, silencing the other man with a roar. He waved at his gunmen and every one of them raised their rifles, taking aim at the assembled group. "Show everyone," he said, glaring at the Russians, the Americans and the Chinese. "Show the world what I sold you!"

One of the Chinese agents was the first. He reluctantly unfolded the page and held it out. Lucy's heart froze in her chest when she saw the words *NEW YORK CITY* written there. But if that meant the video from NYC had been of the real Exile device, then the others—

Simonova offered up her page. The location of the bomb was shown as *BEIJING*.

With growing alarm, the CIA operative who had taken the other envelope showed his paper to the rest of the group. Lucy heard Simonova draw in a hissing breath as the word *MOSCOW* became visible.

And then the room was awash in contemptuous laughter once again.

A shell game.

Marc stiffened as the full clarity of it shocked through him. There had never been any devices in the three cities. The videos, the demands, all of it had been a ploy by Ramaas to keep his enemies off balance, a way to make sure that he could fight them on terms that best suited him rather than those that favored the global superpowers.

"He lied to us all," said Saito, a hint of admiration in his voice. "I suppose you must respect his audacity, in its own crude way."

"Where is the weapon?" The North Korean officer was crimson-faced and livid. "We made a deal! You have reneged on your promise!"

Ramaas's feral humor flickered into rage for a brief instant, and he knocked the man down with a quick, brutal slap. "Of course I did! I am a liar! I am a criminal!" He opened his hands, daring anyone to decry him. "I am a pirate! I am what you have made me!"

"You're a dead man, is what you are." The words slipped out of Marc's mouth before he realized he had given voice to the thought, and they caught in the air in a random moment of pause amid all the jeers.

Ramaas glowered at him. "I beg to differ."

"Really?" Marc squared off in front of the warlord, fighting down the fear in his gut. "Correct me if I'm wrong, but you just scammed not only the largest military forces on the face of the planet, but also a bunch of the most ruthless extremist groups as well. In what version of that story do you come out of it alive?" He shook his head. "You're insane. Even if you kill everyone in this room, you've signed Somalia's death warrant!"

Ramaas let that slow, predator's smile come out again. "Don't you want to know where it *really* is, policeman?" He wandered back to the raised platform at the rear of the compartment, talking as he went.

"I have learned one truth in life. God has taught me this. The only things a man must respect are money and strength . . ." He rubbed at the skin beneath his dark eye. "Now I have both. I have taken it from these fools."

Ramaas moved to the tool chest he had been using as his makeshift throne and flung open the lid. From inside, he drew out a bulky steel suitcase and set it down. The room fell silent as the warlord opened the smaller case's latches and revealed the complex nuclear detonator mechanism within.

A vivid memory flashed in Marc's mind. *The duplicate steel cases in the boot of the sports car. Four of them.*

"So what now?" The enforcer from the Los Noche cartel spoke up. "You gonna start the bidding again, *hombre*? Is that even the real thing?"

By way of reply, Ramaas's skinny hacker wandered over with a Geiger counter and waved it in the direction of the device, the detector returning a sullen chorus of metallic clicks as he pointed the scanner head at the case's innards.

"No more money, no more shouting and posturing like some politician," said the warlord. "You want this? I will let you take it. The price is blood."

"You want us to . . . fight you for it?" Saito appeared to find the prospect interesting.

"Me? *No*." Ramaas chuckled. "Each other? *Yes*." He came forward and rested on a safety rail, as his gunmen drew back. "Each of you put in your best. The last man standing gets this." He waved in the direction of the steel case. "I've seen your money. Now I want to see your strength."

"All your lies," spat the North Korean. "Why should we believe you will keep your word now?"

"Because only a man who fights is worth my respect."

A ripple of anticipation went through the assembled gunmen. Marc saw some of them muttering to one another, others already trading folds of cash in anticipation of placing bets on the outcome.

"You don't seriously expect us to kill each other for your entertainment?" The CIA operative stood tall, his arms folded across his chest.

"The United States does not exist to amuse you, Ramaas." The American turned to meet the gazes of the others. "Listen to me, if we all refuse to—"

Marc saw the annoyance in the curl of Ramaas's lip; he saw the warlord throw a nod toward a pair of men standing behind the Americans. He tried to call out a warning, but a clatter of gunfire briefly filled the compartment as the armed thugs shot the two CIA men in the back with bursts from their AKMs.

"You refuse, you die," Ramaas said impatiently. "Now show me blood!"

Simonova threw off her jacket and the taciturn man at her side caught it. She shook out her arms, limbering up, and stepped forward.

"You're doing it?" Lucy hissed. "Are you out of your mind?"

"This is his arena," said the Russian. "He makes the rules." She turned and looked Lucy in the eye. "And I have my orders, Keyes. If I do not leave here with the weapon, this place will be destroyed in order to deny it to anyone else." Simonova flicked a glance at the watch on her wrist. "If I were you, I would get away now, while you still can."

Lucy followed her, clutching the assault rifle close, but Simonova was already walking into a wall of lusty shouts from the baying crowd. The tattooed Los Noche enforcer saw her coming and came around, bringing up his hands—too slow. The Russian landed a hard uppercut—the first blow of the new game—that hit him square in the gut and the cartel's representative staggered back drunkenly.

Ramaas's men roared their approval and it was the starting bell for the melee. Suddenly, there were fights breaking out all across the rusting machine room. Lucy saw one of the Chinese agents execute a brutal throat chop on one of the other representatives, sending the man down. She heard the sharp crackle of breaking bone.

Lucy drew back, using the distraction to cover her as she slipped around the edges of the compartment, moving toward one of the open hatchways. She could see Marc standing by a steel pillar, and as she watched him the Brit's eyes were darting back and forth as if he was searching for something.

I know that look, Lucy thought, and her heart sank. *He's going to do something reckless.*

"It's time to end these childish games," said Saito. He slid out of his combat webbing vest and pushed past Marc. "The Combine want the weapon. I'm going to get it."

"What, you're going to beat everyone else?" Marc snapped.

"I will do what is needed."

"Ramaas hates everything the Combine stands for," said Ruiz. "He'll deny it to you out of spite."

Saito nodded. "That's why I will kill *him* in front of all these animals. He said they respect strength—they will respect me when I break the brigand's neck."

"You'll never get close!" Marc watched him step forward, into the ersatz ring that had formed in the middle of the crowd. "When did this turn into *Gladiator*?" he muttered.

"Ah, these boys, they like the cut of it," said Ruiz. "It's all their kind know."

The Japanese mercenary did not hesitate to show his colors. He threw an overarm strike at the Saudi who stood up to oppose him, making the other man dodge—but from his vantage point, Marc could see it was a clever feint, and Saito's other arm came up in a bullet-fast punch that landed in his opponent's ribs. The Saudi reeled back as all the air in his lungs was expelled in a choking grunt. Saito walked to him, unhurried, and grabbed the thinner man by the throat. The Saudi clawed at the mercenary, trying to reach his face, failing. Saito put his long-fingered hand over the mouth and nose of the other man and smothered him.

"One down," said Ruiz, with a sour grin. "I've seen him do this before. Always an education."

Saito let the Saudi fall to the deck. Marc couldn't tell if the other man was still breathing, but the mercenary was already moving on to his next target, one of the Europeans. They fought close at hand, this time in a flurry of short, sharp strikes. Trading attacks, the two of them spun about at the edge of the crowd and the gunmen shouted as they came near, shoving them back toward the space in front of the raised platform.

Ramaas stepped down and walked among his men, sharing their elation, their savage joy at the display before them. The hatred in the air was a palpable thing. The brigands wanted nothing more than to watch these foreigners destroy one another.

Saito got his arm around the European's neck and twisted it with slow, steady pressure. His opponent's face turned purple and Marc heard a sickening crackle as the mercenary crushed his trachea.

"Two down," reported Ruiz. "*Madre,* I should have bet on him . . ."

"You think he's getting tired?" Marc said aloud. He wasn't looking at Saito or the other fighters anymore. He was staring at the hacker and his laptop, and the prize itself, the steel case atop the tool chest.

"What are you saying?" Ruiz gave him a sour look.

"Never mind." Marc took a breath and mantled a rusted switching gear on the deck, sliding over it and into the middle of the fighting space.

The crowd bellowed their approval at the sight of a new challenger, even as the rational part of Marc's mind was screaming at him that this was *the stupidest fucking thing you have ever done.* Saito heard the shouts and he was turning, momentary confusion written across his face.

Marc dragged up the muscle-memory of all those months of Luka Pavic's fight training at the gym, moving into the fast, sharp steps of a Krav Maga pattern. It was all about speed, about the application of maximum damage as quickly as possible. There was no way in hell he would beat Saito in a stand-up fight, no way he could second-guess him. His one, slim line of advantage was surprise—that, and the fact that the mercenary didn't consider him capable of it.

He went for a hard hit to the kidneys, mustering his strength and channeling it so that the punch landed in exactly the right place. Marc's fist connected with Saito's torso, but it was like hitting a wad of knotted rope. He got a grunt of pain from the mercenary, more from shock than actual hurt, and followed it up with hits in the same place.

If I can knock him off balance, if I can stay outside his reach—

Marc didn't see the backhand strike that hit him. It was a glancing shot, Saito's iron-hard knuckles clipping his brow and snapping his head aside. The mercenary followed it with a swinging kick that landed on Marc's knee joint and the second blow sent an electric shock of agony through his body. He stumbled backward and fell into the crowd, who parted and let him crash to the metal deck.

Marc blinked away the bright spirals of pain, and saw Saito rock on one foot, as if he was considering the value in coming in to finish the job. Then the mercenary flinched aside as the Chinese operative came at him and for a moment Marc's brief assault was forgotten. Some in the crowd spat on him and then turned away, disappointed by his performance.

Hands grabbed at his arm and hauled him up to his knees. He saw a dark red shemagh around a face and familiar eyes glaring out at him. "You're an idiot," Lucy grated.

"I know . . . what I'm doing." He dragged himself the rest of the way to his feet. Something he had said to Saito moments ago was running through his head, or perhaps it was the first signs of a concussion. "You'll never get close. I've got to get close."

"What?"

"Going back in," he said, lurching forward. "Trust me."

"Then for cryin' out loud, take this!" Lucy jammed something cold and metallic into his hand and Marc's fingers closed around it.

Marc stumbled back toward the edge of the crowd and the men around him parted. They gleefully helped him on his way, shoving Marc back toward the fighting floor.

The Chinese operative was still breathing and struggling to get up, although Saito had done something to the man to make his right arm hang wrongly from the elbow. Marc saw the Russian woman across the way in the middle of a boxing match with the Los Noche enforcer, the pair of them landing blow after bloodied blow on one another.

Saito rounded on him. "Are you going to make me end you? I'm sure I could find another pilot."

Marc circled the mercenary, until he was standing with his back to the dais. He could see Ramaas out in the audience, grinning wider with each blow struck. "Come and have a go," Marc snarled, "if you think you're hard enough."

Saito came at him in a rush, much faster than Marc had antici-
pated, leading with the same move he'd used on the Saudi. It showed
how little respect he had for Marc's abilities, lazily using the same
feint to set up for the hammer-strike that he would use to put him
down.

Marc met him halfway with a high punch to the chest, but clutched
in his fist was the weapon that Lucy had pressed into his grip. The
silver dagger was long and slender, a rod more than a blade.

Misericorde, Marc remembered. The clinical, analytical layer of his
mind retrieved the name from the depths of his tech-nerd recall, where
the stats for dozens of guns, the arcane forms of programming languages and a million other bits of trivia were stored. *Used for killing
champions.*

The tip went into Saito's body just below his right clavicle, the force
of his forward momentum making it sink in all the way to the hilt.
He screamed in agony and struck out with hysterical force, slamming
away his attacker with all his might.

Marc reeled back as though he had been kicked by a mule, as the
crowd let out an enthusiastic whoop. He struck the guide rail around
the raised platform and rolled over it, colliding with the pirate hacker
and knocking him sprawling.

And then the thugs were fumbling to bring up their weapons again
as Marc elbowed the rifleman guarding the steel case in the belly and
he folded. Marc snatched at the device, hauling it up and around in
front of him.

He clutched the case to his chest like a shield, opened outward so
everyone could see his hands gripping the shell of the detonator frame.
"Back off!" shouted Marc, retreating until he was flat against the steel
wall of the compartment.

"What . . ." Saito was finding it hard to breathe with six inches of
dagger stuck in him. "Are you . . . going to do?"

Marc visualized the technical diagrams from the NATO Exile files
in his mind's eye and the fingers of his right hand splayed across the
workings of the bomb, blindly feeling for a thick nest of wires connecting to the explosive detonator matrix. His left hand cupped the cylinder
that contained the nuclear payload of the device, the hemispheres of

enriched uranium that would be shot into one another to unleash the horrific fires of a fission detonation.

No one was shouting now.

He heard Jalsa Sood's dying words in the silence. *Right cylinder. Nine rods.* Marc's fingertips brushed over the cold metal of the frame and he counted out the numbers as his thumb brushed over the tips of the rods.

"Put it down," Saito ordered. "Before you . . . destroy us all."

"Piss off," said Marc, and he grabbed the bundle of wires in his fist. "I'm not sure what will happen if I rip these out. Who wants to see? I guarantee you won't want to be this close!"

From the far side of the compartment, Ramaas brought his hands together in a slow clap. "Very brave, policeman. How long do you think you can hold it?"

"Not long," Marc admitted. The case was heavier than he expected, and he was gripping it awkwardly. "Better start swimming."

Some of the warlord's gunmen were backing away, and Ramaas snarled at them in the local dialect.

"Release the device," said Saito. He was pale and sweaty, but still unswervingly on-mission. "Turn it over to me."

"It belongs to the Russian Federation," said the GRU agent.

The surviving North Korean delegate pushed his way forward. "It belongs to us!"

"Policeman won't pull the wires," snorted Ramaas. "He does not have the courage to go to God and take us all with him."

Marc sniggered, a sudden nervous urge to laugh fighting its way up out of his chest. *Damn, this case weighs a ton!* He grinned wildly at the room. "Here's the thing, Ramaas. You've lied about everything, every time. Just hiding one lie underneath another. And I reckon this is no different."

He yanked hard on the bundle of wires. They came away in his hand with a fizz of electric discharge and Marc let the case drop to the deck.

In that second, any sound would have been thunder.

── TWENTY-THREE ──

The detonation would look like a second sunrise to the early-morning fishermen who had sailed from the coast of Puntland and Galmudug. Men looking toward it would be permanently blinded by the flash of nuclear fire out in the Gulf, and those on the shore would hear the echo of the explosion, the sound reaching as far north as Raas Casayr and all the way south to the streets of Mogadishu. Satellites in orbit would see it happen, a ball of sun-hot plasma engulfing the derelict gas rig in a millisecond, atomizing thousands of tons of steel and concrete and seawater—

The idea of it overwhelmed Lucy and suddenly she couldn't breathe. She pulled the shemagh from her face, her disguise forgotten. Marc's name was forming on her lips, but he was already doing it, he was already tearing out the detonator wires from the weapon.

He let it drop and the case clattered loudly to the floor. No one dared to utter a word, as if they were afraid a single breath would set it off.

And then the tension snapped like a cord reaching breaking strain. "It's a fake!" Saito bellowed the words across the compartment, the Japanese mercenary's emotionless exterior finally cracking. "Another lie!"

The same hot second of terror Lucy had felt in Dubai during the highway pursuit briefly flared and faded in her heart, a voice in her head screaming that she was *not going out like this* suddenly swept away by the truth.

Dane was right, damn him. Each fake-out Ramaas served up was the cover for the one after that and the one after *that*.

She grasped the full truth of it; this whole charade had *never* been about the bomb or the money. It was about turning the screws on the first-world nations that had used up Somalia and thrown it away, and who wanted to do so again. It was about Ramaas's vengeful need to humiliate and degrade them, publicly and violently.

She remembered the boy Rio and the way the old doctor's deeply buried hatred had boiled to the surface. Ramaas was speaking with the same voice. He had been all along, but nobody had seen it. *Nobody but Marc,* she reflected.

The warlord's dark face was like captured thunder and he roared the next, inevitable command to his men, furious that the Brit had put a sudden end to his game. *"Kill them all!"*

Every gun in the room opened up, and anarchy erupted as cordite stink filled the air. The surviving delegates scrambled for cover or dived at the nearest riflemen to get weapons of their own. Time slowed as adrenaline flowed into Lucy, and the familiar, icy rush of an unfolding fight spread through her body.

As she pivoted, she saw the Hispanic mercenary Ruiz fall to a torrent of bullets that ripped into him and spun him about before he went down. Lucy glimpsed Saito taking a hit in the torso before he vanished from sight behind the frame of an old generator unit. Across the compartment, Simonova and her comrade were fighting for their life against a gang of brigand thugs armed with AKs and machetes.

Lucy let instinct take over and she dropped to one knee, flicking the selector switch of the AKM in her hands to fully automatic fire. She pointed the assault rifle's muzzle at the ceiling and squeezed the trigger. Gripping the gun tightly so that its recoil didn't jerk it away from her, Lucy sprayed an entire magazine of 7.62mm bullets into the corroded metal of the roof and the broken ductwork hanging beneath it. Yellow sparks cascaded from the rust-chewed steel as it came apart, and whole sections of the ceiling caved in. The collapse brought with it a flood of oxidized dust and pieces of corrugated iron that fell on the men on the suspended catwalks and the compartment floor alike. Amid the melee, some of Ramaas's thugs began to panic and fire in all directions, fearful that a retaliatory attack had begun.

Lucy vaulted forward, coughing as the metallic dust choked her. She discarded the AKM's spent magazine as she moved, slamming in a new one by feel and pulling the slide to ratchet a fresh round into the chamber. She found Marc on the deck, in the middle of a tussle with Ramaas's gangly hacker sidekick. Marc swung a punch that missed and the youth hit him hard across the face with the flat of his laptop computer. It sent him sprawling and she cursed, running to his side even as the youth sprinted away.

"Get up," she snapped, grabbing for him.

"Forget about me!" Marc retorted, shrugging off her hand. "Get that tosser!" He jabbed a finger in the direction of the fleeing hacker.

Lucy spun around, leading with the rifle, in time to see Ramaas and the youth disappear through a hatchway, with a handful of his men following. He was bugging out, once again leaving nothing but chaos in his wake.

"Go, go!" shouted Marc.

Her jaw set and she ran, moving and firing short bursts to clear their way. Marc came after her, and she heard him swearing with each quick, limping footfall he took.

They made it out of the killing room with shots chopping at their heels, and Marc gave a groan as he leaned on a hatch to shut it behind them and block the path, swinging it closed under his body weight. He dogged the latches as heavy blows rained down on the frame, and lurched away. The pain in his knee was a razor across bone, but he couldn't falter, not now.

"This way." Lucy pointed down a narrow, shadowed corridor with the blade of her hand. "Sure you can keep up?"

"Easy," he said, through gritted teeth, going after her as she set off again.

As they moved, Lucy had her rifle close to her shoulder to aim down the AKM's iron sights. "I cannot believe that shit you pulled back there. Did you even think for one second what would happen if you were wrong?" She almost choked on the word.

"I wasn't wrong," he replied.

"You are either stupid or incredibly lucky," she retorted. "We get out of here alive? We're gonna go to Vegas and find out for sure . . ."

"Sod off," Marc retorted, and shook his head. "I'm not going to waste it on playing blackjack. I'll save it up for the important stuff, thanks." He coughed out stale air. "Anyhow. I wasn't lucky, I was *right*. That's all there is to it. Soon as I saw the case, I knew he was playing us for fools."

Something clanked off the deck up ahead and both of them instinctively flattened themselves against the walls. The reaction saved their lives, as bright muzzle flares in the gloom up ahead briefly illuminated the snarling faces of Ramaas's shooters.

Lucy fired back and heard a strangled cry as one of them fell. "They're running interference for Ramaas! He's gonna rabbit, I know it!"

"He doesn't matter," said Marc. "That laptop, though . . . We have to get it! Anything else is secondary!"

"Did you forget we still don't know where the weapon is?"

"And you reckon Ramaas will actually tell us? After all this?" Marc shook his head. "Not gonna happen. But we take the computer and this ends."

"Why?"

"Because a machine can't lie!" Marc shot back, flinching as a bullet shrieked off the wall near his head. "I know why Rubicon didn't pick up any cell chatter from Ramaas and his lieutenants . . . It's 'cause they don't use phones! They're on voice-over-Internet comms, all digital. That's how we track the bomb!"

Lucy ducked down to take a breath. "When did you figure that out?"

"A minute ago," Marc admitted. "When laughing boy clocked me with the laptop." The answer had literally smacked him in the face.

Lucy's eyes narrowed. "Okay." She launched herself out of cover with a yell and darted across the corridor, firing a long burst from the AKM on the run. There was another strangled scream and the heavy fall of a body.

Marc raced after her, moving as fast as he could manage. He almost stumbled over the gunmen Lucy had taken out and blinked in the smoky dimness. Glancing around, he picked out debris-choked stairs, one set leading up toward the top decks of the old rig, another down toward the concrete support pillar and the lower tiers. The metal steps rattled and echoed, making it hard to be sure where the sound was coming from.

Lucy aimed the rifle up, listening. "Someone there," she said. "Moving."

"Yeah . . ." Marc crouched and pulled an AKMS—the folding-stock version of the rifle Lucy was carrying—from the hands of one of the dead men. The gun was dirty with salt-water corrosion and strapped together with threadbare wraps of duct tape, but it was better than being unarmed. He checked the gun and searched the corpses for ammunition clips, divided what he found with Lucy. Then he froze, holding his breath "You hear that?"

Back along the corridor they had traveled down, the noise of rusted hinges sounded sharply. "They're coming up behind us," Lucy told him, heading for the stairwell. "C'mon, we gotta go."

Marc held out a hand to stop her. "*Wait*. We go up, what's there?"

Even in the dimness, he could see the look on her face was saying, *What do you think, idiot?* "The helipad. Ramaas gets on one of the choppers and he's gone." As she said the words, both of them heard a clanking noise from high above—a hatch closing.

"And if that's another fake-out?" He leaned close. "Ramaas is a sailor, yeah? He's under pressure . . . He's going to go for a boat, go for what he knows." Marc pointed down the stairwell, in the direction of the docking platform below decks.

"You sure about that? A helo would be the smarter option."

"I'm not sure," he admitted, and Lucy swore under her breath. "But we can't chance it. You go for the helipad, I'll go down to the dock." He scrambled over the debris and slipped down onto the descending staircase.

"Do not get killed," Lucy called after him.

"You and me both," he called back, heading into the darkness.

It was hard to move quietly. The metal stairs were choked with trash that had been left behind from when the drilling rig had been abandoned, and Lucy picked her way around slumped panels and sections where whole steps were missing entirely.

Two levels up, she started to get a little more light leaking in from along the corridor, but the morning sun was still low and if anything it made the places where the shadows fell run deeper and darker. In the distance, she could hear the cries of the pirate gunmen as they argued with one another and scoured the decks of the platform for someone else to kill.

She hazarded a glance at the glowing hands of her tactical watch. How long did they have before someone decided to come looking for their people? Lucy guessed that the militaries who had sent men in to meet with Ramaas would not wait forever for their operatives to contact them. And with all their radios and comms gear at the bottom of the rig's central shaft, that wasn't going to happen any time soon.

Metal clattered on metal, back in the direction of the machine room. Lucy whirled and aimed toward the source of the sound. A sliding hatch juddered open and two figures emerged. She was a heartbeat away from gunning them down when she heard a gruff male voice curse in coarse Russian.

"Rada?" She didn't let the gun drop. "That you?"

"Keyes?" Simonova came into view, her taciturn comrade moving awkwardly behind her. "You got out of there. I shouldn't be surprised."

"Same here." Lucy could see that Simonova's associate was bleeding badly from a wound in his torso. "That looks nasty."

"No, Dmitry always looks that way," said the other woman. "Where is your friend?"

"Around." Lucy wasn't about to completely trust the GRU operative, but then again they had already come to something approaching a temporary détente. "Job's not done yet."

"It is for us. Let me remind you of my earlier advice." Simonova pushed past her, dragging a liberated rifle of her own. "Don't be here. A contingency is already in progress."

"Care to elaborate on that?" Lucy asked the question, but she already knew the answer. Somewhere out there, the Russians were preparing to destroy the derelict rig. For all she knew, there could be a

flight of ship-launched cruise missiles on approach, hugging the wave-
tops to stay beneath the radar detection threshold. She shook off the
worrying image. "Okay, fine. Follow me . . ."

"Great minds think alike," said Simonova.

The deck plates beneath Marc's feet creaked alarmingly with each
footfall, and here and there he could see right through rusted holes in
the metal plating and down to the sea a few hundred meters below.
The lowest level of the rig was clamped to the underside of the platform's engine-block silhouette, festooned with gantries that led down
to the boat dock floating on the water's surface, and conduits that had
once held heavy-gauge pipes for transferring natural gas to waiting
ships. Like a lot of Calypso XV's structure, the rig was riddled with
voids where valuable machine sections had been cut out and removed
for scrap after the site was deserted.

The only ambient illumination was coming from the sullen reflection of the sunrise off the water, and right now Marc would have traded
anything for a flashlight. Wind whistling up through the holes in the
hull made everything creak and moan. It was impossible to be sure if
someone else was walking around out there, with every grind of metal
on metal the possible signal of an incoming attack.

He was sweating, and an instinct he couldn't fully articulate made
him halt in place. Marc dropped quietly into a crouch and held his
breath, listening. He laid a hand flat on the steel grid plates of the deck,
feeling the irregular vibrations through the metal.

He heard a sound, like a shallow intake of breath—and it was close,
dangerously so. Marc's splayed fingers touched something, a discarded
bolt lying forgotten on the edge of the walkway. He gathered it up,
and then with a quick dice-throw toss, he sent it skittering away over
the deck.

The bolt bounced off a section of wall and ricocheted. Twenty
meters distant along the walkway, twin fountains of fire erupted out
of the darkness as two guns opened up in the direction of the noise.

Marc pointed the AKMS a few degrees back past the point of the
nearest muzzle flare, aiming to where he hoped the shooters would

be. Holding the rifle sideways, he fired, knowing that the sound and fury of his own weapon would immediately give away his location.

More shrieking rounds flashed off the frames and the decking, and the first gun fell silent. Marc couldn't see the man he hit, but the shooter was mortally wounded and screaming in horrible agony. The sound cut into Marc and made his gut twist, but he was already moving as the second shooter turned in place to fire back in his direction.

The floor vibrated as he ran across it, and he felt a section lurch as it shifted under his weight. Marc vaulted forward and rolled away in time to see a sheet of corrugated iron and a length of decking fall and crash into one of the Zodiac inflatable boats moored down below.

The man he shot continued to scream. Marc followed the path of the suspended walkway until he came to a blind corner with low head-room, choked by snarls of pipework. Feeling his way, he ducked down as random shots sizzled past him. The second gunman was close, but he didn't know exactly where he was.

In the near distance, the injured man's screams changed tone and then suddenly ceased in the bellow of single heavy-caliber gunshot.

Still low, Marc pressed himself into meager cover behind a disabled switch box and aimed the AKMS in the direction he had just come. He picked out a shadow, bobbing and moving, as the second gunman tried to figure out where he had gone. There was too much pipework between them for a clean shot. Marc would have to wait for the man to come to him.

He heard a shout in Somali, but no reply. Then a terse, exasperated sound. The shadow moved; the second gunman was walking into the trap.

Marc waited for the man to emerge from under the pipes, close enough that there was no way he could miss. He pulled the Kalash-nikov's trigger and it rewarded him with a dull click.

The gun was too heavy to be empty, but it had been poorly cared for and now the inattention of its last owner turned Marc's makeshift ambush into a disaster. He yanked on the cocking handle, but it didn't give a millimeter. Something in the gun was jammed solid.

The shooter gave a cry of rage and came at him. Marc reacted with-out thinking, slamming the AKMS on the deck in a last vain attempt to get the corroded gun to work. The cocking handle suddenly slipped free and he pulled on it, just as the angry shooter tried to crack open Marc's skull with the wooden butt of his own rifle.

Two decades old and a Chinese knock-off of the Russian-manufactured original, the rusted AKMS performed its final service with a clatter of shots that went point-blank into his attacker's chest cavity. Fluid and bloody matter burst from the other man's back and he died instantly, folding into a twitching heap on the deck. Blood began to drip off the walkway and spatter on the iron weather shrouding beneath.

"*Fuck*." Marc tasted copper and dragged his hand over his face, sickened by the brutality of the kill. He got shakily to his feet and forced himself to control his fast, panting breaths.

Back in the direction he had come, Marc heard a heavy footfall and then a low growl of a voice speak a command in Somali.

"Your boys are done," Marc managed, keeping his tone steady.

"Policeman," Ramaas called from the shadows. "Why do you keep coming? When will you learn?"

"I admit it," he said. "It's a character flaw." Marc was moving, slowly and quietly, mentally gauging his position.

His directional sense had always been excellent, and he knew that up ahead was the western end of the platform. Beyond that was an open-frame stairwell that descended the rest of the way down to the boat dock. He positioned himself with his back to the blank steel door that opened onto the stairwell, aiming into the gloom of the lower compartment. Thin razors of sunlight entered through the cracks around the door frame, cutting across the space before him.

"You got no way out, mate," Marc called. "Give me the computer and you can piss off with your winnings, I don't care. I've had enough of all your bullshit."

A deep, basso chuckle echoed off the walls. "Who wants money?" said Ramaas. His loud, booming voice made it hard to be sure from which direction it was coming. "In the end, the greed for it only causes more problems. The money was just something to hurt you people with, you see? It was another kind of weapon. One you Westerners gave me yourselves."

"We never paid you a fucking penny," Marc shot back.

"I am going to kill the men who brought ruin to my homeland," Ramaas said, after a moment. His tone became flat and matter-of-fact. "You know this. It has already happened."

Marc's blood ran cold. *Could that be true? While we've been out here playing games with this asshole, has he set the nuke off somewhere?* But the warlord's next words suggested otherwise.

"They will live the way I have lived. The way my people have lived." Ramaas sounded close enough to be standing right next to him. "The men who came before me? They loved only riches. They took money so your people could sink your toxic ships off our coast. You treated our home like your garbage dump, and it sickened our children. My children . . ." The warlord fell silent and Marc strained to hear him. When he spoke again, he was distant, his words echoing. "I know the names of the souls who did this. The Combine, who let the money change hands without notice. The criminals who let it happen, who found the crooked men with their filth to be disposed of and sent the ships . . ." His tone was a slow, steady burn of vehemence. "They ruled Somalia once. Then they poisoned it. But we don't forget. We don't forgive."

Marc ran his hand over the rifle's frame and tested the cocking handle for play, but it remained resolutely stuck. *Jammed solid.* He needed to act fast if he was ever going to come out of this alive, never mind get the better of the warlord. The man was out there in the dark, stalking him, and if it came to a one-on-one fight there was no way he would be able to defeat Ramaas. Marc took a shaky breath, feeling the tension of every single pulled muscle, every abrasion and blossoming bruise he had accumulated over the past few days. Trading punches with Saito was bad enough. If he tried to fight Ramaas, the bigger man would end him.

He remembered something that Franko Horvat had told him back in Croatia, in the casino. *You are in trouble. You are out of your depth.* In this moment, the corrupt cop's words had never seemed more truthful.

But I don't get to choose when I tap out, Marc told himself. *That's not how this works.* He took a slow step forward, trying to spread his weight on the deck, but the floor gave a grinding creak that betrayed him.

He fought back a wave of fatigue. He was tired of chasing this man, tired of running down one blind alley after another. He was tired of asking the same question over and over. "Where's the bomb?"

"So many places it could be," Ramaas replied. He was moving closer. "Paris. London. Rome. Berlin. All the rest. I wish God had given me enough weapons to strike them all. But I will be satisfied with what I have. A city full of thieves will be burned to ashes and all who gave them succor will suffer for it."

A city of thieves. Something about the phrase connected to a possibility in Marc's mind and his thoughts raced, his analytical nature seizing on it. Suddenly, he was looking at all of Ramaas's threats and boasts through a new lens, the truth just within his grasp if he could assemble the pieces correctly.

But then without warning, the hard metal muzzle of a large-caliber revolver jammed itself in the back of Marc's neck. "I keep seeing your face, policeman," said Ramaas. Somehow, the hulking warlord had managed to skirt around the edge of the walkway and blindside him, quick and silent. "No more. Make your peace," he continued.

Marc heard the oiled click of the pistol's hammer pulling back.

Lucy kicked the hatch that opened out onto the helicopter deck with enough force that it swung back as far as it could go and clanged loudly against the metal frame.

Simonova's comrade gave a furious snarl and surged forward, spraying fire from his rifle as he strode out onto the deck. He didn't appear to feel the wound in his gut that was leaking red all over the shirt and jacket he wore, powered forward by a kind of mad endurance that set Lucy's teeth on edge. The two women came out after him, as the first shots chewed up the deck at their feet.

Lucy saw figures crouching in the cover of a parked Mi-8 helicopter, with only their feet and lower legs visible around the wheels of the aircraft. She threw herself at the deck and landed hard, rolling across into an untidy half-prone stance that brought her AKM up and onto target. Flicking the fire-selector to single shot, she lined up the iron ring sight on the Kalashnikov and started shooting. The gun was poorly maintained and the aim was off by a couple of degrees, but she corrected automatically. With the Russians giving her supporting fire, Lucy picked off the men in cover by planting rounds in their ankles, through-and-through shots that blasted boot leather, bone and meat into a ragged mess.

Simonova crabbed forward, finding anyone who was alive and making certain they didn't stay that way.

Lucy hauled herself up as another target flickered in the corner of her vision. She saw the hacker burst out of cover and run toward the drop ramp at the rear of the black Combine VTOL. He had a snub-nose revolver in his hand and he fired it blindly in her direction as he sprinted.

She flicked the fire-select back to burst and drew a line across the helipad directly in the young man's path, emptying the mag of its last few rounds. He stumbled and fell over his own feet in an effort to stop himself getting shredded, and she sprinted over to him. Lucy stamped on his hand so he couldn't raise the pistol and poked him in his ribs with the AKM's red-hot muzzle.

"Where's the king?" she asked. "Tell me or you're dead."

"You won't win this," said Marc. He gripped the inert rifle in his hands, tensing himself for the killing shot. "You won't live to spend any of that money you stole. And your country and your people will be the ones who pay for what you've done."

Ramaas pressed the muzzle of the Python revolver deeper into Marc's flesh. "I have already won. You don't learn. You never do. Revenge is better than riches, policeman. Poor is poor . . . but dead is dead."

Marc turned slightly, the gun still against his throat. He could see Ramaas as a towering black silhouette against the weak light filtering through the door frame behind him. The warlord's shark eye glittered in the dark. "God didn't choose you," Marc told him. "You chose God as a way to excuse all you've done. You wanted a reason to justify it, but the truth is, you're just an amoral thug and you'll never be anything else."

Ramaas showed his teeth. "A day from now, the whole world will know my name. You won't live to see it."

Marc forced out a rough snort of derision, planting his feet firmly against the deck. He would only have one shot at this. "What you've gotta understand, mate, is that you're not the only one who knows how to set up a trick." As the last word left his mouth he twisted in place, jerking his head back and away from the barrel of the Python, bringing up the rifle like a club.

The revolver spat fire and noise, the thunderous blast of the round deafening Marc in one ear. The hot exhaust gas from the muzzle seared his flesh, pain rippling across his skin, but the shot missed. Crying out, he smacked the jammed AKMS into Ramaas's bicep, hitting the other man with all his might in the spot where Jalsa Sood had landed a bullet back in Dubai.

Ramaas howled in agony and let something fall, spitting his fury. Marc was aware of the laptop dropping from the warlord's grip, but he had no time to do anything about it as Ramaas fired again, the flicker of orange fire-light dazzling as another heavy round sparked off the rusted metalwork.

The bigger man swatted at Marc and caught him hard enough to unseat the jammed rifle from his grip. He staggered and Ramaas grabbed him, crushing his shoulder with fingers like iron rods.

In the hot, dusty dimness, Marc made out the shape of the revolver coming up again. Ramaas was going to bury it in his belly and kill him point-blank. He grabbed at the warlord's collar and held on tight, then let his legs go slack.

With no resistance to stop him, with the weight of Marc and his own momentum pulling him forward, Ramaas lurched across the walkway and the two of them crashed into the stairwell door. It whipped open beneath the force of their impact and they were suddenly outside on a creaking steel balcony.

Inside the confined corridors of the rig's under-levels, everything had been dark and filled with shadows; outside, the Western face of the drilling platform was bathed in the orange-yellow radiance of the rising sun. For Ramaas, with the damaged iris of his eye, stepping into the abrupt flood of harsh light was like a dagger being driven into his skull. Briefly blinded, he clawed at his face with one hand, flailing with the other.

Marc tried to disengage, but the butt of the Python cracked him across the ribs, knocking the wind out of him. Then in the next instant, there was a sickening lurch as the rusted walkway beneath their feet tilted, corroded bolts popping out from support frames as the two men cannoned back and forth against the safety rails.

Gravity snared them both. Marc and Ramaas spun over the edge of the collapsing stairwell balcony, and fell through a six-meter drop that landed them on a gangway beneath with a clatter and screech of tortured metal.

"Ramaas is gone! You won't stop him!" spat the hacker. He answered Lucy in American-accented English.

Her heart sank. Marc had been right about this as well. Lucy grabbed the youth by the collar and dragged him up. "Forget your boss, then. Where's the computer?"

"I gave it to him. He will keep it safe." The hacker showed his teeth in a wide grin, and he pointed a hand at her like it was a pistol. "You have nothing, bitches!" he added, spitting out the words in English.

"Then he's no use to us," said Simonova, as she walked up behind them. The Russian agent's rifle barked and the hacker was blown back by a shot that caved in his chest. He toppled over the edge of the heli-pad and Lucy jerked forward, watching his body windmill down to the ocean below.

"Shit!" She shoved the other woman out of her way. "I gotta find Dane . . ."

"No time," Simonova told her. She nodded toward Dmitry, and Lucy saw the other Russian standing half-in and half-out of the heli-copter's cockpit. He was talking animatedly into a radio handset. "Our pickup has arrived. You are going to come with us." Simonova's rifle wasn't aimed at Lucy, but the threat of what would happen if she did otherwise was clearly implied.

Lucy fixed the other woman with a hard glare. "I won't leave my guy here." She thought about Dane going through the same motions over her back in Mogadishu.

Simonova's tone cooled. "Do not mistake what I said for a request, Keyes."

Stalling for time, Lucy looked up into the cloudless sky. She searched for the sight and sound of an approaching aircraft, but there was nothing up there.

"Not like that," Simonova corrected and she jutted her chin in the direction of the sea. "The orders were clear," she went on. "We are going to initiate damage control. Believe me, coming with us will save your life."

Far out beyond the shadow cast by the rig, Lucy caught sight of a sudden churning in the water.

A squared-off conning tower made of matte black material burst through the calm surface of the ocean, rising to reveal a length of curved deck beneath it. The submarine rolled gently in the swell. It had to have been monitoring the rig for days, floating silently below the surface, waiting for the right moment.

"Move," grated Dmitry, gesturing toward a deck elevator on the far side of the platform.

Lucy let the empty AKM drop and held her hands out to her sides. "You're making a mistake, Rada. If we work together, we can still pull this back from the edge!"

Simonova shook her head. "It is already too late for that. All trace of this place and of Abur Ramaas is going to be wiped off the face of the earth."

"And when that suitcase nuke goes off?" Lucy snarled. "What then?"

"Those devices are a myth. Propaganda and disinformation," said the Russian. "That will be the truth from now on."

Pain kept him from blacking out, great tidal surges of it that rolled over him in waves of pressure, gathering in the joints of his legs and his knees. Just the act of turning on to his side was an agonizing experience, and Marc clawed at a support stanchion to haul himself up to a sitting position.

He had hit the gangway straight on, landing on his right shoulder. The meat of it felt spongy and swollen, and when he tried to move that arm more than a little, a jab of fresh pain shot down the length of his nerves. Nothing was broken and he accepted that small mercy with gratitude. Pulling on the support again, he saw that the frame ended in the blunt rod of a half-dismantled safety rail, one of dozens spaced along the gangway. A half-meter to the right, and he would have fallen right onto it.

Casting around, he found Ramaas lying sprawled further along the decking. Grimly, Marc saw that the warlord had not shared his good fortune.

A bloody spar of corroded metal was protruding from Ramaas's chest, just below his sternum. His shirt and gun vest were awash in dark fluid that pooled on his belly, soaking through his clothing.

Each step was an effort, but Marc hobbled toward him. Ramaas's chest rose and fell in stuttering jerks, and a wet gurgle escaped his lips with each breath. The metal rod had gone through his lungs and the color of the blood suggested it had slashed into his heart.

"You were right." Ramaas forced out the words, pink foam collecting at the edges of his lips. "I won't . . . survive . . ."

Marc sagged against the deck, breathing hard. "Where is it?" He threw the question at the other man. "Don't do this. *Please don't.* Just tell me where the weapon is."

Ramaas turned his head to look at Marc, a moment of confusion on his face. "This is not the way it was supposed to end." He looked down at the spike through his chest and spat out a pain-filled laugh. "But God knows. The world balances . . . on the bull's horns. I fell . . ."

"Ramaas!" Marc shouted his name in a rush of burning rage. "Answer me!"

"Tomorrow," he began, and the big man shifted, pressing his hands down on the deck with one last, massive effort. "It will be over."

Marc only understood what Ramaas was doing when it was too late to stop him. The warlord cried out as he hauled himself up and off the rusted metal spar. With nothing to staunch the flow, his blood gushed out in a fatal rush and Ramaas rolled over, choking out a last gasp of air before he fell still. His blank eyes stared up at nothing.

The climb back to the deck above was hard going, but Marc forced himself on, putting one foot in front of the other, ignoring the distant shouts of angry men and the sporadic chugs of gunfire.

The ruggedised laptop was still where it had fallen, and Marc experienced a brief surge of elation. He hobbled to it, dropping clumsily to the deck to look over the portable computer. More than anything, he wanted to boot it up at that moment and start rooting around inside the device. What Marc held in his hands was the last possible chance to find and neutralize the rogue Exile device, and he couldn't risk any mistakes. *Can't do this here,* he thought, *have to get back to Rubicon. They'll have what I need . . .*

The gunfire was getting closer. Soon, Ramaas's men were going to figure out that their bandit king was dead, and then there would be no telling what would happen next—but for a foreigner, an enemy of their pirate nation, there would be no good outcome.

The whole stack of the rig was between him and the helipad on the top of the platform, and if he went up he would be walking right into the gunmen. *Lucy could be up there,* said a voice in the back of his mind. *You want to leave her a second time?*

He shook off the traitorous thought. *She will understand. The job is the first priority.* Marc grabbed the laptop and limped away, back down the stairwell toward the floating dock, and he hated himself a little more with every step he took.

By the time he reached the boat dock, the sun had risen high enough to throw the drilling rig's shadow across the platform. There were bodies down here too, and from what he could tell a disagreement had broken out between some of the pirates that had ended badly for all of them. A few of the smaller vessels had already been scuttled, skiffs and rigid inflatable boats half-swamped by the rise and fall of the waves, and in other places Marc saw where mooring lines had been cut by those desperate to escape.

There was a low-slung black inflatable at the far end of the dock and Marc started toward it, but he had only taken a step when he saw that the boat was already manned. A cluster of armed men in tactical gear turned toward him and raised their rifles. Marc held up his hand, still clutching the laptop, trying to project a non-threatening air.

He heard them speaking Russian as they approached, and the distinctive digital camouflage pattern of their uniforms and the marine-variant Vityaz-SN submachine guns they carried confirmed it. These men were Russian Navy commandoes.

The closest one barked an order at him and then repeated it in thickly accented English. "Identify yourself!"

"My name is Marc Dane. I'm a British citizen," he replied.

"Civilian?"

"More or less." There seemed little sense in lying about it. He and Lucy had deliberately inserted into Somalia with no identity documents of any kind on them, real or otherwise. "I was brought here against my will." Another commando circled behind Marc while a third tore the laptop from his hand, drawing a shout from him. "*Hey!* Be careful with that! It's important—"

The commando who had spoken before silenced him with a throat-cutting gesture and muttered into his throat mike. After a brief conversation, he gave orders to the others and they moved back toward their boat. The commando's SMG never wavered from its aim at Marc's chest, and his pulse quickened.

"You come with us," the commando said finally. "Move!"

"*Spaciba,*" Marc managed. He couldn't afford to let the laptop out of his sight, not now, not after everything that had happened.

The Russian RIB raced away from the floating dock at full throttle and Marc sat low in the boat's gunwale, looking back toward the drilling rig as they left it behind at a rate of high knots. He saw an Mi-8 cargo helicopter perform a shaky take-off from the helipad and rattle away overhead in the direction of the distant coastline, but all he could see of the Combine Osprey was a thick pillar of black smoke where the V-22 had been. It appeared the VTOL had been torched, and Marc wondered if Saito was still on the rig, or if he had perished in Ramaas's killing room.

He turned away, scanning the horizon for signs of a ship, and a low black shape close to the wave tops revealed itself as the sail of a *Kalina*-class diesel-electric submarine. Marc knew the vessel well. In his earlier career, before his time in MI6, Marc had crewed helicopters for the British Fleet Air Arm, trained to seek and destroy subs like the *Kalina* for the Royal Navy. He had never expected to see one this close, however.

The RIB pulled into a hard turn and slid in alongside the sub. Crewmen on deck hauled Marc and the commandoes back on board, then dragged the boat up with them onto the dorsal hull.

"So I guess you need a lift?" said a familiar voice. Lucy pushed her way past the deck crew and came to Marc, laying a hand on his shoulder. "You okay?"

"I fell off a thing," he told her, with feeling. "And I hit another thing." Marc leaned in and pointed at the commando who had taken the laptop. "I got the machine."

"Ramaas?"

"Dead and gone," he said. Admitting it felt like a minor victory. "But we are not out of the woods yet."

The Russian woman from the rig was coming up behind Lucy. "Get below. Captain's orders."

They descended through the hatch and into the cramped confines of the sub's upper deck. Marc experienced a brief, odd sense of nostalgia at being on board a naval vessel, but then he shuttered it away. As familiar as it was, this was not friendly territory.

"So, introductions." Lucy nodded toward the woman. "Rada Simonova of the GRU, Marc Dane. He's my . . . consultant."

Simonova looked Marc up and down. "You're working with him? Not your usual type."

"I've got hidden talents," Marc retorted. "I want that laptop back, you get me? Or else we're all in the shit."

"We are all, already, very much in the shit," Simonova replied coldly. "That laptop is now the property of the Russian Federation."

"And what are you going to do with it?" Marc pressed. They moved down the sub's central walkway, making space as the deck crew came scrambling back inside in rapid order. "By the time you've shipped it back to Moscow for the GRU's cyber-division to pick over, the suitcase nuke your government insists does not exist will have blown up a major city!"

Lucy was nodding. "Yeah. And I reckon I know where he's going to hit . . ."

Overhead, the hatches were sealed shut and Marc felt a shudder through the deck as the sub's engines turned over. An alert klaxon sounded and a rough voice called out a warning over the intercom.

"What's going on?" said Lucy.

Marc didn't speak Russian, but he had served with the Navy long enough to know what a ship going to battle stations looked like. He glared at Simonova. "You're going to torpedo the drilling rig."

"*Da.*" As she said the word, a low thud of pressure rumbled down the length of the sub from the bow once, twice, three times. "Ramaas's pirate haven will be a bad memory."

Marc became aware of the commandoes advancing toward them, their weapons in their hands. "Don't do this," he told Simonova. "You lock us up, we can't help you."

"You will assist us with our inquiries," she replied. "When we make port."

"*Rada.*" Lucy looked the other woman in the eye. "As one operator to another, listen to me. You're making the wrong call."

Simonova shot a look at her watch. "You have no idea where the weapon is. Only guesses. I need facts."

Marc held out his hand and played the last card he had. "Then give me the laptop! I can dig out the location. And we can end this so that *everyone* walks away clean."

"He's pretty damn good," Lucy added.

The Russian's icy expression thawed, and she snapped her fingers, summoning the man carrying the portable computer. "You understand, if you fail in this, the blame . . . all of it . . . will be made to fall on your heads?"

"Yeah." Marc took the laptop and turned it over in his hands. "How fast can you get us back to Europe?"

Through the hull, there was a distant snarl of detonations, shattering concrete and crashing steel.

TWENTY-FOUR

The VW Transporter rocked on its shocks as it rolled over cobbles, heading northward along a narrow avenue. The van's battered exterior made it look like one more commercial vehicle on the city's busy noonday streets, but the cargo it carried was anything but ordinary.

Marc sat on a narrow bench welded to the VW's interior, with his back to the driver and his shoulders hunched forward over the laptop. The computer had been his constant companion for the last fifteen hours, and bit by bit in that time he had tamed the stolen machine and made it his own.

Little Jonas had layered it with a dozen levels of encryption—in the process of suborning his computer Marc had learned the name of the skinny hacker Ramaas recruited to run his tech—but he hadn't been quite as good as he thought he was.

There was a lot of material in the device's hard drive, and more floating around out there on remote servers in Nigeria that appeared to be the off-site dump for all of the pirate warlord's less relevant data. A complete analysis of the intelligence gleaned from the laptop would take a digital forensics team months to sift through. But if Ramaas had been on the mark about his promises, there were only a few hours left on the clock to deal with the immediate threat of the nuclear device.

Marc looked up as he sensed Lucy leaning closer. She sat across from him, between Simonova and one of the unsmiling GRU operatives who had met them at the airstrip on their arrival in Italy. Four more Russian agents were squeezed into the back of the VW, all of them making their final preparations for the task at hand.

"Level with me," said Lucy. "How big a roll of the dice are we making here?"

He eyed her. "I didn't just pluck this from the air, Lucy." His reply came out terser than he wanted, and he frowned. "Sorry."

Lack of sleep was making him irritable, and the drugs that he had been administered back on board the submarine were wearing off. A morose navy medic had poked and prodded them both, before prescribing injections of painkillers and stay-awakes. It had seemed like a good idea at the time, but now Marc was beginning to regret it. If they made it to sunset, he was going to crash hard and sleep for a week.

"This is the target," he concluded, for what felt like the hundredth time that day.

In the wake of the Calypso XV drilling rig's destruction, the sub that had been sent to recover Simonova's team sailed south to Tanzania, and a few hours later they had been put ashore on an empty stretch of beach to be met by yet more grim-faced men. During the short voyage, as the GRU agent won over her commanders with a plan to recapture the Exile device, Marc was hard at work on breaking down the firewalls on Jonas's machine. The kid showed talent, that was clear—but ultimately Ramaas had put his trust in a script kiddie whose programming skills talked a better game than they played. Cracking the basic levels of encoding was easy enough for someone trained in data intrusion, but it wasn't until Simonova provided him with a portable satellite router that Marc was able to get online and truly start to dive deep.

An Aeroflot cargo plane had picked them up at Nyerere International in Dar es Salaam and then it was a straight run up toward Europe. Lucy slept as much as she could, but Marc was too wired to take anything more than broken fragments of rest. When he was away from the computer, he was still thinking about it, mulling over the digital barriers that were keeping him from getting into the heart of the machine.

Marc kept a private cloud server from which he could download a set of intrusion tools from anywhere in the world, and he had used them to unpick the firewalls as the jet flew high over the Sahara and across the Mediterranean.

Reaching out into the pirate digital network, he found that parts of it were dead and unresponsive, either by design or thanks to the cobbled-together structure Jonas had put in place. Marc located a half-dozen bank accounts tied to clan-affiliated hawala brokers in the States that had gone dark in the last day or so; when he told Lucy that, she grinned and spun him a story about poisoned virtual dollars, a greedy uncle who drove a cab in New York and the way she had sneaked aboard the derelict drilling rig. But the network corroborated his analysis. A swell of money had moved into Europe over the last few days, dozens of anonymous payments covering transport, food, accommodation. All the logistics you would need to mount a covert operation.

The Russians kept Marc and Lucy on a short lead, and there was never a moment when one of Simonova's men was out of sight. But this was his playground, and he knew how to manipulate it to his advantage. Under cover of his work on Jonas's machine, he got around the monitoring software built into the Russian satellite router and threw out a message to one of Rubicon's dead-drop email servers. There was little he could do other than tell Solomon's people that he and Lucy were still alive.

That, and warn them that the city of Naples had less than a day to live.

"Explain it again," ordered Simonova.

"Why?" Marc scowled at her. "You think I'm hiding something from you, that's why you keep asking the same questions?" He gestured at the city passing by around them. "We're here now. You're way past time for any doubts."

"Indulge me," said the Russian.

"Fine." He gave a reluctant nod, and patted the laptop. "Ramaas used voice-over-Internet protocol for his communications, digital sat phones rather than cellular ones. It's harder to track unless you know exactly where to look for it. I found a series of calls from Jonas sent through a dark web server over an anonymity network . . ." He paused.

"Stop me if I'm using too many technical words." Simonova's jaw hardened and she indicated for him to continue. "Okay. So Jonas wasn't as smart as advertised. Long story short, I tracked the messages back to an Internet café here in Naples."

The Russian looked at a digital tablet in her hand, where a map was displayed. "On the Via Tarsia, *da*. We are five minutes away."

"Right. And that's where we're going to find Ramaas's local contact."

"If he is there. None of what you say confirms that the device is in this city," she added. "But you still insisted that we come here."

He spun the laptop around so Simonova could see a data window on the screen. "You're looking at transit data for a cargo ship called the MS *Valerio Luna*. It docked in Naples yesterday. It sailed here from Split, in Croatia. That's where Ramaas acquired the weapon."

"You're sure of this?"

Marc nodded grimly. "I was there, I'm bloody positive." At first it had been gut instinct, but hard-won experience had taught Marc to listen to that base, animal sense.

"The *Valerio* was one of the probable vectors we looked at after Ramaas escaped Eastern Europe," said Lucy. "Damn, but he was a slick son-of-a-bitch. All that crap with the videos from New York, Beijing and Moscow, the case he had on the rig . . . Fakes, all of them. He tracked down Jalsa Sood in Dubai and gave him the Exile blueprints so the Baker could build him a smokescreen . . ."

"And all along, the real nuclear device never left Europe." Marc tapped the screen. "While every major global counter-terror agency was on a tear trying to run down blind leads, the bomb was on a slow boat to Naples." His lip curled. "This is his revenge. Ramaas coerced his connections in shipping to do the job for him."

"A Somalian bandit warlord who believes he is on a holy crusade takes it into his head to plant a stolen nuclear weapon in Italy's second largest city." Simonova laid it out in cold, emotionless terms. "A very specific objective."

"Yeah," agreed Lucy. "From a man with a very specific grudge."

"Ramaas blamed the rest of the developed world for Somalia's ills— and for his personal burdens too," said Marc. "But beneath all that, his real hate was reserved for men who live here. *The Camorra*." The warlord had targeted the home of Italy's most notorious organized crime group.

"He wants to wipe them out like a Somalian clan would deal with one of their rivals back home," Lucy went on. "It's just the scale that's changed. For years the Camorra and their Mafiosi pals took money to sail ships full of radioactive waste and toxic materials into African waters and scuttle them. All that poison is in Somalia's water table now. It's ruined the lives of hundreds of thousands of people. Increases in birth defects, cancer rates . . ."

Marc nodded again. "And the Combine made it happen. They brokered the deals, they took their nice fat percentage, yeah? Ramaas wants his payback for all that, even if he takes it from beyond the grave." He paused as the van negotiated a sharp corner. "Clear enough?"

Simonova eyed him. "So you understand. I do not care about one man's holy mission, or revenge, or whatever it was Ramaas believed he was doing. I do not care about this city and the people in it, criminals or not. What matters to me is Russia. I will not see my country take the blame for his actions." The consequences of a Russian-made nuclear device exploding in a European city, the same city where the United States Navy headquartered their Sixth Fleet, would be grave indeed.

"Maybe your bosses should've dismantled all the devices like they said they would." Marc's reply was blunt. "Then we wouldn't even be here."

Simonova ignored the barb. "So, Dane. If you are not right about this intelligence, if we fail here today because of an error you have made . . . That is something I *will* care about a great deal."

The light from the work lamps illuminated the inclined walls of the artificial cavern, and Zayd looked up into the shadows where the ceiling vanished into darkness twenty meters above their heads.

The other men were uninterested in the place, content to sit on discarded oil drums and smoke their noxious European cigarettes, talking or playing dice. None of them were known to him; all were locals from the immigrant community who had performed minor services for the clan in the past, ex-soldiers and former bandits. That was fine with Zayd. He didn't want to speak with anyone. His mind was fully and completely on the mission.

He wandered away, to the far end of the excavated chamber. The space was wide enough to fit a pair of trucks side by side if one could have got them down here. The yellow-gray rock all around him was rough hewn and cool to the touch. The air had a dense, slightly damp quality to it that sat heavily in Zayd's chest when he breathed in. Despite the size of the excavation, he still felt uncomfortable within it, too enclosed to be at ease. His natural arena was an open space with sky above, sighting across clear sea or over the rooftops of a city. He tried not to think about the tons of stone above his head, closing his eyes for a moment.

Zayd heard the distant rumble of a subway train passing, as if it were some massive animal stalking through a nearby tunnel. The mental image disturbed him and he pushed it away.

This place was a tomb. That was what fascinated him the most about it. The contact had said that the tunnels were ancient, cut out of the living rock a thousand years ago, but none of that mattered to Zayd. He reached the sheer wall that marked the cavern's blank end and turned around, sighting down the length of the chamber that extended away into the dark. More work lights were scattered along the distance.

This place seemed *unnatural* to him. The still and lifeless air. The strange echoes. Even the feel of the ground under his feet. It felt far removed from life.

Close to death, he thought. As if he could be physically near such a thing. *Buried underground with the corpses.*

Zayd made a negative noise in the back of his throat and shrugged off the notion, unwilling to follow it where it might lead him. He returned to where he had left his gear in the rusted-out hulk of an old car, moving aside the long fishing rod bag and placing a hand on the steel suitcase.

Still there. It was foolishness to keep checking it, but Zayd could not help himself. Ramaas's last words to him echoed through his mind. *I have never asked you to do anything more important than this, brother. Do not fail me. Do not fail God.*

He considered opening the metal case, then thought better of it. Zayd pulled the walkie-talkie radio handset from its clip on his belt and made sure it was switched on and ready to receive.

His gaze dropped to the watch on his wrist, the glowing numerals there steadily advancing. *He should have made contact by now,* said the voice in his head, the same voice that talked of tombs and death and burial. *If he has not, what does that mean?*

Zayd let the question fester, and after a while he reached for the steel case once again.

As the van started to slow, Marc tapped the laptop's keyboard and the data window he was looking at closed, revealing another active panel that he had forgotten was open.

The window was the same nuke-map utility that Kara Wei had used back in the Rubicon office in Monaco, only here it had been reset to show the effect of the Exile bomb on downtown Naples. An above-ground detonation would atomise the heart of the city, coring it like an apple and flattening everything within a two-kilometer radius. With the day's strong northeasterly wind, a dagger of radioactive fallout would cut right across the local countryside toward neighboring Caserta and the Matese Mountains.

The data graphic was sobering and Marc's mouth went dry. Out of nowhere, he thought of his sister's face and realized with a jolt that he had not heard her voice in over six months. For a brief instant, all he wanted was to talk to Kate again, to connect back to something good and honest and true, something far removed from the danger swirling all around him.

"We're here," said Lucy, and the moment faded. The van lurched to a halt a few meters up from the corner of Via Tarsia and Via Toledo, mounting the narrow curb in front of a shuttered clothing store. The Internet café was a couple of doors away, an illuminated sign in the window showing it was open for business.

As one, the Russians stood and Simonova gave them a last, terse order. All of them were dressed in dark, deliberately nondescript street
clothes that were clearly too much for the warm Neapolitan morning.
The GRU team wore light body armor under their jackets, they carried Serdyukov SPS pistols that ended in boxy suppressors, and Marc
had little doubt they were prepared to use the guns on anyone who
got in their way.

Simonova glanced at her digital tablet. On it was the data Marc
had gleaned from Jonas's laptop, identifying the IP address of the
computer the Naples contact had been using. "This machine is in
there," she said.

Marc got up. "I can take you right to it—"

Simonova did not let him finish, pressing him back with the flat of
her hand on his chest. "You and Keyes will both remain here while
we execute the objective. If I need you, I will bring you in. Do not interfere with this operation."

She handed her tablet to one of the agents—a younger guy with
dark, close-cropped hair—and Marc knew she was ordering him to
stay behind to watch them. The man threw her a nod in return. Simonova produced a pair of glasses and set them in place. On the tablet
a video window appeared, showing a remote feed from a micro-camera
in the frames. The GRU operative closest to the sliding door in the side
of the VW counted down from three, and the Russian team were out
and gone in less than a second.

The door slammed shut and Marc blew out a breath. "Huh. *Stay
in the van*. I thought I was past all this . . ."

Lucy looked out of the tinted windows in the back of the vehicle,
watching the Russians move quickly and carefully down the block toward the target. "That building is a rabbit warren. There's gotta be a
dozen exit routes. Must be why he picked it . . ."

Marc closed the laptop and leaned across to peek over the GRU
operative's shoulder. The tablet relayed Simonova's point of view as
she entered the cramped confines of the café, panning around to
show dozens of old PCs with large, outdated monitors lined up before
users who were intent on sending emails, surfing the web or engaging
in video chat. The business largely catered to African immigrants,

which meant it would be a perfect place for a Somali expat to blend in.

He watched a stocky, barrel-chested man interpose himself in front of Simonova, demanding to know what she wanted there and in the corner of the shot, a dark-skinned guy with a panicked expression suddenly bolted from his chair and vaulted over the next row of computers. There was a flicker of motion and Simonova was on the move, glimpses of her men at the edges of the image showing them keeping pace. The agent ran up a narrow set of stairs, onto a landing, and slammed open a door.

"Here we go," said Lucy. The patrons of the café were spilling out onto the street in rapid order, doubtless convinced that this was a police raid of some sort.

The GRU operative was speaking quickly into a microphone concealed in his collar, and on the screen Marc caught a glimpse of Simonova's silenced SPS semi-automatic as she aimed it ahead of her.

It was like playing a first-person shooter video game, but without any direct control of events. Simonova's gun bucked in her hand as she fired in the direction of a dark blur. She was moving again, running through a shady apartment hallway barely wide enough for one person. Marc heard shouting coming from down the street.

Somewhere above them, glass shattered loudly, raining down on the top of the VW; then a heartbeat later the van sank hard on its shocks as a weight slammed into the top of the vehicle, deforming the roof with a wide, circular dent. Footsteps resonated across the metal and a figure jumped down, hitting the ground in a rolling sprawl. As the man came up, Marc saw the same face he had glimpsed through the Russian's video feed.

"That's him!" He reacted without hesitation, rocketing off the bench and through the rear doors of the van. Behind him, Marc heard a warning shout cut off mid-flow as Lucy intervened to cover his exit, but he was already on the move, sucking in a deep breath as the fugitive dashed away down the side street.

The aches in his legs were still there, but they were a distant thing dulled by doses of military-grade painkillers. Marc forced the sensation away and concentrated on one thing—the runner.

The Russians were still reacting, still scrambling to double back and snare the target. If Marc waited for them Ramaas's contact would be lost.

They sprinted up the rise of the street, barely a few meters between them as they threaded between blank concrete walls covered in fly-posters and plastic recycling bins crowding the side of the pavement. The runner hopped over an iron safety bollard and veered across the road. Marc came after him, but he almost collided with a teenage girl riding a scooter down the low hill. She leaned on the horn and cried out in dismay, and Marc lost precious seconds getting around her.

He shot a look over his shoulder and saw Lucy coming after him, one hand pointing after the fugitive. "Keep going!" she shouted.

The road ended abruptly in a T-junction and the runner cut the head off the turn, going over a low wall and on to the first of a couple of steep hairpin switchbacks. Marc kept on him, seeing his target vault up and over a battered green Fiat Panda, much to the vociferous response of the irate driver.

Marc was closing the distance as they hurdled the next turn, dodging around a heap of uncollected rubbish and discarded building debris piled on the corner. He was just a moment from getting close enough to grab at the other man, his muscles crackling with each impact of his feet against the rough, cobbled street.

On the turn, the runner wrenched a metallic object from his pocket—a cell phone—and threw it in the opposite direction. Marc saw the phone go spinning over a low wall and vanish. "Get that thing!" he yelled and pointed, and kept on running, hoping that Lucy would understand what he meant.

The pursuit passed into the shadows as they ran into a tight, single-lane street, hemmed in on both side by terraces of five-story tenements. The runner snatched at a dining-table chair left out in front of a doorway, and hurled it blindly back in Marc's direction.

Marc sidestepped and gritted his teeth, forcing himself into a surge of speed to close the distance and bring the other man down. Despite having been ordered to remain in the van, Marc and Lucy had still been kitted out with the same Kevlar vests as the GRU team and the armor was working against him, slowing his pace. If he didn't catch this guy in the next sixty seconds, he wasn't going to catch him at all.

As they came up on the graffiti-daubed mouth of a blind alley, the runner dared to shoot a glance over his shoulder and Marc saw the raw panic on the other man's face.

The man was looking the wrong way when the water truck came out of the crossway and slammed into him, square-on. The truck's brakes shrieked as the terrified driver brought it to a skidding halt, and the runner was thrown back across the intersection as if he were a lure jerked on a fishing line.

Marc got to the man and stumbled to a stop, his chest heaving with the effort of the chase. The fugitive was lying on the cobbles with his neck at an appalling angle, blood seeping from his mouth and nostrils. He resembled a broken, discarded puppet.

"Bollocks . . ." Acting quickly, Marc dropped down and pretended to check the man's pulse while patting him down. He found a wallet and pocketed it.

Lucy came up behind him as doors around them started to open. People were coming out onto their balconies, having heard the horrible sound of the accident. "Ah, sucks to be him," she muttered, beckoning Marc to back away from the body.

"Sucks to be *us*," he corrected. "Our only lead just killed himself."

"Not exactly." She showed him a battered digital satellite phone with a shattered screen. "Still in one piece. Can you hack it?"

"Reckon so," he said, taking it from her and turning it over in his hands. The case was dented but still intact, which meant there was a good chance the internals were still in working order.

"Company," said Lucy. Two of Simonova's men came running up the street toward them, but their guns were hidden away as they approached. The locals were gathering around the dead man and the driver, who was ghost white and shaking with shock. Attention started to turn toward Marc and Lucy.

"We must go," said the crop-cut Russian from the van. "Police will arrive. We cannot be here then."

"Yeah, copy that," Marc agreed, heading back the way they had come.

* * *

By the time they returned to the Net café, Simonova's crew had locked the place down and she was in the middle of interrogating the owner, the stocky character who had been caught on the video stream.

She broke off her questioning as Lucy entered, with Marc following behind and their two GRU minders flanking them, in case the urge for another run came over them.

"What part of *remain in the vehicle* did you fail to comprehend?" Simonova snarled. "I will personally shoot both of you if you try anything like that again."

Lucy gave her a sideways look. "Nah, you want to try that another way, sister. Repeat after me: *Hey, thanks for going after that guy we were too slow-ass to catch*."

One of the other agents told Simonova that the runner was dead, and that didn't go down well. "You got him killed. Yes, I can see how that is something I should be grateful for." She shook her head. "The Polizia won't take long to track him back to this place, which means we have to abort. You have single-handedly ruined this operation."

Marc walked over to the computer that the runner had been using. "Not yet, we haven't."

"But the day is young," Lucy added, with an unfriendly smile.

The Brit gave the PC a quick once-over, tapping at the grimy keyboard. His expression told the tale. "Yeah, this is the machine Ramaas was sending messages to. It's got a VOIP program installed on it. Very basic but also low-bandwidth. Easy to piggyback behind something else." He glanced at Lucy and the Russian woman. "The exact same software is on Jonas's laptop."

"The owner says the one who ran was waiting outside when he opened up this morning," offered Simonova. "He's been here since then. Drinking apple tea and watching YouTube. He didn't use the video chat."

Marc gave a slow nod. "He had the VOIP program running all the time in the background . . . But it didn't connect to anything, incoming or outgoing. He was just waiting. Waiting for somebody to call in." Something caught his eye and he reached behind the keyboard.

His hand came back with a walkie-talkie in it. "Hello. Our boy must have left this behind when he bolted."

"Why'd he need a walkie if he had a sat phone?" said Lucy.

Marc turned the radio over and examined a label on the case. "Check this out . . ." He tossed it to her, but before she could grab it, Simonova interposed herself and plucked the handset out of the air.

"*Proprietà di Napoli Metro,*" said the Russian, reading it aloud. Simonova weighed the radio in her hand, considering something. Then she used the device's antenna to point at the café's owner. "He says the contact was a night worker for the city Metro service."

Lucy nodded in the direction of the main road. "And we're just around the corner from the nearest subway stop."

"Yeah. Dante Station, in the piazza," added Marc, as he rifled through the dead man's wallet. "There's a prepaid travel pass in here. But he didn't have any work ID on him, or anything, just a CIE . . ." Marc held up the dead man's national identity card for all of them to see. He trailed off; then suddenly he was working at the broken phone, manipulating the device. "There's a bunch of deleted texts on here, but I can fish them out of the recent memory." Marc was silent for a moment as he worked. "Okay, here we are. Looks like, maybe, times of the day?"

"Orders for a meeting," Simonova suggested.

"Last one was this morning," Marc continued. "Three a.m. . . . That's well before the Metro officially opens, right?"

Lucy nodded. "A phone signal, that wouldn't reach someone underground in a subway tunnel." She thought it through out loud, assembling the connections. "But a radio would be enough."

"Computer, satellite telephone, radio." Simonova ticked off the items one after another. "Our dead friend was acting as message hub."

"Not just that," Marc said, with a grim nod of agreement. "He gave his contacts *access,* don't you get it?" He pointed at the ground. "I know where the weapon is."

They left two men with the van to clean up and intimidate the café owner into keeping his mouth shut, and the rest of the group broke into pairs. Temporarily splitting apart, they made their way to the Pi-azza Dante, approaching the square from a variety of angles, each of them taking a different route down into the Metro station.

Marc walked with the crop-haired GRU agent, forcing himself not to move too hurriedly in case it drew attention. He scanned the open space, devoid of the vendor stands that usually choked the place on a market day. Behind metal railings in the middle of the square was a white marble statue of Dante Alighieri on a high pedestal, the poet gesturing languidly with one hand. Marc recalled something of his writings on hell, and scowled at the thought of an apocalyptic inferno erupting right beneath the statue's feet.

They approached a glassed-in entrance, and when Simonova's agent was momentarily distracted, Marc slipped the damaged sat phone from his pocket and thumb-typed a quick message. He input the number for the Rubicon digital dead-drop and pressed SEND, hoping that the device was still able to transmit.

"What are you doing?" The GRU operative glared at him as they descended below street level and into the station proper.

"Checking this," Marc lied. "In case there's more information, yeah?"

"Keep your hands where I can see them," he was told.

Simonova and Lucy were already engaged in a conversation with a man in a station manager's cap. The Russian woman had a good grasp of rapid-fire Italian, and she flashed him a fake Interpol badge. Marc caught the word *terrorista* and that opened the floodgates. In a few seconds, the manager's manner changed from aggressive and obstructive to obedient and worried. He released the ticket barriers and let all of them through without another word.

"What did you tell him?" Marc asked.

"We showed him the runner's identity card," explained Lucy. "He said the guy's name was Eddie. And apparently, he—or someone who looked like him—took a work crew down into the lower levels of the station several hours ago. Our pal over there was about to call it in. They're overdue for clocking out."

"Eddie gave his Metro ID to someone else." Marc frowned. "The person on the other end of that radio." He briefly considered trying to

draw out the intruders by initiating contact with them, but then discarded the idea. If they had a code in place, it would alert Ramaas's
men that they had been compromised. The only advantage in play
right now was the element of surprise.

The station was sparsely populated at this time of the day, in the
lull between rush hours, and the team moved quickly toward the lower
levels. Brash, brightly colored murals and artwork covered the walls
of the crossway, leading down to wide platforms where boxy trains liv-
eried in silver and yellow pulled in to deposit or gather up groups of
tourists.

The safety gate at the top end of the southbound platform was un-
secured, and Simonova ordered them into a single-file formation.
They moved into the semi-darkness of the train tunnel, hugging a
narrow maintenance walkway.

"We're going in here with you, Rada," Marc heard Lucy say quietly. "How about you equip me and Dane as well?"

"I gave you a vest," said the Russian operative. "That's all. You are
here to observe and assist. I hope this time I have made it clear enough."

The younger guy with the close-cropped hair was leading the way,
panning around with a powerful Maglite torch. He saw something
and held up his hand to halt them.

Marc crouched along with the rest of the team as another Metro
train screamed past them, less than half a meter from his face. The
suction of the train's passage plucked at his jacket as it vanished into
the station, and as the noise of it died away, the GRU agent moved
forward to highlight a hatch sunk into the side of the rail tunnel.

The oval of light from his torch passed over the remains of a cut
padlock lying on the ground, the ends of the metal bright and shiny.
Their quarry had come this way and breached the door.

"What's on the other side of that?" Lucy voiced the question forming in Marc's mind.

Simonova looked at her tablet screen. "The older tunnels beneath
the Metro network. There are kilometers of them down here."

The other GRU agent cracked open the door and slipped through.
"It is clear," he called back.

One by one they followed him, and as Marc stepped across the threshold, his surroundings changed from newer poured concrete slabs to a narrow conduit sliced out of the yellow "tuff," the dense volcanic sandstone rock that underpinned the entire city.

The Metro system was just one more network of tunnels built amid those of previous generations. From what Marc knew about Naples, there were underground passages below its streets that had been cut in the 1950s, which threaded among others dating back to the fifteenth century and ancient reservoirs cut by the Greeks more than a thousand years before that. It would take days, weeks even, to conduct a full survey of the tunnels, and that was time they didn't have.

The conduit was steep, with steps fashioned from the stone, and the air became moist as they descended. At the end of the passage, it opened out onto a wider tunnel filled with ankle-deep water. Beams from the point-man's flashlight swept over the curved ceiling and the far wall, revealing the mouths of other passages across the way.

"We keep moving," said Simonova. "Watch your step."

"How we gonna find these guys?" Lucy said quietly. "You got a radio direction finder in your pocket?"

Marc shook his head. "We narrow it down. Think like them. Where would you want to put the weapon so it did the maximum amount of damage?"

"Somewhere that'd cause the biggest cave-in . . . ?" She stopped and frowned. "Think like Ramaas. The question we gotta ask is, what was he angriest about?"

"The poison." The word floated to the top of Marc's thoughts. *They ruled Somalia once. Then they poisoned it. But we don't forget. We don't forgive.* Ramaas's words came back to him. "Destruction won't be enough. He'd want to salt the ground, make it totally unliveable."

"A nuke will do that," she agreed, "for a couple hundred years at least."

"Yeah . . ." A bleak possibility occurred to him. "But if the weapon went off in an aquifer below the surface, it would irradiate the water table for the whole region. It wouldn't just destroy Naples, it would get into the underground rivers and poison everything for miles around." He rushed forward and grabbed Simonova's shoulder, splashing across the shallows. "I need to see the map."

The Russian operative gave him a searing glare of irritation, but she handed over the tablet device and Marc looked down at the illuminated screen. He saw immediately what he was looking for. "There! That's where they're going to be. This dead-end tunnel is right above one of the largest natural reservoirs, and it's close enough for them to have a clear line of escape once they kick off the timer."

"Assuming their master has not told them to perish in the holy fire," muttered Simonova.

"*Stoi!*" The point-man called out a warning and everyone froze. His torch beam was glistening off a tripwire suspended above the waterline. It led away into the gloom, and Marc could make out a dark box lying on the far side of the tunnel. *A claymore mine or something equally unpleasant,* he guessed, a booby-trap set to neutralize anyone who might come after the men with the weapon.

The point-man produced a multi-tool to cut the cable and let it fall harmlessly into the water, then resumed moving forward. Simonova and the pair of GRU operatives fell in step, but Marc saw Lucy hesitate.

"What?"

"Everything so far, what's it been?" she whispered. "One fake-out after another. Misdirection, every single time."

Marc's blood chilled. "You reckon—?"

As he spoke, the point-man's right foot touched on a pressure-pad switch that had been hidden on the bottom of the silt-choked tunnel. Seated ahead of it beneath the surface of the shallow water was a single OZM-3 anti-personnel mine, a nasty piece of Russian military surplus that Ramaas's men had smuggled into the country for just this purpose.

The mine triggered, ejecting a charge canister that burst out of the water, spinning up to chest height, trailing a spool of wire behind it.

Marc and Lucy both reacted without conscious thought, diving into the water as the mine's charge detonated in the confines of the stone tunnel. The echoing crack of the blast threw out a storm of razor-edged shrapnel that sliced through armor, flesh and bone.

TWENTY-FIVE

The thunder of the landmine's detonation rumbled through the tunnels and into the chamber, making Zayd's head snap up.

The other men scrambled for their weapons, looking his way for guidance. He jabbed his hand in the direction of the sound. "Go! Whoever you see, kill them!"

"If it is police—" began one of them.

"I told you what to do!" Zayd shouted, and his snarl was like a starting gun. The men sprinted away into the shadows, leaving him alone in the echoing gloom.

The steel case was where he had left it, resting atop the black sports bag he had used to carry it down here. Zayd kicked away the covering and hauled the case up, dragging it behind a low stone wall. His hands shook as he fingered the locks and unlatched the lid.

My hands do not shake. It was a frightening sensation for him. The sniper had been afraid to think about the weapon, to really consider what it would do, as if the device was like a mythic demon that could drive him mad with a look. Just to say the name of it was to invite the worst fortune.

And yet he couldn't stop himself from wanting to stare the monster in the eye. Zayd opened the case and revealed the complex mechanism within. The thick steel cylinder inside, webbed with wires, reminded him of a giant, blunt-headed bullet. *A kill-shot that can end thousands of lives.* He ran his fingers over its surface and it was warm to the touch.

To prepare during the journey to Italy, Ramaas had given Zayd papers to read and memorize. The documents showed how to arm the weapon. A simple matter of entering a code seven letters long and then activating a preset countdown. Those papers were ashes, burned and destroyed days ago, but the process was indelibly etched in Zayd's memory. As if he were being controlled by a force outside himself, the sniper flipped up the safety switches and slowly input the code, letter by letter.

He could hear shouting and gunfire, but the acoustics of the cavern made it difficult to be sure of how close it was. The enemy was here, that was all he needed to know. And if that was so—.

Then Ramaas has failed. But he would not fail . . . So he is dead.

The impact of that possibility shocked through Zayd. There could not be any other explanation. The warlord would never have willingly given up the location of the device, Zayd believed that with all his heart and soul. No price would ever be high enough to assuage the blood cost the West had taken from their people.

Revenge is better than riches. Ramaas had said those words to him the first time they had met, when Zayd was still a stringy teenager with a sharp eye and the will to do violence. Ramaas had not been a warlord then, just a gifted and brutal pirate working his way up through the ranks of the clan. Zayd had been isolated and alone, constantly belittled by an elder cousin who always took credit for the youth's kills and shorted him on his share of the prize money each time they took a ship.

Ramaas, clever and insightful, had seen through the cousin's lies. And one dark night, on a hijacked car carrier out of Indonesia, it was he who gave Zayd the impetus he needed to free himself from his inferior status.

Zayd remembered it, as if it had happened a day ago. *Ramaas handing him a gift: the Russian-made SVD marksman rifle. "You have a good eye." His words wrapped around a wide, predator's smile. Showing Zayd the guard post at the distant stern where the cousin who made his life a misery stood taking a piss into the ocean. Smiling again. "Try it. See how it feels."* Zayd made the mark with one clean shot, and his cousin did not come home from that sortie.

Ramaas had been right. Money was good, but vengeance was without price. Zayd owed it to the warlord to make sure that his revenge was complete. He finished typing in the code and looked at the preset timers. Ramaas had told him to set the weapon for two hours and then escape, knowing that it would be enough to get the sniper beyond the kill zone.

But now Zayd was thinking about how many would die from this, how many souls would go to the next world because of a trigger that *he* alone would pull. The part of him that wanted to see it happen was reaching forward, enrapt by the idea of being at the heart of such chaos and destruction.

He activated the timer's reset function and slowly dialed the numbers downward.

Lucy burst from the acrid water with a gasp, rolling over and taking a wet breath.

Light from the torches flashed off the yellow stone walls. She glimpsed shadows moving here and there, and struggled to right herself. The mine detonation had set her ears ringing, but the blast hadn't injured her. Her fast reactions and the attenuating effect of the water had saved her life.

The point-man wasn't so lucky. He had taken the brunt of the explosive force and it had ripped him open, shredding his Kevlar vest and the body beneath. The man looked as if he had walked into the blades of a propeller, his face an unrecognizable mess of red, his torso a ruin. Blood was misting the water around him where his corpse lay half-in and half-out of the murk.

She looked away and found Marc dragging himself out of the silt and shaking off the water. "Are you all right?" Her voice was woolly and thick behind the ringing in her ears.

Marc nodded, breathing hard. He had cuts on his cheek and his hands but he appeared unhurt. "I'll manage. The others . . . ?"

Simonova had collapsed against the far side of the tunnel, and by the way she moved to pull herself up, Lucy knew that the Russian had taken a glancing hit from the shrapnel scattered by the mine. Another GRU agent was helping Simonova stand, but the last man in her team—an older guy with a salt-and-pepper beard—was limping painfully, barely able to stay on his feet.

Lucy moved to offer him a hand and the bearded man warily accepted the support. They managed two or three steps between them before Marc shouted out a warning.

"Contact right!" Four figures burst from the mouth of the service tunnel on the opposite side of the flooded passageway, men in the dark jackets of the Metro company uniform with semi-automatics in their hands. They came out firing, and once again the tunnel was filled with a roaring turmoil. The bearded agent brought up his SRS pistol and managed to get off a shot, but the round keened off the stone wall and only served to make him a target for two of the gunmen.

His last act was to shove Lucy behind him, out of the line of fire, before a staccato drumbeat of rounds hit him in the throat and chest. He fell back against her, becoming a dead weight as she caught him by reflex. Lucy grabbed at the SRS before the silenced weapon could drop from his nerveless fingers, and aimed it back toward the gunmen. She pulled the body of the GRU agent to her chest and used him as a shield, firing back.

The pistol chugged, ejecting empty shell casings into the water, and despite her off-balance aim, Lucy caught one of the gunmen across the shoulder and heard him cry out in distress.

She glimpsed Marc ducking low as the operative with Simonova—a narrow guy with a severe face—tracked and shot dead another of the gunmen. The man he hit toppled off the ledge on the far side of the tunnel and crashed face-first into the shallow water.

Lucy let the bearded man drop, unable to hold on to him any longer, and pulled his pistol into a two-handed grip as the gunman she had winged drew a bead on her. She fired first, a bullet penetrating his nasal cavity and blasting a jet of blood and brain matter up the stonework.

The other two shooters fell back the way they had come, firing as they retreated. As the echo of the brief gunfight died away, Lucy took up the grim task of searching the bearded man's body for more ammunition, before reloading the weapon as she waded to the far side of the tunnel.

Marc was already there, turning over the dead gunman's weapon in his hand, checking the magazine. "Czech CZ 75," he said, squinting at the gun's frame. "Serial numbers have been taken off with acid. I'd swear this was from the Kurjaks' stocks."

"Likely," she told him. "How long was Ramaas dealing with them before he iced those two? They would've sold his boys guns . . ."

Simonova refused her colleague's help and hauled herself painfully up onto the raised stone bank. In the glow of the flashlight, Lucy could see she was pale with shock. "Don't wait for me," she snapped. "Get after them. *Go!*" She barked the order again in Russian and the other agent nodded, reloading his weapon.

"Your men . . ." Marc started to speak.

"We'll all be as dead as them if you don't stop this," Simonova said tersely. The Russian was pale and shaky, her legs covered in lacerations from the mine blast. "*Dane.* Wait." She reached inside her collar and came back with an abstract metal key on a chain, pulling it hard enough that the links broke. She glared at Marc. "You told me you are familiar with the device's mechanism."

"More or less," he admitted.

Simonova pressed the key into his hand. "Use this. Do not let them succeed."

The shouting and the gunfire were getting closer.

Zayd pushed the steel case away from himself and dropped into a crouch beside the black fishing rod bag he had been carrying with him since he left Mogadishu. It had been difficult to get the bag all the way here without some security man or police officer taking too close an interest in it, but the effort had been worth it.

Zayd unzipped the side and folded it open, revealing the long, skeletal shape of his "dragon," the Dragunov SVD marksman's rifle.

The gun was rake thin and lethal, the mirror of the man who used it, and he knew it as well he did his own body. The rifle was a part of Zayd, in a way. He had an almost symbiotic relationship with the weapon, knowing intimately the action of every moving part and its unique quirk. By feel and muscle memory, he loaded a box of 7.62mm bullets into the magazine well, running his hands over the careworn wooden stock and handguard. His cohorts in the clan would sometimes make fun of him when they thought he couldn't hear them, talking about the rifle as if it was his wife instead of his weapon, mocking the care and painstaking attention he gave it. But Zayd ignored them, and said nothing when their ill-maintained guns jammed or took off their fingers with a misfire. He unrolled a leather pouch containing the rifle's bulky PSO-1 scope and attached it with quick, economical movements. Dropping into a prone position, he aimed down the length of the tunnel as it extended away from him and proceeded to adjust the sights.

It was right that he should have his dragon with him, now when death was close at hand. How many lives had he ended with it? The notches etched on the stock told that story.

Zayd put his eye to the scope. They would be coming, very soon.

The tunnel narrowed and then widened again, becoming an open area that reminded Marc of the bottom of a vast well. Sullen light leaked in from high up above, and supporting ribs cut out of the rock cast shadows and provided cover as he kept close to the walls. Lucy moved out the other way around the edge of the chamber, while Simonova's agent came up through the middle.

The Russian saw something in the same moment that Marc heard the scrape of a boot on the sandy floor, and he shouted a warning.

A man came out of the dark, firing as he moved, unaware that his enemy was only a meter away. They saw each other and the gunman's eyes widened in shock. He twisted, but Marc yanked the trigger on his stolen CZ and sank two rounds center-mass in the man's torso. The gunman fell with a cry.

Across the way, the second fleeing gunman broke cover and sprinted toward the far side of the circular chamber, firing wildly over his shoulder as he made for a gap in the far wall. Lucy and the Russian ducked low and shot back, taking out the runner in a crossfire.

The GRU operative came over as Marc warily approached the man he had shot and kicked his gun out of reach. He was badly wounded but still breathing—at least, he was until the moment the Russian aimed his silenced pistol at the man's head and finished the gunman with an execution shot. The GRU operative glared at Marc, as if daring him to say something.

"Is this it?" said Lucy, moving carefully toward the gap in the wall.

Marc nodded. The map he had seen on Simonova's tablet showed the only entrance to the next chamber, the one closest to the underground reservoir. He held his breath as a low rumble sounded in the distance. "Train coming . . ."

"We go when it's loudest, right? Stay close to the walls. There won't be much cover in there, and this place is a goddamned rat run."

"Got it." Marc muttered the acknowledgment under his breath and pressed up to the wall near the gap. The little cuts on his face stung from where tiny razors of metal had cut him in the wake of the mine blast.

The sound of the passing train built to a crescendo, and Lucy gave a curt nod. The three of them burst through the entrance into the dead-end chamber and started running.

Marc saw a cathedral-like space with a high ceiling, the floor dotted with discarded oil drums and the rust-chewed frames of abandoned fifties-era coupés. His mind took it in like a snapshot. Spread out along the length of the artificial cavern, there were thick stone supports close to the walls that were big enough to hide behind, and he aimed straight for the nearest one.

At the far end of the chamber, maybe a hundred and fifty meters distant from the entrance, he glimpsed a low stone wall, more piles of debris, a quick blink of light off a disc of glass.

A rifle scope—?

A loud gunshot sounded and Marc heard the whirr of a heavy-caliber rifle round slice through the air, close enough to make him flinch. Another shot rang out in quick succession as he slammed into the support with a gasp, and spun in time to see the hit strike the pelvis of the GRU operative coming up behind him. Before the Russian stumbled to the ground, a third bullet hit him in the chest and he landed in a messy heap.

Marc swore under his breath and looked away, finding Lucy against the opposite support on the other side of the tunnel. She was holding her pistol up, straining to listen as the thunder of the shots died away.

"7.62 round," she said quietly, just loud enough that he could hear her. "Single shot semi-auto. Best guess, shooter down there has got a scoped SVD trained right on us."

"You can tell that all from the sound of the shot?"

She gave a wan nod. "You got your geek skills, I got mine." Lucy was silent for a moment. "So if he's a shooter with good judgment, he's not gonna spray and pray. Not at this range. I'm guessing he's got a five-round mag. Any more adds too much drag on the rifle . . ." She held up her hand, fingers spread, then folded three of them. "Get me?" She pointed with her thumb and forefinger like a pistol. "We go at the same time."

"What if he's got a ten-round magazine instead?"

"We'll find out the hard way."

"Wait. . . ." Marc began, but he ran out of breath. What was he going to say? *Don't run? Don't risk your life?* It all seemed trite.

"One. Two." She began the count and Marc sucked in a lungful of air, tensing for the break. "Go!"

They burst out of cover and sprinted forward, racing toward the next two support blocks, a third of the length down from the end of the echoing stone chamber. Marc concentrated on the pace, trying to weave and present a difficult target as he moved around a couple of overturned drums. He heard the rifle discharge and the sound of it was such a shock to his system that for a terrible moment he was afraid he had been hit. But then he collided with the stone support and almost knocked himself down with the force of it.

Marc turned around and the first thing he saw was Lucy lying on her back in the middle of the chamber, her gun lying out of her reach. Color drained from his face as he feared the worst, but then she coughed and moved slightly. He could hear her wheezing, struggling to take in each labored breath.

His first impulse was to dash out and go to her, try to drag her out of the firing line, and Marc had to physically stop himself from following through. This was an old sniper trick, he knew. Wound a soldier so that others in the unit would be waylaid trying to help them.

He's stalling for time, thought Marc, and that could only bode ill. He stuffed the CZ 75 into his jacket and found the damaged sat phone, turning it over in his hand. The digital camera on the back of the handset was still operating and he toggled it to a live view. Holding it at an angle so he could use it to peek out around the edge of the stone support, Marc extended a little of the phone's length out of cover and took snapshots of the chamber beyond.

He glanced at the images. There was part of a boot visible by the side of the tumbledown wall on the right. The shooter was there, concealed by the cover, and dug in hard. Marc tried the trick again, holding out the phone, this time turning it so he could get a different angle.

The gunshot and the pain came in the same instant. Perhaps it was light glittering off the camera lens, or maybe a flicker of movement, but the sniper saw the object and instinctively shot at it. The phone was blasted out of Marc's grip and he cried out as the splintering glass and the broken aluminum case lacerated his hand.

He hissed in pain, closing the hand into a fist, and in the dying echo of the rifle shot he heard another distinctive sound. An oiled snap as a receiver locked open, followed by the soft click of metal on metal.

Reloading. Lucy had been right. Five shots, and the shooter had emptied their magazine. In seconds, the rifle would be ready to fire again and this tiny fraction of opportunity would be gone.

He was running. Marc wrenched the Czech pistol from his jacket with his left uninjured hand and fired at the low wall as he hurtled across the last twenty meters toward it. All the wounds and contusions, bruises and strains he had earned over the past few days now worked in concert against him, a force of drag trying to pull him to the ground before he could get close enough to take out his target.

The shooter saw him coming and swung the long rifle around, yanking back the slide to charge a round into the weapon's chamber. So close, he didn't need to use the scope, pulling it into his chest to aim by instinct.

But Marc was already firing, marching the last rounds from the pistol up the stone wall and onto the rifleman's torso as the gun's recoil pulled up the muzzle.

A shot hit the rifleman in the sternum and another cut across his neck. His arm jerked with a wild nerve impulse and he fired the SVD into the dirt, even as the slide on Marc's pistol locked back and the gun ran dry.

Marc's headlong momentum sent him over the low wall, mantling the stonework and coming down hard. He brought the spent pistol down like a cudgel and cracked the rifleman across the face with it, blood flicking up as the two of them reeled back. The shooter gasped and coughed up blood as Marc stamped on the rifle, feeling the pressed-metal frame distort under the heavy blow.

Behind the wounded man was the same steel case Marc had seen a dozen times over. In the images from the NATO Exile intercepts, the snapshots in Jalsa Sood's workshop, in the trunk of the fleeing Mercedes, Ramaas's threat videos and the rusting space of the kill room. The same silver bulk, scuffed and dented, promising destruction.

He sank to his knees next to the case and with bloody hands, he felt for the latches to open it. Marc felt that terrible, inexorable pressure inside his skull once again, as if he were somehow sensing the apocalyptic force contained in the device, desperate to break free.

The case opened easily and revealed the workings inside. The timer mechanism was already active, the numbers on the digital display spooling down toward zero and detonation.

Marc saw *275* on the clock. Less than five minutes remaining until the trigger point. He fumbled for the arming key Simonova had given him.

A shadow fell across the open case, and droplets of blood spattered on the sandy ground. Marc whirled, barely fast enough to avoid the keen tip of a diamond-shaped kunai blade burying itself in his back. The rifleman was a mess, bleeding profusely from the wounds on his chest and face, but he was still alive, still coming at Marc on pure rage, the hollow fury in his eyes stark and wild.

Marc rolled away from the case as the rifleman slashed at the air between them, trying to force him into a corner. He lost the key as he desperately backtracked, and the rifleman trod it into the sand, ignoring it.

The blade came at him in a sideways arc and Marc grabbed the man's wrist, struggling to hold him back. His attacker was wiry but strong, and driven by adrenaline. The man brought up his other hand, flipping a second dagger into his grip by the iron ring at the end of its shaft, and swept it up. The tip scraped across Marc's armor vest and cut into his undershirt as he tried to block the second blade's advance.

They struggled against one another, neither man gaining or retreating. Marc let out an angry yell and slammed his head forward, butting the rifleman in the face where he had hit him moments before. His assailant hissed in pain but his death-grip didn't slacken.

Marc was afraid to look away to the case, afraid to see the number on the countdown timer, afraid he would give the rifleman the opening he needed to stab him through the heart before the nuclear fire claimed them all.

Then a suppressed pistol chugged twice and the other man stiffened in shock as two bullets hit him squarely in the back. All resistance fled from his body in an instant and he tumbled to the floor, leaving Marc to rock back against the stone wall.

"Fuck that guy," growled Lucy, the smoking SRS semi-automatic in her hand. Her face was slick with sweat and she was clutching her side, clearly in great pain as she shuffled across the tunnel.

"Are you all right?" Marc took a step toward her, but then his brain caught up to him and he crouched, digging the arming key out of the dirt.

"Vest took most of the impact," she explained. "Might have broken some ribs . . ." There was blood on her hand. "Ah, man. Popped my stitches too."

"If this doesn't work, that'll be the least of our problems." Marc crouched over the open case and felt across the workings of the nuclear device. His fingers brushed the metal cylinders of the core and Jalsa Sood's dying words echoed in his memory. *Right cylinder, nine rods.* He counted the components and found *ten* rods on both sides. Any lingering doubts he had about the device in front of him faded.

Marc found the control panel mounted in a shock-resistant frame in one corner. He located a cover latch and flipped it open with his thumb. Beneath it was a slot for the key.

The countdown clock showed the numerals. *153. 152. 151 . . .*

Marc turned the key over in his hands, and now that the moment was on him he was frozen. *What if it was rigged? Could Ramaas have done that, booby-trapped the bomb so it would go off no matter what happened?*

Was there one last lie above them all?

"Do you have a good reason for waiting until the last goddamn minute?" Lucy snapped. The effort of the words drained her and she slumped against the stone wall.

Marc's heart thudded in his chest as he held up the key. The sliver of metal had been bent slightly when the rifleman had stood on it. "This . . . may not work." But Lucy was right—he had no time to waste. Marc inserted the key and it went in halfway before jamming. He tried to turn it, but it wouldn't rotate.

The timer was at *110.*

"For cryin' out loud," puffed Lucy. "You disarmed bombs before, right? I know you did. I was there."

"Kind of. But those weren't nukes," he corrected absently.

"Does it matter?"

Marc had to fight down the adrenaline rush cracking though his hands, willing them to stay steady. In less than two minutes, the Exile device would initiate nuclear fission and then nothing that they had done up until this point would matter. Marc's struggle to prove himself right about the Kurjaks, Rubicon's race to isolate Ramaas and his "piece of the sun," all of it would be erased by the murder of hundreds of thousands of people and the slow, lingering poisoning of thousands more. One man's arrogant belief that he had been chosen by his God as a tool of vengeance would be all that remained.

"I do this wrong, we're dead. Everyone is dead, Lucy." Admitting it hollowed him out.

"I trust you, Marc," she gasped. "C'mon. Be lucky. For everyone this time."

"Not luck," he told her. "It's a calculated risk." And then before she could reply, Marc slammed the heel of his hand into the key with every bit of strength he could muster. Metal twisted and rivets popped, making Lucy flinch back by reflex, but the key went all the way in. Marc twisted it hard, glaring into the weapon's innards, daring it to defy him.

With a buzzing click, the clock turned dark.

"I take back what I said," Lucy offered, breaking the silence that followed. "You're not lucky. You're off the goddamn chain."

"It wasn't a punch," he insisted. "I didn't punch a nuclear bomb."

If it hadn't been for the steady, throbbing pain that was wrapped tight around her chest, Lucy might have actually laughed at that. "Whatever you say."

They trudged up the stalled escalator to the ticket hall of the Dante Metro station and the two GRU agents Simonova had left at the van were waiting for them. One of the men gestured urgently toward the exit.

Marc, Lucy and the Russian were clustered together, each supporting the others, although Simonova had insisted on personally carrying the defanged suitcase nuke up from the old tunnels. She pushed herself away from them and spoke to her men in a harsh, rapid tone.

"How is this going to get covered up?" muttered Marc. "Whole bunch of dead guys in the caverns under Naples? The Italians aren't going to be pleased about that . . ."

Simonova heard him and turned to give Marc a cold stare. "It is a better trade-off than a radioactive pit where their city used to be. My agency will talk with theirs . . ." Then her manner shifted and Lucy saw what was coming next. Simonova nodded at her men, and the other two agents turned their guns in their direction, still holding them close to their jackets. "The Russian Federation and the Intelligence Directorate thank you both for your assistance in recovering our property. However, you will need to accompany us for a debriefing."

"Seriously? We told you everything back on the sub," Marc shot back. "There's nothing else."

"That ain't it," said Lucy, with a frown. If the GRU decided to consider the two of them as loose ends in need of tying off, this would not end well.

"Move," growled one of the agents, gesturing with his gun. His comrade came in and snatched the SRS pistol Lucy had taken, prodding her roughly in the shoulder when they didn't walk fast enough.

"We started this mess in a black-site prison," said Lucy in a low voice. "Really don't want to end it in another one." But Marc shot her a sideways look and something in the Brit's manner gave her pause. "What?"

"We're not done yet," he said wearily, and as much as she wanted to believe him, they were both nearly dead on their feet.

If it came to *fight and run,* she wasn't sure how far they would get—but that didn't mean she wasn't going to try.

They emerged from the Metro's north entrance and the VW van was parked a short distance away on the edge of the piazza, engine running, and the driver staring straight ahead. Simonova's men hid their weapons and came in close. If any of the shopkeepers, tourists or pedestrians passing by on the pavement saw anything troublesome, none of them remarked on it.

When the group was two meters from the van, the sliding door on the side opened to reveal a pair of policemen in dark blue tactical gear and balaclavas, each holding an MP5 submachine gun. They were NOCS officers, members of the Polizia di Stato's elite SWAT division.

"*Arrenditi!*" shouted one of them, jumping down to train his weapon on the Russians. The other cop spoke into a radio mike clipped to his gear vest and suddenly blue and white patrol cars flooded in from all directions, disgorging more armed officers. Ambulances and police vans blocked off the ends of the road in a chorus of hooting horns.

The Italian cops surrounded the group in moments and Lucy raised her hands, shooting Marc a look. "Why am I thinking you had something to do with this?"

"I made a call," he admitted. "I reckon someone heard."

An armored van from the *Polizia*'s bomb disposal squad halted at the curbside as the regular police fanned out, pushing back the civilians to a safe distance. Lucy saw Marc's shoulders sink as a dour-looking man in a smart jacket climbed out of the vehicle and strode toward them. A second guy, doughy and thickset, trailed after him, blinking in the sunshine. As he approached, the man fixed an identity pass to his jacket and Lucy glimpsed a United Nations logo on it.

"You know those two?"

Marc gave a weary nod. "We used to work together."

"Dane," said the man in the jacket. "You never cease to disappoint. You couldn't just follow the orders you were given, for once?"

"I did quit," Marc retorted. "Didn't you get the memo? But a thank you would be nice, de Wit. Because I'm about to give you the prize of your bloody career." He looked across at the other man. "Jurgen. I got something for you." He jerked a thumb at the steel case on the ground.

De Wit's face froze and it took him a moment to re-gather himself. As the NOCS officers demanded the Russians surrender their weapons, figures in HAZMAT gear hovered nearby, aiming particle detectors and other handheld sensors at the case.

The doughy guy, Jurgen, peered at the case warily. "Is that . . . ?"

"Exactly what I said it was," Marc said firmly, then his tone shifted. "I'm sorry I got you into the shit, man. But I hope you can see why . . ."

Jurgen snatched a radiation counter from one of the suited figures and trained it on the case. His eyes widened. "I really hoped you were wrong."

Marc looked back at de Wit. "Now the way I see it, you've got two choices. Take this fucking thing and dismantle it and make sure it never troubles the world again, or let the Russians walk away with it. Your call."

Lucy looked across at Simonova, who stood in a tight cluster with her men, all of them still holding their weapons. The Italians outnumbered them two to one, but she couldn't be certain if the GRU operative was willing to commit to another firefight.

"That item is the property of my government," Simonova announced, carefully producing an identity card. "My men and I have diplomatic immunity in this country. We are leaving with it and you will not interfere."

De Wit glanced at Marc and then at the Russians. Jurgen spoke quietly to him and he nodded. "I'm afraid not," he said, at length. "Your status is acknowledged, and you are free to go, although I imagine there will be repercussions . . ." De Wit directed the HAZMAT team with a wave of the hand. "However, that device falls under the jurisdiction of the United Nations Division of Nuclear Security. Please feel free to report to your government on your return to Moscow that my department will complete the disassembly and disposal of the unit. I'm sure that the Russian Federation's failure to do so, despite signing a treaty to that effect several years ago was just . . . an oversight?"

Lucy gave a pained grin. "Hey, I like this guy."

"That is how you wish to conclude this?" Simonova studied de Wit, and then turned her icy glare on Lucy. "Very well. Watch your back, Keyes. You and the African." She holstered her weapon and her men followed suit. The Italians reluctantly parted to allow them to board the van and the VW roared away, disappearing past the cordon.

Paramedics arrived to give the two of them a look-over, and Lucy submitted to having her ribs taped up and her wounds cleaned and bandaged. Across from her, Marc sat staring into space as another medic did the same for him.

"So now we've pissed off the GRU," he said quietly. "We should start a record of all the three-letter agencies who have us on their shit-list . . ."

"Be happy," Lucy told him. "No one else died, so that's a win."

Nearby, de Wit was barking orders into a mobile phone and shot a look up into the sky.

"He's calling in a helicopter to take the device to a secure location," said Jurgen. "Can I take it that it was you who asked them to bring me down here?"

Marc nodded. "De Wit can't deny it if you back up what he's seeing. And hopefully this'll go some way to getting you off suspension."

The other man gave a wan nod. "Yes. Thank you so much for making sure I am in close proximity to a nuclear bomb."

"Sorry," Marc repeated, and Lucy knew he meant it. If they hadn't been able to find the device in time, Dane's friend would have perished along with everyone else in the city, and that had clearly weighed heavily on him. "Again. About everything."

De Wit finished his call and approached, giving the paramedics a look that told them to get lost. "You two will need to come with us."

"Let me guess, for a debriefing?" Marc broke in. "That's the second time I've been told that today and I'm still not interested." He started walking away toward the edge of the piazza, and Lucy walked with him.

De Wit was on their heels. "Perhaps you don't understand," he insisted. "That wasn't a request!"

"Who called you in here today?" Marc shot back. "You'd know nothing about this if I hadn't kept Rubicon in the loop."

Lucy raised an eyebrow. "How's that?"

He glanced at her. "Remember I said I sent a message to Solomon's digital dead drop? Well, that message pretty much said, *Contact the NSNS, get those dicks to come to Naples, make sure Jurgen Goss is with them.* I counted on Solomon following through on that."

"He always does," Lucy noted.

A scowl creased de Wit's face. "The Rubicon Group provided some intelligence to us, that is true. They have assisted the division in the past . . ."

Marc pulled out the damaged sat phone and tossed it to Jurgen, who caught it awkwardly. "Before we went underground, I sent another message. *Piazza Dante, right now.*" He pointed at the phone. "You're going to want to get Goss there to give that the full soak. Probably a lot of good intel on it, and he's the only person you have who is smart enough to do it."

They approached an open-fronted tourist café that had been emptied during the police's evacuation of the area. "Got any money?" Marc demanded.

De Wit's frown deepened, but he handed Marc his wallet. Lucy watched him pluck out a few euro notes and give it back. "What are you doing?" she said.

"I dunno about you . . ." Marc reached behind the café's counter and helped himself to a couple of cans of San Pellegrino soda, glasses and ice, leaving the cash by the register. "But I am dry as a bone."

He sat heavily in a chair and poured the drinks. Lucy joined him, wincing at the tight pull of the bandages.

"Just give us a minute, yeah?" Marc told de Wit. "We need a breather." The man muttered something unpleasant in Dutch beneath his breath, and stalked away toward one of the police cars.

"He's not happy," noted Jurgen.

"Is he ever?"

Jurgen gave a brief smile and gestured with the phone before he set off after the other man.

The pain in Lucy's ribs was dulled but steady, but still in that moment the orange soda tasted like nectar and she briefly forgot about her aches. "Are we done?" She ventured the question, afraid that the answer might not be what she wanted it to be. "Are we actually done with all this?"

The conversation halted briefly as a police Jet Ranger swept in low over the boarding school that backed onto the square and made a quick landing. Lucy saw the HAZMAT team clamber aboard the helicopter with the Exile device sealed inside a heavy bomb-disposal container, and then it took off again, on a speed course toward the nearest military base.

"Let's say yes," said Marc. "I am *finished*."

"Are you?" A familiar figure in a red leather jacket approached them, toying with a matte black smartphone in one hand. Kara Wei pulled a pair of Ray-Bans down her nose to look over the gold frames at the two of them. "Wow. You kids look like you've had fun, huh?"

"Hey, girl." Lucy offered her fellow Rubicon operative a fist-bump, which Kara returned. "I was wondering where you were. I figured if Marc called, you'd be here."

"Malte is around too," she explained. Kara placed the phone on the table and tapped it. "Go ahead, sir."

A rich, stentorian voice issued out of the smartphone. *"Lucy. Mr. Dane. You are safe . . ."* There was a note of genuine concern in Ekko Solomon's voice. *"When you went off the grid in Mogadishu, we feared the worst. I am pleased you were able to make contact again. Has the situation been contained?"*

"Done," Lucy explained. "All threats neutralized."

"Good. Kara will take you to the extraction."

"When you've finished your drinks, that is," Kara added, cocking her head. "But that is only an option for Rubicon employees. And technically, Dane, you were just part of this operation as a . . . consultant, am I right?"

Lucy offered a smile. "She has a point."

Marc downed the rest of his drink and stood up, crunching a piece of ice between his teeth. "That's true." He shrugged off his battered, water-stained jacket, and looked around. He seemed to be weighing his options, looking for a way out.

Did I misread him? Lucy wondered. *Was I wrong to think he wanted to be part of this?*

Not everybody was wired to do what Solomon's people did. She could tell Dane liked the rush of adrenaline, and she was sure he wanted to be somewhere where his actions made a difference. But seeing the sharp end of it like this, being a breath away from making the wrong choice and risking innocent lives . . . Not everyone had the heart for that. *I wouldn't blame him if he walked.*

Marc picked up the smartphone and studied it. "Mr. Solomon. You remember what you said to me a year ago, back in London?"

"I believe I offered you a job—"

He spoke over him. "I'll take it." Marc hit the END CALL button and cut off any reply, then wandered away, tapping at the phone's screen.

Kara and Lucy exchanged glances. "Did he just—?"

"I think he did."

"—hang up on the boss?"

Lucy rose to follow him. "Marc, where are you going?"

He waved her off. "I've got to call someone. It's important, yeah?"

She accepted that with a nod and he kept walking. Lucy heard the ringing of another phone, then a faint click and a woman's voice.

"Hey, Kate," Marc began, and there was something lonely in his voice Lucy had not heard before. "I was hoping we could talk."

— TWENTY-SIX —

The traffic on Moskvoretskaya Embankment was bumper to bumper, moving in sluggish fits and starts through the slushy snow rolling down from the low cloud above. A frigid polar wind off the river came up and spattered the thick, wet flakes along the flank of the black limousine crawling slowly in the direction of the Bolshoy Moskvoretsky Bridge and Red Square beyond it. Outside, temperatures were dropping as the evening approached, but inside the darkened cabin of the limo it was warm and comfortable amid the soft leather upholstery and glassy accessories.

The man in the back seat brushed a speck of lint off the front of his suit jacket and prepared himself a generous glass of Stolichnaya Elit, swirling the vodka in a thick-based tumbler before taking a mouthful. He glanced out of the window as they crawled past the grand edifice of Moscow's Imperial Orphanage, contemplating his next move.

The digital tablet on the seat next to him chirped, and he frowned, picking it up. As the device automatically scanned his fingerprints, he spoke his name into a pinhole microphone to complete the security protocol. "Pytor Glovkonin."

The screen blinked and presently an elegantly dressed woman appeared on the display. *"Good evening,"* she began. Her aristocratic French accent was soft and always alluring, but the frown on her face marred her usual beauty.

"Celeste." Glovkonin saluted her with the glass. "An unscheduled contact? It is always a pleasure to hear from you, but . . . should I be concerned?"

"The operation centered on the Exile device has been concluded," she explained.

"Your tone tells me that it did not go our way."

"No." She shook her head. *"The committee wanted me to inform you. Despite our best attempts, the second phase of the project was a failure. It appears that the device was deployed in Naples by the criminal who stole it, but circumstances led to its capture by investigators from the United Nations."*

"Distressing," he offered. "After so much preparation." He kept his tone even, despite the annoyance that simmered beneath his calm exterior. His personal investment in the operation had been extensive, in part as a plan to regain some of the costs incurred by the failure of the Washington project a year earlier.

Glovkonin was already well aware of the events in Naples, thanks to his contacts in the GRU, just as he had recently learned that the threat of a nuclear device being deployed in Moscow had been a bluff. But he saw no reason to reveal that. The Combine's governing committee did not see fit to bring him fully into the fold, so he saw no reason to give them more than he needed to.

It continued to frustrate him. Glovkonin was one of the richest men in Russia, and he was not accustomed to the idea that there were certain things he could not have. His association with the Combine had added considerably to his personal fortune, but he wanted more. He wanted to be part of the inner circle, to know the names and faces of the committee's members.

They showed no interest in making that happen, however. The clandestine network operated on a cellular structure, making sure that no member knew more than the identity of one or two others. Celeste was Glovkonin's contact, but he wanted dearly to know who ran her, who she answered to. *Patience,* he chided himself. *That will come soon enough.*

"At least we can take heart that Fedorin's removal was expedited correctly."

Celeste nodded. *"That met our expectations,* oui. *The committee commended your assistance with that phase of the project. The general's re-*

placement is much more aligned with our group's needs. That will prove useful in the future."

"I was happy to help." He took another sip of vodka. "How will the disruption of the operation affect us, moving forward?"

She eyed Glovkonin, as if unwilling to share a confidence with him, but then relented. *"Key agents have been lost. A facilitator in Italy was assassinated. One of our field operatives was badly injured extracting from the situation in Somalia . . . But the device, yes . . ."*

"There were plans for it," he prompted.

Celeste nodded again. *"Indeed. It sets back one of our projects a year, perhaps more. Other options will need to be explored instead."*

"However I can help . . . ?"

"Noted." The limo jerked and started moving smoothly again as at last it pulled free of the traffic bottleneck. *"I should make you aware of one other thing. During the operation, an outside factor became involved. One that played a large role in the failure. A group you may be familiar with."*

He knew what she was going to say. "Rubicon. I will be honest with you, Celeste—ever since Ekko Solomon's people interfered with the Washington operation, I have been agitating to prepare a project on him. We need to assemble an option to neutralize."

"Agreed," she replied. *"Be aware that your suggestion has been taken under advisement."*

He saw his opportunity and seized it. "I would be happy to lead that initiative—"

Celeste showed a patient smile. *"We will keep that in mind. Au revoir, Pytor."* The screen went blank.

A low, lion's-growl chuckle sounded from across the limo's cabin. The other occupant of the vehicle shifted and became briefly illuminated by the glow of a passing street light. He was handsome and steely, but there was a darker streak of cruelty that glittered in his eyes. "How you must hate to be at their beck and call."

Glovkonin smothered an angry retort with a wan smile. "One does what one must to survive and prosper, Khadir. You of all people should know that."

"Why am I here?" said the other man. He nodded at the inert tablet. "To witness that exchange? Your Combine mean nothing to me."

"It is not *my* Combine," Glovkonin replied. "Not *yet*. That is going to change."

Khadir's lip curled. "Much was promised and still our attack on America failed. I listen now and I hear of more failure. Why should I care?"

"Who has helped you survive, Khadir? Over the last year, who is it that has kept you alive while the United States is hunting down and executing your brethren in Al Sayf?" He didn't wait for an answer. "We have a future together, you and I."

"We are not allies," spat the other man.

"There is no such thing," agreed Glovkonin. "Only men whose interests align for a time." He toyed with the glass in his hand. "My interest is to be the hand that guides the Combine. Yours is to watch the world burn." That got him a harsh look from the terrorist, but he pressed on. "We can both have what we want. If we align."

Khadir looked away, out across the river, and was silent for a long moment. "Who do you want killed?"

"I have a few suggestions." Glovkonin glanced at the tablet. "It may take a while to put things into place . . . But the woman will have to go. And there are others. The African."

"Solomon?" Khadir glanced back, a flicker of interest in his eyes.

Glovkonin smiled. "I see I have your attention."

ACKNOWLEDGMENTS

First, a thank you to everyone at United Agents, Bonnier Zaffre, and Tor/Forge who took me on and gave me the chance to tell these stories: Robert Kirby, Kate Walsh, Joanne Hornsby, Margaret Halton, Jonathan Lyons, Mark Smith, Joel Richardson, Kate Parkin, James Horobin, Emily Burns, Christopher Morgan, Marco Palmieri, and the rest of the team—your hard work and confidence in me is eternally appreciated.

This novel is a work of fiction and while I tend to err on the side of drama, as much as I can I've tried to maintain a sense of authenticity. With that in mind, my appreciation goes to John Boyle, James M. Bridger, Rosie Garthwaite, Adam Goldman, Johann Hari, Ross Kemp, Tom Kington, Justin Marozzi, Jonathan Medalia, Sgt. Dan Mills, Martin Roach, Jeremy Scahill, P. W. Singer, Richard Wheeler, Richard Whittle, and the International Atomic Energy Agency for the various articles, papers, and books which were of great use in my research for this novel.

I must also thank the friends, colleagues, and family who have been greatly supportive of my writing, as I introduced Marc Dane to the world.

And last but always first and most, all my love to my parents and my better half, Mandy.